BE MY

HERO

LINDA KAGE

Contact Information : linda@lindakage.com

Publishing History
Linda Kage, August 2014
Print ISBN: 1500454559
Print ISBN-13: 978-1500454555

Credits
Cover Artist: Kage Covers
Editor: Rosa Sophia
Proofreader: Shelley at *2 Book Lovers Reviews*

Published in the United States of America

DEDICATION

THIS ONE IS FOR ALL MY WONDERFUL READERS.

For those of you craving more Mason: Here you go! He is smothered all over this story!

For those of you who love Reese: She is too, and she's the same quirky goofball as ever!

For those of you who need more funny business: I present to you Reese's homicidal version of the *The Wizard of Oz*!

For those of you ready to dive into Pick: he's ready to share his secrets.

For any young, new mother: Eva can totally relate.

For everyone patiently waiting for Ten's story: He's preparing for his time in his usual loud-mouthed, obnoxious way!

For all the Noel fans: Even he has some cameo scenes.

For anyone who might want more Forbidden Men: I think I can dig up at least one more.

And for that one reader who has claimed Quinn as her very own: Well, Linz, you might have some competition for him after this.

My greatest hope is that all of you go away with at least one thing you came to receive when you start this story, because this one's for you. Thank you for giving me yet another chance to entertain you for a little while!

1

PICK'S PROLOGUE

MEET PICK RYAN

As Harvey and I crouched behind the lilac bushes in front of the old decaying house, a stiff breeze burst upon us, stirring a batch of dead leaves around my knees and freezing the fuck out of my arms.

I had decided coats were overrated after last week. I'd asked Vern, my newest foster dad, if he'd buy me a jacket since the weather had turned cold and I'd outgrown last year's winter coat. He'd told me he'd consider it—if I sucked his dick.

So being a human icicle wasn't the worst thing that could happen to me.

"Jesus, Pick." Shivering beside me, Harvey wrapped my last year's coat tighter around him—since it actually fit him—and burrowed deeper into its warmth. "Did you feel that? She must know we're out here. She's already casting some kind of voodoo shit spell on us. Let's bounce already."

"It's called wind, you moron." I smacked him lightly

1

on the back of the head. "I seriously doubt she can make the wind blow. And we're not leaving until it's done."

"Bet she can. She's a witch. She can do anything. Just look at what she did to Tristy."

My teeth clenched. What had happened to Tristy was exactly why I wasn't budging until my mission was accomplished. I wasn't leaving this place until the witch had paid for what she'd done.

Spurred on by the fresh wave of rage Harvey had instilled in me, I tightened my grip on the brick I was holding and darted out from behind the bushes. Spotty clumps of dead brown grass made the ground uneven, but even that didn't deter my step. Sprinting for all I was worth, I reached the huge bay window of Madam LeFrey's home and wound back my arm.

She'd get the message I'd tied around the brick. *Leave Tristy Mahone* alone. And she had better abide. Tristy had been through enough already.

Tristy and I hadn't lived in the same foster home for over a year, not since I'd called the social worker on my last foster family and told them what was happening to her. But we still kept in touch, and I looked out for her. So when Harvey had told me why she was in the hospital, I felt as if I'd failed her. I never should've let her visit Madam LeFrey, who never gave anyone a cheerful fortune reading. I should've prevented it somehow.

But what was done was done, and I had to placate myself with paybacks. The shatter of breaking glass told me my avengement was complete.

"Oh, shit." Harvey's voice carried from the bushes. "You did it. You really did it."

Shit, I really had. I'd never been the perfect choirboy type, but this was my first stint at vandalism. I thought I'd feel satisfied. Vindicated. But Tristy was still in the hospital with her wrists taped together. And I was still a low-life deadbeat who'd never amount to anything. Madam LeFrey would no doubt continue to freak kids out by giving them doomed fortune readings.

I stood there like a complete dumbass just staring at the cracks spider-webbing through the parts of the glass that were still intact. But now I was more pissed off than before because breaking a window had accomplished absolutely nothing.

Madam LeFrey's porch light sprang on, jolting me out of my rigor mortis. As the ancient paint-chipped front door creaked open, Harvey screamed for me. Anxiety spurted through my veins in a panicked mess; I needed to reach him. Protect him.

I scrambled toward him, but to get there, I had to pass by the front porch where the witch was rushing from the house, toting—holy fuck—a shotgun that looked bigger than she was.

I skidded to a stop so fast the wet dead leaves under my shoes gave way, and I slid down, landing hard on my ass. I caught myself with one hand; my fingers dug into the muddy cold earth before I found enough purchase to push myself back up.

While I was busy wiping out, Madam LeFrey was equally busy wracking a shell into the chamber. The distinct sound of a loading gun echoed through my ears until that was all I heard. Springing upright, I stumbled away before I'd regained my footing. If I could just make it to the corner of her house, I was sure I could get out of her view long enough to find a nice dark shadow to escape into and be able to evade the mad old woman.

But I never made it to the corner.

I stepped on something solid that made a metallic click before it gave way and sucked my foot down. Sharp, knife-like teeth bit into my ankle and trapped me. I shouted out as I collapsed. The cold, wet earth enveloped me, and I curled into a fetal ball, clutching my shin. Waves of agony screamed up my leg while the ankle trap held me prisoner.

"Pick!"

Panicked and scared, Harvey's voice shot another dose of fear into me. I'd let him follow me here tonight. If anything happened to him, it'd be on me. I glanced past the witch inching toward me, the barrel of her gun aimed between my eyes, and saw him hesitating at the edges of the bushes, wavering as if he didn't want to leave me behind but didn't want to stick around either.

"Go," I choked out, waving him away.

The kid didn't hesitate. He spun around and took off.

With him out of harm's way, I finally looked up at my captor, ready to face my fate. She had to be the ugliest woman I'd ever seen. Her frizzled gray hair stood out in a crisp silhouette with the lights from her porch shining in around her, making her look as if she'd stuck her finger in an outlet and the electrical shock had split out every end in a different direction.

The loose moo-moo she wore only emphasized how wide and stoop-shouldered she was. And her moles looked like pieces of fruit wobbling around in a JELL-O mold. I caught sight of them dotting her second chin as she stepped close enough for me to make out her wrinkled, snarled-tooth sneer.

Blood left a coppery tang in my mouth. I must've bitten my tongue or lip. But my pain receptors fired too strongly in my ankle for me to feel discomfort anywhere else.

Mud and withered leaves clung to me as I panted on the ground in front of her, glaring up with all the defiant bravado I could muster.

Shuffling closer, she pressed the end of the barrel against the center of my forehead firmly enough that it'd no doubt leave a ring-shaped indention for days—if I survived that long.

Knowing this was probably it, I closed my eyes and gritted my teeth, my nostrils flaring because I couldn't stop breathing so hard.

I was going to die. Right here. Right now.

But at least it'd be quick. I probably wouldn't feel a thing. I *hoped* I wouldn't feel a thing.

The sad part was a sense of relief flooded me. The pathetic excuse that was my life was finally over. I didn't care that I'd die a virgin or that Harvey, who was a year younger than I was at thirteen, had already bagged a girl before I had. After being chained and forced to watch Tristy get raped so often, I was kind of turned off to the whole subject of sex, anyway. Using my hand and sneaking peaks at nudey pictures in magazines suited me just fine.

There were other things I had wanted to try before

dying, though. Driving. Getting a tattoo. Growing old enough to finally move out on my own. Or maybe finding a good family to adopt me.

Okay, damn. My life must really be flashing before my eyes, because I hadn't thought up the whole maybe-someone-will-adopt-me-and-love-me dream since I was nine. It was lame and useless to want such a thing.

"Did you throw a brick through my window?" Madam LeFrey asked, her voice thick and guttural, and nearly impossible to understand. She nudged the barrel harder against me as if she thought she didn't already have my undivided attention.

"Yes," I gritted out from between my clenched teeth. "Did you tell Tristy Mahone no one would ever love her, and she'd die a miserable death, young and alone?"

The old bat's shoulders twitched in what I assumed was her version of a shrug. "Like I know the name of some silly girl who came to me for her fortune."

"So you give that reading to *everyone* who comes to you?" What a complete bitch.

"I say what I see. No more. No less. If your friend got a bad reading, then your friend's a bad girl. She doesn't care for anyone."

"Doesn't care for anyone?" I repeated incredulously. Anger caused me to shove the gun out of my face so I could give her the full intensity of my glare. "Yeah, she didn't care *so much* that she went home after what you said and tried to kill herself. She cut her wrists open and almost bled out before someone found her. If she didn't care about anyone or anything, do you really think she would've taken your words to heart like that?"

The witch made a gurgling sound in the back of her throat as if she wasn't surprised to learn what Tristy had done, as if she felt no accountability or sympathy at all for Tristy's near-death.

"You almost killed her, you fucking bat!" I swiped out again like the wounded animal I was, hurt and cornered, fighting back for my life.

Instead of shooting me as she probably should've done in return, Madam LeFrey scurried a couple steps away until she was well out of my reach. At the same moment I realized her feet were bare, I also realized tears were matted to my cheeks.

A strange surge of surrealism passed over me, making my head light and woozy. A barefoot woman was about to kill me, and I was bawling like a baby. That was just so fucked up.

My vision blurred. I blinked as Madam LeFrey cocked her head to the side, studying me intently.

"You love this girl?" she asked.

I rested my cheek in the mud and fisted my hand around a clump of grass. The pain was beginning to make my stomach revolt and my thinking dull. But I tried to come up with an answer to her question because, hell, I don't know why. Maybe she'd put me out of my misery if I replied.

Did I love Tristy? God, no. Most of the time I didn't even like her. We'd survived through hell together, though, and you didn't just turn your back on a fellow hell survivor. They became a part of who you were and left you bound to always keeping watch over them.

"She's under my protection," I managed to answer, my words slurring for some strange reason. I had no clue if the pain was whacking me out, or if Madam LeFrey was pulling some voodoo crap on me, but I sure as fuck did not like being this vulnerable in front of her.

When ice-cold, gnarled fingers touched my pulse, I jerked under the pressure but couldn't seem to pull away. Turning my face, I opened my lashes and looked up at her. Pale, watery blue eyes held me captive as she peered straight inside me.

"Your friend doesn't care enough, no," she said. "But you . . . you care too much."

A hollow laugh escaped me. Here I was, ready and willing to die, and she was calling me caring. Yeah right, not giving a shit sounded real compassionate.

I had no clue what had happened to her gun, but it was nowhere in sight. If I had spotted it in that second, I might've grabbed it from her and pulled the trigger myself. But there was only me and her now. Her freaky pale blue orbs saw everything and more, making me shiver and wish she'd just put me down already.

"Please," I begged, my words slurring in the cold breeze.

"You've had a hard life but possess a pure soul," she said, ignoring me as I begged for death. "Hope drips from you like water in a leaky bucket. If it dries up, you'll turn hard and brittle. Like your friend." Her fingers shifted toward my eyes. I squeezed them shut right before she pressed both her thumbs into each of my sockets.

"What the fuck?" Was she going to pluck my eyeballs out? That sounded like it'd hurt. And I just wanted everything to stop hurting.

I grabbed her wrists to pull her off. "Let go." But as soon as my fingers latched around loose skin draped over frail bone, something happened and I couldn't move. My fingers locked into place around her, and I couldn't retreat, couldn't attack.

I was paralyzed.

"Don't worry." Her voice echoed between my ears as if she were speaking inside my head. "I'll give you your hope back."

That's when it happened. I have no idea how else to explain it except I was transported, sucked right out of my body on that cold wet ground with my ankle on fire and bleeding until suddenly, I was warm and dry, without a pain in the world and stretched out on a bed, buck-ass naked while the softest skin of the girl under me slid against mine.

Whoa! I was having sex with someone on silky sheets and a comfortable mattress. And fuck. Sex felt good after all. It wasn't as demented and perverted as that bastard who'd raped Tristy had made it look. It was sweet and warm, and just . . . really, *really* good. Better than good. Amazing.

Connected to my partner in the most unspeakable way, I buried myself deeper into her. Her sharp fingernails bit into my ass to keep me there. Desire rippled through my bloodstream as the sweetest, tightest wet heat hugged my dick. The link between us seemed to strengthen as her smell, her softness, her throaty sounds of pleasure attacked all my senses. I glanced down into her face, needing to see what she looked like.

She was beautiful, so beautiful. Probably in her early twenties, though I had a feeling I was too, and she had pale corn silk blonde hair that looked glossy and soft.

Dumbfounded by such pretty hair, I sank my fingers into it as I cupped her face in my palm. Grinning, she parted long, dark lashes to reveal the most amazing set of eyes I'd ever seen. Almost turquoise around the pupils, their color fanned out, turning stark blue and then a bright navy close to the rings of the irises. It didn't seem possible that eyes could change three shades of one color like that, but they did.

Her features were flawless, matching her unique eyes to perfection. With olive skin that wasn't pockmarked by blisters and sores as most of the methed-up girls in my neighborhood, she looked clean and wholesome. Pure.

"Tinker Bell," I said, my voice shocking me because it was deeper and more grown-up than I'd ever heard it before. I was no longer fourteen.

She smiled and breathed out a sigh, staring up at me as if she—

"I love you," she said, actually voicing the words I was aching to hear. It was the first time anyone had said that to me.

A shudder tore through me. Overwhelmed by a blasting warmth and a strangling, overwhelming desire to say it back, I pressed my forehead to hers and pumped my hips with an age-old rhythm that seemed as natural as breathing. Her wet warmth clamped even more snuggly around me and her spine arched up, smashing a set of full breasts against my chest as she gasped and threw her head back.

She was coming.

Most magnificent sight ever.

I had no idea how I knew what was happening to her, but I did, and the knowledge spurred my own body to respond. My balls tightened and my dick began to contract.

Before I could follow her into oblivion though, I was sucked away. Panicked, I clawed out to return to her, the perfect girl with the perfect body who said she loved me.

But then, there she was again. The bed under us disappeared and we were no longer naked. At least we were still twisted together—on a couch this time—and my chest still felt as weightless and free as it had in the last scene, as if I had nothing to worry about. I was . . . shit, I was happy.

So was she. Squirming underneath me, she tried to twist out of my grip as she laughed. I kept tickling her because I loved that sound, and I swear I loved her too. I had no idea how I knew that. I just knew. She was everything to me.

"Patrick Jason Ryan," she scolded me. "I'm warning you." But there was too much warmth and joy in her voice to be of any real threat.

She loved this as much as I did. My body responded, and I was ready for more of that sex I decided wasn't so bad after all.

But just as I leaned in to kiss her, a small voice asked, "Mama? Daddy? What're you guys doing?"

Startled the fucking shit out of me.

I wrenched my head around to find a little girl of four, five, hell, maybe six years old standing in the doorway, watching us curiously as she hugged a pink stuffed pig to her chest and sucked on her thumb. She was freaking adorable. Startling blue eyes, just like the woman on the couch with me, but darker hair.

Kind of like mine.

"Skylar." The woman gasped, unable to break free of me. "Help me, baby. Tickle Daddy. Get him!"

Daddy?

My eyes widened, but the wider I tried to make them, the less I saw. With a bright flash of white, I was jerked away from both girls.

The woman returned, thank God. She had coiled her pale hair up into formal silky rolls with white pearls woven through the locks and a veil trailing down her back. I sucked in a breath as I saw the wedding dress she wore.

Surrounding us, hundreds of people became a distant muted blur as they milled around the large reception hall just as the deejay started a new song. Our song.

9

"And this one's for the happy couple." The deejay sent me a nod, telling me I was up.

Ignoring how stiff the shoulder pads in my tux jacket were, I held out a hand to the blonde in the wedding dress. "Mrs. Ryan," I said, feeling as if everything inside me was going to burst out through my pores. "May I have this dance?"

This was my wife. My fucking wife. I couldn't remember ever feeling more gratified than I did in that moment when she gave me a giddy grin and took my hand. I pulled her close and twirled us onto the dance floor as I lowered my mouth to her ear.

"Tink. God, I love you. So much."

When I noticed the letters P.I.C.K. tattooed in neat black script just behind her ear, my heart pounded from all the emotions rushing through me. I buried my nose in her pearl-coiled highlights and breathed in the fresh scent of lilac.

She pressed her mouth against my neck, and I swear the impression of her kiss followed me as I was sucked into yet another scene, a backyard with vivid green grass that was perfectly trimmed on a warm, sunny day. I'd never lived in a neighborhood with a lawn so immaculate, which made me swell with pride because I knew this was my lawn. My home.

I was so fucking happy, even though the pair of scrawny arms wrapped around my neck were nearly choking me into unconsciousness. The weight of the small body pressed into my back made it worth it.

"Faster," a boy's voice encouraged in my ear. "Come on, Dad. Faster."

So I spun faster, making my boy laugh as I whirled us in a circle on that amazing, lush lawn. The world around us blurred into a blissful oblivion. When I finally stopped after making us both dizzy, I bent down, resting my hands on my knees so he could slide off. And the little girl from the earlier vision—Skylar—immediately appeared before me, tugging on my elbow.

"My turn next," she begged, her mommy's blue eyes making it impossible for me to say no. "Please, Daddy."

But from the house, the sliding glass door opened and

the woman—*Tinker Bell*—appeared in the opening. She wore a bright red t-shirt that bulged over her very pregnant belly, but she radiated with a jovial glow that made everything inside me brighten.

"Pick!" she called. "Julian. Skylar. Time for dinner."

And just like that, the vision was gone. In the next, a paper mask over my mouth and nose caused my hot breath to moisten my cheeks as a prickly cap wrapped snug around my head itched my scalp. When I realized I was wearing surgical scrubs, I arched an eyebrow. What the hell? Was I a doctor now?

But that voice—*her* intoxicating, amazing, love-filled voice—from the bed next to me had me turning until I saw her. My Tinker Bell lay on a hospital bed. Her face was flushed and damp but her tired eyes were lit with love as she grinned up at me. Cradling a small, wiggling bundle in her arms, she lifted the infant.

"Pick, come meet Chloe."

A sense of peace and joy filled me.

Before I reached for our child, I cupped my wife's cheek in my hand and just looked at her, trying to convey to her how much I loved her. "You did good, Tinker Bell."

I was about to reach for my daughter, our little Chloe, when the darkness sucked me back in.

I cried out, scrambling, desperate to return to any of those visions, but I found myself back on the cold, wet ground in the witch's front yard.

Madam LeFrey released her fingers from my eyes and I flopped limply to the ground, shuddering from loss and confusion. Keeping my lashes closed, I panted, willing myself back to wherever she'd just taken me. But the pain in my ankle kept me grounded to the bitter present.

Shuffling beside me told me Madam LeFrey was standing up and moving away, but I didn't care about her anymore. My brain was jumbled, shifting between the pain in my leg and the memories stirring in my head.

"There. You have your hope back now." Her ragged old voice angered me.

I opened my eyes and managed to glance up at her. "Wha . . . what was that? What did you do to me?"

"I gave you a glimpse."

"You gave me a *what*? What the hell is a glimpse? What does it mean?"

"Mean?" She cocked her head as if confused by the question. "Maybe nothing. Maybe everything. It shows you what your life would look like if you lived it to your heart's content."

My yearning heart thumped hard in my chest. "So . . . so that's going to happen to me? That's my future?"

Shit. It didn't seem possible. I had never done anything good enough to deserve a life like the one I'd just had a glimpse of. Elation roared through my veins until the fucking witch shook her head.

"No. It's only your future if you live to your heart's content," Madam LeFrey repeated solemnly.

"So..." I gulped, wanting to deny it. "It's not true then? It won't really happen?" More tears filled my eyes. Would I never meet that girl? Would I never have a beautiful backyard with plush green grass? Never have three perfect children who meant the world to me? Never belong to a family?

"The future is not ours to know. I only showed you what could happen if you lived happily ever after. It's up to you to make that happen."

"But . . . " I reached for her, desperate for answers. "How do I do that? I don't even know that girl. I've never seen her before in my life. How do I find her?"

The witch had been busy picking her shotgun off the ground. But she paused at my frantic questions. "Girl?"

"Yes! The *girl*. The girl you kept showing me. Who is she? Is she even a real person?"

With a confused shake of her head, the old bat stared at me as if I was crazy. "I showed you only you. Five glimpses of you. That's all. If you saw another in one of your visions, that means you love that person."

"But I . . . she was in *all* of them, not just one."

Stepping closer, Madam LeFrey eyed me as if I was a new species she'd never heard of. "Can it be?" she whispered in awe.

"What?" I demanded, almost panicking. I wanted to know more about that girl and how I could live that life with her where I'd been so fucking happy. I'd never been that content before.

Madam LeFrey shook her head as if unable to believe what she was about to tell me. "A soul mate," she rasped. "How very rare."

"What? She's my soul mate?"

I was a little giddy over the idea. A soul mate sounded good. Soul mate, someone to love me, a happy future, a place to belong. *Family.* Now, all I had to do was find her.

Except the fucking old bat looked concerned. She grabbed my arm. "Find her," she told me, urgency lacing her voice. "You're not complete until the two halves come together. You're only half a soul."

I tugged my arm out of her grip. "Well, where is she?"

Instead of answering, she jerked backward as if I was tainted. Stomping on something by my ankle, she released the trap I'd been stuck in. I cried out from the rush of blood that shot to the injury and created a shit ton of pressure. As I gritted my teeth and clutched my leg, Madam LeFrey turned her back on *me.*

"Go away now," she said, as if she were afraid of me. "Don't come back."

"But . . . *wait*! How do I find her? What's her name?" When she didn't even slow down, I growled out my anger and pain. "Damn it. Can't you do some spell to draw her here? I just want what you showed me." Why would she show me that if she wouldn't help me get it?

When she reached the porch, she glanced back. "No spell can touch this. It's bigger than any spell. It's fate."

Before I could say anything else, she scurried into her house and slammed the door, leaving me to find my own way home on a bum ankle.

Though I was no longer held prisoner, I just stayed there. Breathing hard and rattled in more ways than one, I held onto my injury and filled my head with all the damn glimpses the witch had given me. A cool mist on my face told me it had started to rain.

I knew I'd never be the same again. Up until tonight, I had convinced myself that my life would always be shitty and hopeless. But Madam LeFrey's glimpses made everything even worse. Because now I wanted something. I wanted it so damn bad I could taste it. I wanted that future and happily ever after. And if I never found that girl, if I never found even a portion of those glimpses, the disappointment would probably kill me.

EVA'S PROLOGUE

Meet Eva Mercer

Five Years After Pick's Prologue

I snuck in the back door half an hour after curfew. Someone had turned off the lights in the kitchen, so I hoped everyone had already gone to bed.

To be on the safe side, I slipped off my sandals with the extra-hard heels that were *über* noisy and padded barefoot across the cool tile. But when I reached the entrance to the back hall, I noticed the light in Daddy's office was on.

He'd left the door cracked open too, which he never did, so I guessed he was waiting up for me, trying to catch me coming in late. Again. A shiver of dread curled up my spine as my limbs went cold.

Even though fear made my breathing quicken, I wasn't about to give up on my attempt to sneak in. Tiptoeing with each step, I held my breath and tried to become one with the floor. I'd just reached the large

Oriental rug when the first creak under my toes gave me away. I halted in my tracks, closing my eyes and cursing in my head.

Please don't let him have heard that. Please, please, plea—

"Eva." The baritone I hated most in the world boomed from Daddy's office, making me jump. "Get in here. Now."

For the briefest moment, I considered running. Maybe I could outrun him this time. Maybe—

I bit my lip and shook my head. Running was bad. He'd only come after me; the fucker loved a chase. And he'd catch me, he always caught me, and it always ended worse when that happened.

But lately, I'd been able to talk my way out of it. Maybe I could reason with him tonight.

Swallowing the dread rising up my throat, I pulled back my shoulders and lifted my chin with all the false confidence I could muster. I hadn't been confident about anything—especially myself—since I was twelve, not since the first night he'd snuck into my bedroom. But I'd been bluffing my courage for two years now. All I had left was one big fake bluster. So I bluffed my confidence all the way to his office.

Setting my fingers on the cool surface of his door, I opened it just enough to peek inside.

When I saw the whiskey decanter on his desk sitting beside the crystal tumbler full of ice and that dreaded amber liquid, my hopes crashed. I inched a step in reverse.

Yeah, no way was I talking him out of anything tonight, not when he'd been imbibing that. My breathing increased its pace. It'd been four months since he'd last touched me. They'd been a good four months. I wanted to make it to five months.

He sliced me with a lethal glare when I crept backward another step. "Sit down."

My hands balled into fists at my sides. Oh, how I wanted to defy him. How I wanted to spit in his direction and tell him to go fuck himself. But with a single arch of his brows, he held me captive. I was powerless but to obey his command.

An urge rose for me to wrap my arms around myself and hide away every bit of flesh I exposed. I hadn't meant for *him* to see me dressed like this; I'd worn the short, tight skirt and halter-top for all the boys who'd been at the party I'd attended. I'd wanted *them* to watch me and want me. I'd needed one of them to take me to some private corner and erase haunting memories of other, awful hands.

I'd gotten my wish too, but now it seemed to be coming back to bite me.

It didn't matter to me that all my friends called me a slut behind my back, or that I was only fourteen, a month shy of entering high school, but had a more active sex life than most twenty-year-olds. It wasn't like I was pure by any means and needed to preserve the sanctity that was my untouched body. Dear old Dad had made sure I was no longer a virgin.

I just craved the blissful void that came over me whenever a boy got me alone. I could escape into the safe place in my head where nothing touched me while fumbling hands did whatever they wanted. For a short time, I felt free in that place. Free from everything. Especially him.

"I said sit down," Daddy snarled.

My nerves rattled under his harsh tone, but I made damn sure that outwardly I appeared unruffled. He could physically hurt me all he wanted, but I still had something he couldn't touch. Attitude.

Tossing my blonde hair over my shoulder, I sauntered to the couch against the far wall and settled onto the soft cushion. When his gaze skimmed over my legs as I crossed them, I wanted to vomit all the beer I'd chugged earlier before I'd let Jimmy Santos explore under my skirt.

I sneered and picked at my cuticles. "Whenever you're done ogling your own *daughter*, I'm ready for the lecture I know you're just dying to give."

Even as I smarted off those words, my heart leapt into my throat. I'd never been quite so smarmy and bold with him. With everyone else, yes. With him, no. But I

17

don't think I'd ever been quite so intoxicated when he'd caught me alone before either.

His jaw went hard. After picking up his drink and tossing back the rest of the contents, he slammed the tumbler down on his desktop. "I thought we'd already been over this. You're not really mine, remember?"

Ah, yes. He'd made that quite clear the first night he'd stumbled into my room, right after having an argument with Mom and learning one of her faithless encounters had brought me into the world. The whole thing had been to exact revenge against her. And it *had* pissed her off. I'd heard them arguing about it many a night, but it never prompted her into leaving him, or getting me out of his clutches and saving me.

A marriage in our respected, affluent neighborhood wasn't supposed to end in divorce. Husbands and wives simply had bigger closets built so they could hide away more of their skeletons and dirty little secrets.

And so Mother kept sleeping around, Father kept drinking and visiting my room because I guess once he got a taste of little girl he just couldn't stop. And I turned into someone I didn't recognize or like.

I sent him a little smirk. "Yeah, because calling it molestation and pedophilia sounds *so* much better when you don't tack on the incest."

The rest of the world thought of him as my biological father, and he was the only father figure I'd ever known, so to me, it was just as bad. Just as disgusting. Just as traumatic.

Eyes narrowing, he drummed his fingers against his empty glass. "Be careful, Eva. Or I'll put that smart mouth of yours to better use."

I gagged a little on my own puke. Despite wanting to back off and curl into a ball until he finally left me alone, I kept my back ramrod straight as I glared back.

No. I wasn't going to fold to him anymore. And the liquor flowing through my veins had already provided me with all the courage and bluster I needed. So I just kept digging my own grave with more attitude.

"Oh, I'm sorry." I set my fingers over my chest with sarcastic regret. "Did my honesty offend you?" I dropped my hand as well as the fake cringe of apology and shrugged. "I guess you've exhausted all your intimidation tactics on me. I'm just not that scared of you anymore."

"Is that so?"

When he rose slowly from his chair, air hissed from my lungs, replaced with a fear so thick I couldn't breathe. Fuck attitude. This wasn't funny anymore. But I wasn't sure what to do now, so I remained seated in my casual, who-gives-a-fuck pose, even though my head went dizzy from terror and my instincts told me to run.

"Well, let's see." I twirled my finger through my long hair and tilted my head in thought. "You can no longer tell me everyone will know what a naughty, naughty girl I am if I tattle on you. They already think I'm the slut of the century. And you can't use Mom against me. She's never really cared what you did to me." As I rattled on, he crept out from behind his desk and inched unnervingly closer. "I guess you could stop putting money into my account, but then I'll just go to the police. And even if they didn't believe me, the mere hint of such a scandal would probably ruin your career. So you see, old man, I hold all the cards now."

I was mostly bluffing. I would never go to the police. I didn't want anyone to know what had happened to me, least of all a bunch of officials who'd make it public.

But my father didn't know that. He leapt at me.

I squeaked out a scream I hadn't meant to let loose and flew off the settee. My scramble toward the doorway was deterred when my bare feet slipped on the polished wooden floor. I went down and banged my knee against a solid plank. The pain made my stomach rebel, but I was so desperate to escape, I kept going anyway.

He beat me to the door.

Surging in front of me, he pressed it shut with his back, successfully trapping me inside the office with him. This was his way. He liked playing spider and letting me get caught in his web before he actually pounced.

I slammed to a halt, breathing hard as all my hair flew into my face. Shoving it out my eyes, I stared up at him while he sent me a triumphant sneer.

"Now, what were you saying again about not fearing

me?" He stepped away from the door toward me, and I couldn't help it, I shrank backward. "And what was that about not being intimidated?"

I clenched my teeth and lifted my chin as I backed up for every foot he came forward. "Fuck you. You're an evil, disgusting old lecher, and you make me sick."

The insult only caused him to chuckle. I was down to my last bag of defiance, and he knew it. "Where were you tonight, Eva?"

"Out of this house," I growled. "Away from you. That's all that matters."

Realizing he'd backed me into a corner of bookshelves, I let out a whimper that only made the foul glint in his eyes brighten. He was taking away my attitude, my bluff. The only things I could control were slipping through my fingers.

"You drank at this party," he said, hovering inches away and making my breathing spike out of control. "I can smell it on you. Did you have sex too?"

I wanted to keep being Brave, Defiant Eva and hiss something like, *"What? Are you jealous?"* but with him this close, my courage fled with my smart-mouth and my insolence. I was nothing but a pathetic quivering ball of distress. And I hated him for that.

His gaze dropped to my cleavage. Shuddering, I bowed my head and wrapped my arms over my chest. I also hated being an early developer. I hated my d-cup breasts. And I hated how he always looked at them.

"I know what you're trying to do, baby doll." The whiskey on his breath choked me and made my eyes water. "You think being with all those boys is going to wipe me off you, but it won't. I'll always be there. I'll always be your first. My touch has forever stained you."

When his fingers grazed over my shoulder and down my arm with a soft, slimy caress, I lost it.

"No!" With nowhere to run, I fought, swinging out and catching him across the face.

I'd forgotten I was still holding my sandals in a death grip. The hard, pointy heels caught him in the cheek, jerking his face to the side and slashing open a gash that had my eyes popping wide and my jaw dropping with shock.

Oh, shit. I'd never struck him before. He was so going to kill me for this.

He roared out an enraged bellow and lifted his palm to his cheek. As his attention slowly rotated around to focus on me, I backed more snugly into the corner, cowering from him. He lowered his hand and looked at the blood on his fingers. When I saw his arm tremble, hope surged to life inside me. I'd scared him . . . or something, something shocking enough to give me a slice of hope. A slice of power.

Brandishing my sandal in a threatening manner, I lurched forward, making him stagger away.

"You will never *ever* touch me again, do you hear me?"

"You little bitch." Seething, he brought his fingers to his face and applied pressure to the wound, making blood gush out the sides. "You're just like your mother. I'm the head of his household and if you do anything to embarrass us, I'll see that you regret it for the rest of your life. Do *you* . . . hear *me*?"

I didn't answer. I was too busy circling around him until I was the one closest to the door. Then I turned tail and raced for the exit. Once I made it out of his office, I dropped my shoes and dashed up the stairs. I didn't slow down until I reached my room and locked myself inside. Backing away from the closed door, I brought my hand to my mouth, waiting for and expecting him to come pounding and shouting. He had a key; he could get inside if he wanted to.

But he didn't.

After nothing happened for a solid five minutes, I sank onto my mattress and hugged myself, shaking uncontrollably. Then I curled into a ball and nestled my head on my pillow, allowing myself to drift away and dream. I wouldn't be here forever. Someday I'd leave this house. I'd leave Florida. And I'd be free. I'd be whatever the hell I wanted to be.

I just had to be patient and wait. But it would happen.

It had to, otherwise, what was the point of suffering through this day in and day out?

1

-EVA MERCER-

Five Years After Eva's Prologue—Present Day

All men were bastards.

As I watched my cousin's boyfriend begin to lose his temper, I rubbed my swollen belly, relieved the baby inside me was a girl.

Okay, fine. I would've loved her no matter what gender she was. I think it was impossible not to love this thing growing in there that wiggled around day and night and got hiccups at the oddest hours, or jumped when a loud sound startled her. But at least I was relieved I wouldn't have to watch her grow up to become one of the bastards.

"I'm just saying," Mason gritted out from between clenched teeth as he gripped handfuls of his hair and paced the small kitchen. "We can't afford to keep buying all this baby crap for Eva. Why does she need a changing table anyway? Why can't she change a damn diaper on the floor, or the bed, or hell . . . *anywhere?*"

I'd give him this; he'd lasted longer than I'd expected he would. But eventually, every guy had a breaking point where he couldn't hold it in any longer. He had to let his bastard side out. Couldn't hide it forever.

Crossing my arms over my chest, I glared at him while Reese—my cousin, best friend, personal hero, and Mason's girlfriend—sat at the kitchen table, looking guilty as spit while she huddled in her chair, hugging herself. I hated how bad he was making her feel when I'd been the culprit and begged Reese to buy me that stupid changing table in the first place, because it had matched the crib they'd gotten me, and I . . . damn it, I just wanted the best for my baby.

But I kept forgetting I wasn't a spoiled little rich girl anymore, and the money in this household didn't flow like water as it had back home. It was going to take me time to realize I no longer had Daddy's blackmail money to squander. Except I wished I could hurry up the pace and straighten myself out because I hated watching Reese take the blame for my spendthrift transgressions.

I opened my mouth to defend her, but she sliced me a quick, threatening glance. I'd promised before moving in that I would never interfere in any fight she had with her boyfriend, which hadn't been all that hard of a promise to keep up until now, because usually Reese and Mason were disgustingly happy together. It didn't seem normal that they rarely fought.

And that's why I trusted Mason least of all. Just like my father, he could put on a good front. He could smile and bat his pretty boy eyelashes, and people adored him. Out in public, he could do no wrong. Even Reese freaking worshiped him as if he were some kind of saint.

But I knew he had to have a bastard hiding in there somewhere. He had a dick; it was inevitable. And since he was so good at hiding his rotten core, I was extra cautious around him.

He'd even been a complete gentleman to me one night at a party a year back when I'd tried to get into his pants . . . way before Reese had ever met him, of course.

I'd heard the rumors. People said he was a gigolo, he had sex with women for money. That alone lit him up on my radar as a candidate to take me to my safe, numb place. But then he'd turned me down, and he'd been freaking nice about it. He'd told me I'd been drinking too much, and he'd even offered to drive me home. That's when I knew he was worse than most of them. He was just another Bradshaw Mercer—a bastard hiding under the façade of a gentleman.

I'd been living here with Reese and Mason for three months now. And every night, I'd stayed up late, waiting for that inevitable moment when Mason would try to sneak into my room and get handsy. Just like my father had. I'd even piled empty soda cans in front of my bedroom door so it'd make a racket and wake Reese. She could catch him in the act and finally boot his bastard ass out.

But he'd never once done anything against me.

After three months of occupying the same apartment with him where he didn't try a damn thing, I was beginning to wonder if maybe, possibly, there were actually a few good guys in the world after all.

But then tonight happened. When Mason opened the credit card bill, he totally lost it, and now he was moments away from revealing his inner jerk. Once he did, everything would be right with the world again. I could go back to knowing I was dead-on: all men were bastards.

"I'm sorry," Reese said, her blue eyes swimming with misery as she looked up at him. "We can return it, I swear. I just got carried away. I wanted her baby to have everything and be spoiled rotten."

There was another reason I loved Reese. She already adored my little girl as much as I did.

"But it's not *our* baby," Mason muttered. "It's hers." He sent me a contemptuous glare, and I could feel just how much he resented having me around.

How Reese had ever talked him into letting me move into their snug, two-bedroom duplex apartment in the first place, I'll never know. He'd never made me feel welcome, not that I blamed him. I had completely invaded his love nest and fucked up his happily ever after. I'd resent me too. I would ignore me whenever possible. And when I was forced to talk to me, I'd probably treat me with cool disdain as well.

That was fine; he could hate me all he wanted. But he was not allowed to treat Reese with anything less that absolute adoration.

Except I didn't like where this conversation between them was headed.

"*She* should be the one to take care of that kind of shit. We're already providing a roof over her head, all her utilities, food, everything. And we can't even afford *that*."

"I know. I know." Reese began to wring her hands. It made my skin itch to watch how placating she was being. "Maybe I can . . . I'll find a job. Something that pays."

She already babysat Mason's little sister between her college coursework, but ever since they'd started dating and she'd moved here from Florida, she no longer took money for watching Sarah.

"No," Mason muttered with an irritated growl as he spun away to rub his hands over his face. "Your time's already stretched way too thin as it is. I don't want anything else cutting into your school work."

Aww, there he went, trying to act like a nice guy again, pretending to want what was best for Reese. The bastard. Determined to flush out his inner monster, I finally spoke up.

"Well, I guess *I* could get a job." I spread my arms apart so I could put my big, pregnant belly on display. "What do you think? If I took after you and sold myself on the street, would anyone buy an hour with me in this condition?"

I knew that was a low blow; I really should get a job. But my words were also completely uncalled for. Another rule Reese had made me adhere to before letting me move in with her was that I never, ever mention what he used to be before they'd moved here. But I wanted to push him over the edge already, so my cousin could see just how much of a bastard he really was.

I realized I'd made a mistake a second too late, right around the moment Reese gasped and slapped her hands over her mouth.

Mason sliced me with a glare. He stared at me so intently I held my breath waiting for him to finally lose it. My brain skipped around the kitchen, wondering what kind of gadget I could use to defend myself if he turned violent. His scowl told me just how much he wanted to wring my neck.

But instead of saying or doing anything, he turned away. Shoulders rigid and hands fisted at his sides, he marched from the kitchen, into the small living room and yanked open the front door of the apartment.

Reese leapt out of her seat. "Mason?"

He paused as if the tremor in her frightened voice held him captive, but he didn't turn around. Lifting a hand over his shoulder, he grated out, "I have to go." Then he fled the apartment. He didn't even slam the door in his wake.

Both Reese and I gaped at the closed exit. Well, I certainly hadn't expected him to do *that*. I'd pushed him past the limit. I'd made him angry enough to release his bastard, but he'd chosen to walk away instead of engage.

Shit. That wasn't good. A bastard definitely would've engaged. Why hadn't he engaged me in a fight? Called me a bitch? Taken a swing? Kicked me out?

This was all wrong.

Reese whirled toward me, her eyes wild. I tripped a step backward. Oh, double shit. She was beyond pissed.

"Why did you *do* that?" she cried. "E.! I told you not to ever, *ever* mention anything to do with that again. You *know* how much it bothers him."

I wrapped my arms protectively around my stomach, though I have no idea why. Reese wouldn't do anything to hurt my baby. I just couldn't help it. Old habits die hard.

"He . . . he was being a jerk to you."

"No, he was not. He was freaking out about the credit card bill . . . for a damn good reason. Money is a very sensitive issue for him."

I already knew that. Reese had confided to me months ago why Mason had become a male prostitute to begin with, how he'd felt the need to see to his family's security and how his landlady had blackmailed him into servicing her.

It all sounded heroic the way she told it, making him out to be this really good, stand-up guy. But I was so stuck on my theory that inside every male lurked a selfish, devious, evil prick, I just couldn't think of him in noble terms.

Except now that he'd opted out of releasing his anger on me, I was confused.

"I never should've bought that stupid baby changing table. Damn it, we haven't even gotten diapers yet. How the hell are we supposed to use a changing table if we don't even have diapers?"

My throat felt raw as I watched her break down. This wasn't her fault. It was mine. Every stressful issue for her in the past few months had been my fault because I was here, invading her life and mooching off her and her boyfriend.

But I pushed my guilt aside because knowing what I *should* do—leave her and try to make it on my own—scared the crap out of me.

"I can't believe he just left," I said, still stunned.

"Me neither." Reese lifted her face and pinned me with a strange stare as if a new idea had struck her right before her face drained of color. "Oh, God. What if . . . what if he doesn't come back?"

I started to shake my head. Impossible. Mason was just as addicted to Reese as she was to him. Bastard or not, he'd never leave her. But tonight had been a breaking point for him. Maybe he couldn't forgive her for letting me move in with them. What if, because of me, he just couldn't take this anymore?

Reese must've seen the worry on my face, because she let out a whimper and sank into the kitchen chair, covering her mouth with both hands.

"Ree Ree?" I stepped toward her with my arms open. "I'm sorry. I'm so sorry."

I didn't apologize often—rarely ever—but for Reese, I would. She was the only person on earth, other than the little girl swimming around in my belly, who I loved.

But she held up her hand, warding me off.

I stopped in my tracks, watching helplessly as tears slid down her cheeks. "Just leave me alone."

Backing away to respect her wishes, I retreated to the doorway where I'd watched her and Mason fall apart to begin with. But that wasn't enough for her.

"Go . . . *away*," she screamed.

I scurried around the corner and pressed my back to the wall just out of sight of her. Then I slid down until I was sitting on my butt, and I listened to her weep into her hands. Hugging myself, I just sat there, feeling like crap and rubbing my belly for my own comfort.

Reese had gone above and beyond for me; I never should've broken her rules.

Then again, we probably wouldn't even be in this predicament if she hadn't come to Florida in the first place.

I'd had everything planned out. A few of my things were discreetly packed, money had been tucked away, and my escape plan was complete. As soon as I graduated from high school, I was going to leave Bradshaw and Madeline Mercer for good. I was going to be free.

But then Reese had run into trouble. Her loser boyfriend at the time—another bastard, of course—had tried to kill her, and she'd needed a safe place to stay until everything blew over and he was put behind bars for good.

I had snorted when I'd heard that one. Safe place? Here? Whatever. But my mother had already made plans with her sister—Reese's mom—and Reese came to the Mercer home to stay with us whether I approved or not.

Well, I didn't approve. I didn't want sweet, innocent, fun-loving Reese anywhere near my father. I somehow talked Mom into making her stay in the loft above the garage, so at least she wouldn't be sleeping under the same roof as him. And then I delayed my plans to leave. I was probably the worst kind of safeguard between her and Bradshaw Mercer ever, but I wasn't leaving her alone with that monster.

So I enrolled into the local community college with her, and took classes with her, and I kept dating Alec, the egotistical asshole I'd had a summer fling with. I totally didn't plan for her to meet Mason and fall head-over-heels in love with him. And I didn't plan to get knocked up with Alec's kid. And I most certainly didn't plan to get shot by Reese's psycho ex-boyfriend who finally found her. But I'd been through a lot of shit I'd never planned on happening. So I had to evolve and deal with what I got.

By the time Reese moved back home to Illinois and took Mason with her, Alec—who turned out to be the typical bastard—had dumped my ass, and my parents had demanded that I quietly get rid of the little embarrassment I'd created with him.

But that's one thing I hadn't been able to do. I'd never thought of having kids. I'd never wanted to be a mommy. I was too fucked up for that kind of shit. But now that there was a baby growing inside me,. nothing else mattered but taking care of her. I was not going to hurt my child, a little piece of complete innocence I was supposed to love and nurture. I refused to become my parents. I was going to devote my life to this kid and make sure nothing bad ever happened to her.

So I had forgone the abortion my mommy and daddy had tried to pressure me into. Instead, I ran to Reese, begging her to take me in. It was too bad I'd already exhausted most of the money I'd saved for my escape. I could've helped Reese and Mason with some of their financial worries, but I wasn't used to saving, so I had nothing.

Sitting on the floor in the hallway of their apartment as I listened to Reese weep, I wondered why she didn't just boot my ass out now. It seemed like every time I'd ever tried to help her, I'd screwed the whole situation up and only ended up hurting her more. Me and helping someone other than myself just didn't mix. I'd always been too concerned with conveying a certain image so no one would ever know my secrets to worry about anyone else, and now that I did care, I was a complete bumbling idiot about it.

I don't know how long I sat there, listening to her sniffle and blow her nose over the mess I'd caused, but it gutted me. My hands began to tremble as I rubbed circles over my stomach a little faster. My throat went so dry it burned.

When the front door came open, I jerked hard in surprise, making the baby inside me start too.

"Reese?" The worry in Mason's voice was evident as he shut the door. "What's wrong?"

I scooted sideways on the floor just enough to peek around the corner of the hall and into the kitchen. Mason fell to his knees in front of Reese and gathered her hands into his, pressing them against his mouth.

Fresh tears welled in her eyes. "What do you mean, what's wrong? You . . . you *left*."

Air whooshed from his lungs and his mouth fell open. Shaking his head adamantly, he said, "No. No, I didn't leave you. I would never leave you. Christ, Reese. I'm sorry." He scooped her into his arms and hauled into his lap so he could cradle her close. She burrowed against him and buried her face into his shoulder as he kissed her hair.

"I didn't mean to upset you. I just . . . I was so mad I couldn't see straight. If I'd stuck around a second longer, I would've said something to her, and I knew that *would* upset you. I was actually trying *not* to distress you."

She nodded her head against him but didn't look up as she sobbed. "I didn't . . . I didn't know if you were ever coming back."

"Sweet Pea." He tucked her even closer and pressed his cheek against her temple. "I would never leave you," he repeated. "I was coming back. I was always coming back. I just needed to cool off. I love you, Reese. You're everything to me. I'm sorry."

"Don't ever leave like that again."

"Okay." He kissed her temple, then her cheek, working his way to her mouth. "I promise. Never again."

I inched away to give them some privacy, but also because it was just too sweet, too heartbreaking for anything I was used to watching. Closing my eyes, I pressed the back of my head against the wall and listened to them continue to make up.

"She just, when she said that—"

"I know," Reese murmured. "I'm sorry. I—"

"No, you didn't do anything wrong. And neither did Eva, really."

My eyes sprang open. Say what? Of course I'd done something wrong. I'd been the catalyst for their entire fight.

"I mean, she didn't say anything we all weren't thinking anyway, right? *Why doesn't Mason just go back to doing what he was doing before?* We wouldn't have money problems then."

Wait, I totally hadn't said that. I hadn't even thought it. Why had he assumed I'd suggest such a thing? Crap. Probably because I was me, and I usually said whatever I thought would hurt a person most.

Hurt them before they hurt me.

He sounded so forlorn and upset, I put my knuckles to my mouth and bit down hard. Damn, I'd only been trying to unleash his inner jerk; I hadn't actually intended to *hurt* him.

"I never once thought that," Reese said. "My God, Mason. Were you . . . were you actually *considering* it?"

"No," he mumbled. "I would never do that to you, but the thought was there. I could probably solve all our problems in one night. I could take care of you and . . . and it seems to be the only thing I'm good for, because I freaking suck as a bartender. If they don't give me more hours at the club, I'm going to have to find something else, except the only thing I've ever done that pays better than working there is—"

"Stop," Reese commanded, her voice soft yet firm. "Just stop thinking this way. Right now. There is so much that you're *good for*, Mason Lowe. What happened to you back in Waterford does not define you. You're an amazing, wonderful man, and I feel lucky to wake up every morning wrapped in your arms. Now just admit you're amazing, damn it. Because you are. I wish you could see you the way I see you. That bitch, Mrs. Garrison, brainwashed you into thinking you were only good for one thing when she violated you and forced you into becoming something you hated."

My eyes popped open as Reese's words echoed

through my head. *Violated you. Forced you into becoming something you hated.*

I sucked in a silent breath as it hit me. He *had* been violated by the woman who'd blackmailed him into having sex with her. And he *had* turned into something he hated because of it. Just as I had. We were like two peas in a pod. Well, except for the fact I'd turned into a pretentious bitch that acted like I was better than everyone else so I could conceal my dirty, dark secrets, and he remained a nice guy. But, whatever. We'd both suffered from a similar kind of abuse.

Tears rolled down my cheeks. Holy shit, Mason Lowe really wasn't a bastard. I didn't even know how to process that. All these months I'd been waiting for him to show his true colors, and he'd been showing them the entire time.

In the kitchen, the sound of kissing paused just before Reese quietly asked, "Do you want me to send her away?"

My insides coiled tight, and fear seized my throat when I realized she was talking about me.

"What?" Mason sounded clueless, though.

"Eva," Reese whispered, making me tremble. She'd done it, then. All these months, she'd never taken sides. She had more reason to hate me than anyone, yet she'd remained my friend and stood up to her boyfriend to help me out. But now . . . now she was choosing him over me.

I didn't blame her, not one bit, but it still infused the fear of God in me. If Reese and Mason kicked me out, I didn't know where I'd go, or what I'd do. I wasn't hardwired to take care of myself. I wouldn't even know how to start. And with a little one on the way, I wasn't ready to start such a task. Close to Reese was the only place I felt safe.

But she kept talking. "I know how you feel about her. I've always known. But I was so guilty after she got shot by my crazy, stalker ex; I thought I owed her *something*. And you were always so awesome about it, even though I knew you hated the idea and probably even hate her. And I know she has her problems, but she's my cousin and . . . Seriously, Mason, if having her here is too much for you, I'll make her go. I will not lose you because of her."

Covering my mouth to hide the sound of my crying, I waited with bated breath for Mason to decide my future. I wouldn't blame either of them for making me leave. They'd already put up with more from me than they should have, but I still prayed he'd have mercy, that he'd give me one more chance. I could be a better person; I knew I could.

I touched my belly. For this little bundle of joy, I'd be anything I had to be.

"You would really kick her out?" Mason sounded stunned. "For me?"

Reese gave a soft laugh before I heard a loud kiss. "Of course. You mean more to me than anyone."

I brushed the tears off my cheeks and drew in a deep breath. I could survive this. No matter what happened, I'd survive, even if it landed me and my baby on the streets.

"Jesus, Reese," Mason muttered. "Don't put this on me. You know I don't want her here. But I want to make you happy. And shit, where else is she supposed to go? Didn't your mom already say she wasn't having any part of it?"

"Yeah, but maybe my sister or one of my friends . . . " Reese trailed off as if she realized neither of those options would work.

"Aside from what she said tonight, she seems to be changing," Mason argued, as if he were actually coming to my defense. "I don't . . . I mean, you taught me that everyone deserves a second chance. That's something I love most about you. How freaking forgiving you are."

I nodded, agreeing with him. Reese forgave too easily. But since she'd forgiven me for things I didn't deserve to be forgiven for, it was one of the things I loved most about her too.

I tried to sniff up some of the tears leaking down my cheeks, but I realized too late that they'd heard me. Before I could push to my feet to escape to my room, both Mason and Reese appeared in the doorway.

When they saw me bawling on the floor, my face heated mercilessly. I lifted a hand in apology, trying to excuse my behavior. "Sorry. Ignore me. Freaking pregnancy hormones."

"Oh, hell, E." Reese knelt next to me and pulled me into a hug. "How much did you overhear?"

"All of it," I admitted, wiping my cheeks and hugging her back before I looked up at Mason. "I'm sorry," I told him. "And I'm not just saying that to try to get you to let me stay. If you want me to go, I'll go. I totally understand, but I . . . really, I'm sorry. I shouldn't have said it. I didn't understand. I don't think I wanted to understand. But I do now, and it'll never happen again."

He closed his eyes and blew out a breath, his jaw hard and unforgiving before he muttered, "Damn it," and got down on the floor to sweep both of us girls into his arms for a hard family hug. "It's okay," he reluctantly admitted, not meeting my gaze before he pulled away, touching Reese's back while he did as if he needed to feel her for support.

She smiled at him and nodded her approval. In that moment, he became the only male I'd ever considered not evil. And for the first time since Reese and he had hooked up, I was actually jealous of her. She'd found a diamond in the rough. She deserved it more than anyone I knew, but a part of me still felt covetous. Now that I knew there was actually such a thing as a good guy, I wanted one too. I wanted some white knight to be my hero.

Screw girl power. I wasn't strong. I wasn't anything. I needed help. A lot of help.

Clearing my throat, I tucked a piece of hair behind my ear. "I can leave now," I offered. It was the very least I could do. I had no idea where I'd go, because Reese was the last person I could turn to. But there had to be some kind of shelter in this town where I could stay the night. Right?

"You don't have to go," Mason mumbled. "We said we'd help you until you could get out on your own. And we will."

More tears flooded my cheeks. "I don't know how

long it will take. I'll look for a job as soon as the baby's born, and I'll chip in on the bills and—"

Mason covered my hand briefly. The warmth and compassion in his fingers startled me. "Just . . . take care of your kid. The rest will come when it comes. We'll help you."

His kindness and willingness to give me a second chance pulverized me. For the first time in years, I finally felt free. I didn't have to worry about any male in my own home trying to get at me. I could just live, focus on my baby, and begin the rest of my life. Except, now that I could finally be me, I felt lost.

I had no idea who I really was.

2

-PICK RYAN-

I had sacrificed a lot over the years to help friends out. I'd dished out my own hard-earned money to get people out of trouble. I'd gone cold all winter to make sure others had coats. I'd stayed up all night with a baby so someone else could get a little shut-eye before I had to head into work at the ass-crack of dawn the next morning. But I had to admit, I'd never given up sex for anyone before.

That's exactly what I was about to do.

Sitting outside the judge's chambers in the court-house, I tapped my toe against the floor as Tristy and I waited for them to call our names. Next to me, she sneezed and scratched a spot on her shoulder. She used to scratch her arms all the time when she was tweaking. Drugs had made her do all kinds of weird shit.

Hoping she hadn't started that up again, I shot her a sharp glance as she dropped her hand. I thought I'd been careful, keeping a close eye on her. She said she'd been clean for the past six months. But I knew I couldn't watch her all the time, not when I was working two full-time jobs and pretty much only came home to sleep.

Catching my stare, she frowned. "What?"

I shook my head and turned away. She had assured me she'd stopped the drugs, so I chose to believe her. But she better not fuck with me on that issue, because I was sacrificing a lot—my fucking sex life included—to help her out.

Closing my eyes, I rested my head against the wall behind me and tried to remember the last time I'd actually had sex. The memory could be my way of saying goodbye to it for the next couple of months or—shit, I hoped not—years.

My buddies at Forbidden, the bar where I worked, thought I got laid damn near every night. While that might've been nice, it wasn't anywhere near the truth. Ten out of ten times, I didn't touch the girls the guys saw me take home from the bar, nothing beyond a hug or kiss on the cheek, because they were drunk when I drove their cute asses home. No self-respecting guy took advantage of a wasted chick.

I couldn't even remember the last time I'd been inside a woman, how long ago it had been or even with whom, so of course my mind brought up an image I never forgot. And it was as if I was still fourteen, being fed the glimpse by that old witch. I saw unique blue eyes first, then her blonde hair, her smile, the hint of lilac.

A sigh eased from my lungs.

My Tinker Bell.

But thinking about *her*—whoever she was—only made my chest ache. If Madam LeFrey were still alive, I'd look that woman up and cuss her out. It'd been ten years, and she still had me dreaming about those goddamn glimpses. Ten years, and I still wanted Tinker Bell to be a real person I could really meet. Ten fucking years, and I still thought my happily ever after might come true.

Fucking bullshit.

Wishing Madam LeFrey were toasting in a nice fiery pit in hell right about now, I opened my eyes when a small whimper came from the floor between me and Tristy. The car seat began to sway as the baby inside woke, thrashing his arms and legs.

Tristy moaned and sent the kid a glare. "God . . . *damn* it. He just went to sleep. Why can't he just stay the fuck asleep for ten full minutes?"

I scowled at her before leaning forward. "I got him." She didn't attempt to stop me as I pushed the handle out of the way and unbuckled him from his carrier. When he looked up at me and kicked his legs as if glad to see me, I couldn't stop a smile. "Hey there, Fighter. You have a good nap?"

Tristy snorted. "Like he's going to answer you."

I ignored her and focused on cradling the three-month old to my chest. He rooted around at my shirt as if he were seeking something to eat, which was strange. Tristy sure as hell had never breastfed him. I have no idea how the kid even knew he could get food there.

I chuckled and stroked my hand over dark curls. "You hungry, little man?"

Thank God Tristy didn't berate me again for asking him a question as I bent forward and dug inside the diaper bag to find the bottle I'd put in there before we'd left the apartment. I probably would've snapped something rude back at her, and grooms really shouldn't snap at their brides, especially on their wedding day.

But she was definitely in a mood. I had no idea what had gotten her so pissy. Maybe all women went through a grouchy stage right before they got hitched. Not that there was going to be anything conventional about the piece of paper we were about to sign, legally binding us together.

With a baby who required regular medical check-ups, Tristy needed insurance. She hadn't passed governmental approval for the free stuff, and since my boss at the garage where I worked during the day had recently signed me up for a nice insurance plan, one I could put Tristy and her little man on—if we were husband and wife—I'd come up with the idea to marry her.

I knew it was in name only and not a real marriage. Tristy wouldn't care if I went on a date with someone else. But that didn't seem fair to whomever I might go on a date with.

I could already imagine how it'd play out. *Shh, baby, we gotta keep your orgasm quiet. Don't want to wake my wife in the next room. Or her kid.* Yeah, that was not going to happen.

Besides, in the eyes of the law, this was the real deal, so I had decided I'd be celibate until she finally got her life back on track and we could annul things amicably. It was anyone's guess when that would happen, but she'd been staying clean and doing well since she'd given birth. Hopefully a couple months, half a year, and she could get out on her own.

Aside from my dick going cold turkey, the marriage thing wouldn't change too much else in my life. I'd already been letting her crash in my guest room since she'd been three months pregnant when she showed up on my doorstep crying and destitute. So the only thing that would really change was her last name, my insurance plan, and yeah . . . my very pissed off penis.

Tristy had actually gotten pregnant two times before. The first two had ended up in miscarriages because she hadn't been willing enough to clean herself up. But this time, I'd had enough. I'd watched her like a hawk to keep her off drugs while she was carrying, and she'd only had a couple setbacks. Surprisingly, the third time was a charm. This baby made it, and now he was already three months old.

I called him my little fighter.

I needed to call him something because it pissed me off that Tristy had named him Julian. She'd liked the name ever since I'd gotten it tattooed on my chest years ago, right alongside the names Skylar, Chloe, and Tinker Bell. Though honestly, I don't know why it mattered what she named her kid. I was never going to meet Tinker Bell, so our three children together were never going to exist.

If Tristy wanted to steal my baby's name . . . whatever. It didn't matter.

At least, I didn't want it to, which was probably why it bothered the hell out of me so much.

And why did I keep thinking about Tinker Bell and our non-existent future together?

Probably because I was about to get married—even if it was just a marriage of convenience—and she was the only person I'd ever imagined as my wife. I wanted to stop thinking about her. I wanted to stop feeling guilty as if I was betraying her for helping out a friend. I wanted... fuck, I wanted her to walk through the door this very second so she could sweep me away to happily ever after, and I could leave this shitty life behind.

But the only woman who poked her head through the doorway was a short, plump, gray-headed clerk who said, "Ryan?"

"That's us." I smiled at her as I got to my feet, keeping a happily drinking Julian cradled in the crook of my arm.

"Aww," she said, smiling my way. "There's nothing more precious than watching a handsome young man taking care of a baby."

As I sent the old gal a flirty little wink, Tristy snorted and plowed past her into the judge's chambers.

Irritated that she hadn't gotten the carrier and diaper bag while my hands were full, I gritted my teeth. "*Thanks, honey,*" I was tempted to call after her. But I sucked it up and tucked Julian back into his car seat, tried to prop the bottle into his mouth so he could keep eating and slung the bag strap over my shoulder before picking up the carrier.

Then I followed the sweet old gal into the small room, where Tristy and I got married.

It was over and done about as soon as it started. Afterward, my stomach churned miserably. Ever since that damn glimpse, or whatever the hell it'd been, I'd always thought of marriage as forever, as love, and happily ever after, sacred and binding. But this had been none of that.

It left me empty and restless. Trapped.

Tristy and I didn't even talk to each other as I dropped her and her son back off at the apartment before I returned to work at the garage. When five o'clock came around, I stamped my time card and drove home, only to find her sitting on the couch, typing away on the laptop I'd gotten her. An afternoon talk show played on the television, barely muting Julian, who fussed in the swing.

I pulled him out and found his diaper almost leaking through it was so full. After carrying him back to my room, I changed him and plunked him onto my hip so he could join me in the kitchen where I whipped up a quick supper.

"I'm making a sandwich," I called over my shoulder while Julian slobbered all over my grease-stained pinstripe shirt and happily pounded his chubby fists against my chest. "You want one?"

"Yes!" Tristy yelled back. "No mustard this time."

I rolled my eyes but repeated to Julian in a playful baby voice, "No mustard, you hear that, Fighter? Your mama's gonna fire us if we don't get it right."

He gurgled and cooed in response, so I spent a moment cooing back, rubbing my nose against his until I got him to smile and wave his arms. He'd only started smiling a week or so ago. Tristy claimed she still hadn't seen one, even though I'd caught it on camera. I had to hold my tongue to keep from telling her she actually had to look at him to notice it.

After we men made the sandwiches, I warmed a bottle for the little guy. Back in the living room, Tristy took her sandwich with a half-hearted grunt, and Julian and I settled into the rocking chair. While we all ate, I watched Tristy madly type, pause every few seconds to read something on the screen, then nibble from her ham and cheese before typing some more.

"What're you doing, anyway?" I asked, mildly interested. "Writing a book?"

She speared me with a short scowl before she went right back to typing. "I'm talking to someone on Facebook."

I lifted my brows. I hadn't known she'd joined the network. I'd never had the time to myself. "Who?" I asked, wondering who the hell else from our neighborhood got into that shit.

With another glare, she muttered, "None of your damn business."

Well. I lifted my eyebrows but let the issue drop. After I finished eating, and Julian was nearing the end of his bottle, I pushed up from the chair and sighed. That was the one break I'd have today. "I'm working at the bar tonight," I reminded Tristy, carrying the baby back to his swing. "So I'm going to take a shower and push off again."

She groaned and sent her son a glance brimming with disgust. "Can't you take him with you while you get ready? I've had him all fucking day."

I clenched my teeth and popped my jaw but acknowledged her request with a strained, "Sure." Picking Julian back up, I carried him down the hall and set up a bouncer seat next to the tub for him to wiggle in while I took a quick shower. As I dried myself afterward, shaved, and ran a quick comb through my hair, I talked nonsense to the kid, telling him about who'd come into the garage today and what was wrong with some of the cars I'd worked on.

Tristy might think it was stupid to talk to someone who didn't understand a word I said, but he responded to me more than anyone else who lived in this apartment, so I kept talking to him. Besides, he was too cute not to talk to him. He watched my mouth when I spoke as if every word was divine; he was mesmerized. Kinda made me feel important.

I slipped on my Forbidden Nightclub uniform—which was actually just a snug black T-shirt and blue jeans—and checked the kiddo's diaper one more time before I carried him back into the front room.

"Here you are," I told Tris. "He's clean and fed and ready to go." I tried to hand Fighter to her directly, but she shot me a dirty look. So I sighed and settled him back into his swing. I bet he hated that damn swing.

I would not lose my temper. I would not lose my temper. No matter how much she neglected her own child, I would not yell at her.

That had become my mantra these past few months.

Kissing Fighter on the forehead, I wished him a quiet farewell, then I waved goodbye to my wife of six hours, who remained seated cross-legged in the same spot on the couch she'd been in when I'd walked in the door, and I left to start my second job of the day.

As usual, I was late for work.

"Hey, look who finally decided to join us," my coworker, Noel Gamble, called as I ambled inside. He and the new guy, Mason, were already behind the bar, which meant I got to wait tables tonight. Fine by me. I made more tips working the crowd anyway, especially on Thursdays when it was ladies' night. The ladies loved me.

"I decided you'd miss me too much if I didn't show," I hollered back to Gamble. Sending him an air kiss, I tapped my chest with both hands and then spread my arms wide. "So here I am, baby. Just for you."

He snorted and shook his head. "You'd need bigger boobs to interest me."

Chuckling, I turned to find a complete stranger fumbling to tie a waist apron around his hips but messing up so bad he had to start again.

"Whoa. Wait." I took it from him. "It's like this."

After I showed him how to properly tie the thing on, he looked up and smiled appreciatively. "Thanks."

"No problem." I gave him a nod before adding, "Now who the fuck are you?"

I wasn't rude about the question. I mean, yeah, I might've dropped the f-bomb, but mostly I was just surprised to see another face working tonight. Grateful but surprised.

The guy skittered away from me, though, clearly intimidated, even though he was a good six inches taller than me and twice as wide.

Maybe my tattoos and multiple facial piercings put him off. Who knew?

"Uh . . . I'm Quinn. Quinn Hamilton. This is my first night."

I nodded. "Huh." Chewing on the side of my lip, I studied him from head to toe. "So, where the hell did Jessie find you? Hiding under a pew at church?" He looked like a freaking choirboy, his hair all gelled and styled and his face fresh and pure as if he'd just come from a confessional to blot all his sins away. All two of them.

I was surprised Jessie—our temporary boss—could even find a kid as clean-cut as him.

"Gamble hired him," Ten said, popping up beside Hamilton to pat Hamilton's shoulders from behind. Ten had a purple ring around one eye; I wondered where he'd gotten the shiner. Probably at football practice. "He's on the team with us."

"Really?" A college boy. That figured. But a football player? Ten had to be pulling my leg. "He looks like a fucking virgin." Even if he did have the size to play a mean game of ball.

Ten just laughed and slapped Hamilton's shoulders again as the poor virgin newbie blushed hard. "We don't hold that against him. Kid knows how to tackle like a motherfucker. And he can throw a ball almost as good as Gamble over there."

Kid. That was exactly right. The boy didn't look old enough to work at a bar, but he had to be at least twenty-one, which still made me the old guy. Mason, Gamble, Ten, and apparently Hamilton here were all barely twenty-one while I'd had my twenty-fourth birthday a couple months back.

In truth, I felt decades older than the four college boys I worked with.

Oh, well. Being around them made me laugh. Though I never hung out with any of them outside of work, I considered them some of my closest friends. And yet, I didn't bother to tell any of them I'd gotten hitched earlier today. It didn't seem like anything to brag about.

Tying on my own apron, I got to work, and showed Hamilton how to unlock the door to let the masses in. It really did feel like a flood tonight too. Busier than usual, the place exploded with noise and people. My tips went through the roof, and thank God, Hamilton had worked in a pizza parlor before, so he was decent at waiting tables.

I noticed some contention at the bar when Ten was up there trying to get some orders. Gamble sent him a brief glare before completely ignoring him, and Ten had to wait until Mason was free to get his drinks. Ten and Gamble were roommates as well as football players together, so I asked Gamble with my next trip, "You two love birds have a fight, or what?" Hell, maybe Gamble had given Ten the black eye.

Gamble merely pierced his roommate with a glare before refusing to answer me. I let it drop but studiously watched the two for a while until I saw a little brunette I knew Gamble was interested in enter the bar. When Ten spotted her as well, he turned tail and hurried away in the opposite direction.

Interesting. I wondered if the two guys were fighting over her. Sticking my nose where it didn't belong, I approached her, even though she'd just turned Hamilton down for a drink. Hey, I needed something more stimulating in my life than conversations with a three-month-old. So I snooped into my coworkers' lives.

At first, I pretended to treat her like any other customer. "Hey there, pretty lady. Can I get you drink?" Then I looked into her eyes and hoped to God my impression of a double take looked genuine as I pointed at her. "Wait, you were here a few weeks back, flirting with Gamble, weren't you? He's working the bar tonight."

I led her up to the bar and called for Gamble to get his attention. When he caught sight of her, his eyes lit up, telling me that if he and Ten had been fighting over her, he'd definitely won the match.

It was like watching a soap opera. Ten avoided the bar while she was there, and Gamble decided flirting with her was a job requirement. Since I didn't know Hamilton yet, I sidled up next to Mason to tip my chin toward Gamble and his woman. "So, what's up with those two?"

I was hoping for a *Ten-Gamble fight to the death* story, but Lowe shocked the shit out of me when he said, "She's his literature professor."

"Really?" Pretty little thing like her didn't look like any literature professor I'd ever seen before. But then I narrowed my eyes. "He's not doing her for a grade, is he?" I had no patience for men who used, manipulated, disrespected, or in any way hurt a woman.

Mason only smiled and shook his head. "Not that I

can tell. I think he really likes her."

"Hmm." That was good, at least. "What's Ten's problem, then? He into her too?"

"I don't think so." Mason gathered up a row of used glasses sitting on the bar. "I'm guessing he just knows more about their relationship than he's supposed to, and that makes Gamble nervous. Big time."

Knowing Ten and his smart-assed, lewd mouth, I figured Lowe had to be right. Ten had no doubt said something offensive enough to rile Gamble into giving him a black eye.

My shoulders slumped now that I knew what was going on. Well, that turned out to be a bummer of a dead end in the entertainment department.

I delivered my drinks, and a couple drunk girls flirted with me, inviting me back to their places. It put a strain on the celibacy pact I'd made with myself, even though I would've turned them down anyway. But then I got a nice, fat tip right before closing that made up for the rest of my dud of a night.

We closed up shop and kicked everyone out, except Gamble's teacher girlfriend. I was a little loath to go home so I took my sweet time sweeping the floor. I had a bad feeling I'd find Julian passed out in his swing, right where I'd left him before leaving for work. And it wouldn't be the first time.

I knew Tristy was having a hard time dealing with being a new mom, but damn, sometimes I wished she'd just hold him, or make nonsense faces at him, or change his damn diaper more than once a day.

I was trying my hardest to help her out and be patient because the moment I said something to piss her off, she was going lose it and probably fall of the wagon, turn to drugs, and then I don't know what. But every damn day, it got harder and harder not to just shove her son in her face and demand that she love him, and coddle him, and spoil him rotten already.

A commotion at the bar jerked me from my thoughts. I stopped sweeping to find some other chick had come in after we'd closed. She was a little older, probably in her mid-forties and looked like the rich, polished type.

Definitely not a typical Forbidden college student customer.

The way she paid attention to Mason told me she wasn't here to get her party on. She was here solely to see him.

"Fine," she snarled. "Since you're forcing me to speak out among your friends, then I will. I'm pregnant. And you're the father."

I was about ten yards behind her so I couldn't see what she was revealing when she swept open her coat, but I assumed it was a decent-sized baby bump by the way Mason's mouth dropped open as he stared in horror.

Suddenly, I regretted wanting something a little more exciting to happen tonight because I didn't want to think of Lowe as a cheater. He'd talked sweet about his girlfriend, Reese, as if he were a faithful, dedicated guy. I had liked that about him. But he turned away from the woman, and marched out from behind the bar and then down the hall to the bathroom in a guilty kind of trance. He'd definitely had sex with her.

Abandoning my broom, I followed him, pushing open the bathroom door to see if he was okay, and hopefully to find out he hadn't fucked around on his woman. Maybe all this was a big misunderstanding and—

Shit. He was too busy vomiting to talk to me. I heard the heaving from inside the stall and turned right back around.

The virgin was opening the front door for Mason's baby mama to leave as I returned to the big room.

"Well, he's puking his guts out," I told Gamble, thinking the cheating bastard Lowe deserved it. "Impending fatherhood must not suit him."

Gamble's teacher girlfriend made a sound as if she wanted to disagree with me, but she ended up holding her tongue. Gam glanced her way. "What?"

She gave a small shake of her head and sent him a tight smile. "Nothing."

They stared at each other a couple seconds, and had some kind of silent conversation that only a couple in a committed relationship could have, which made me want to gag because today was not the day I wanted to invest in true love, and soul mates, and happily fucking ever after.

A cell phone by the cash register started to ring, jerking me from my bitter thoughts.

Ten tipped his chin toward it. "Is that Lowe's phone?"

Everyone left in the club glanced at each other. We all knew Mason's shit was hitting the fan right now. Nothing on the other end of the line could be good news.

Gamble, the leader of our merry little crew, stepped toward it. "It's Reese."

Fuck. "That's his girlfriend's name."

Hamilton glanced at me, then at Gamble. "Should we answer it for him?"

Snorting out a dry laugh, Gamble lifted his hands. "And say what? Sorry, but your man can't come to the phone right now; he just found out he's going to be a daddy . . . to another woman's kid."

So no one answered the phone. Its ring seemed to echo through my chest, telling me with each vibration that Mason's woman knew exactly what had just happened.

I wondered if she was raging mad, or hurt so bad her spirit felt crushed. Poor girl. I wanted to kick Lowe's ass for her.

When the ringing stopped, it continued to ricochet through my head, making me feel evening guiltier. *Shit.* She deserved to know what had happened.

When the phone started up again, I couldn't take it. "I have a feeling she's going to keep calling," I told Gamble. "She must know something's up." If he didn't answer it, I would.

He sent me a scowl, and then looked at his woman for another one of their silent conversations.

I was about to hop behind the counter and grab the fucking phone myself when Gamble finally acted.

But as soon as he answered it, fucking Ten yelped, "Shit! Are you really going to tell her some old chick just came in, claiming Lowe knocked her up?"

Gamble sent Ten a death glare and promptly hung up the phone.

"You moron." I slapped Ten on the back of the head.

"He'd already answered the phone; she probably heard everything you said."

"Oh . . . fuck." Ten glanced at Gamble. "My bad."

"You mean, *Lowe's* bad," Gamble muttered. He pinched the bridge of his nose. "Damn it."

I ran my hands through my hair. This was going to end badly. And I could only picture one person getting hurt: Mason's girlfriend.

When Mason finally came out of the bathroom, I was ready to pin him to the wall by the throat and demand answers.

When we all turned to him, he jerked to a halt and rasped, "What?" Then his face went sheet white. "Jesus, she's not gone, is she?"

"Um." Gamble sent him a guilty cringe. "No, *she's* gone, but . . . uh, we might've just . . . accidentally told your girlfriend what happened." When Mason only stared at him, Gamble cleared his throat. "Your phone rang . . . and then it rang again. I was only going to let her know you were away for a minute, but . . . yeah . . . sorry, man."

Mason rushed to his phone like some kind of prick who was about to spill every excuse in the book to his unsuspecting girlfriend. But as soon as he said, "Reese?" the front doors of the club banged opened.

"Let me guess," a girl with straight, long dark hair said as she stormed into Forbidden. "Mrs. Garrison just showed up to announce you'd put a baby in her."

I was so busy gaping at Mason's girlfriend I didn't notice someone had come in with her. And when I did, I didn't immediately glance at the second person because I was too busy trying to gauge Reese's reaction. Surprisingly, she didn't look as pissed or hurt I as thought she would. She looked more resigned, as if she'd expected this to happen all along.

From the corner of my eye, I noticed the person following her had a huge stomach. Wondering if the pregnant cougar had followed Reese inside, I lifted my face to see a blonde wearing a bright pink shirt with Disney's Tinker Bell on it, instead of the older, dark-headed woman. I started to look away, dismissing her, when I did a double take, studying her shirt.

Tinker Bell?

A strange buzzing filled my head, and my skin suddenly felt about five times too small. Lifting my face from the cartoon fairy on her shirt, I took in her face.

Oh, hell.

Dumbfounded, I stood like a freaking statue, staring at the way-too-familiar vision that followed Mason's girlfriend up to the bar. For a second, I wondered if I'd gone delusional and was seeing things. No way was this woman real. But then I saw Ten glance at her. He lifted his eyebrows as his gaze traveled to her stomach.

Holy shit. If he was seeing her too, then she must be real. Right?

I froze as she passed right by me without even looking at me. When the hint of lilac wafted off her, I went dizzy from the shock.

No way. This wasn't possible.

I tried to shake my head, tried to get my vision to clear, because I couldn't be seeing what I was actually seeing. But my eyes soaked in every detail of the pregnant blonde.

I wasn't mistaken. Every inch of her was the same as I remembered. Even her lilac scent.

Tinker Bell from my glimpses was real.

3

-Eva Mercer-

About the same time Mason finally accrued more working hours at the club where he bartended and more money started trickling in, Reese's car went kaput.

I was quickly learning things never came easily in this household. It was so unlike the Mercer residence where there was never a financial concern. But that's what I loved most about living here. I'd rather worry about money any day of the week over what I'd worried about before.

The mechanic they took Reece's junk bucket to shook his head and quoted an astronomical price to fix it. So Reese and Mason began carpooling everywhere in his Jeep.

One Thursday evening when Reese wanted to go grocery shopping while Mason worked, she dropped him off at the Forbidden Nightclub and agreed to pick him up again at closing.

It was late when he clocked off, so I probably should've been in bed asleep. But my baby girl had been kicking, and punching, and doing chin-ups from my ribs for the past two hours; plus I'd been suffering from cabin fever because I hadn't gotten out of the apartment in a good three weeks, aside from checkups with the doctor and grocery store runs. So I asked if I could tag along when Reese went to pick him up. She claimed to be grateful for the company, ergo the ride together worked for both of us.

Plus, by the end of the night, I'm glad I was there for moral support.

Riding in Mason's Jeep felt strange, though, as if I was encroaching on his territory. Things had improved between us; I no longer got the cold shoulder and he said more than three words to me at a time, but . . . yeah. Now that we'd decided we didn't totally hate each other, we were kind of at a loss of how to treat one another. We certainly weren't friends, but we definitely weren't enemies, so it just felt awkward speaking to him.

But Reese had a way of smoothing the waters. And she eased the why-was-I-in-Mason-Lowe's-Jeep nerves by trying to guess the name I'd finally decided for my baby.

"Gabriella? That one's pretty."

From the passenger seat, I grinned and shook my head. "Nope."

"No Gabby? Okay then." She pulled into the parking lot across the street from the bar and had to slam on the brakes when a pair of stumbling drunk girls walked right in front of the headlights.

As I watched them sling their arms around each other and giggle together, leaning heavily against one another and wobbling in their high heels, it struck me: I could've easily been one of them. If I hadn't gotten pregnant, I would've remained a party animal to this day, living it up every night and getting wasted, trying to find something loud and boisterous to fill the void that was my empty life.

But instead, here I sat, rubbing my huge belly and talking baby names with my best friend. The strangest part of all was that I felt grateful to be where I was.

"Next," I said, after the girls passed in front of us and Reese could finally drive again.

"How about Hayleigh?" she guessed. She liked going through the alphabet and coming up with a name for each letter.

Grinning because I knew Isabella would be next—she always guessed Isabella for the *I*—I laid my head back and closed my eyes. "Do you realize if I wasn't pregnant right now, we'd probably be talking about some cute pair of shoes we wanted to buy, or the next party we wanted to attend, or I'd be making fun of some person I didn't like while you'd be defending them?"

Reese made a humming sound in the back of her throat as she parked. "What a difference a few months makes, huh?"

"I was so shallow." Shame washed over me.

Her warm hand covered mine where it rested on my stomach. "You were not shallow. You were . . . "

When she couldn't come up with a complimentary description within five seconds, I opened my eyes and glanced at her. As I lifted my eyebrows expectantly, she colored, and then cleared her throat discreetly. "Okay, you might've been a teeny tiny bit . . . self-absorbed. But that was . . . that was *before*. Now your life has meaning, and substance, and—"

"I want to be a good mom," I said to stop her rambling. "I want . . . I just want her to be happy, and content, and proud of who she is as a person." Completely unlike the way I'd been raised.

Reese let out a small sigh before patting my fingers and squeezing them. "You will. The way you already put her before everything else, I know you'll be a great mom. And I think she'll be lucky to have . . . "

When her words trailed off and she stared transfixed out the front windshield, I turned to look too but didn't see anything out of the ordinary. The way we were parked, the Jeep faced across the street toward the front entrance of the club where Mason worked.

"What?" I asked.

"I just . . . " She shook her head. "No. I must've been

seeing things. It couldn't have been her." Bringing her index finger to her mouth, she began to chew on a fingernail. Since I'd never known her to be a nail biter before, I turned back to the bar and tried to scan for whatever—or whoever—she was talking about.

I was about to ask her who she thought she'd seen, when she began to ramble to herself, which was definitely one of her nervous ticks. "I must be totally losing it. I mean, it's dark. The shadows could be playing tricks on my eyes. And we're all the way across the street, way too far to be sure it was her, and—"

Unable to handle a second longer of her panic attack, I lost it. "Oh my God, stop! *Who* do you think you saw?"

"I don't . . . I'm not . . . " She turned to me, her eyes huge and almost scared. "That lady who just entered the club, wearing a trench coat . . . I don't know, but I swear to God, she looked just like . . . Mrs. Garrison."

I blinked, and it took me a second to place where I knew that name. When it hit me, my eyes widened. "Mrs. Garrison? You mean, *Mason's* Mrs. Garrison?"

She gasped, and the hard expression on her face told me she was a second from clawing my face off. "Don't you ever call her Mason's *anything*. That bitch has no claim on him whatsoever."

"Okay." I lifted my hands in surrender and cringed out an apology. "Sorry. I just . . . I meant, Mrs. Garrison, the . . . the rapist?" When Reese's shoulders relaxed at that label, I frowned. "But what would she be doing here? Florida is a good nine hundred miles—"

"What do you *think* she's doing here?" Reese exploded. "She's stalking my man. What else has she ever done? She's obsessed with him. She's probably never going to leave him alone until someone finally takes her out."

Eyes lighting with intent, she grabbed my hands and squeezed them hard. "Oh my God, E. Let's take her out. Together. We're in a big-ass Jeep." Her fingers clamped even tighter around mine. "When she comes back out, let's gun the engine, pop this curb and run her wicked ass over. Oops, total accident. What was she thinking by jaywalking across a busy street in the middle of the night? And then . . . " She nodded, as if coming to the best part of the story. "While the car's lying on top of her and the only things poking out are her glittery red Christian Louboutins, I say we steal her shoes and run."

Wow, what was this, the homicidal version of *The Wizard of Oz*?

While, yes, I had to agree Mrs. Garrison, Mason's rapist—er, I mean, the rapist of Mason since she wasn't Mason's *anything*—was the Wicked Witch of Florida, that still didn't mean manslaughter was a good option.

And hello, how had *I* turned into the rational one?

"Yeah . . . " I said slowly before shaking my head. "No, I think maybe we should shy away from anything involving . . . murder."

"Murder?" Reese snorted. "It wouldn't be murder. It'd be . . . it'd be doing society a favor to rid that kind of evil from the world. It'd be a public service."

Crap, she was beginning to scare me. "But you weren't sure it was her, remember? The shadows. The dark. She was all the way across the street. It was probably someone else, sweetie."

Reese took a long, deep breath, physically calming herself. But she wouldn't stop staring at the front doors of Forbidden.

"How about you guess another baby name," I tried, suddenly glad I had refused to tell her what I'd decided to name my little girl; now I had something to use as a distraction. "You're on the letter *I*, remember? Maybe you could try to come up with something different than Isabella this time."

"Idiot," she hissed.

"What! Why would anyone name their kid Idiot?"

"No. *I'm* the idiot. I was so sure moving us halfway across the country away from her would get her out of his hair and free him from her forever, but—oh God. There." She pointed. "There she is." She covered her mouth and whimpered. "It's her, E. It's really her."

I'd never actually met Mrs. Garrison before. Never even seen her. I'd only heard Reese's horror stories. The woman was Mason's living nightmare. Sorry, I meant, the living nightmare *of* Mason.

It was dark, and I barely saw her face. But she did have a certain air about her that reminded me of my father. Rapists were all the same—predators.

"Are you sure? I can barely see her," I insisted, trying to keep Reese calm so her reactions wouldn't throw me into a panic attack, because that atmosphere about her freaked me the hell out.

"Yes," she said with steely determination as she reached for the keys still dangling from the ignition.

"Whoa. No." I reached out and caught her hand. "This is not . . . you shouldn't . . . " Damn, I was no good at this. We really needed Mason here. I'd never seen my cousin this unhinged before, but if anyone could draw her back from the ledge, it'd be him.

"Mason," I gasped, an idea hitting me.

Reese glanced sharply at me. Wow, even his name broke through her haze.

"What about him?"

"He's inside. If she went in there, she probably saw him, right? So don't you want to make sure he's okay?" I snatched her phone off the center console and thrust it at her. "Call him."

He'd make this better. He'd tell her she was mistaken, his blackmailing rapist was nowhere near Illinois, and everything was fine.

Blowing out a shaky breath, Reese nodded and dialed his number.

"Put it on speaker phone," I demanded, beginning to chew on my own nails as I turned to stare at the opening of the club, where the wicked witch lookalike had thankfully disappeared down the block.

Reese complied and I listened to the phone ring and ring, and ring. When it went to voice mail, she cursed and hung up.

I bit down a little harder on my thumbnail, wondering why he hadn't picked up. Mason always answered the phone when Reese called. It was all part of how disgustingly adorable they were together.

"Call again," I ordered.

She did. Then she did again. Baby Girl must've noticed the growing unease in me because she stirred in restless agitation. I smoothed my fingers over her, my palms naturally ironing down the image of Tinker Bell I had on the nightshirt I wore.

When the ringing stopped and the line clicked on, Reese and I sat up straighter and shared a relieved look. Until a muted voice as if it were a distance away from the receiver shouted, "*Shit! Are you really going to tell her some old chick just came in, claiming Lowe knocked her up?*"

"Say what?" Reese cried.

Immediately, the line went dead.

"Oh, no, they did not." Reese redialed.

I wasn't at all surprised when no one answered. Gulping in absolute worry for her, and even a little for Mason, I tried to calm her. "Maybe . . . maybe they meant . . ."

Reese glanced sharply at me. I winced. She muttered a couple more obscenities before grabbing her phone and shoving open the driver's side door.

"Ree Ree?" I squawked, not sure how I was going to physically restrain her if she actually did try to kill someone. I lurched out of the Jeep behind her, waddling pathetically in an effort to catch up. "What're you doing, sweetie?" I tried to sound soothing.

Totally didn't help.

"I'm going to find my goddamn boyfriend and figure out what the hell is going on."

Oh, double crap. I hurried after her. Her phone began ringing as soon as we hit the sidewalk. She answered without hitting the speaker to let me hear this time.

As she shoved open the front doors of the bar, she growled, "Let me guess. Mrs. Garrison just showed up to announce you'd put a baby in her."

I followed her inside, only to pause briefly in the entrance. Since the place had already closed, it was cleared out save for five guys—all employees because they wore the same kind of black T-shirt Mason always wore to work—and one woman. They had gathered around the bar in the back.

On the other side of the long counter, Mason dropped his phone from his ear and let out a long sigh. "Yeah.

Pretty much," he confessed, looking more troubled than I'd ever seen him.

Worry gnawed at my stomach. I'd just decided Mason wasn't the anti-Christ and now this? According to Reese, if he had knocked up Mrs. Garrison, it wasn't because he'd wanted to be with her. But still, how could Reese stay with him after learning he'd fathered a child with someone else?

Even more shocking, I didn't *want* them to break up.

It was such a perplexing thought for me since I'd spent the first six months of their relationship trying to get them to do exactly that.

But they loved each other, they were good for each other, and they gave me hope that happily ever after existed. Or at least they had up until now.

"I had a feeling we hadn't gotten rid of her so easily," Reese said as she hurried toward her man.

I bumbled after her because, yeah, I felt totally out of place being seven months pregnant and pretty much wearing my PJs—a nightshirt and gray yoga pants—while inside a bar with a bunch of complete strangers. I mean, sure, every guy in the place was hot, but they were still strangers.

"I say, if a stake through the heart doesn't work, we try cutting her head off."

I rolled my eyes and gave a soft smile. Only Reese would say that.

Mason laughed as if relieved by the way his girlfriend was taking all this. But he just as quickly sobered and shook his head. "I am so . . . so sorry."

When I saw the hint of tears in his eyes, I had to blink and glance away because I'd never seen Mason anywhere near tears before. It was hard to watch him like this. Lately, I could not let anyone cry alone. I even wailed over those dog adoption commercials, and I totally wasn't a dog person.

Freaking pregnancy hormones.

Too-forgiving Reese merely shrugged. "Hey, if there isn't some insurmountable obstacle in our path, we wouldn't be us, would we?" But there was still a tremor in her voice, letting me know she was just as freaked out as Mason was.

He didn't seem to want to be forgiven quite so easily, though. He brought her hands to his mouth and shook his head. "You shouldn't have to deal with this. You shouldn't—"

"I think she was lying," I blurted out, unable to watch them go through this torture. I felt so strongly against the whole idea, I absolutely refused to believe this could happen to Reese.

Winded from chasing her across the street, I plopped down on a stool at the bar beside Reese. When I spotted a bowl of beer nuts, the pregnant munchies struck with a vengeance.

I reached for them, not even caring how much the salt in them was going to make my ankles swell. Already tasting the tart nutty flavor, my mouth began to water. But mere inches away from scooping up the biggest handful I could manage, I was shut down. Warm fingers wrapped around my wrist, stopping me while another hand yanked the bowl away.

Ack! My nuts! That yummy, yummy salt and—

I looked up, ready to lambaste whoever was keeping the famished pregnant chick from her food.

But the dark brown eyes of the guy staring back at me caught me totally off guard. Wow.

He was—

I didn't even know how to describe him. A surface description would be tattooed and pierced. There was a metal hoop caught in his eyebrow, and two right next to each other through the corner of his bottom lip. His tats spread down both arms, making him look like he was wearing long sleeves instead of a short-sleeved shirt and one colorful design flared up the right side of his neck.

He appeared to be a bad boy straight from the wrong side of town. But there was something *not* bad boy about him. He simply didn't look like the type who didn't give a damn about life. His deep brown eyes held too much compassion and vivacity.

Then he winked at me, confirming he was definitely no typical careless, brooding antihero. "Let me get you a fresh batch, Tinker Bell. Who knows what kind of filthy fingers have been in these all night."

Nice. My pajamas had just won me a stupid pet name. Go me.

I began to roll my eyes, but I stopped, my mouth falling open as he jumped over the bar. Like jumped *over* the bar, the same way Sam and Woody had done in all those *Cheers* reruns I'd seen. It was so hot I might've drooled a little.

After he tossed the old bowl, he pulled up a big box full and sprinkled out a new pile. Just for me. When he slid the untouched beer nuts my way with an indulgent smile, I continued to stare at him in utter awe.

That might've been the sweetest, most thoughtful thing anyone had ever done for me.

But seriously, who was that sweet and thoughtful to a complete stranger?

I'd had plenty of guys be nice to me before when they'd wanted to get into my panties, but that was seven months of pregnancy ago. He surely knew there was zero chance of scoring with me now, and why would he even *want* to score with a pregnant girl? Maybe he was a total creeper.

I guess he could've been acting decent because I was so obviously knocked up. People did smile and hold doors open for me a hell of a lot more now than they had before. Even so, I was overwhelmed with how charming, yet totally suspicious his actions were.

Around us, the conversation continued, but I didn't hear a word of what anyone said. I was too busy caught in a staring contest with Mr. Considerate. He stared right back with a blatant curiosity that made my knees weak.

I had listened to Mason describe his coworkers to Reese when he'd first started. I knew of some guy named Gamble. He was the star football quarterback at the university where both Reese and Mason took classes. And then there was someone called Ten. There was also a Bick, or Rick, or Dick, something like that. He hadn't mentioned a fourth male coworker, though.

The man before me didn't look like quarterback material. I wouldn't have called him scrawny by any means, but he didn't have the usual beefy bulk of an athlete. His muscles seemed wiry, lean, scrappy and street savvy. Yeah, I'm not sure what I meant by 'street-savvy' muscles either, but the term seemed to fit him.

So, he probably wasn't Gamble.

Mason had referred to Ten as squirrelly and loud-mouthed. This guy didn't seem to fit that bill either. He was too laidback and . . . I don't know, friendly and open.

"I think she was lying, too," said the only other woman present besides Reese and me.

"Exactly." Whirling toward her, I sent her a *thank you* gesture for backing me up. Stuffing nuts into my mouth because Mr. Considerate was still staring as if I was some kind of ghost, and making my stomach churn even more than it already was, I went on. "I mean, hello. She'd have to be nearly as far along as I am, right?" When I glanced at Reese for verification, she nodded. *Right*. So . . . "Everyone I needed to tell about my baby was told months ago. Why would she wait this long to drop the bomb *now*?"

Reese turned to Mason, her body vibrating with eager hope. "Eva has a good point. And what about her fiancé? How does she know it's not his?"

Mason merely winced as if he didn't want to get his hopes up. "Maybe it took her a while to find me."

"Yeah, right." Reese snorted. "You know good and well that bitch has known every step you've made since leaving Waterford. She found out everything there was to know about me within a month. There's no way she lost track of *you*."

"So wait, wait, wait." One of the other bartenders stepped closer, waving his hands. "Lowe, you seriously fucked another woman, maybe even knocked her up, and you," he set his gaze on Reese, "aren't pissed as hell right now?"

Now *that guy* was definitely Ten, I decided.

"Oh, I'm pissed," Reese told him. "But not at Mason. Besides, this particular . . . event happened before we hooked up." Then she cleared her throat and lowered her face before mumbling, "Technically."

Looking helpless, Mason smoothed his hand over her hair before leaning over the bar to kiss her temple. "I can't believe this is happening. You are the only person I've ever wanted to have babies with. Jesus, Reese . . . " He squeezed his eyes closed and pressed his brow to hers. "Can't we just rewind everything so I can do it right the first time?"

Again, I had to look away. Their misery was just too intense. But when I turned my attention forward, Mr. Considerate caught my gaze. His brown eyes filled with sympathy, and he opened his mouth as if he wanted to say something to soothe me.

Sucked back into the staring game with him, I studied his face some more. He was handsome in an unconventional way. His face wasn't as filled out as most faces. It seemed gaunter as if he had to prowl the streets each night for food. But it worked for him. The hollow dips and lines gave him character, adding to his appeal and making him look even hotter.

All the metal in his face made me miss the hoop nose ring I'd had for a few months. I'd taken it out when I'd gotten shot and had to stay in the hospital. I had only gotten it to piss off dear old Dad, but I'd ended up liking it more than I thought I would.

Without warning, Mr. Considerate popped forward closer to me and rested his elbows on the bar so he could lean over the counter and check out my belly.

"You *do* have the most adorable baby bump I've ever seen," he murmured, as if answering someone else's observation. His voice stirred something in me that no one had ever awoken before.

I shook my head, wondering why the heck he'd said that, until the other chick responded, "And the other woman's breasts didn't look nearly as swollen as hers."

"I'd say," he shot back, lifting his gaze to meet mine. He didn't check out my tits, but my nipples burned and responded as if he had.

I'd never gotten turned on so easily before. Actually, I wasn't so sure if I'd ever been turned on in the first place. Usually I disappeared into my blank void when I let a guy do me. If I'd ever responded to one of them during our encounters, I was too busy chilling in my numb place to remember or feel it. But I know I'd never tingled from head to toe before just because a man was looking at me.

The foreign sensation freaked me out.

"Who the hell are you, anyway?" I demanded, needing a little more control over my own body than I had.

4

-EVA MERCER-

Mr. Considerate didn't seem perturbed by the snap in my voice when I commanded him to tell me his name. He just grinned, and said, "Pick."

Huh? "Pick *what*? I'm not picking out your name." *What the hell?*

"No." His smile only spread, reaching up into his eyes and making the beautiful brown orbs twinkle. "That's my name, Tinker Bell. Pick, short for Patrick Jason Ryan. You like?"

Like? This guy totally blew my mind. Why would he care if I liked his cool-ass, unique name?

"*Anyway . . .* " The woman I still didn't know cleared her throat, gave the two of us a strange glance, and turned back to the group. "She didn't have any of the water retention this girl has in her face."

I gasped and covered my cheeks so hottie boy Pick couldn't see how fat I'd become. Oh my God, how hideous did I look? And why would Reese let me leave the apartment this way? I swung to her for immediate support. "I have *water retention*?"

"What? No! No, sweetie. Barely any at all."

Oh my God! Barely any at all was so far away from none that she might as well have called me a bloated whale. "So I *do* then?"

Reese fumbled a moment before sending the other woman a scowl. But as she opened her mouth to calm me, Mason grabbed her arm. His face paled as he stared at something over her shoulder.

I glanced around to find a new person entering the nightclub—in a long tan trench coat.

Oh, hell. My best friend was going to go to jail tonight for murder.

"Anyone have a hatchet handy?" Reese growled, stepping away from the bar to face off with Mrs. Garrison. "Because I'm feeling a compelling need to hack a bitch."

"Dude." Ten bumped his elbow into the fifth bartender who might be Gamble—or not. Hell, I didn't know who was who anymore. "Chick fight. Awesome."

As I reached for Reese to stop her and failed, Mason jumped over the bar, much the same way Pick had hopped over it to fetch me more beer nuts. He had more success at catching Reese than I'd had and curled his arm around her waist, keeping her from attacking.

"I told you not to come back," he snarled at Mrs. Garrison. "And I made it crystal clear before I even left Florida that I never wanted anything to do with you again. Why are you doing this?"

She ignored him, smiling evilly at my girl. "Reese," she murmured, nodding her head in acknowledgement. "It's been too long since I last saw you."

"I know, hasn't it?" Reese answered with the same fake pleasantry before she sneered. "My hand's stopped ringing from the last time I bitch-slapped the shit out of you."

"Ohh!" Ten cried, smacking his hand on his knee and hooting. "*Burn*."

Mrs. Garrison narrowed her eyes. "You need to release him, dear. He doesn't belong here."

Everything went incredibly tense then. Mason and Reese ganged up on the rapist, trying to get to her to leave, telling her they didn't believe a word she said. And Mrs. Garrison just oozed evil as she ripped open her coat, revealing a swollen stomach.

"If I'm not pregnant, then how do you explain this?"

"Oh, please." I rolled my eyes and waved my hand at her. "That's the fakest pregnant belly I've ever seen."

When Mrs. Garrison swiveled my way with a scowl, I slid off my stool and pooched out my little girl. "This is the real deal, honey. So why don't you stop picking on Mason and my cousin Reese, crawl back home to Florida, and find someone new to harass. In fact, look up Madeline and Shaw Mercer why don't you? They actually deserve your brand of attention."

Ooh, I would just love to watch the two rapists go head to head. Might actually be a bit of a challenge for my father to chew Mrs. Garrison up and spit her out. Might take him a whole hour to destroy her.

She narrowed her eyes. "I should've guessed you were Reese's snooty little Mercer cousin. Eva, isn't it? The one who tried to trap Alec Worthington into marriage by getting herself knocked up—"

"Okay, that's enough," Reese snapped, and I'm grateful she intervened because just hearing Alec's name made me tense and shut down. But what the hell? Did everyone back home think I got pregnant on purpose to trap him into marriage? Eww. No way on God's green earth had I wanted to settle down with an egotistical ass like Alec Worthington. I wouldn't let that man back into my life now if he came crawling, begging, and offering money for me to forgive him.

While my head still swam, wondering what all my old cronies back in Florida really thought of me now, Reese and Mason and Mrs. Garrison went 'round and 'round some more, until the woman I soon learned was named Dr. Kavanagh pulled a pregnancy test out of her purse and told Mrs. Garrison to supply some physical proof.

Once the rapist finally agreed to pee on the stick, there was some debate over who'd accompany her back to the bathroom to oversee her test taking. When I tried

to chime in and say I'd gladly escort the wicked witch—
so I could be the first to laugh in her face when all her
lies were revealed—Pick whipped out his hand and
reached across the bar to grasp my elbow, halting me.

"I don't think so, Tinker Bell. If Lowe doesn't trust *his*
woman alone with that broad, then you sure as hell
aren't going near her. Not in your condition."

I blinked at him, startled into silent stupidity. Not in
my *condition*?

Really, just who did this guy think he was to act so
proprietary of me, making sure I had clean food and
stayed away from evil rapists? No one was ever that *nice*
for no reason at all. Made me wonder what his ulterior
motive was. I jerked my elbow from his grip, glaring him
down.

Men equaled bastards, and he was most definitely
male.

Blinking rapidly, his gaze zipped up to mine. He was
obviously startled by my anger. Maybe even a little hurt
by it.

I wavered, silently debating whether I actually had
the right to be mad at him. Let's see. He'd grabbed me,
twice now, and had made decisions for me as if he owned
me. Humph, owned *me*?

No one owned Eva Mercer, so I was going to be ticked
at him for trying.

The bastard.

The problem was I wasn't all that bothered. I couldn't
think of him as a creeper because everything he'd done
had been attentive and protective. Even his staring had
been more curious and seeking, as if he were trying to
recognize me from somewhere, or he wanted me to
recognize him. It certainly hadn't been creepy and
leering as if he were visually undressing me. Not that
anyone would want to visually undress a pregnant chick
with water retention while she was wearing Tinker Bell
pajamas. But there were all kinds of weirdos out there.
This I knew well.

Frankly, I didn't want to be on anyone's radar as
much as I seemed to be on his, so I forced my gaze away
from him, even though I was acutely aware of every

move he made. Of every breath he took. Of every—God, my reaction to him was so powerful it was irritating.

Only seconds after Mrs. Garrison followed Dr. Kavanagh and who I realized was Gamble down the hall toward the restrooms, she came storming back into the bar area. Without looking at anyone or saying anything, she marched toward the exit and left.

"Oh, going so soon?" Reese taunted after her. "I'm so sorry to hear you're not pregnant after all, you fucking lying *bitch!*"

The front door slammed, and the nameless bartender hurried after her to lock the doors.

Mason and Reese hugged, murmuring to each other. Relieved this round with the rapist was over, I rubbed my belly, wondering why some people perjured themselves the way Mrs. Garrison just had. I mean, I knew why *I'd* always lied and pretended and said things I didn't even mean. I had dirty, dark secrets I didn't want anyone to discover. But this . . .

I began to wonder what kind of childhood Mrs. Garrison must've gone through to turn her into such a loose screw. Then I stopped myself because I didn't want to know what made her a raping sociopath. As long as Reese and Mason were done with her for good, I never wanted to think about her again.

Reese dashed down the back hall to thank Dr. Kavanagh for helping her get rid of Mrs. Garrison. When Mason, still looking shaken, slumped forward to cradle his head in his hands and rest his elbows on the bar top, I opened my mouth to ask if he was okay. Then I decided against it, reminding myself we weren't friends.

"So, how far along are you?"

At Pick's question, I jumped. He remained on the other side of the bar, watching me intently.

"Look." I drew in a breath. "I don't know what you're trying to do, but you need to stop."

He opened his mouth, then shut it before shaking his head. "I need to stop what exactly?"

"I just said. I don't know. But cut it out, okay?"

Instead of turning pissy, he grinned. "So, you don't know what I'm doing that's obviously pissing you off, and I certainly don't have a clue, but I definitely need to cut it out?"

I scowled because when he said it like that, he made me sound like a complete idiot. "Okay, fine. You've touched me. Twice now. That's just not cool. Then you told me *what* I couldn't eat and *where* I couldn't go like you freaking owned me. Which you definitely don't. And now you're trying to make polite conversation as if we're friends. I don't know you. I've never met you before in my life. We are not friends."

"E.," Mason said, his voice sounding like a dog owner who was commanding his snarling pet to heel. "Leave him alone. He's always protective of women. He's fine."

Oh. I shrank back, guilt seeping into every pore. God, there I went again, automatically assuming every man alive was a bastard. I really needed to cut that out and start giving people the benefit of the doubt. Bad Eva.

"Sorry," I mumbled, ducking my chin and tucking a piece of hair behind my ear because this apologizing business was still so new to me. "I guess if Mason says you're fine, you're fine."

Brows furrowed, Pick opened his mouth to answer me, but Mason snorted out a laugh. "Wow. I cannot believe I just heard those words come out of Eva Mercer's mouth."

I turned to tell him I was at least *trying* to change, but I got a little distracted by how pale and upset he looked, still slumped against the bar and holding his head. "Are you okay?" I reached for his elbow and drew him to a barstool. "You look like you're going to pass out."

"Yeah, Lowe." Pick grabbed a glass from the back of the bar and filled it with water. "Why don't you sit down?" He slid the water in front of Mason. "Here. Drink something."

Mason sat, but he didn't move to take the glass, so I picked it up and tried to help him . . . to which he sliced me an annoyed glare. "Really?" He snagged the cup from my hand and drank on his own.

Confused by his irritation, I turned to Pick who winced and shook his head. "Bad move, Tink. Don't emasculate the poor guy by helping him drink."

I lifted my hands. "I was just trying to help."

Amusement flittered across his face. He leaned across the bar to talk in a quieter tone. "I know that. And you know that. But Lowe . . . " He shook his head. "He didn't know that."

He was so close I could make out a small chip in the silver paint on his eyebrow ring. I studied it a moment before my attention wandered to other features. But when I got to the deep, chocolate brown of his eyes, I was surprised to learn how much they were studying me in return.

I cleared my throat. "So, yeah." Shifting away so we weren't quite so close anymore, I glanced toward Mason, but he seemed lost in his own thoughts. "Sorry again for being a complete bitch. I just . . . I haven't met a lot of guys who aren't total bastards. So, I'm pretty much leery of everyone."

"Been burned a couple times, huh?" Sympathy ruled his tone.

My throat grew too dry to answer, so I didn't.

"Well, if this is as bitchy as you get, I'm not scared off. I've definitely met worse."

I snorted, meeting his gaze without meaning to. "I seriously doubt that, but thanks for trying to cheer me up."

"No, really." Grinning, he shook his head. "I'm dead serious. This friend of mine puts on a bitch front constantly." He rolled his eyes. "She was raped a lot when she was young, so she's built up this shitty attitude where she degrades everyone around her. It's become like this security shield she hides behind so no one can see the real her and know how broken she feels."

For a moment, I stared at him, unable to move, or breathe, or react. Sensation left all four of my limbs, as a cold blanket of fear covered me. It was the strangest thing, but I could feel the color drain from my face. I gaped at Pick Ryan, wondering how he'd just described my entire life to a perfect T.

Exposed, unable to hide, and feeling like a frightened rabbit with nowhere to run, my heartbeat fluttered in my chest. I swayed away from him.

And I saw the very moment he realized what he'd done. The smile slid from his lips, and his eyes bulged with shock. "No," he whispered as if absolutely horrified.

Oh my God. This was awful. No one had ever guessed this before. And outside of my parents, no one *knew*. How could he . . . after less than five minutes of talking to me . . . ? *No*. There was no way possible he could pluck that out of my brain just like that.

But, holy shit. He had. And he knew it.

"Tink?" His fingers skated across the bar, headed in my direction. I tried to jerk my hand away, but he caught my wrist. "No. Don't."

His voice was so soft and understanding, trying to coddle me as my eyes filled with tears. Dear God, I was going to turn into a blubbering mess if this kept up. "Let go," I pleaded, desperate to stop this.

"But—" He cut himself off even as he refused to let go of my hand. His face blanched of color as he met my gaze. Finally, he squeezed his eyes shut before opening them and saying, "I'm sorry. I didn't mean to crack open that little egg of information."

He looked about as torn up as I felt. I swear, if I had burst out really crying in that second, he would've joined me.

The force of his empathy was sweet, but it was a little too much for me.

"It's okay," I reassured him as I tugged at my hand, hoping to break free from his warm grip. "But you need to let me go."

He gave a watery laugh and shifted his gaze toward the ceiling. "Let you go," he repeated as if the suggestion were ludicrous. When he met my gaze, he seemed completely rattled. "Easier said than done, Tink."

Yeah, so that confused the hell out of me. I opened my mouth to ask what he meant when Reese exited the hallway.

"I don't know about anyone else, but I'd like to get the H-E-double-hockey-sticks out of here now."

Mason surged off his stool. "Amen."

"Right behind you," I said. As soon as I broke free of

Pick Ryan.

I looked up at him expectantly. He didn't let go, but he eased his grip enough for me to tug myself free, and still he made sure his fingers slid against mine the entire way.

I expected some kind of farewell from him, but he didn't even say goodbye. The sad longing in his brown eyes told me he couldn't say the words; they hurt him too much.

Out of my depth with this man, I ducked my face and turned away, trailing after Reese and Mason. When we reached the doorway, I glanced back, and I was as unsettled as I was thrilled to find his gaze still on me.

It was a quiet, tense ride to the apartment. Trying to make myself as small as possible in the Jeep's back seat because I knew this had to be the worst time ever for Reese and Mason to have a third wheel hanging around, I tried not to think about Mason's tattooed coworker.

But I did. Why had he been so intrigued by me? Why had I been so intrigued back? How had he so easily figured me out? Why . . . ?

Hell, it didn't matter.

Things had changed too much in the last few months. Back in September, I wouldn't have thought a thing about some guy staring at me as if he thought I was amazing. I would've expected it and flashed him a little more skin just to be mean and stir him up. But getting pregnant and finally growing up a little had killed all that. Knowing my face was swollen, my stomach was forty-five inches around, and my waddle was anything but seductive, I had no idea what could be so amazing about me.

But, like I said, it didn't matter.

Once we reached the apartment, I hung back as Mason and Reese went inside together. I was glad they'd already gone to their bedroom by the time I made it through the front door. I wasn't sure if I had the strength to watch the struggle those two had to go through to get over this bump in their lives.

After a quick bathroom break, I holed up in my room and crawled into bed. But even though Baby Girl was settled and not shifting anymore, I still couldn't fall to sleep.

Pick Ryan knew about me. I didn't like that.

ʃ

-PICK RYAN-

I found myself following in Lowe's footsteps and emptying my stomach in the nightclub's bathroom, which totally sucked ass. The room reeked of piss, and shit, and an accumulation of other guys' puke. Awesome.

After I was done, I stumbled into the kitchen to wash my hands. The cook had been gone for hours since they closed the kitchen at midnight. The quiet gave me a moment to breathe in some fresh air and digest everything that had just happened and everything I'd learned.

But shit. *She was real. She was real. She was really fucking real.*

And pregnant. And Christ, had she really gone through something similar to what Tristy had gone through? The way she'd turned sheet white told me yes, but I was still in complete denial over that part, so I chose to ignore it for the time being.

I had plenty else to freak out about, anyway. Namely the fact that the woman Madam LeFrey had told me was my soul mate was really fucking real.

I was dizzy with the knowledge of it. My Tinker Bell was real. And damn, now I knew why I'd even given her that pet name to begin with. She'd been adorable in her huge T-shirt with a picture of Tinker Bell stretched over her bulging belly.

But double shit. Pregnant? I had not expected that.

My Tinker Bell was pregnant. But *not* with my baby. Not my Julian. Not my Skylar. Not my—

Fuck, I probably shouldn't feel jealous as hell right now, should I? I probably shouldn't wonder about that baby's father or want to cut his dick off with a dull spoon. And . . . man, I hoped her pregnancy wasn't the result of her rape.

My stomach revolted again. I dashed to the nearest trashcan, but I'd already emptied all the contents in the bathroom, so nothing but dry heaves came up.

Suddenly plagued by memories of all the times I'd been forced to watch Tristy be brutalized, I gagged some more. I didn't even want to consider the possibility that Tinker Bell had gone through anything remotely similar. No. Just . . . no.

But I kept remembering all those times I'd been there to clean Tristy up afterward. Who'd been there for Tink? Who'd taken care of her and—

Dammit. It hurt too much to even ponder.

A cold sweat plastered itself to my brow and my hands wouldn't stop shaking. I absolutely could not believe—

"Yo, Pick!" Ten popped his head through the kitchen entry. "The virgin and I are taking off. You good with closing?"

No. I wasn't good with shit right now. But I waved him away, and forced myself into action, shutting down all the lights and locking up the place. It was a routine that helped keep me focused on the here and now, because thinking about—

I couldn't believe she was real. She was pregnant. She'd been violated.

I was still rattled by the time I let myself into my apartment twenty minutes later.

Fighter was awake and crying in the swing where I'd left him. Cursing, I hurried to him and pulled him into my arms. When shit and piss splattered my arms as the diaper that could contain no more disintegrated and plopped to the floor, I almost puked from the rank smell. Thank God I only had dry heaves left in me.

"Damn it." Dodging the mess, I hurried him to the bathroom to clean him off. After a quick wipe down of both of us and a good scrub to the floor, I carried him back to my bedroom where his crib and his baby stuff were kept because I'd promised Tristy I would get up with him every night. "Damn it, damn it, damn it."

My rage helped keep me centered on Julian and getting him taken care of.

Had Tris not even heard him crying? I wanted to shout at her, strangle her, and hell, I don't know. But this was no way to treat a child. I knew she was dealing with a lot of baggage, but three months ago, Julian had become a higher priority to me than she was, and I was so close to the end of my rope with her, my anger scared me. I was shaking from it.

I had never thought that would be possible. After watching her get shit deal after shit deal in life, I figured I'd always want to protect her and take care of her. I would always be patient and understanding. Except now, I just wanted to rip her fucking ass for the way she handled her own son.

Julian still fussed as I got him a new diaper. I knew he had to be starving, so I started for the kitchen to get him some food. But first, I paused at Tristy's door and tried the doorknob to see if she was even home, because fuck, he'd been crying pretty loudly. How could she not have heard him?

She'd locked herself inside, so I hoped that meant she was still here, but I didn't break the door down to make sure. I still had Julian to take care of. I'd deal with her later.

The kitchen was a disaster. My new wife must've gotten the major munchies after I'd left for Forbidden.

Bags of potato chips and empty cookie packages had been pulled down from still-open cabinets where they littered the countertop. Cans of soda were lying on their sides with sticky puddles splattered under them. And the dishes were probably at least two weeks old. But I had no time for fucking dishes.

Still seething as Julian and I fell into the rocking chair in the living room with a full bottle, I plugged his mouth with a plastic nipple and closed my eyes with relief when he finally stopped wailing.

"I hear you," I told him, exhaustion draining from my tense shoulders as I kept my lashes shut. "I'd like nothing more than a nipple in my mouth right about now too, kiddo."

But nipples in my mouth made me think of sex, and sex made me think of . . . yep. Just like that, there came Tinker Bell, flooding my head. Except I saw her as she'd been tonight. Not as she was from my glimpses.

Pregnant and defensive, nowhere near as happy as she'd been in any of my visions.

I could not believe she was real. Or maybe she wasn't.

Yeah, I liked that idea. The girl I'd met tonight couldn't be Tinker Bell. Not *my* Tinker Bell. She was just some doppelganger for the woman Madam LeFrey had shoved into my head. Lots of people had exact lookalikes in the world. No way could Eva Mercer be my soul mate. Except, shit, she'd been wearing Tinker Bell on her shirt. And she'd smelled like fucking lilacs. How could that be a coincidence?

In no way did I want to believe all that voodoo shit, like glimpses and predestined soul mates. If only that old bat had just been full of it ten years ago, wanting to scare a teenage boy into cleaning up his act, I could get past this. But everything inside me had seamlessly aligned into the proper place when she'd looked up into my eyes for the first time. It felt as if we belonged together, and not just because I'd spent the last ten years looking for her in every woman I saw. Eva Mercer and I had serious chemistry.

Damn, it was weird thinking of Tinker Bell as anything other than Tinker Bell. But her face finally had a name. A true, legitimate name.

Stunned I had not just one but several names to work with, I blew out a breath. Eva Mercer, Alec Worthington, Madeline and Shaw Mercer, Reese and Mason Lowe. I had filed each one into my head when I'd heard them tonight. I certainly hadn't meant to, but I'd turned into a sponge the moment I'd seen her, needing to soak up every detail.

When I spotted Tristy's closed laptop sitting on the arm of the sofa within reaching distance, I snagged it and situated it onto my lap.

Finished eating, Julian twisted his attention to see what I was doing, so I turned him around and sat him upright, propping his back to my chest so he could watch the screen with me.

"Better?" I asked.

He didn't answer except to reach his chubby fingers toward the keyboard when I flipped up the lid.

I chuckled. "Oh, yeah. You must be thinking exactly what I'm thinking. Let the typing begin."

I wiggled my fingers for a moment, acclimating myself to Tristy's home screen before clicking onto an internet search. The first hit for Eva Mercer was a Facebook page. I clicked into it and realized Tristy had never logged off, so I came in on her account. But it wasn't the Eva Mercer I was looking for.

Damn, I hated the disappointment that sucked the joy right out of me.

Using the Facebook search engine, I typed in her name again and scrolled through a page full of Eva Mercers before I spotted Tinker Bell about fifteen profiles down. My fingers shook as I hovered the pointer over her picture. God, did I want to do this?

Torturing myself by finding out more about her was stupid.

Nothing could ever happen between us. Being as pregnant as she was, she obviously already had someone in her life—Alec, the Prick, Worthington—and I was fucking married.

A derisive laugh choked from my throat when I remembered it'd only been earlier today that Tris and I had gone to the courthouse. Fate hated me. It figured I'd finally meet my soul mate on my *wedding day*.

"Fuck it," I muttered under my breath and clicked into her page. I'd dreamed about this girl for the past one hundred and twenty-five months, and I didn't know a single thing about her. I deserved *some* dirt. Anything.

Her profile picture was a selfie of her wearing shades and an electric blue string bikini on a beach, or at least somewhere sunny and outside. She had taken the snapshot from above and was looking up so the camera aimed straight into her generous cleavage. And my, what fine cleavage she had. Damn. Not a single tan line marred her perfect golden skin while the wind blew a few tendrils of sunbaked blonde hair into her face. She was so flawlessly gorgeous she took my breath away.

The cover banner showed a line of hot, plastic-looking girls with their arms draped over each other's shoulders as they all tipped their heads back to take what looked like JELL-O shots. Tinker Bell—*er, Eva*—was right in the middle of them. Her face was flushed as if she were already drunk off her ass.

Defeat ran like acid through my veins. This wasn't the kind of girl I'd imagined she'd be. My Tink had always been sweet, loving, family-oriented, untouched by rape.

Fighter must've found my fingers around his chest holding him upright interesting because he began to play with them. I let him wrap his hand around one and draw it into his mouth. As slobbery gums clamped onto my knuckle, I pointed to the picture of her.

"See that woman right there, kiddo? That was supposed to be your mom."

Pain shot through my gut as soon as I said the words. This wasn't fair. It just wasn't fair at all. Unable to keep looking at her picture, but unable to leave her page, I scrolled down, learning as much as I could about her. But all I saw was this self-absorbed, rich party girl. She was either drinking it up at some immaculately lavish home with a bunch of carbon copies just like her or she was snapping pictures of new purchases she'd made at the mall. All her status updates were bashing someone she didn't like, talking about her latest shopping spree, or figuring out where she wanted to get drunk next.

Though her page hadn't been updated in five months, probably around the time she'd learned she was going to have a baby, there were no pictures of any family members, no talk of anything good she'd done, and— *shit*.

When I came across a seven-month old picture of her hanging all over some clean-cut, dark-haired prick in Dockers and a collared Polo shirt, I stopped and stared, unable to shed the jealousy that gnawed at my gut.

Was this him, then? When I shifted my finger to run the cursor over the frame, the name Alec Worthington appeared. My jaw popped. I wondered if the cougar had just been talking out her ass when she'd said Eva had tried to trap him into marriage by getting herself pregnant, or if it was true. But I seriously doubted he'd been the one to rape her. She wouldn't have let a picture of him stay on her page if he had been. Would she?

Either way, I still hated him. I hated everything he represented. But most of all, I hated what he meant to her. He was obviously the type she preferred: rich, pampered, entitled. He was everything I wasn't.

White-hot envy burned deep in my gut. I just couldn't believe she was already taken or that she was the kind of person I usually resented.

None of this made sense. If fate had really labeled Eva Mercer as *my* soul mate, then why did we come from worlds so far apart it was frankly a miracle we'd ever crossed paths? Which made me wonder how a girl from the yacht club kind of life had ended up at the Forbidden Nightclub at two in the morning on a Thursday night, six or seven months pregnant. Mason's girl was obviously her cousin but . . . fuck, it didn't matter. I'd never see her again.

I didn't want to think about this anymore. It didn't matter how long I wondered about anything; I wouldn't get any answers. Why was I torturing myself like this?

Reaching out to shut the lid to Tristy's laptop, I paused when a little message box popped up in the bottom right-hand corner of her page.

When I saw it was from Quick Shot, everything inside

me went cold. Quick Shot had been one of Tristy's drug buddies back in the day. I'd suspected he might've been her supplier too, but I'd never been sure. Until now.

The message read: *hey babe u stil lookin for a hit?*

My hands balled into fists and my muscles went so taut Julian shifted restlessly, letting me know he'd fallen asleep.

Counting to ten, I forced myself to breathe deeply and not lose it. Then I set my fingers to the keyboard and mechanically typed: *No.*

The fucker replied instantly. *wi not? ur ol man kach u?*

I assumed *kach* was idiot-speak for catch, so I answered: *Something like that.*

Mabe latr then.

Jesus, learn how to spell, you dip shit.

I slammed the laptop shut, startling Julian. Drool ran down the back of my hand as his mouth lost contact with my knuckle.

Blowing out a breath to calm myself, I tossed the laptop onto the couch and eased from the chair. After carrying the baby to my room and settling him gently in his crib, I covered him up and then stood there a moment, watching him sleep before I felt composed enough to confront Tristy.

I shut the door behind me as I stepped into the hallway. After I reached the barred entrance to her room, I waited another moment, trying to keep my shit together.

And then I began to pound on her door.

"Get up, Tristy. We need to talk." I'm sure I was loud enough to wake her, but when she didn't open the door within a minute, I completely lost my temper.

"*God dammit*," I bellowed, pounding hard enough to rattle the entire doorframe. "I swear I will break this fucking door down if you don't open it within ten seconds."

Five seconds later, I began to shout, "Ten. Nine. Eight."

The door flew open, and my lovely bride of less than a day glared at me, wearing an old ratty pair of boxer shorts and a too-large T-Shirt covering the fact she hadn't lost any of her baby weight since giving birth.

"What the fuck is your problem?" she muttered, rubbing her eyes and shoving ratty tangles of red hair out of her face.

"Are you still talking to Quick Shot?" I demanded, folding my arms over my chest.

"What?" she croaked in the middle of a yawn. Dropping her arms to her sides, she muttered a curse. "Jesus Christ. You woke me in the middle of the night to ask *that*? I thought the fucking building was on fire."

"Answer the question, Tristy."

"What? No. *No*, I'm not talking to that shithead anymore. Haven't seen him in months."

I arched an eyebrow. "Really? Is that why the time on the Facebook message you sent him, begging for a dime bag, says four *hours* ago? Is that why he just fucking asked if you were still looking?"

Tristy's mouth fell open. She shook her head once before saying, "No . . . wha . . . Wait, what were you doing on my Facebook page?"

Great. Of course, she'd twist this around to make it all my fault. That's what she always did. Gritting my teeth because I felt caught, I muttered, "I was trying to look something up and you were still logged in. Then these messages started popping up and, fuck! You've been fucking lying to me." Grabbing handfuls of my hair, I gritted my teeth to keep myself from reaching out to shake her. "Damn it. I've been busting my ass to keep you clean and safe, and you do *this*? With *Quick Shot*? The dick who left you abandoned in an alley the last time you overdosed?"

If it hadn't been for a complete stranger calling the cops, who'd in turn called an ambulance and rushed her to the hospital, she'd probably be dead right now.

"Keeping me safe?" Tristy snorted and folded her arms over her chest. "You've been keeping me prisoner is what you've been doing. I've been trapped in this goddamn apartment for—"

"You have *not* been trapped. You know damn good and well you can do whatever the fuck you like. You're free to come and go as you please."

Tris snorted and rolled her eyes. "As if I could go anywhere with a *baby* strapped to my hip. I have no freedom. No—"

"*You* got yourself knocked up. And if you ever need a break from Julian, I'll find you a fucking babysitter. Damn it, Tris. This is no reason to go to Quick Shot for fucking drugs!"

"It's what I know, okay. Those people, that life, that's what I know. Who I am. And you're trying to change me. Turn me into something I'm not. Into *her*."

I gritted my teeth and glanced away when she mentioned Tinker Bell. I regretted the night we'd gotten drunk together and I'd spilled everything to her about Madam LeFrey and the glimpses she'd given me. She'd never forgotten, never let me live it down.

"I'm not trying to change—"

A pounding on the front door of the apartment interrupted me. "Police. Open up."

I closed my eyes and hissed out a breath. Of course, someone had called the cops on us. The walls in this building were paper-thin. Someone probably heard me every time I sneezed.

Fuck.

"Are there any drugs in my apartment?" I asked quietly. "Don't lie to me, Tris."

When she answered, "No," I opened my eyes and sent her a hard look. She scowled and hissed, "There's not. I swear to God."

"There better not be. Because if I get arrested tonight, you have nowhere to go. *Julian* has nowhere to go."

"If Quick Shot was asking if I still needed a hit, that meant I hadn't gotten anything yet, right?"

If anything, she at least managed to look guilty that she'd just confessed she'd been planning to bring drugs into my home . . . the one thing I'd made her swear never to do.

I sniffed and shook my head. "Unbelievable." Whirling away from her, I stormed down the hall to the front door and yanked it open.

Two officers stood in the hallway, and one of them

had arrested me the last time I'd gotten into a fight. "We received a domestic disturbance call from one of your neighbors."

"Yeah, I'm sure you did." I pulled the door open wider to let them in. After growing up in the foster care system, I was well aware how this worked. When the cops showed up at your place, you cooperated, you didn't turn belligerent, and you answered whatever questions they asked. Nothing more.

They stepped over the threshold and immediately turned their attention to Tristy. "You okay, ma'am?" the shorter one asked.

Tristy clammed up in the presence of cops, mostly because we'd always been treated like suspects, even if we were the victims.

"I'm fine," she mumbled, ducking her head, which only made her look like an abused spouse.

God, this better not end badly for me. She might regret my interference in her life and feel as if I was keeping her prisoner, but without me, she'd be on the street right now and Julian would probably be dead.

When she wasn't any more forthright than that, the men turned to me. "So what's all the commotion about?"

"I shouted," I confessed. "And I pounded on her bedroom door, trying to wake her up so I could talk to her. But I wasn't even loud enough to wake the baby."

"And just what did you need to talk to her about at . . . four in the morning?"

Four? It was already four? Nice. I was going to have to get up in four hours to get ready for my day shift at the garage.

I shoved my hands into my pockets, feeling the need to be belligerent but trying to hold it back.

"Hands out of your pockets," they barked at me together.

I jerked my hands free and lifted them to show I didn't have a weapon.

"Why did you need to wake her up and talk to her?" the taller one with more attitude repeated.

Glancing away from him, I ran my hand over my face. "I found some messages from another guy on her

Facebook page. And I didn't like what they said."

There. I made it look like a lovers' quarrel. I don't know why I covered for her since she'd been planning to sneak drugs in behind my back. But I didn't want to see her go to jail either.

The ball-buster cop, the one who'd arrested me seven months ago, stepped close to study my face. "I've dealt with you before, haven't I?"

"Yes," I admitted. "For battery and assault."

I had looked up the guy Tristy was seventy percent certain was Julian's biological father because he'd been hitting her, and I'd bashed his face in.

Almost disappointed that I was being so cooperative and not giving them any lip, the men turned away from me, eyeing Tristy.

"Are you sure you're okay, ma'am? Did he hit you or touch you in any malicious way?"

She drew even further into herself.

I sighed and rubbed my forehead, ready to get this shit over with. "Tristy, just let them look you over so they know you're okay."

"No!" she screamed, stomping her foot and glaring at me. "I don't want anyone to fucking *look* at me. I don't want anyone to fucking touch me. JUST . . . LEAVE . . . ME . . . ALONE."

Down the hall, Julian's muted wail made me hiss a curse. "Now *that* was loud enough to wake the baby," I told the officers before I started down the hall to fetch him.

The short cop followed me. "Anyone else home?" he asked, glancing into Tristy's room when he passed it.

My gut clenched as I hoped to God Tris hadn't been lying about there being no drugs here, because if they found anything in my apartment, Julian would end up in foster care. That was the very last thing I wanted to happen to him.

"No," I answered as I opened the door to my room. "It's just the three of us." I kept the light off so the sudden blare wouldn't hurt Julian's eyes, but the cop flipped it on as he stepped into the room behind me. And of course, the baby's wail grew louder.

"Hey, little man," I murmured. "Did Mommy wake you up? I know she did, you poor thing. And you just got to sleep too. I'm sorry, bud." Kissing his hair as I cuddled him against my chest, I swayed on my feet, hoping to rock him back to sleep. With my nose buried in his dark curls, I slid my gaze to the cop who wouldn't stop gawking.

"That kid's black," he blurted out, shocking the shit out of me.

I blinked, wondering what Julian's ethnicity had to do with anything. "Gee, really? I hadn't noticed."

At my sarcastic answer, he shook his head. "But . . . you're . . . why are *you* the one coming back here and taking care of him when he's obviously not yours?"

For a split second, I saw red. Just because my blood didn't flow through this child's veins didn't make him any less mine. I loved this kid more than just about anyone.

"Because no one *else* is going to take care of him. And he *is* mine. He's my stepson."

Eyeing me strangely, the cop nodded slowly. Something akin to respect glinted in his eyes before he said, "Next time you get mad at your old lady, keep your tone down, will you? If we take too many calls at the same address, someone eventually goes to jail. And that someone would be you."

I nodded, realizing he was trying to give me a break and a friendly heads-up. Some people would've taken it as a threat, but I knew how these guys worked.

"I hear you," I answered.

He lingered another moment, his gaze returning to Julian who'd closed his eyes and was snuggled peacefully against me. "Cute kid," he finally said.

I grinned and shook my head. "I'd say thank you, but he didn't get his looks from me. *Obviously.*"

Sniffing out a short laugh, the cop tipped his hat. "Keep the volume of those arguments down." And then he was gone.

Listening to them bid Tristy a farewell as they left the apartment, I continued to pace the floor with Julian. I knew all too well that if he were even the slightest bit awake when I laid him down, he'd holler his head off. He had to be completely out of it.

When Tris appeared in the doorway, her arms folded over her chest as she stared into my room at us, I sighed.

"Okay, maybe I shouldn't have yelled and pounded on your door," I confessed before she could start in on me. "And yes, I could've waited until morning. But, shit, Tris. Are you really that miserable here? Is it so bad that you'd rather go out and get high, not knowing where you're going to wake up, what's going to be done to you, or who you'll end up with than having a roof over your head, a clean bed to sleep in each night, and a constant supply of food?"

Tears filled her eyes. She wiped the back of her hand across her cheek, smearing them. "No, but . . . Damn it, Pick. I get so . . . so sick and tired of being cooped up in this place all day. And I thought it'd be okay if it was just marijuana. Nothing heavy. It's just . . . the kid's always *here*. There's just no break. You get to go off to work; you don't have to constantly listen to him cry and demand shit all day."

I blew out a breath and closed my eyes, resting my cheek on Julian's head. "I wish you had come to me and told me this instead of looking up Quick Shot. Damn, Tris. If you need a break, I can get you a break. I can watch him every evening I have a night off, and you can go out and do whatever. Plus, I'm sure Mrs. Rojas next door can babysit one or two times a week."

When Tristy's eyes lit with excitement, I knew I'd said the right thing. "Really? You'd do that for me?"

"Tris." I rolled my eyes. "When have I not done everything within my power to get you whatever you needed?"

"That's true," she admitted with a sheepish shrug.

"If you promise not to contact Quick Shot again, I'll make sure you have more . . . freedom. Okay?"

"Okay." Then she stepped in the room, looking relieved. "I can walk with him for a little bit if you want?"

Her offer shocked the shit out of me. "Uh . . . yeah. Sure." We fumbled awkwardly as I tried to pass the sleeping kid off to her. Julian stirred but didn't wake.

When his head was securely propped on her shoulder and she patted his back in a motherly manner, I stared openly, unable to look away.

"What?" she asked, giving me an irritated frown. "Am I doing something wrong?"

"No." I grinned and shook my head. "Nothing. You're doing great. I'm going to change into something to sleep in and get a snack. Be right back."

When she nodded, I grabbed a T-shirt and a pair of sweats and darted out of the room. I couldn't stop grinning as I changed in the bathroom and then ransacked the kitchen, looking for food. I finally just smeared butter on some saltines, sandwiched them together, and called it good. After tossing all the disposable trash I found on the counters, I stacked the dirty dishes so there was some counter space left and hurried back to my room.

I'd been gone five minutes max, but that must've been too long for Tristy. She'd already settled Julian back into his crib and returned to her own room.

With a disappointed sigh, I stroked the sleeping kid's head before settling into my own bed, where I dropped crumbs all over my sheets as I polished off my snack. I guess I couldn't expect too much from the new mommy yet. So for now, I'd take five minutes. She'd touched him and held him. That was progress.

6

-EVA MERCER-

My roommates were driving me crazy. A week after the wicked witch of Florida had swooped in to mess with Mason and Reese's life, the awkwardness in our apartment grew so thick I was sure it'd smother all three of us. And it was Mason's fault entirely.

Reese tried, she really freaking tried to move past it, to shrug off Mrs. Garrison's visit and get on with her life. But Mason just wouldn't let her. He kept acting like some kind of abused dog who'd been kicked in the ribs one too many times. He shied away from Reese, couldn't look her in the eyes, stopped touching her completely. His guilt was so tangible it left a nasty aftertaste in *my* mouth. Despite her normally upbeat personality, even Reese had stopped attempting to be cheerful.

They were both so miserable; I hated it.

So when Mason walked into the kitchen one evening while I was fixing myself a snack—carrots, apple slices, and celery smothered in peanut butter because I wanted to deliver a healthy kid—I dropped my butter knife on the counter and grabbed his arm, yanking him close. I'd had enough of this shit.

He tried to jerk back in surprise, but I wouldn't let him go.

"This has to stop," I hissed, glancing warily toward the opening of the kitchen in the hopes that Reese didn't walk in any second and catch me chewing him out.

"What? I just walked into the kitchen." Pulling his arm away, he managed to free himself as he scowled back.

I snorted. "As if. Your non-stop moping is sucking the life out of Reese. I hope you realize that."

His face drained of color, telling me how much he'd noticed it . . . and hated it, too. But the way his jaw tightened said he was pissed I'd brought it up. Stepping in close, he whispered, "What the hell am I supposed to do about it? I can't stop what happened. It already *happened*."

"Yes, it did. But it's over and done with. All you can do is control how you react to it. And you're having a *really* bad reaction. It's dragging Reese down with you."

His eyes filled with torment. "Don't you think I know that? It's killing me to see her every day with all that pain in her eyes. But I don't know how to stop it. There aren't enough apologies on earth to make up for what happened. And there's no way to fix it. No way to—"

"Just stop right there." Rolling my eyes, I set my hand over his mouth to shut him up. "You're thinking about this all wrong. Looking for forgiveness from her is not what you need, because newsflash, numb nuts: she's already forgiven you. That's the amazing thing about Reese. She *forgives*. And an even more amazing thing about her is that she *moves on*. Just think about it. Were you able to tell her ex-boyfriend had tried to kill her and nearly succeeded just four *months* before you met her? No, because she has this super power of being about to get past awful, disturbing, traumatic events. It's all part of the beauty of who she is. She would've gotten past this last episode with Mrs. Garrison too, but you're not letting her. Every time you pull away, or refuse to meet her eyes, or dodge a conversation, it *kills* her."

Mason closed his eyes and covered his face with both hands. He gulped audibly and took a moment to regain his composure. Then he blew out a breath and dropped his fingers.

"I swear to God, Eva. The last thing I want to do is hurt her, but I just can't . . . *God*." He swiped the heels of his hands over his eyes. "I don't know how to get past this. I don't deserve her forgiveness. I don't . . . how the hell do I touch something so pure and amazing when I'm so fucking filthy?"

I bit my lip when tears began to swim in my eyes. Freaking pregnancy hormones. They just wouldn't leave me alone, would they? But my heart was breaking for poor Mason. The man could not forgive himself for what he'd been.

Picking up a piece of peanut-butter coated apple, I took a bite and began to munch, trying to act as cool and collected as I didn't feel. While Mason tried not to emotionally fall apart in front of me, I licked my fingers clean of my snack and then wiped my mouth with the back of my hand. Finally, I cleared my throat.

"So, I've been reading all these new mommy, expecting-your-first-baby articles online lately. And they're really cool. They go week by week through your pregnancy, telling you how big your baby is compared to a piece of fruit." Setting my hands over my bump, I grinned. "Baby Girl's about the size of a pineapple right now, by the way."

Mason blinked and stared at me as if I'd lost my mind. But I did have a point, and I was about to get to it.

"The advice that helped me stop freaking out the most was about dealing with all the mistakes I'm going to make as a mother. They say it's inevitable, you know. No matter how great I want to be, I'm going to mess shit up. And I'm going to worry that I'm destroying my child's life. But I read this thing that said as long as I love her and try to make her happy, the rest will fall into place. Discipline, temper tantrums, all of it. Instead of drowning in my mistakes, I'll learn from them. And the more joy I bring to her life, the more I'll bring to my own." Reaching out, I grasped Mason's hand hard.

"Are you listening to me, Mason Lowe? Just love Reese and make her happy. And when you bring joy to her life, it'll bring joy to *your* life. Instead of wallowing over everything you did wrong, you'll forgive yourself and move on from this, because making her happy is the ultimate priority. Everything else is just bullshit."

He gently squeezed my fingers in return. "I want to do that," he assured me, his voice low and filled with sincerity. "I do. I just want to show her how much I love her and bring a smile to her face, but I . . . " He shook his head helplessly. "Right now, I can't even imagine what I could do to accomplish that."

My lips spread wide as an idea hit me. "I'll tell you what you're going to do. You're going to dig out that engagement ring you have hiding in the bottom of your shirt drawer, and you're going to propose to her. Tonight."

"Wha . . . " Mouth falling open, Mason sputtered a couple seconds before he scowled at me. Stepping closer, he sent a quick glance toward the opening of the kitchen before he whirled back and quietly hissed, "How the hell do you know what's in my shirt drawer?"

I snorted and waved an unconcerned hand. "Oh, please. If you want to hide something from your girl-friend, next time put it in a better place than you did. Reese loves wearing your shirts when you're not here. She found the ring months ago."

"She . . . " He shook his head, denying it, and then tried to speak, but nothing intelligible came out.

"You should've heard her," I went on. "I'd just fallen asleep when this *scream* ripped through the entire apartment. I thought someone was killing her. By the time I scrambled into her room, she was dancing around and trying to put it on, but her fingers were shaking so badly she kept missing. She was so happy she was crying. I don't know if I've ever seen her that ecstatic before in my life."

Mason caught his breath. His eyes filled with wonder. "She liked it?" He sounded so hopeful and yet uncertain, so I punched him in the arm.

"Liked it? Hell, no, she didn't like it. She freaking *loved* it. And FYI, Lowe, you have immaculate taste in jewelry. I mean, holy God, who knew you'd pick out such a beautiful ring? I'm seriously impressed."

He grinned so hard his entire face lit up. "Really?"

"Yes. So dig that bad boy out and make it official already, will you? That, I know for certain, will make my Ree Ree happy."

Mason nodded. "Okay." He started to turn away as if to follow my instructions that very moment, but then he paused. "Wait. I can't. I still haven't planned the perfect proposal. I keep thinking I need to take her to a fancy restaurant and somehow have the waiter bring it out with her food, or—"

"Don't you dare be so cliché. This is Reese we're talking about. She'd prefer something simple, yet private, just between the two you. Maybe a picnic—oh, hey. She loves that park across the street as much as I do. There's this big-ass tree by the lake. You could spread a blanket out under it, feed a couple of the ducks, eat a romantic little snack, and then, you know . . . do your thing."

Biting his lip, he seemed to consider my suggestion. "I don't know how to ask, though."

"Oh, whatever." I shoved his arm right where I'd just punched it. "Every time I've ever heard you tell her you loved her, you've always spit out some big, flowery speech that would put a romance novel hero to shame. Just start talking, and the words will come. I promise you."

"But I want it to be perfect."

I sighed. "Reese doesn't want perfect. The poor, confused girl wants *you*. So . . . give her you."

He mentally debated a moment longer. The guy looked positively thrilled by the idea, yet utterly frightened by it. It made my own stomach flutter with anticipation. I was about to shove him again and demand, "*Just do it already*," when he nodded.

"Okay. I'm going to do it."

I almost peed I was so excited. But the anxiety in his

gray eyes made me wary. "Tonight," I ordered.

"Yeah," he said. "Tonight."

I about hugged him, but that would've been way awkward because the last time I'd tried to *touch* him, I'd reached for his junk to show Reese he was a cheating bastard just like every other dick out there. But he hadn't been a cheating bastard; he'd knocked my hand away, and Reese had turned on me as if I was the backstabbing whore of the century. Not wanting to relive any of those memories, I cleared my throat and ran my fingers through my hair, glad when Reese entered the kitchen.

"So what're we doing for supper?" she asked, completely clueless as to what Mason and I had just discussed.

Mason jumped because his back was to the doorway and he hadn't seen her enter. When he whirled toward her looking as guilty as spit, I snorted. Time for me to set the wheels in motion before he blew it.

"You two are driving me crazy," I said, taking control. "Both of you have been moping around the house all week, and it's enough already. I'm officially kicking you out for the evening. I'd leave myself, but . . . I hate walking too far in this condition, ergo, you guys have to go. I'll pack you a picnic supper, but you better not come back until you're both freaking approachable again. Got it?"

Reese lifted her eyebrows and sent me a withering stare. "Wow. I'm so sorry our drama is messing with your life, E. Let me just get right on—"

"Sweet Pea." Mason stepped toward her and swept an arm around her waist, making her look up at him in surprise.

As her startled blue eyes grew wider, he forced a tense smile. "Let's just . . . let's listen to her and go out for a couple hours, anyway. Just the two of us."

She started nodding immediately, but it took her a few seconds for her to say, "O . . . Okay. Yeah, that sounds good."

"Great." His smile was slow and devastating enough to make Reese visibly melt. I swear the girl almost let out a dreamy smile.

Then he kissed her forehead and released her. "I'm going to grab my . . . my hat from the bedroom. Be right back."

As soon as he was gone, a grinning Reese whirled to me. "Did you just see that?" she demanded and began bouncing on her toes. "He touched me. *Ohmigod*, Eva. I think he's starting to come around again."

I had to turn away before I spilled the entire surprise, but I was so happy for my best friend. I couldn't wait to see her face when she and Mason returned from their picnic. "So, what kind of food do you want?" I asked, already opening the refrigerator and yanking out deli meat. Sandwiches sounded like a nice light meal for the simple kind of proposal Reese would prefer.

She tried to assist me in packing the supper, but she was so eager to get going and too busy jabbering about what might've cheered Mason up that she mostly just followed me around as I bagged up some fruit and veggies along with some of her favorite chocolate chip cookies.

When Mason returned to the kitchen, he slid a hand into his pocket and leaned a shoulder against the doorframe. I noticed he'd totally forgotten to put on a hat as he said he was going to do, but Reese didn't. She just smiled adoringly.

A knowing grin lit his face as he studied the brilliant sheen on hers. "About ready?"

"Yep," I answered for her, waving a mini bottle of wine behind Reese's back so Mason could see the last thing I shoved into the hulking lunch bag before I zipped it closed. "I think you guys are good to go. Have fun. Don't come back until it's late, and feed the ducks for me while you're there."

Slinging the strap of the bag over my shoulder, I put my hand at the base of Reese's back and propelled her toward Mason. He straightened up in time to catch her around the waist and pull her close. Then he grinned at me and took the lunch bag. "Thanks, E."

Reese suddenly sent a suspicious look between the both of us. I swallowed, hoping she hadn't caught on to what was happening. But then she whirled to me. "You're really eager to get rid of us. Are you planning to throw some wild party while we're gone?"

I snorted. "Yeah, I'm having my secret boyfriend come visit and we're going to practice for baby number two." But as soon as I said that, an image of Mason's co-worker, Pick, popped in my head. But I smacked him right back out and rolled my eyes at my cousin as I patted my belly. "Wow, why are you so paranoid?"

"Yeah, Reese." Mason slid his hand down her arm and laced his fingers with hers. "Who cares why she wants us gone? Let's just go have fun."

She turned to him, and I could tell she'd already forgotten who I was. "Okay," she said. "I guess I'm ready."

I'm glad she was already wearing a cute outfit. She never would've forgiven me if I'd let her leave the house for her proposal wearing something sloppy and old. But even her hair looked adorable in a perky ponytail.

I followed them to the opening of the kitchen as they crossed the living room hand in hand. Neither of them glanced back as they left. But strangely, instead of feeling left out, I felt full and content. Huh. I guess that article I'd read knew what it'd been talking about. Make someone else happy and the feeling came back to you tenfold. What a wonderful discovery.

Still wishing I had a crystal ball so I could eavesdrop on their picnic and watch the big proposal, I settled on the couch with my healthy snack and pulled Reese's computer onto my lap so I could look up more baby sites.

I'd stumbled across this do-it-yourself-mommy web-site I was absolutely in love with. Since I was finally learning I couldn't go out and buy whatever my spoiled heart desired, I had started making all kinds of neat things to get my baby what she needed in an affordable way.

Reese let me have one of her old knock-off Dolce and Gabbana bags to transform into a diaper bag. It was black, gold, and leopard print, but I was thinking it needed a splash of pink along with a couple more pouches for all the necessities I was going to need to carry around for my baby girl.

As I stitched, my mind wandered back to Mason's coworker. It still bothered me that he'd guessed my past somehow. Like a constant itch under my skin, I hated knowing what he knew about me. And I wasn't so sure I liked the way he affected my hormones either. I'd just been getting used to the fact that I never had to use a guy again to go to my numb place. I wanted to wipe sex from my life completely. So why was I wondering what Pick looked like shirtless, or just how many tattoos and piercings he had under the rest of his clothes?

I wished there was a way to wipe my feelings and his knowledge about me completely from existence. Brooding, I kept sewing and thinking, and coming up with no good plan. Not that it mattered what I did about Pick Ryan. I doubted I'd ever even see him again. Who cared what he knew about me?

Unless he told Mason.

Oh, shit. He could not tell Mason. Mason would tell Reese. And if Reese knew—

I had to convince him he'd assumed the wrong thing, that what he thought wasn't true at all. Yeah. Next time I saw him—and I *would* find a way to see him again— that's exactly what I'd do.

When the front door of the apartment opened, I jumped, surprised to realize how much time had passed. Reese and Mason blew into the living room, full of smiles and laughter.

I had quite the mountain of material, scissors, a needle and thread piled up around me on the couch. I was so engrossed in sewing an *R*—the last and final letter—into the side of the bag that I screamed and stabbed my finger when the door burst open.

"EVA! Ohmigod, ohmigod. Look! *Look!*" Reese hurled herself at me, hand spread and waving as the diamond glittered from her second finger. "Can you believe it? Can you just believe it? *We're getting married!*"

I made a spectacle of studying the ring we'd both already oohed and awed over months ago. Then I looked up and dryly reported, "I'm . . . shocked."

Reese yanked her hand free and frowned at me. "Oh. You're no fun. This is happy news. *Amazing* news."

Grinning, I rolled my eyes. "And I'm happy for you. Honestly. Congratulations."

As Mason shut the door to the apartment and leaned against it to watch us on the couch, I glanced up at him and arched an eyebrow. "Well done, Mr. Lowe."

"Mr. Lowe," Reese sighed the name as she slid her hand from mine and launched herself off the couch toward him. "And I'm going to be Mrs. Lowe. Mrs. Reese Lowe. Teresa Alison Lowe. *Ohmigod*, I love it!"

She hugged him and began to kiss him all over his face. He laughed and caught her head in his hands so he could hold her still long enough to press a soft, lingering kiss on her lips. "What? Did you actually doubt this was going to happen?"

"No." Sighing, she melted against him and rested her cheek on his shoulder. "Not really. But I still can't believe it's here. It's happening now, and it's finally *real*."

"Of course it's real. I love you, Reese." He closed his eyes and pressed his mouth to her temple. "I'd do anything to show you that."

A big wad of jealousy caught in my throat. The only way I was able to swallow it down was from thinking about how fulfilled I was after playing cupid for them. Doing good deeds really was an amazing sensation. And I was even more satisfied because it was Reese I'd helped make happy. But why couldn't I be happy like that, too?

Because I didn't deserve it, I reminded myself.

"Give me two minutes," Reese told Mason as she pulled away from him, the look in her eyes making it obvious what she had planned.

His gaze heated and he held her fingers for as long as he could before she stepped back out of his reach. "Yes, ma'am," he murmured before grinning like a guy about to get laid.

When Reese giggled, I snorted. I think they'd both forgotten I existed. As Reese turned away, bounding from the living room, Mason sighed in contentment and met my gaze. Seeing me tempered his mood instantly. He cleared his throat and tried to blink the desire from his expression, but didn't quite succeed.

"So," he said, nudging his toe at a scrap of fabric that

had fallen to the floor. "Thanks."

Shrugging as if my intervention had been no big deal, I went back to sewing my *R* into place. "It's the least I could do."

"Yeah, but . . . you freaking saved us. Reese and I were drowning until—"

"Oh, don't be so dramatic." I couldn't let him get all mushy because then I'd get all emotional and have to blame a whole new batch of tears of my poor, innocent pregnancy hormones. "You guys love each other. Nothing was going to change that. I just knocked a little clarity into your head."

"Well, it's the knock I needed, and I'll be forever grateful." He stepped closer and tipped his head to the side to see what I was sewing. "Is that the baby's name?"

I gasped and covered the word with my hand, even though he'd already read it . . . and knew. "Don't you dare tell anyone," I warned him. "Especially Reese. She's been having fun trying to guess."

His gray eyes glittered silver as he grinned at me. "My lips are sealed. But only because I owe you one." Then he glanced toward the doorway leading into the hall, which led to his and Reese's bedroom. "You think it's been two minutes yet?"

"I think it's only been thirty seconds, you big horn ball."

Scowling, he shoved his hands into his pockets and grumbled around a moment before muttering, "Well, I can't wait anymore." Then he was off, hurrying down the hall in pursuit of his fiancée.

I smiled and shook my head. I liked their kind of love. I enjoyed watching them make it past this obstacle, and I liked knowing they were going to live happily ever after. But it also depressed me.

I knew I had my baby girl. Once she was born, I'd probably be too busy raising her to want what Reese had with Mason, but a part of me still ached, a part of me wanted to be loved like that, too.

7

-PICK RYAN-

Exactly two weeks had passed since I'd gotten married and discovered Tinker Bell's real name, and it felt as if my entire universe had flipped on its axis.

Not much changed at home aside from the fact that Mrs. Rojas, mother of four and our neighbor to the left, agreed to watch Julian three days out of the week. With a little more 'freedom' as Tristy called it, her moods brightened considerably. It put a bigger strain on my budget, but to live with a happier, drug-free Tris, it was worth it.

Nothing changed at my jobs either. Cars still came in needing repairs at the garage, and customers still came in looking for drinks at the club.

It was me who suffered.

Internally, I went haywire. I felt restless with all this energy to burn but nothing to exhaust it on. I couldn't stop thinking about Tink. I knew it was stupid. The real

Tinker Bell—Eva Mercer—wasn't the kind of person I thought she was. We would never click, probably wouldn't be able to carry on a single conversation together if we ever even saw each other again. She no doubt stepped right over lowlifes like me and kept on walking without even realizing she'd crushed them below her name-brand heels. I should've completely forgotten about her.

Except I couldn't help myself. Every time I worked with Mason, I had a mental battle with myself over whether or not to pump him for information. Where did she live, how in love was she with that fucking prick boyfriend of hers, what were her biggest hopes and dreams and fears in life? I wanted to know everything. But no matter how many times I talked to Lowe, I stopped myself from finagling my way into asking about his girlfriend's pregnant cousin.

She hadn't even told me when her baby was due. I wondered how close she was now, or if she'd already given birth. Was it a girl or a boy? Damn, there was so much I didn't know. And worst of all, it was Thursday. I knew I was going to be working with Mason again, the one guy who held so many of the answers I sought.

He was behind the bar when I strolled into work. I was actually early because I was hoping to get some chatty time in with him. There had to be *some* inconspicuous way to get him to mention her without revealing how desperate I was to know everything.

I fully expected Noel to begin shouting something about the apocalypse coming because, for once in my life, I wasn't late. But no one said anything, and there was nothing to do but wait for my shift to start. I realized I'd even beat the football star to work. But Ten was setting up tables, and if he was here, then Noel should be too because he always caught a ride with his roommate.

"Where's Gamble?" I asked.

"Heartbroken." Ten moodily shoved a table into a better position on the floor so we waiters could move around easier between them later on in the night.

Aw, hell. This was the third night this week Gamble hadn't come in. "He and Professor Girlfriend didn't make it, huh?"

"He's a complete mess," Hamilton said with a sad shake of his head. "I've never seen anyone so upset after losing a girl before. He really loves her."

"Damn." I shook my head.

What a shame. I'd been jealous of Gamble and his woman two weeks ago when she'd come into the bar to see him. They'd had this intense connection between them. It was upsetting to know the bond they'd shared hadn't kept them together. And it gave me no hope whatsoever for my own situation. But it didn't keep me from my plan either. Mission Extract-Info-From-Lowe was definitely a go.

Glancing at him as he slotted the money drawer into the cash register, I tried to gauge his mood. Thank God *he* didn't emit any heartbroken vibes. He'd seemed pretty melancholy after his confrontation with the cougar. I hoped like hell his girl hadn't dumped him, because then he certainly wouldn't give me any information about her cousin.

But tonight, the man looked pretty damn perky. He was whistling some tune I couldn't name under his breath. So I opened my mouth to ask what had him in such a good mood when Ten made a gagging sound behind me.

"Dude, what the hell is that on your shirt?"

Hamilton appeared next to him a second later, grimacing as he stared at my back as well. "Looks like someone puked down your back."

"Shit." I grabbed the shoulder of my shirt and tugged at it while I craned my head around to see. And yep, Julian had lost his supper all over me before I'd taken him over to Mrs. Rojas's tonight. "My kid must've spit up on me."

Ten's jaw fell open. "Excuse me? Did you say kid? Since when do you have a *kid*?"

I frowned, still trying to twist a glance over my shoulder to see how bad the damage was. "Since about three months ago."

"Shut the fuck up." Ten kept gaping stupidly. "Why the hell did you never tell us you were a *dad*?"

I stopped twisting and shrugged. "I don't know. I didn't figure stories about diaper changings and crying spells were something you cared to hear about."

"Well, no, but . . . " He shook his head, still dazed. "Damn, man. Did you forget to wrap it up or what?"

I sighed, realizing how long it was going to take to explain my situation—for which I'm sure Ten would raze me for taking on someone else's kid—when Jessie, our boss until her dad recovered from his heart surgery, strolled out from the back hall that led to her office.

"Good. You're all here." She clapped her hands together gleefully. "Wait." She paused as she glanced at the four of us. "Where's Gamble?"

"Sick," Ten hissed at her. "Leave him the fuck alone."

"Damn." She chewed on her bottom lip. "I was going to have you do an auction night since we hadn't done one in a while, but if there's only going to be four of you working—"

"We can handle it," I was quick to speak up. Auction nights brought in a shit ton of cash, and I could always do with more cash, especially since I was going to be spending more on a babysitter now.

"Well, then . . . handle it." Jessie waved a hand in my direction, which basically told me I was in charge. Then she turned away and marched toward the exit, leaving us to 'handle it' by ourselves.

"What's auction night?" Mason was the first to ask after she was gone.

"Oh, baby, are you in for a treat." Ten rubbed his hands together gleefully. "The customers have a little bidding war—only on a ladies' night, mind you—for some lucky woman willing to pay the most to have the bartender of her choice personally cater to her for the rest of the evening."

"The best part is the guy who's chosen gets fifty percent of the take," I told him.

Mason's eyebrows furrowed and he glanced over at Quinn, whose eyes had grown to twice their normal size.

"We're going to auction off . . . *ourselves*?" Quinn sounded scandalized.

"Hey, it's fun." Ten knocked him in the shoulder,

roughing him up a little. "All you have to do is flirt and talk to the broad until closing and make sure her drink never runs out. All the chicks dig it."

"And you get *fifty* percent of the haul," I repeated.

But neither Quinn nor Mason seemed all that enthused by the idea.

"Dude." Ten pointed at my back and shook his head. "You might want to clean that shit up. No woman's going to choose you with baby crap on your back." Then he shook his head and muttered something about me being a dad before he loped off to finish rearranging the tables.

But, shit, he was right. I pulled my phone from my pocket, hoping Tristy would be willing to run a new shirt down to me. No way did I have enough time to go home, change, and hurry back before we opened. Except she must've already taken advantage of her freedom for the night. She didn't answer the apartment phone, and I'd never gotten her a cell phone because I just couldn't afford one for her too.

"Dammit." I disconnected. After shoving my phone back into my pocket, I grabbed the back collar of my shirt and ripped it off over my head so I could see just how bad off I was.

"I'm going to try to rinse this off," I told whoever was willing to listen. But when I looked up, it was Mason I caught staring.

"Whoa," he said, gaping at my bare chest. "You have the words Tinker Bell and Skylar tattooed over your heart."

I slapped my hand over the tat, protective of it. I think I would've rather listened to him bash my nipple ring than mention that specific tattoo.

"Yeah," I said, furrowing my brow and ready to kick ass if he made one disparaging remark about the family I'd always craved but was starting to realize I'd never get. "What about it?"

"Nothing." He shook his head but kept staring at the area I continued to conceal. Lifting his gaze, he finally added, "It's just . . . strangely ironic. I mean . . . " He squinted slightly. "Isn't Tinker Bell what you kept calling Eva the other week when she was here with Reese?"

Fuck.

My mouth went bone dry as I stared back at Mason. But how the hell had he remembered that? He should've been preoccupied with that cougar claiming she was carrying his kid.

"E . . . Eva?" I croaked, frowning as if I had no idea who he was talking about. "She was the pregnant blonde, right? Your . . . your girl's cousin or something like that."

Damn it, now I was being overly stupid. He was going to know I was faking it. And yep, he narrowed his eyes, probably wondering what the hell was up with me.

I shrugged. "She had Tinker Bell on her shirt. What else was I supposed to call her?"

"Nothing, I guess. I don't know." Mason waved a hand. "Ignore me. It was just a shock to see that name on top of Skylar, that's all."

I crinkled my brow, totally confused. "Wait. Why? Who's Skylar?"

Mason let out a breath before saying, "No one. I mean, not yet. That's what Eva's going to name her daughter when she's born."

"*What?*" I plopped onto a stool and gaped slack-jawed at him. But, no. No, no, no. This couldn't be happening. My vision went momentarily black. I thought I was going to pass out, but all too soon, I blinked Mason back into focus.

"Hey, are you okay?"

"I . . . " I patted my chest a few times. "Yeah," I finally choked out. "I'm fine. Great. So . . . she's having a girl, huh? Eva?"

He nodded slowly, eyeing me funnily. "Yeah. Actually, she refused to tell anyone the name she chose, but I caught her sewing it into something last week and she swore me to secrecy."

"Swore you to secrecy?" I scowled, still pressing my hand to my chest, trying to keep all the broken pieces inside from falling out, because shit . . . Tinker Bell was really having a little girl named Skylar. And I had nothing to do with it. "If she swore you to secrecy, then why the fuck did you tell *me*?"

Mason pulled back in surprise at my barked question.

"Uh . . . probably because I didn't see how it'd matter if *you* knew. I doubt you'll ever cross paths with her again."

God, did he have to rub that into my face quite so hard?

Clearing my throat, I glanced down at the shirt in my hand. "Yeah," I said, my voice hoarse. "Good point." Waving my pukey clothes, I started away, needing to escape. "I'm going to see if this'll rinse out."

I don't remember the walk down the hall to the bathrooms. I don't even remember turning on the water in the sink. I just knew I suddenly looked up from the shirt I was scrubbing under the freezing running faucet and saw my own reflection in the mirror while I lost it.

"Fuck," I muttered and threw the slopping wet shirt at my image. "*Fuck.*"

Backing up until my spine hit the wall, I gripped my pounding temples and slid down until I was sitting on the floor, holding my head in my hands and resting my elbows on my knees as I tried not to hyperventilate.

How could this be happening to me? Julian, Tinker Bell, and now Skylar all ended up being real people and none of them were fucking mine. Not my woman, not my children, not my anything.

They were supposed to be *mine*, damn it. My family. *My* happily ever after. Jesus . . .

Madam LeFrey hadn't been lying when she'd said she'd given me my hope back. For ten years, I'd blindly yearned for all these things, things I wasn't even sure I wanted. A wife? Children? That wasn't really my style, but I'd still craved them with every breath I had because I'd craved the way I'd felt in those glimpses. I craved the rush of love, the pride of accomplishment, the tenderness of being adored by others, of finally having somewhere and someone to belong to. And now . . . now there was nothing. No love, no happiness, no satisfaction.

My hands began to shake and I squeezed my eyes closed. I had gotten by for a full decade, banking on the mere hope that maybe those stupid glimpses might come true. I'd kept my nose clean, which was no small feat where I came from. It took a goddamn lot of effort to be good when you lived where I'd lived, where everyone around you cheated and stole to get ahead. It would've been so easy to follow that path. But I wanted to be a good person, a person who would eventually deserve my Tinker Bell.

Except there was no way in hell I'd ever be near good enough for that rich, pampered girl I'd seen on Facebook. Not that it mattered. She already had someone else. And the fucking prick had put a baby in her; he'd put *Skylar* in her.

My Skylar.

Throat closing over, I lifted my face to bump the back of my head against the wall. After concentrating on pushing air through my lungs, which beat the nausea away, I crawled back to my feet and fished my wet shirt out of the sink, soaking my hair when I slopped it on.

I had a shift to begin and an auction to win. My happily fucking ever after certainly wasn't going to come to me, so I guess I'd have to keep working my ass off to make up one of my own.

8

-Eva Mercer-

"Okay, so I know I should totally be working on my final World Masterpieces essay tonight, but ugh, I'm too brain-dead." Reese plopped onto the couch beside me. "Let's watch a movie instead."

Leaning across me where I was working on my newest craft project to make a diaper holder to hang from my crib, she snagged the remote. "So what're you in the mood for? Jake Gyllenhaal, Channing Tatum, or Zac Efron? I'm voting for Zac since he looks the most like Mason."

Wrinkling my nose, I paused on the chunk of fabric I was hacking away at with a pair of scissors. "Mason looks nothing like Zac."

"Excuse me? They're both hot. That's close enough." Settling herself down, Reese tossed her legs over the armrest and used what little space was left of my lap as a pillow. I totally envied her for being so flexible.

Someday, I'd be able to move like that again too . . . as soon as I got this extra thirty pounds off my waistline.

"They still look nothing alike." I went back to chopping, giving the fabric a ragged, fringed look.

"Fine. Then which actor do *you* think Mason most resembles?"

Ugh. I didn't care who Mason looked like. Ever since she'd gotten engaged, Reese had been even more annoyingly in love with him than usual. It was beginning to drive me batty.

"I don't know," I said. "Maybe a young Tom Welling, Tyler Hoechlin, or ooh . . . Danny off *Baby Daddy.*"

"God, yes. Danny is hot. Mason could definitely be a Danny."

"I wonder what his real name is," I pondered aloud. "Danny, I mean." Poor guy probably got tired of people calling him Danny when he was actually someone else.

"Who cares," Reese announced. "He's hot, that's all I know. Though he seriously needs more shirtless scenes on the show."

Finished with my cutting task, I set the cloth and scissors in the bag beside me and snorted. "He's shirtless in, like, every episode."

"I know." Reese aimed the remote at the television and started flipping through channels. "It's totally not shirtless enough."

With a laugh, I put my project on hold for a while so I could enjoy this quality time with my bestie. Lifting a chunk of her dark hair and beginning to braid it, I realized that soon we wouldn't have these moments together anymore. She'd be married to Mason, and I'd have Skylar. We were headed in entirely different directions. Better, but different directions. All the same, I'd miss the hell out of her.

"Hey, what about this one?" Having found a movie on Amazon Prime, Reese waved her remote at the television screen to gain my attention.

I lifted my face only to frown. "That doesn't have Jake, Channing, *or* Zac in it."

"But it's got Chris Hemsworth. So . . . same thing. We're watching it."

"Okay, Sweet Pea," I agreed, using the name Mason called her. "Whatever my adorable, precious bride-to-be wants."

But as soon as she pressed play, her cell phone rang.

Reese leapt off me with the agility only a non-pregnant girl could accomplish and jogged into the kitchen for her phone. "It's Mason," she called, only to answer with a low, seductive, "Hey, most handsome man in the world. How're *you* doing?"

After listening for a moment, she paused and sent me a significant glance. "Oh, he does, does he?" An ornery grin spread across her face. "Well, sure. Eva and I would just love to deliver *Pick* a new shirt."

At that name, I sat up straighter, paying rapt attention as my blood raced with interest.

Reese met my gaze, and arched an eyebrow as she kept talking into the phone. "'Kay. Sure. Love you too. Bye." When she disconnected, her smile was a little too smug. "Well, well, well."

"What?" I demanded, needing to learn whatever little scrap of information I could about Mason's coworker. "Why are we delivering Pick a new shirt?"

"I knew it!" She snapped her finger and pointed at me, crowing, "I just knew it. You're totally into him, aren't you? *Aren't you?* Yes, you are!"

My face flushed as I ground my teeth. "Give me a break," I muttered. "I'm seven and half months pregnant. The last thing I want is any kind of involvement with some guy."

Except maybe that *guy.* Ugh, why couldn't I get him off my mind? We'd had one brief encounter weeks ago, and that was it.

"I don't know," Reese murmured, tapping her chin idly as she studied me. "Becca said she'd never been so horny in her life as she was when she was pregnant."

I scowled. "Yeah, except there's something seriously wrong with your sister." Though maybe that *was* my problem. My freaking pregnancy hormones were making me horny. But why had Pick been the only one to set them off?

"He is pretty hot," Reese said as if answering my

unspoken question. "I mean, not as hot as Mason. But there's definitely some notable steam rolling off him. The tattoos and piercings make him seem all wild and uncontrollable."

"Whatever," I snapped, sending her an incredulous glower. There wasn't a single thing wild about him. And besides, "He's way hotter than Mason."

Crap, I'd totally just admitted I was attracted to him, something I shouldn't even be thinking about. I didn't want guys on my radar. Even considering men and relationships when I was a little preoccupied with become a single, first-time mother was just plain ridiculous. What was wrong with me?

Reese didn't seem to notice the panic on my face; she was too busy choking on her disagreement. "Not even possible. No one—I mean, *no one*—is hotter than Mason."

I patted her hand sympathetically. "Yeah, just keep telling yourself that, sweetie. Now, what happened to Pick's shirt?"

I was dying of curiosity over here. Had some female customer ripped it off him? Not that I'd blame her. I was curious to know what he looked like bare-chested, too. He was probably more of a Jake Gyllenhaal lookalike . . . with more tattoos. *Yum.*

"Well, apparently, your lover boy came to work tonight without knowing he had dried baby puke running down the back of his shirt." When I pulled back in surprise, she arched an eyebrow. "Did you know he had a baby?"

"No." I shook my head, feeling almost betrayed, which made absolutely no sense because I was carrying around thirty extra pounds of my own kid over here. "Keep talking."

She rolled her eyes, but complied. "Anyway, he doesn't have any time to run home and fetch a fresh clean one, so Mason wanted to know if I—but I'm including you in this errand too because I love you and know you want to see him—could grab one of *his* shirts and speed it down there for his friend to wear."

"Of course, we will." I struggled to get off the couch,

feeling like a freaking beached whale that couldn't move as my arms floundered for help.

Reese had mercy and took my hand, tugging me upright.

I smoothed my shirt over my bulging waistline and gave a breathless, "Thanks. I just washed and folded laundry today. I think there's a nice clean shirt sitting at the top of the pile in the basket on the washer."

As I hurried into the hall to fetch it, Reese followed me. "You really *do* like this guy, don't you?"

With a snort, I snagged the shirt that would soon be pressed up against Pick and brushing against his naked skin. Oh, *le sigh*. But I kept pretending I wasn't affected for Reese's benefit because frankly, I was still freaked out that I *was* affected.

"I don't even know him." I just *wanted* to know everything about him.

She smiled and lifted her eyebrows as we started for the front door. "Oh, don't think I've forgotten how he flirted with you that night. Big time. I mean, 'don't eat those nuts, Tinker Bell. Let me get you a *fresh* batch.'" When she drew out a dramatic swish of her hair and fanned herself as she tried to imitate what he'd said, I snorted and rolled my eyes.

"You are so lame."

"Whatever. I might've been temporarily preoccupied by wicked bitches from Florida flying in on their broomsticks," Reese went on, "and then getting engaged to Mason, and—oh my God, I still can't believe I'm really engaged. It's really happening, E. Mason and I are getting married."

With a happy squeal, she stuck out her left hand so she could show off the ring I swore she hadn't taken off since Mason had put it on there, probably not even to shower.

"Isn't it just the most beautiful diamond you've ever seen?"

Smiling because she'd so easily become preoccupied away from the Pick-and-I subject, I nodded. "Yes, sweetie. He did good." I opened the door to let her lead the way to the ancient old car she and Mason had bought this week.

I'd be surprised if the clunker lasted a month.

"*Good*?" She looked at me as if I was on crack. "He did *amazing*. If there were ever a symbol to show how much he loved me and wanted to be with me for the rest of his life, this is it. This is *sooo* that symbol."

She kept gushing until we were almost to the club where the ringing of her phone interrupted her. My stomach tightened with worry that it would be Mason, calling us off because Pick had already gotten a shirt from someone else. *I* wanted to be the one to provide for him and take care of him.

Hmm, those must be the pregnancy hormones channeling some kind of motherly instinct through me, because I'd certainly never wanted to cater to any guy before, for any reason. Strange.

I could tell it was Mason's mom on the phone from listening in on Reese's side of the conversation. "Okay. Change of plans," she told me as she hung up the call and tossed her phone into the center console. "Sarah has a fever, so Dawn needs me to run by the drug store and pick up a prescription for her."

Mason's mom, Dawn, usually freaked out whenever her daughter, Sarah, suffered from any little issue since she had cerebral palsy. More than once a week, either Reese or Mason had to charge over there to help them out. I know I had no place to talk since I was currently sponging off Mason and Reese myself for . . . well, everything, but to me, it really felt like Dawn relied on her son way too much. It was no wonder he'd felt pressured into selling his body to his evil landlady, or as Reese was currently calling her: the Wicked Bitch of Florida.

"But what about Pic—" I started before Reese held up her hand.

"We're only a block from the club. I'll just drop you off at the front door, head to the drug store, pop over to Dawn and Sarah's, and then come back to pick you up on my way home."

She'd have to do a lot of driving out of her way to come back for me, but I knew she always felt a sense of urgency whenever Mason's mom needed something from her. So I kept silent.

"Okay." Tucking Pick's shirt into my purse, I bobbed my head as she slowed to a stop at the curb.

"And remember." Reese sent me a wink and a grin. "It's totally okay if you want to rip all those clothes off that tattooed piece of man candy and just . . . lick him. You're pregnant. Your hormones are all out of control. It's not your fault."

I rolled my eyes, my pregnant hormones stirring at the visual my best friend had just painted in my head. "Thanks so much for your permission." Opening the door, I added, "But listening to my hormones is kind of how I got into this situation in the first place. So, I think I'll pass."

"But Mason actually likes this guy. He says Pick is his favorite coworker . . . not only because he's a hell of a worker, but because of the way he treats women. I guess the man knows how to make each and every one of them feel special."

Staring at her, I tried to ignore the disappointment that bit me in the ass. So he treated *all* women well, huh? I knew that was supposed to be a good thing. I mean, it *was* a good thing. But it also meant he hadn't singled me out. I hadn't been special at all, just another nameless, faceless female he felt the urge to pamper.

Shaking my head, I told myself it didn't matter. I was staying away from all men, anyway. Focusing on nothing but babies over here.

But inside, it still hurt. I'd probably meant nothing at all to a guy I hadn't been able to stop thinking about for two weeks straight.

With a shake of my head, I shook off my disappoint-ment and blew Reese a kiss. "Bye, sweetie. Give Sarah this kiss for me, 'kay?"

"Okay."

As Reese pulled away, I turned and looked up at the bright neon lights of the Forbidden Nightclub. They had ten more minutes until opening, so I hurried forward and knocked on the glass of the front door until the guy who's name I'd never learned appeared on the other side, peering out at me.

I pulled Mason's shirt out of my purse and waved it like some kind of peace offering until he unlocked the door and opened it.

"Hi," I said, sending him an uncertain smile. "You're Gamble, right?"

"Quinn," he corrected.

Score. Got his name. "Quinn," I repeated. "Right. Hey, I don't know if you remember me. I'm Mason's cousin, Eva." *I would be soon, that was.* "I'm here to deliver a shirt."

"For Pick?" he asked, opening the door wide for me.

"Yep." I stepped inside, holding my breath for that first moment I'd get to see him again. "For Pick."

But I didn't spot Pick anywhere. Aside from Quinn, only Mason and Ten filled the large, quiet club. I started for Mason, who was doing something behind the bar with his back to me.

"One black T-shirt," I announced, making him jump and whirl around. "Freshly cleaned and folded."

When I lifted it, he scowled at the article of clothing before glancing behind me. "Where's Reese?"

"Change of plans." I seated myself at the bar and spotted a bowl of beer nuts. I tapped my fingers along the countertop for a few seconds, trying to resist temptation, before I just couldn't handle it any longer, and I reached out. "Your mom called." My next words were muffled as I chewed. "Ree Ree had to do a pharmacy store run for Sarah. So she dropped me off and will be back once all that's out of the way."

Worry leapt onto his face. "What's wrong with Sarah?"

I shrugged. "Fever. Or something. I'm not sure."

Completely dismissing me, he yanked up his cell phone and started dialing. As he was busy calling Reese, Ten plopped onto the stool beside me.

Hitching his chin my way, he wiggled his eyebrows. "So, you going to breastfeed that kid once it pops out?"

When his gaze fell to my swollen, milk-filled boobs, I sighed. I'd dealt with this exact kind of immature moron way too much in my life. Shifting closer to him, I gave him a flirty smile. "Why, yes. Yes, I am." Touching his arm, I fluttered my lashes. "Hey, do you think you could watch me do it sometime, tell me if it looks right, because . . . " I lifted my fingers to bite one fingernail. "I'm just so new at it, I don't know how to make anyone suck on my tits."

He nodded, dumbly, his mouth falling open. "Hell, yeah, I could watch. You serious, honey?"

"*God, no*, I'm not serious, you loser." Shoving him hard in the arm, I pushed him off the bar stool he was sitting on. "Get a life and stop hitting on pregnant women. *Gah!*"

After tripping over his own legs, he landed on his ass, hard. With a mouthful of muttered curses, he scrambled upright and dusted floor grime off the back of his jeans as he scowled. "Jesus, I was just asking. All you had to do was say no."

"No," I said, eyeing him with some serious warning.

He lifted his hands and backed away. "Fine. Whatever. Your loss, milk tits."

When he turned away, Pick finally appeared, striding out of the back hall and running a harassed hand through his damp hair as if something had upset him. A sizzling wave of energy passed through me. I popped off the bar stool so fast I made myself dizzy.

"Hi." I rushed out the breathless greeting.

He lurched to a stop and jerked his head my way. As he stared without responding, I grew nervous.

"I . . . you . . . here. Shirt."

Oh my God. What the hell had I just said?

His eyebrows crinkled with confusion as he looked down at the shirt I was thrusting at him. When he looked up again, I blew out a breath. "Mason called," I finally said with some decorum, even though my cheeks were burning up with embarrassment.

I couldn't believe I was acting like such a ditz. I was Eva Mercer, the queen of cool and collected, unaffected and always hard-to-get. I was supposed to have goddamn *attitude* here. If I'd just thrown myself at Pick's feet and begged *take me, I'm yours*, I don't think I could feel any more pathetic than I did now.

"He said you needed a shirt and asked if we could run one of his down to you," I added more calmly. "So . . . *voila*! Here you go. Cleaned it myself, just today."

He didn't take the shirt. Frowning, he asked, "Mason called *you*? Wait, you do his *laundry*?"

I wasn't expecting such questions, and I was a little thrown off by the accusation in his voice.

Blinking and sputtering, it took me a moment to answer. "Well . . . yeah, I do their laundry. If I'm going to live with them and sponge off them, the least I can do is wash their clothes. And it wasn't like he called *me*, exactly. He called Reese and asked *her*. But she's . . . otherwise occupied at the moment, and I was just sitting around on the couch, you know, waiting for my baby to be born. So, I volunteered."

He began to smile as if pleased to hear I'd actually *wanted* to fetch him a shirt. But then another frown marred his brow. He shook his head. "Wait. You live with Mason?"

"What?" My eyes grew big as I blurted out, "No. Not at all. I live with Reese . . . who . . . lives with Mason." When he lifted an eyebrow, I bit my lip. "So, okay, technically, I guess we reside under the same roof. And eat in the same kitchen, and share one miniscule little bathroom, but . . . I don't *live* with Mason. Nothing like that." When I gave a nervous little laugh, he grinned.

God, I loved his smile. I loved how it made his eyes light up and how his stretched lips made the rings in them shift and move. I just felt so full whenever he looked happy like this.

"Well, thanks for clearing that up. And thanks for the shirt."

He reached out and wrapped his fingers around a portion of cloth. But I wasn't so ready to give up this moment. When he tried to slip it out of my hand, I didn't exactly let him take it. We found ourselves both holding onto the same item, neither of us letting go, playing a seriously hot game of tug-of-war.

"You're welcome," I said, noticing how the drenched shirt he was wearing now clung to his torso. And, wow, who knew someone so slim could have such a defined chest? And was that the outline of a nipple ring I saw through that wet cloth? Oh holy hosanna, the boy had a pierced nipple. Kill me now.

"Honestly, though," I told him, my voice winded. "The wet shirt look is totally working for you. You sure you want this dull, old dry one?"

Surprise filled his brown eyes before he gave a slow, hooded smile. Using the shirt we were both holding onto to rein me in closer, he lowered his voice. "Why, Eva Tinker Bell Mercer," he murmured, his tone a teasing scold. "Are you flirting with me?"

"What? No!" With a gulp, I realized—Good God—I was. How freaking mortifying. Letting go of the T-shirt, I jerked a step back. "Crap. I'm sorry."

"Why?" Disappointment filled his face. "I didn't say I minded."

"Yeah, but you . . . I . . . " I frowned, not remembering why flirting with him was such a bad idea again.

But he seemed to get it because his eyes filled with understanding. "You already have a boyfriend."

"Huh?" I shook my head. "No. What would make you think that?" When his gaze drifted down to my stomach, I cleared my throat. "Oh, right. *That*. Yeah, no. No, I'm definitely not . . . not at all. That guy's . . . an asshole." I waved out my hand to indicate that Alec was long gone until it struck me how strange I must look, blathering on like an idiot and flailing my hands around. I dropped my arms to my sides, feeling like Reese when she went into goofball mode.

"Five minutes 'til opening," Ten called from across the room.

Behind me, Mason muttered, "Shit."

Pick and I exchanged glances before we turned together to watch Mason curse as he tried to fit a fast pourer onto a bottle of rum.

"You okay over there, Lowe?" Pick asked.

Mumbling under his breath, Mason nodded as he shook spilled alcohol off his hands. He totally did not look okay.

"Hmm," Pick began before he tapped me on the arm with the shirt. "I'm going to go change. Be right back."

I nodded but kept my attention on Mason.

"What is wrong with you?" I asked as soon as Pick took off.

"Nothing," he snapped. "Damn it. I spilled some on my jeans." As he spread his arms and looked at the single wet spot on his thigh as if it were the end of the world, I arched an eyebrow. He was definitely not acting like normal Mason.

"Okay, something's going on. *What is your deal?*"

He shot me a glare just as Quinn approached the bar. "Man, are you as nervous about this auction tonight as I am?"

I turned curiously to the tall guy who reminded me of a teddy bear. Huge and bulky, but too cuddly to hurt a fly. Hmm, maybe he was more like *Baby Daddy's* Danny. "What auction?"

"It's *nothing*." Mason's bark told me the opposite.

"Dude, it is *so* not nothing." Ten slipped back onto the stool next to me as if I hadn't just shoved him off it five minutes ago. "Auction night is a guaranteed money-maker . . . that is, if the winner chooses you. And I'm getting fucking chosen tonight. There's no Gamble around to cock-block me."

"Wait. I'm confused." I turned to Quinn, since I had a feeling Mason would only bite my head off again if I asked him, and I really didn't feel like talking to Mr. Milk Tits. "What happens on auction night?"

"We get auctioned off," Quinn explained quietly, the look in his eyes telling me he did not look forward to that. "At least, *one* of us does. Whoever wins gets to pick whichever one of us she wants."

A familiar feeling of dread sunk heavily in my stomach, and this had nothing to do with the pineapple-sized kid living there. I glanced at Mason, but he refused to look my way. So I turned back to Quinn. "The winner picks you to do *what*, exactly?"

He shrugged. "I'm not really sure. Serve her all her drinks and pay attention to her and stuff, and stick around her all night. Ten said something about flirting, but . . . " He sent me an uneasy glance.

Spinning to Ten, I set my hands on my hips and

glared. "Well, you can count Mason out. He's not selling his body for *any* reason."

Ten just stared at me. "Jesus, you make it sound like we're going to turn into a bunch of gigolos."

The very word made me bristle. I could only imagine what it did to Mason. But I refused to glance his way, in fear I'd somehow oust him.

"We act attentive, that's all," Ten continued. "We don't have to sleep with the chick, or kiss her, or hell, even touch her. Especially if she's dog ugly." Pointing at me, he turned to Mason. "I thought the dark-haired broad was your girlfriend. Not this one."

"She *is*," I spoke up, poking Ten in the arm. "But as the *dark-haired broad's* cousin and best friend, I know exactly what she'd say right now if she were here. And she'd say, *no fucking way. Mason's not doing this.*"

"It doesn't *fucking* matter what you think, anyway," Ten shot back in the same pointed tone I'd just used. "Because the winner's going to choose me, not him. *Pick*," he called as Pick emerged from the hall, wearing Mason's shirt, which—*sigh*—was a little too loose on him. "Make this crazy preggo cool her damn jets, will you?"

"Hey, watch what you call her." Pick moved toward Ten as if he wanted to get into his face and have a serious showdown, but I grabbed his arm.

"Pick," I pleaded. "Please don't make Mason participate in this auction."

He swerved toward me and looked down at my hand on him before lifting his face, his eyes glazed with shock. Then he shook his head. "I . . . It's not up to me, Tink. Our boss made the call."

"Then I want to talk to this asshole boss."

"Eva," Mason hissed, his jaw taut and eyes flaring with anger. "Shut. Up. It's fine."

"No." I hissed right back because he didn't look fine at all. He looked exactly the way I'd felt way too many times in the past. Turning back to Pick, I pleaded with my eyes. "He doesn't want to do it." I made sure my voice was hushed enough that Mason couldn't hear us.

But Pick totally didn't get it. Grinning, he shook his

head. "It's all in good fun. There's no harm in it, and it's not like he'll be cheating on your cousin. Hell, I'm married. So it's completely—"

My mouth fell open. "You're *married*?"

Oh my God. Cut my heart out.

He froze, the guilt on his face thick and obvious. I suddenly felt like throwing up. I'd just flirted with a married man. And why had I not assumed he was married? I'd just learned he had a *baby*, for God's sake. Daddies did occasionally marry the mothers of their children. Damn, I was such an idiot.

And why did I feel so lost all of the sudden? As if he'd betrayed me.

With a small clearing of his throat, Pick ducked his face and mumbled, "Kind of."

"Kind of?" I arched an eyebrow. "That's like me saying I'm *kind of* pregnant. You either are or you aren't.'"

"Okay, then." He looked up at me, and I swore I saw grief and apology in his eyes. "Yes, I am, then. I'm . . . married."

Oh, hell. The one guy to ever really affect me, and he was *married*. I slapped him in the arm. "Why the hell did you let me flirt with you if you're *married*?"

His mouth opened, but all he said was, "Uh . . . "

I rolled my eyes and sighed. Looking away because it hurt too much to look at him, I saw Mason all upset behind the bar, and I remembered my mission. Turning back to Pick, I whispered, "Please. Don't make him auction himself off. You have no idea what that'll do to him."

Pick glanced at Mason and studied him a moment before shifting closer to me. "Does this have anything to do with that cougar who came in here the other week?"

Wow, he was good. But he'd already proven just how perceptive he was the last time I'd seen him. I gulped and tried not to reveal anything in my expression as I stared at him. But I had a bad feeling I gave the answer away, because Pick nodded as if he suddenly understood. After blowing out a quick breath, he spoke up loud enough for Mason to hear.

"Well, he certainly doesn't have to do it if he doesn't want to. It's not like Jessie will fire him for saying no."

"Really?" Brightening with that possibility, I turned to Mason.

Mason bit his lip, clearly tempted. "You're sure she wouldn't mind?"

Pick just snorted. "She can take it up with me if she does."

Mason nodded. "Then, no, I don't . . . I don't want to participate."

"I don't want to either," Quinn spoke up.

Cursing, Pick closed his eyes briefly before scowling at Quinn. "Jesus, guys. Okay, fine." He blew out a frustrated breath. "Neither of you have to do the actual serving. But this won't work with just Ten and I on the auction block. You'll have to stand up with us throughout the main event and pretend to participate. Then, if someone actually chooses either of you—"

"Which is a total non-issue," Ten called from across the room as he went to unlock the front doors, "because all the ladies are going to choose me."

Pick nodded. "Then we'll just tell the winner you have to work the bar tonight, and she needs to pick someone else."

I blew out a relieved breath. With a quick glance toward Mason, I saw that he had too. Good. There was one issue out of the way. Turning back to Pick, I realized I had one more thing to accomplish tonight.

Reaching out, I grabbed him by the front of his shirt.

9

-PICK RYAN-

"We need to talk," she said.

Eva shocked the shit of out me when she grabbed the front of my shirt.

"Um, o . . . kay." I stumbled into step as she strode toward the back hall, dragging me along behind her. Not that I minded following her. I'd follow her anywhere she wanted to lead me, anywhere I could be alone with her. But the way she took charge and yanked me into action was hot.

Anticipation stole up the back of my neck. I knew what it felt like to thrust inside this woman. I knew exactly how she looked when she closed her eyes and bit her bottom lip when she came, how her muscles clenched around my cock and her breasts arched against my chest. Yet I'd never had sex with her, never actually seen her naked, never even kissed her.

My mind knew that, but my body hadn't caught on

yet. My senses were thrumming with outright arousal. It was impossible to be this close to her, breathe in her lilac scent, and not remember every fucking detail of those glimpses. She'd been the best lay I'd ever had, and it hadn't even been real.

The first time I'd been with a girl, I'd been expecting that rush, that blinding sensation I'd had when I'd been with Tinker Bell in those visions. But it hadn't come. It never came when I was with someone else. I couldn't count how many times I'd searched for the unexpected bliss of burying myself deep into heaven, only to come up with nothing.

Looking at Eva now, I had to wonder if it'd be that way with *her* since she was the woman from my glimpses —my soul mate. My dick definitely thought it would be. The thing was hard as a stone.

She stopped abruptly about halfway down the hall and turned to face me. I had to skid to a stop not to bump into her and accidentally stab her with the horny stone. My body heated, igniting this current that made me beyond painfully hard. Thank God, Lowe's T-shirt was baggy and long on me. It helped conceal it.

"Do you want to win this auction thing?" she asked.

I blinked, still trying to get the vision of having sex with her out of my head. "Yeah," I finally answered. "I do."

"Good. I thought so." Opening a huge purse draped over her shoulder, she pulled out an aerosol can of some kind and shook it before spraying some white shit that looked like whipped topping into her palm, which really sent my dirty thoughts spinning, until she said, "Bend down here," and reached for my hair.

Instead of bending down, I took a leery step back. "What the fuck is that?"

"It's mousse, you moron. AKA, hair-styling gel. I'm going to spiff you up so you can look insanely hot instead of just mildly hot. Now bend your head down so I can finesse your hair into place and help you win this auction."

If she'd wanted to wipe dog shit on me just for the hell of it, I probably would've let her. She was Tinker

Bell; no way could I deny her anything. So I bent my head.

Wait, had she just called me mildly hot? Double wait—

"Let me get this straight. You just about had a coronary to get Lowe out of this auction, but now you're back here, *spiffing* me up, so I'll win it?" I wasn't sure if I should be offended or not. Why didn't she have a problem selling *me* off to some unnamed woman?

But then she sank her fingers into my hair, and fuck... nothing was going to offend me for a good long while. Jesus, she had nice fingers. They felt so damn fine on me. Her nails occasionally scraped my scalp, and each time they did, every nerve ending in my body had a mini-orgasm. My heartbeat pulsed through my throbbing erection until I had to concentrate not to roll my hips with her fingers as she tugged on my hair with these rhythmic pulls, making sure she lathered that foam shit on every lock. And oh . . . holy baby Jesus, it felt good. So. Damn. Good.

Then she spoke, and the tone of her voice was like drizzling chocolate over an already perfect dessert. "You actually *want* to win," she said, "and he didn't even want to participate, so . . . yes. That's it exactly."

What had she said? I think I was little too busy trying not to come in my damn pants. Christ. She could spiff me up every day of the week. I reached out my hand and pressed it against the wall to support myself because all the blood was rushing to my dick and making me dizzy.

"Okay. Look up." Her voice grew huskier.

I lifted my face, sucking in a stuttered breath when our gazes met. Her pupils looked dilated and full of some of the same heat I was feeling. My nostrils flared, aching to draw in her lilac scent, but all I could smell was that fucking mousse.

"You, uh . . . " She cleared her throat and tore her gaze away from mine to focus on whatever she was doing to my hair. Her fingers slowed as if she wanted to draw out our time together. God love her, the dirty tease. "There was actually something else I wanted to discuss with you."

Still refusing to look me in the eye, she sucked her bottom lip in between her teeth, just as she had when I'd been inside her. It was hotter than hot.

"'Kay," I slurred. "Shoot."

"Right." She nodded. "So, the last time we talked, I know you came up with this crazy assumption about me that . . . well . . . " She removed her fingers from my scalp and looked up, searing me with the very blue eyes I dreamed about nightly. "You were wrong, okay? Whatever you thought . . . It was just . . . It's not true. That . . . that never happened. Not to me." She gave me an encouraging, yet tense smile. "Okay?"

I watched her throat work as she swallowed. My gaze fell to her hands; she was wringing them unconsciously at her waist. Lifting my eyes again, I took in the determination and desperation in her expression and nodded slowly. "Okay," I said, giving a little shrug as if it were no big deal.

"Okay," she repeated with a forceful nod, before a scowl line deepened between her eyes. "Wait. I just stressed over this for *two* freaking weeks, unable to stop worrying about what you thought of me and who you were going to blab to. And all you have to say is *okay*?" She set her hands on her hips and scowled.

Her miffed temper was so adorable it made me smile. It reminded me of the Tinker Bell I'd built her up in my mind to be, a sassy soul mate who'd argue with me even when I was trying to be completely compliant.

Fuck, maybe she wasn't exactly as she'd advertised herself to be on her Facebook page. Maybe she wasn't quite the rich, entitled spoiled princess I'd convinced myself she was. Which was bad. Thinking she was more like what I'd envisioned instead of what I'd feared, made my heart think I could actually reach her and have her.

But I couldn't.

With my hand still braced against the wall, I leaned in to her, hovering above her. "What do you want me to say, Tink? That I know you're lying? That I know it really *did* happen, and that the very thought of it rips me in fucking half? That I want to find the monster or monsters that hurt you and destroy them with my bare hands? Is that what you'd prefer?"

Her eyes widened and her breath puffed from her parted lips. "I . . . " She shook her head. "Actually, no. You're right. 'Okay' was a good answer, after all."

"Yeah. It sure as hell was." Then I grinned, loving that I could finally smell her lilac scent again. "Don't worry, sweetheart. I'll keep your secret. If you promise me one thing in return."

She jerked backward away from me, glowering. "I don't make deals."

"Relax." With a low chuckle, I caught a piece of her hair between my fingers and nearly whimpered when I felt how soft it was. It was exactly as I remembered in my visions. "I just want you to tell me you're no longer in danger. If I know he can't get to you anymore, I'll leave it alone and pretend like I'm a clueless dumbass. Okay?"

The vulnerability in her expression made every protective instinct in me kick into gear. I just wanted to scoop her up and carry her away somewhere safe, where no one could ever bother her again.

"I'm no longer in danger," she dutifully assured me, even as her eyes flared with shock, as if she couldn't believe she'd just let me know I hadn't been wrong after all.

I closed my eyes briefly, because I'd still been clinging to the hope that I *might've* been wrong. But now that she'd confirmed it, grief gripped my throat, making my words gritty when I said, "Good." Leaning down, I pressed my lips to her forehead. "Thank God."

She scurried away from me with a gasp. "You shouldn't do that."

I blinked, bewildered. "Do what?"

"Kiss me!"

Blurting out a laugh, I caught her hand and tugged her closer. I didn't like her being more than five feet away. "Pressing my mouth to your forehead isn't—" But my words stalled on my tongue when she looked up at me. Her blue eyes were big and wide, full of heat and fear. I swallowed. "Well it wasn't *supposed* to be anything. Just . . . you know . . . friendly affection."

God, that sounded lame.

But she nodded as if desperate to buy that. "Good, then." She wiggled her fingers out of mine and began to stroke them with her other hand as if my touch had seared her. "I wouldn't want your wife coming after me with a sawed-off shotgun or anything."

Took me a second to remember who she was talking about. It was still ingrained in my head that she was the only woman I'd ever marry. For a moment, I entertained a ridiculous image of her chasing herself around with a gun. It was an animated vision, like something straight off *Looney Tunes*.

I started to smile until I remembered reality. If she was referring to Tris, Tristy wouldn't care if I went home with a dozen girls every night. But I liked having this barrier between us. I didn't want Tink to know what a sham my 'marriage' was. Because for her, I had a bad feeling I'd want to dissolve all my vows and get an annulment or some shit, which I definitely couldn't do. Not if I wanted to keep Julian safe.

"I guess I'll be keeping my mouth off your head, then."

Eva nodded. "Good."

When she turned away and strolled off, I stared after her and gritted my teeth when I took in her ass. Shit, I almost wished pregnancy had done to her backside what it'd done to Tristy's—making it twice as wide—because her taut cheeks looked too good to resist.

She glanced back. "Are you checking out my ass?"

I snorted and shook my head, but confessed, "Of course. And I'm completely confused. Isn't having a kid supposed to make your butt big?" I motioned my finger toward her. "Not deliciously juicy like that?"

"Trust me, honey." She winked as she smacked a hand on her ass. "This *is* huge compared to what it used to look like."

"Dear God in Heaven." I whimpered to myself as she turned away again. A person wouldn't be able to tell she was carrying a kid at all, because from the back, she was curved to perfection. When she put an extra, cocky sway to her hips, most likely knowing I was still gawking, I grinned.

Shit. I think I liked her. Along with her killer body, she had sass and spunk, along with some softness, and a big ol' heart ready to care for people. I grinned, remembering how she'd tried to manually help Lowe drink his water the other week. I had a feeling she didn't even realize how truly compassionate she was.

Popping into the bathroom before I returned to the bar, I checked out what she'd done to my hair. I laughed aloud when I saw that she'd given me a stubby Mohawk.

"Damn," I murmured, carefully touching the gelled spikes. I liked it.

"What the fuck!" Ten hissed as soon as I strode into the bar again. "If you think that *hair* is going to help you win the auction—"

"It is." I patted his shoulder with a placating smile. "Sorry, sucka, but you're going down tonight."

"Fucker." He scowled after me as I strolled away to check on a table full of ladies who looked like they had deep pockets and could afford to win.

Time to start promoting myself.

But I caught sight of Eva at the bar, perched on her stool as she demolished a bowl of nuts. It was strange enough for a pregnant woman to enter a bar when it was closed, but for her to stick around after it opened . . . that did not make me comfortable. If anyone harassed her, I'd be forced to kill them.

Weaving my way to her, I replenished her stock of nuts and rested my elbows on the bar top to watch her gnaw on her bottom lip as she stared at the second bowlful, silently debating with herself if she should eat more or not.

"If you're still worried I'll let any woman *buy* Lowe, I promise you I won't."

She gave in and scooped up another handful before answering me with a perky smile. "Oh, I'm not worried about that at all. I have no doubt you're good for your word."

I swelled with pride. I was a complete stranger who'd majorly unsettled her peace of mind the first time we'd met. Yet here she was, claiming to trust my word.

That didn't explain why she was still here, though. "So, you're sticking around because . . . ?" I lifted my eyebrows. "You want to see who ends up buying me?" I gave a sudden, naughty grin. "You jealous, Tinker Bell?"

She rolled her eyes. "Cute. But, no. I'm waiting for my ride. Reese should be back to pick me up in a few minutes."

Shit. She was stuck here. I loved that because it meant I got to bask in her presence longer. And yet I hated it because my nerves were going ape-shit, knowing there'd be no way to keep a constant eye on her in this crowd.

"You know, if you get uncomfortable out here, I can show you a room in the back you can chill in until she shows up."

She laughed. "Trust me, I'm *pretty* comfortable with the whole bar scene."

"Yeah, but—" When my gaze fell to her stomach, she held up a finger and shot me a look that told me not to even go there.

"If you say anything like *in your condition*, I'm liable to turn into Eva the super bitch and go off on you again."

I grinned. "Duly noted. But seriously, I don't like this. At all." My palm drifted over her belly before falling away. She jumped at the brief contact. "If someone messes with this precious bundle, I'm going to lose my shit."

Her eyes lit and she drew out the word, "Oooh. So *that's* what it's about?"

I blinked. "What?"

"Your overprotectiveness." She twirled out her finger. "I was confused why you were so nice, yet controlling, that first night we met. But now that I know you're a daddy . . . " She shrugged. "It makes more sense."

I pulled back, confused. "What makes you think I'm a daddy?"

"Because . . . " She popped more nuts into her mouth and chewed. "Reese said so. Mason told her you needed a new shirt because your baby had thrown up on the other one."

With a nod, I shifted a step back, reminding myself why I needed to keep my distance from her. Julian needed me. And to keep Julian in my life, I needed to keep Tristy in it. And I couldn't exactly be a good, faithful husband to Tristy if I was here drooling over Eva, the one woman who could make me do anything.

I blew out a breath, not caring for that little reality check.

"Want to see a picture?" I asked, forcing a smile and thinking that seeing a picture of Julian might help cement my faithfulness into my own head.

"Of your baby?" Her face brightened. "Sure."

I pulled out my phone and typed in my password to get into my apps.

Leaning in to watch, Eva gasped and covered her mouth as she zipped her eyes up to mine.

"What?" I asked, dropping the phone to my side. "Are you okay? What's wrong?"

When I reached for her stomach, worried about the baby, she shook her head and slapped my hand away, but continued to stare at me as if I'd lost my mind. Then she motioned toward my phone. "I just . . . you . . . your passcode. One-one-two-zero."

I nodded and shrugged as if it were no big deal. "Yeah. What about it?" But my eyes were intent on her as I held my breath, anxiously waiting to learn why that number was important to her. Because it was sure as hell important to me.

"Nothing," she tried to say, but I knew—

"Oh, no." I rolled out my hand, coaxing her to keep talking. "It's definitely something. Now spill it."

Her face flushed as she motioned to the phone. "It's a date, right? November twentieth?"

My stomach clenched as I nodded. But, shit, if the same thing had happened to her on the same day that it happened to me, I was going to freak.

"Is it your birthday?" she hedged. When I shook my head, she guessed, "Your baby's birthday? Your wife's."

I laughed. "No. It's no one's birthday. It's just . . . a

special date."

The day I'd met her, had sex with her, fallen in love with her, and pretty much became utterly and completely obsessed with her . . . or rather, the day I'd had my glimpses and learned she existed.

"Your wedding day?" she started in with more guesses, not letting up.

Since there was no way I was going to tell her why November twentieth was special to me, I asked, "Why do you care? What's that date mean to *you*?"

She hesitated before meeting my gaze. "It's my birthday."

I gulped. Shit.

What were the odds I'd be shown a vision of her ten years ago on her birthday?

A strange cold prickle rose up the back of my neck. Fucking voodoo shit. This was beginning to creep me out. When I shifted away from her, her eyes widened.

"What? What's it mean to you?" she asked.

"Not telling," I said and quickly re-entered the passcode because my phone's screen had gone dead again. She huffed in irritation, but I distracted her as quickly as I could by pulling up Fighter's mug shot and spinning my phone around for her to see him.

And, yep. Just like that, her mind was jerked elsewhere. Oh, the power of an adorable kid.

"What a little cutie," she cooed. "What's her name?"

My chest swelled out with pride—my boy certainly was a little cutie—right before I scowled. "*His* name is Julian."

She blinked, and then pointed at the picture. "But he's wearing pink. Why do you have a pink onesie on a boy?"

"Uh . . . he's . . . a big supporter of breast cancer awareness?" I posed it as a question, hoping I didn't have to confess that all of my kid's clothes were hand-me-downs from Mrs. Rojas youngest daughter.

Eva laughed, warming my whole heart with the amazing sound. "And apparently he's not at all insecure about his masculinity," she quipped.

With a snort, I shot back, "*My* boy? Oh, hell no. We

Ryans invented masculinity, thank you very much."

She smiled at me, her entire face lighting up. "I think I'm going to like you, Pick Ryan," she stated, making my heart pound in my chest.

No, the real, live woman in front of me wasn't quite as I'd imagined she'd be for the last ten years. But some parts of her were even better. And that glow on her face was one of them.

I had a very bad feeling I was going to end up *more than* liking her in return.

"Yo, Pick!" Ten appeared, thrusting a cordless microphone at me. "You're going to emcee this thing tonight, right?"

"Sure," I said, glad to focus on him before I admitted something completely embarrassing to Eva.

"Well, let's get to it, already," Ten pressed. "I've got some cash to win, fucker."

I turned back to Eva as I took control of the microphone. "I gotta go." I told her, not wanting to leave her side.

Her return smile was sad. "So I see."

I would've stayed, just a second longer. I needed more time with her. But Ten was already dragging me away.

10

-PICK RYAN-

As Ten climbed onto the bar's main countertop, dragging me behind him, I sent Eva a small smile of farewell and followed him up. Once I was higher than everyone else in the place, I waved my hand to get their attention. Then I turned on the mic and called into the sound system.

"*Hello*, everyone! We've got a little something planned for all you sexy things out there to celebrate ladies' night this evening. Can I get a *hell yeah*?"

A round of screams followed, a bunch of chicks waving their drinks in the air and getting in on the fun.

I smiled and pointed at the rowdiest bunch. "Yeah, that's what I like to hear, right there." Crooking my finger at them, I motioned them closer. "So, I'm going to need all you single honeys in the house who're desperate to burn some cash on your favorite bartender to shift closer to the front, please. We're going to have us a little auction."

The women who'd been through this before screamed and scrambled toward the bar. After waiting until a good portion of the room had shoved their way to where they wanted to be to watch the main event, I explained the rules of the auction. And then I introduced the players after motioning Mason and Quinn to join Ten and me.

"Let's get to know your favorite bartenders then. To my right, most of you may remember Wild Thing Tenning. Football star for ESU and crazy freak in the sheets, according to the ladies, Ten likes long walks on the beach and slow, passionate kisses."

Ten's groupies squealed in approval as he lifted his hands to wave and wink. Then he turned his backside to them and twerked out his ass until feminine fingers were reaching up, trying to cop a feel.

Laughing, I shoved him in the shoulder until he straightened up and whirled back to face the front again where he blew more kisses at another screaming brood of women.

"And then we have my sexy self right here." I slid my free hand down my side to put on a provocative display. "But seriously? Who needs any more introduction than this hunka-hunka burnin' love?"

A trio of ladies right below me called my name and reached up their hands to pet my knees since they couldn't seem to get any higher.

Wanting to keep them in my corner but also get their paws off me, I clasped their fingers like some kind of rock star on a stage who was greeting his fans.

But my supporters got a little too enthusiastic and tried to pull me down off the bar and back onto the floor with them, yanking me forward until I was bent over double and my head was at their level.

"Ladies, ladies," I called in the microphone. Laughing nervously, I tried to calm them. "A little decorum, please." Next to me, Mason grabbed my arm to keep me from tumbling off the mock stage, but greedy feminine hands kept pawing at me. Someone caught hold of the baggy shirt I was wearing, and before I quite knew what was happening, the women had ripped it off over my head.

Gaping down at my torso, I found myself completely shirtless. I yanked away, straightening up, and lifted my hands. "Okay, enough of that now, you shameless things. Behave your naughty selves. You gotta actually win before you can sample the goods."

Next to me, Ten tugged off his own shirt, obviously feeling the need to compare chests. More ladies screeched their approval and urged both Mason and Quinn to take theirs off as well. But the two do-gooders refused to budge.

I cast a glance toward the end of the bar where I'd last seen Tinker Bell. Covering her mouth, she laughed so hard, tears trickled down her cheeks. I winked at her just as it hit me that I was shirtless. If she were close enough, she'd be able to read the names tattooed over my heart. But fortunately, she wasn't. To be on the safe side, I turned slightly away from her.

"Moving along to the modest members of the group." I hitched my thumb Mason's way. "We have Family Man Mason. But watch out ladies, he's about to be a daddy."

When I motioned to the very pregnant Eva, Mason spun to me, his glare beating the shit out of me.

"What the hell?"

"Relax," I told him out the side of my mouth as I dropped the mic to my side. "I'm trying to make you look less appealing so no one will want you."

He didn't exactly relax, or stop glaring, but he didn't pounce and try to physically pound me into the ground either. The women reached for him as well, but he stepped to the very back edge of the bar so they couldn't lay a finger on him.

"And last, but certainly not least, we have Hamilton... the *virgin*."

Ten hooted and hollered, laughing his ass off, while Quinn's mouth dropped open, his face turning a very bright, scarlet red.

"Oh, that was harsh," Mason said into my ear, shaking his head in disapproval.

Ignoring him, I asked the crowd, "Any ladies out there willing to deflower this delicate little petal and show him what having a woman's all about?"

When a hell of a lot more feminine voices than I was expecting catcalled, claiming they would gladly take him on, I cringed, hoping my plan to make him look less appealing hadn't backfired on me. But shit, who knew women actually preferred inexperienced men?

I checked on Eva again, wondering if she was as pissed at me as Lowe was by my unappealing introductions, but she was still smiling. She shook her head as if to scold me, but her smile clearly said she forgave me for using her pregnancy for Mason's benefit.

"So, let's get this party started, shall we? Is anyone willing to buy one of us as your very own personal bartender for the rest of evening?"

About fifty woman lifted their hands, cash clutched between their fingers. "Ten bucks," some shouted.

I heard fifty and twenty from a couple of other directions, but I didn't react until a hundred was tossed out among the melee.

Holy shit! A hundred bucks? This was going to be a good auction.

I pointed that way. "Did I hear a hundred? I think I just heard a hundred."

"One twenty," another girl called, rattling me by how easily it had gone over a hundred.

"One twenty-five!"

And we were on. The bidding quickly escalated. We reached two hundred dollars in a matter of seconds. My palms started to sweat, so I rubbed one against the hip of my jeans. More than half the crowd of ladies dropped out at three hundred. But some kept going, hot and heavy. By the time we reached four-fifty, a bead of sweat anxiously leaked down the side of my temple because I was certain the tall redhead below me, who was one of the big bidders, would choose me. But when the price went up to five seventy-five, that woman dropped out. It came down to two ladies I'd never seen before.

"Do I hear six hundred?" I asked, pointing at the woman whose turn it was to raise the price.

She bit her lip, looking undecided and called, "five-eighty," right before her contender immediately said, "seven hundred."

No one wanted to top that. I kept the bidding open a few seconds longer, pointing out past women who'd thrown out a price before, but no one would go over seven hundred dollars. Not that I blamed them. Seven hundred was a lot of fucking money. I glanced at the blonde who was about to win the auction and tried to figure out which bartender she preferred. But I couldn't read her at all.

Unable to help myself, I checked on Eva again. She chewed on her bottom lip, studying the blonde winner as well.

I drew in a breath. "Well, it looks like we have a winner, weighing in at *seven hundred* big ones. Give me your hand, sweetheart, and climb on up here with us."

The blonde reached up for me, and I helped her step onto a stool and then the bar top so she was standing between me and Ten. "What's your name, precious?" I asked before lowering the microphone to her mouth.

She was an attractive thing, tall and slim with big breasts. Ten would have a field day with her if she chose him.

Tucking a piece of hair behind her ear, she leaned forward to announce, "Cora."

"Well, congratulations are in order to you, Miss Cora. You won yourself your very own bartender for this evening. So, who's the lucky guy going to be?"

I held all the air in my lungs as she leaned past me, turning away from Ten. Shit. She was going to pick Lowe. Already trying to figure how to let her down easily, I was shocked senseless when she gestured at Quinn instead.

"Him," she said. "I want him."

I lifted my eyebrows and took in Quinn's reaction. His mouth fell open, and I swear the poor virgin fell into lust that very second. Instantly changing his tune, he stepped past Lowe and grinned shyly at Cora, his face bright red with embarrassment but also glowing with wonder.

"Uh . . . okay," he said.

Still standing between them and holding the mic in

my hand, I announced. "Well, okay then. I hereby announce Cora and the Virgin, bartender and wife. May you two live happily ever after . . . or at least 'til the end of this shift. You may now serve her whatever alcohol she prefers."

Motioning Quinn to move past me, I nudged him and the blonde together as I told everyone else the auction was hereby closed, and thanked them for participating.

"Just for the record, you suck as an emcee," Ten growled into my ear after we were all on the floor again and ready to return to our regular duties. "That chick with the purple hair totally wanted to throw down some major cash for me."

"Hey, she had a chance to give her bid. I'm as pissed as you are, bud. I totally could've used an *extra three hundred and fifty* bucks tonight."

"Yeah, well, you still suck."

I rolled my eyes, and we parted ways. Lowe stayed behind the bar. I had a feeling he was never going to go out on the floor when it was ladies' night.

Fine by me. The tips out here rocked.

"I second Ten," he told me as I slipped my own damp shirt back on and tossed him his dry, borrowed one back. "You totally suck. *Almost a daddy?* What the hell was that about?"

"Hey, the winner didn't pick you, did she?" When he merely scowled, I nodded my head. "I rest my case."

Then I got my ass to work, because all that time we'd taken for the auction had shorted me out of that much tip money I could've been making.

Twenty minutes passed, things returned to normal, and Eva stayed seated on her stool at the end of the bar, sucking down water and orange juice. Mason wandered her way every once in a while to check on her, but mostly she was left to her own devices. I gnashed my teeth, wondering where the hell her cousin was and why she hadn't shown up to get my girl home yet. No one had picked on her, but the longer she stayed the higher the likelihood rose that she would be targeted.

I was busy as fuck, with only Ten and me working the floor and a flustered Lowe taking care of all the drinks.

There was no time at all to stop by for more than a, "how're you doing?"

Eva simply smiled and shook her head as if amused by my concern. "Same as the last time you came by," she kept answering.

She must've grown bored sitting at the bar by herself, or maybe she had to use the bathroom. When she slid off her stool, I freaked. What the hell? Where was she going?

But she merely moved to the old-time jukebox against the wall, and I relaxed.

A table full of drunk girls kept me busy for a couple minutes. One was bemoaning the fact that she'd just caught her boyfriend cheating on her.

"He's an ass," I chimed in, agreeing with her friends. "You deserve so much better than any douche who can't hold it in his pants until he sees you again."

Suddenly, I became the main attraction at that table. In the middle of telling the poor girl what kind of qualities she should look for in her next guy, the first song Tinker Bell had chosen on the jukebox started to play.

I lifted my face to the nearest speaker, my breath catching in my throat. Then I whirled away from the man-bashing table. Eva still stood at the jukebox, flipping through song choices, her back to the crowd.

"Excuse me," I murmured, distracted. Tucking the round serving plate under my arm, I wound my way through too many people until I reached her.

"How the hell did you know this was our song?" I demanded from directly behind her.

She let out a startled squeak and whirled around. When her big blue eyes blinked up at me, my chest tightened. It took everything I had to keep from cupping her face in my hands and kissing her senseless.

Setting a hand on her hip, she arched an eyebrow. "*Our* song?"

I pointed to the jukebox where the Supremes were bellowing out *Baby Love*. "Hell, yes, *our* song. We're going to dance together to this at our wedding reception."

I didn't mean to blurt that out, but I was just so discombobulated that she'd chosen *this* song on the jukebox. Out of all the fucking songs listed, she'd chosen this one. The words had just tumbled out of my mouth.

I didn't panic, though. No way would she think I'd actually foreseen anything. She'd assume I was flirting and teasing.

Good. Great. That was perfect. Let her think I was a tease.

But then I pictured her in the sleeveless wedding gown, the pearls glimmering in her hair, the ecstatic sheen on her face. It all sucked to the forefront of my head until I fell into a surreal state of déjà vu. The room seemed to spin around the two of us, and the two scenes—the here and now in Forbidden, and ten years ago in my glimpses—melded into one.

Oh, shit. I realized in that moment that our wedding reception would take place here, inside Forbidden. How had I not recognized that the first moment I'd walked into this place? I guess I'd always been so focused on her in my glimpses I hadn't paid that much attention to where we were. But why would our reception be *here*? Forbidden never hosted that kind of event.

I shook my head and blinked again until the here-and-now returned.

A fully pregnant Eva frowned up at me as if I was insane. "Did you just say our *wedding* reception?"

I grinned and nodded.

She frowned harder. "But you're already married."

"Pff. Details."

Deciding to just roll with it, I set the serving tray on top of the jukebox and captured her waist with one hand. Then I took her fingers with my other. When I spun her out onto the floor for a dance, she gaped in surprise.

I think she caught a hold of my shoulder more to balance herself than she did to actually dance with me, but that didn't matter to me. We were in the perfect position for a waltz, so I started a bizarre kind of two-step with her.

She didn't shove me away, which was promising, since she was watching me as if I was completely mental.

Tucking her in close until her protruding belly was nestled against me, I swayed us back and forth just as the song hit an intense part.

"*All of my whole life through,*" I sang along with Diana Ross, pitching my voice high and putting my gut into it. "*I never loved no one but you. Why you do me like you do?*"

Shaking her head, Eva laughed. "Oh my God. You're crazy." But she kept dancing with me as I spun her around and bumped her back to me. Laughing again, she wrapped her fingers around my shoulder. "Seriously, do you flirt like this with every woman?"

I pretended to think about her question before shrugging. "Pretty much, yeah. Though to be fair, that eighty-year-old bun-head I helped carry groceries to her car last week might've been the love of my life. I mean, she had a cart full of fruit. I *love* fruit. We could've been meant for each other. Who was I to risk letting her go without testing the waters a little with a couple winks and a pinch to her ass?"

Tinker Bell laughed again. I really liked making her laugh. "Please tell me you did not pinch her ass. Did you?"

"Hey, she pinched mine first." When she laughed again, I winked and leaned in to whisper into her ear. "It was surprisingly firm."

"Oh my God." She had to cover her mouth with her next round of chuckles. "You really are an uncontrollable flirt. You must have one confident wife if she doesn't mind your teasing ways."

With a proud lift of my chin, I preened. "She claims it's my best quality."

Eva opened her mouth to respond, but a little bump nudged me in the stomach, interrupting her.

"What the hell?" I stopped dancing and stepped back.

Color flooding her face, Eva covered her stomach with her hands as if embarrassed. "I'm so sorry. She must like the music."

My mouth fell open. "Are you saying that was the *baby* that just kicked me?"

She nodded. "Yeah. I—"

"Oh, *cool*." I dropped to my knees in front of her and found myself eye level with her stomach as it shifted again. Mouth open in wonder, I placed my hands reverently on either side of the baby bump.

Tristy had never told me when Julian had been kicking her, but I hadn't ventured that close to her to find out, either. No way was I staying away from Eva's belly, though, not after her child had just made contact with me.

"Listen up, little girl," I called above the music. "I'm dancing with your mama right now, but as soon as you're born, you can have your turn. Got it, Miss Skylar? I have the perfect song saved for you and everything."

Another little bulge jabbed out of Eva's stomach in answer. I sucked in an amazed breath and pressed my hand to it. Skylar either high-fived me or kicked me. Still charmed out of my mind and sitting on my knees, I looked up at Tinker Bell to share my awe with her.

"That is just so . . . " I couldn't even fathom a word good enough to describe how much I loved connecting with her baby.

She shook her head, seemingly dazed. "How do you know her name?"

"Umm . . . " Shit. Hopefully, she wouldn't be too pissed at Lowe for blabbing. I climbed back to my feet. "Mason let the cat out of the bag earlier tonight." I hooked my thumb over my shoulder, totally incriminating him as I pointed him out.

"*Mason* told you?" The idea seemed foreign to her, but she smiled slightly and glanced over at him only to startle. "Oh! Reese is here. I should go." She began to step around me, only to pause and bite her bottom lip. "Thanks," she said, awkwardly. Her hand flailed a moment before adding, "for the dance, and you know . . . everything else you helped me with tonight. I really . . . I appreciate it."

A moment of indecision crossed her face before she lunged at me and gave me a quick hug, lasting only long enough for my nostrils to collect her lilac smell, and for Skylar to kick me one last time.

She didn't look as if she wanted to leave as she pulled

away. I sure as hell didn't want her to go. It felt as if Madam LeFrey was ripping me out of my visions all over again. But Ten was already motioning to me from across the room that he needed help serving. Plus it was getting late, and Eva needed to get out of this place.

"See you around, Tinker Bell," I told her a little more solemnly than I meant to.

With a nod, she moved past me and made her way to Reese.

Though I returned to work and took an order from another table full of ladies, I kept my attention on her as she and her cousin bid a farewell to Lowe and left. A strange, crazy depression filled me after she was gone. She had her life and I had mine, and the two didn't seem to be headed in the same direction at all. But it would've been nice if I'd had a reason, one stupid insignificant reason, to see her again. Just one more time.

I wondered if I could get Lowe to tell me when she had the baby. Maybe I'd go visit her and . . . shit, having any more contact with her after this would probably just be needlessly torturing myself. I should stay away.

But after the bar closed and I was helping Lowe clean up, he found a way to suck me back in.

"Thanks for helping me keep an eye on Eva tonight. Reese would've killed me if anything bad had happened to her."

I nodded as if it were no big deal, even though my heart slipped in an extra thump when he mentioned her name. "It's cool. I would've kept an eye on any pregnant woman who wandered in."

Mason moved closer to me as he wiped down the bar with a cloth. "Well, thanks all the same. Hey, uh, Gamble, or Ten, or someone mentioned you work at a garage during the day, like an auto repair shop?"

"Yep." I stacked the last of the clean glasses under the counter before glancing at him. "Murphy's Repair down on Bullview Road. Why?"

"Really? That's great. I mean, Reese bought this . . . we'll call it a car for now. It's a real piece of work. I don't trust it to last a month."

"Sure, I'll take a look at it," I said before he could

even get around to asking. I knew I probably sounded too eager. But for a chance to visit Lowe's place, where Eva was currently staying, I was all for it.

He lifted his eyebrows in surprise, but then a gleam entered his gray eyes as he smiled knowingly. "So, you don't mind coming over some time?"

I shook my head. "Not at all. My next night off is Saturday."

Lowe nodded. "I'm off Saturday, too."

I slid my hands into my pockets and rested my back against the bar, trying to play it cool. "Sounds like I'll be swinging by then."

"Sounds like it."

And that's when Ten chose to appear and slap the top of the bar. "Hey, if you two ladies are done flirting with each other over there, I'd like to clock out sometime tonight and get the fuck home so I can mourn over a bowl of ice cream because no one wanted to buy my luscious body tonight."

"I'm ready to go whenever you guys are," Mason said, glancing over the bar as if to double-check his work. "Just finished cleaning my section."

"Me too." It was late and I should've been beat, but I knew I wasn't going to sleep a wink tonight. Or tomorrow night.

In two more days, I'd get to see her again.

These were going to be the longest two days of my life.

"Hey, where's Hamilton?" Mason jerked me from my anxious daydreams with his question until I too was looking around for the fourth member of our crew.

Ten hitched his chin toward the exit. "He drove Cora home since her ride left her a few hours back."

"He did?" Lifting my eyebrows, I turned toward Mason. We shared a similar look, and I knew he was thinking the same thing I was thinking.

Ten, of course, had to verbalize all our thoughts. "Yep, our baby boy's turning into a man tonight." He sniffed, wiped at a mock tear, and set his fist over his chest. "It's just so heart-wrenching. I'm gonna need a whole gallon of ice cream, I think."

"Damn, put your ovaries away, son." I laughed and shook my head. "Maybe nothing's going to—"

"Oh, yes, it is," Ten cut me off, sending me a telling glance. "He just drove home *Cora the Whora*. That boy is totally getting his cherry popped, if he hasn't already."

"Wait. Cora, the . . . what?" Mason asked incredulously. "Cora the Whore-*uh*? Do you know her?"

"Hell, yeah." Ten grinned at us, nodding knowingly. "She's one of the football groupies, and my God, does that chick like to get *freaky*."

My hope for Quinn to finally enter the world of the sexually active wavered. I pointed at Ten. "So, you've . . ."

He lifted his eyebrows. "Fucked her?" he finished the question for me. "Hello. Did you miss the part where I said she was a *football* groupie? I'm a football player. Of course I've tapped that. Hell, Hamilton might be the only guy on the team she hasn't dug her claws into yet. And maybe Gamble. But she's fairly new to the groupie scene and Gam hasn't partaken from those girls in a couple months. So . . . maybe not Gamble either. But yeah, pretty much the rest of us have. Why?"

Mason and I shared another knowing glance. Finally, Lowe said, "Yeah . . . I wouldn't go telling Quinn that part if I were you."

Ten blinked, utterly clueless. "Why not?"

"Well. Quinn doesn't seem like the type who . . . "

When Mason couldn't seem to come up with a tactful way to put it, I blurted, "The kid waited until he was twenty-one to lose his virginity, you idiot. I'd say the fact he's already shared a woman with . . . well, *you*, isn't something he needs to find out about."

"Wow, now wait a sec. What's wrong with me?" Ten pointed to himself, clearly insulted. "I'm fucking flawless."

I snickered and lifted my hands. "No offence, but I certainly wouldn't want to stick my dick in anything you've already had yours in."

"Amen," Mason seconded.

"Hey." Ten scowled at us. "That's just . . . oh, I get it. I'd get a pussy too stretched out for the likes of your tiny little—"

"Okay, let's just go home before you say anything you'll end up regretting." I patted Ten on the shoulder before shoving him toward the door. "I'm not getting into a dick size discussion with you." Wouldn't want the poor kid to end up feeling deficient.

Mason followed along, chuckling and shaking his head. After we locked up and parted ways, I started for my car, humming "Baby Love" under my breath as I pulled my keys from my pocket and twirled them around my finger. My mind was already far away from Ten and his dick. I couldn't get a pair of amazing blue eyes out of my head.

I knew Eva Mercer was completely forbidden to me, but it didn't stop me from looking forward to seeing her again, more than I could remember looking forward to anything in my life.

Just two more days.

11

-PICK RYAN-

When Saturday arrived, I was antsy as hell. I relieved Tristy in the morning by taking Fighter out to the nearest park, where I sat him on my lap as we swung on the swings. I even took him on the slippery slide once or twice but got some funny looks from a couple moms for that one. I didn't care, though. Julian grinned the entire time, which was all the consent I needed.

The rest of the afternoon dragged. I got a little cleaning done around the apartment, mainly the kitchen and bathroom, but I couldn't calm down.

Lowe and I hadn't agreed on a specific time, so I didn't want to show up too early, but by five o'clock, I couldn't wait any longer. After changing into something that would look nice, yet wouldn't kill me if I got it grease-stained, I carried Fighter into the living room and settled him into his swing, since Tris was busy on her laptop.

"I shouldn't be out too late," I told her as I scooped up my keys.

Her face zipped up as horror lit her eyes. "You're going *out*?"

Jigging my keys in my hands, I opened the door, letting her know that hell yes, I was going out. And nothing she said would stop me. "I'm helping a friend with a car."

"But . . . " She glanced helplessly at Fighter who was happily gnawing on a toy I'd given him. I'd already fed him, bathed him, and changed his diaper; he'd be fine for a while.

When Tristy looked back to me as if I was abandoning her to a tribe of cannibals that were about to burn her at the stake with a nice hickory-flavored barbecue sauce, I shifted my weight uneasily from one foot to the other. I would not let her do this to me. I would not let her make me feel guilty for leaving the house for a few hours. Mason was relying on me to help him with his girlfriend's car.

Shit, that was a lie. I wasn't doing this for Mason. I had to see Eva again, a selfish truth that made my guilt skyrocket.

I ran my hand over my hair, sighing. "It'll only be for a few hours. Damn, Tris. This is the first time I'm actually leaving the apartment since the kid was born."

"What the fuck ever. You leave every damn day."

"For *work*," I bit out. "I have to work. This apartment isn't going to pay for itself. And we need food, and utilities, and car insurance."

"Just cut it out already," she snapped with a glare. "Do I look like an idiot? I know you're going to meet a girl and get laid."

I clenched my jaw, hoping she didn't see anything in my eyes. Spreading my arms open, I asked, "Does it look like I'm going to meet a girl? In this?" I shook my head, confused. "Why would it matter to you anyway?"

She sniffed and lifted her chin. "It wouldn't. Not at all. I had sex just last weekend."

My eyebrows shot up in surprise. "Really?" I couldn't picture her in that way—at all, especially since she'd given birth. She'd never been a great beauty, but she'd really let herself go downhill these past few months. And with the past we shared—no. She felt too sisterly to me to even imagine that part of her life.

When she merely stared at me with a challenging sneer, I shrugged. "Well, good for you. I'll see you later." As I tried to step from the apartment, she cried out my name.

"Damn it, if you're just going to a friend's house to work on a car, can't you at least take him with you?"

I glanced at Fighter. Drool covered his chin and slimed the toy he was steadily gumming. A smile lit my face. I'd love to take Julian, get him out of this place for a while, and maybe let Eva meet him all the while relieving Tristy for a couple hours. But I really did plan on working on Reese's car.

"I can't take him to a grease-filled garage. I'm probably going to be under a car most of the night. That's not exactly a safe place for a baby."

Tristy sniffed and turned away, dismissing me. I was tempted to invite her along so she wouldn't feel left out. But the last thing I wanted to do was let her and Eva mingle. Resigned, I repeated, "I'll see you later."

After blowing a kiss toward the baby, I was free and jogging down the stairs toward the front exit of the building. When my phone rang as soon as I started my engine, I groaned. Someone sure wanted to delay me from seeing my Tinker Bell, didn't they? When I saw it was Ten, I answered with a growl, "*What*?"

"Man, we need your help. Big time."

Fuck. "No," I said instantly. "I'm not working your shift for you tonight."

"Then swing by my place and check on Gamble, will you? Hamilton and I are worried shitless about him. This thing he's going through with his girl really has him messed up, and both Hamilton and I have to bartend tonight, otherwise we'd stay with him."

I didn't answer immediately. My conscience warred with itself. I wanted to see Tinker Bell so bad my pulse wouldn't slow down. But the very fact that Ten had called me with his concern said a lot. Worried about

Gamble, I cursed under my breath.

"Just how bad off is he? Like . . . homicidal? Suicidal? Or just ready to kill *you*?"

"Hardy, har, har." Ten sniffed. "I'd say he's definitely something, though. He wouldn't think twice about participating in an extreme act of crazy right now."

"Shit," I ground my teeth in frustration.

"Hey, if you're that busy, I can call Lowe and ask him."

"No," I muttered. "It was Lowe's place I was headed to."

"Really? So you're all close and shit with Lowe but you never hang out with me after hours? Dude, how insulting."

"He wanted me to look at his girlfriend's engine."

Immature Ten snickered. "I would've checked out his woman's engine, no problem."

"Her *car* engine, you moron."

"Well, whatever," he muttered back. "Take Gam with you. That way both you and Lowe can keep an eye on him."

I couldn't think up a reason why that would be a bad idea, so I agreed and using Ten's half-assed instructions of how to get there, I started toward his and Gamble's place.

Gam answered his door, looking like complete shit. I could understand why Ten and Hamilton were so worried about him. He was never this out of sorts.

It was surprisingly easy to talk him into coming along with me, which was a plus, but the whole detour set me back almost an hour from seeing Eva.

I tapped my fingers impatiently on the steering wheel of my Barracuda as we neared Mason's place. But the closer we got, the further away she felt.

Needing a distraction, I glanced over at Gamble who was staring blankly out his side of the car with his elbow resting on the window frame and his forehead buried in his palm.

"So what's up with you and Professor Girlfriend?" I asked. "I'm guessing you guys split since we've all had to rearrange our schedules for you and now I'm stuck on suicide watch."

Noel glanced over at me and scowled. "You're not on—look, I'm not going to do anything to myself. I'm fine. But yes, we're . . . " He had to pause as his face drained of color. "Over. It's been a week, but I'm past it."

Yeah, right. He was past it, my ass. "Then why are Larry and Curly still worried about you?"

"Because they're pussies?" He lifted his hands and shrugged. "How the hell should I know?"

I rolled my eyes. It was harder to get information out of him than it was to draw blood from a stone. "Well, what happened?"

He began to tap his fingers against his knee, much as I'd been tapping mine against the steering wheel. Must be some kind of chick-induced habit. When he turned to stare out the passenger side window again, I groaned. He was not helping me with my own distraction in the least.

"Might as well tell me," I said. "I'm going to bug the piss out of you until you do."

He let out a belly sigh and glared over at me. "Some anonymous *person* sent a picture of us together to my coach, and she got axed."

"Well, fuck," I breathed quietly. "Why didn't you get into trouble, too?" When his face paled even more, I swallowed. "Or did you?"

Bleakness filled his eyes. "The picture only revealed her face. Mine was cropped off."

I frowned, instantly confused. "Wait. Then how did they even know it was a student she was banging? If they couldn't see you, she could've been fucking anyone."

Noel pushed up the sleeve of his shirt to show me a tattoo I didn't even realize he had. "Back in October, about a dozen of us got these the night before our big national championship game. It was the only clear thing you could see of me in the shot."

I glanced at the tat, read it carefully, and snorted out a laugh. "National champs? Didn't you guys lose that game?"

"And didn't I say we got them the night before?" he growled, shoving his sleeve back down to cover the mark.

I stopped razzing him since he seemed so miserable.

But I still wasn't happy about what I'd just learned. "So, the girl got stuck with all the heat, and you just . . . let her take the fall . . . by herself?"

"No." He slammed a frustrated fist against my dashboard. On any other day, I would've called the prick out for that. No one treated my ride with such disrespect, but he was having a bad day, so I let it slide this time.

"I did not just *let* her take the fall," he said. "By the time I'd found out what had happened, she was already gone. Ten and Hamilton managed to talk me out of confessing to Coach. But that's what I should've done. Damn it. Instead, I went to Aspen's boss and tried to talk him into bringing her back. Big fucking mistake. Let me tell you. Coach would've just kicked my ass off the team and pulled my scholarship."

A bad feeling dropped into my stomach. "But not this prick?"

Gamble shook his head, looking a lot more homicidal than suicidal. "Nope, not this prick. When he learned I was the guy in the picture, not only did he refuse to reinstate her, but he refused to reprimand me. He's a big football fan, you see. So I threatened to leave school and drop out of the team if he didn't bring her back, to which he in turn threatened to go public if I even acted like I was going to leave. So now she's gone, and I'm stuck here in order to save her reputation and make sure she doesn't lose all chances of getting a job anywhere else in the country. But in the meantime, yeah, I look like a complete bastard for letting her take all the heat for our relationship."

"Man." I shook my head and blew out a low whistle. "That's harsh. Sucks to be you right now."

"Yep." Once again, he turned to stare out the side window.

"And you haven't heard from her at all since that went down?"

He sniffed as if trying to hold in some tears. "No. I'm pretty sure she left town. She won't answer her door, and her mail has been piling up."

"You don't think *she* would hurt herself, do you?"

Noel glanced slowly at me, giving me a hard stare.

"Well, I hadn't until now. Jesus, she wouldn't—wait. No. Her car's gone too. If she were in the house, her car would still be there. She's okay."

I wasn't so sure. "Unless—"

"Jesus, Pick," he snapped. "Stop freaking me out. She's okay. She just needs some time."

"Well, if you ever need to get into her place, just to check and make sure, I know how to jimmy a lock."

Gamble shook his head. "God, man. Where'd you learn a handy trick like that? The state pen?"

Wow, let a guy know you'd done a little time and he immediately thought you were some hardcore ex-con. I guess that's what I got for beating the piss out of one of Tristy's tormentors.

"I never went to the pen, ass wipe. It was county lock-up for, like, two weeks. And, no, I didn't learn how to break and enter in jail. You meet all kinds of interesting kids when you grow up in the foster care system."

His eyebrows lifted. "I didn't know you grew up in foster care."

"Yep. From birth until I graduated out of it at eighteen." And that was exactly why I never, ever, not even for one night, wanted Julian put into foster care. I knew exactly what kind of shit he could face.

Spotting the address Lowe had given me for his place, I pulled to the curb, my stomach jumping with excitement. "Here we are."

My adrenal glands spiked. I felt so hyped and alive, ready to see her, a person might've thought I was ready to race in an Olympic competition.

I almost forgot about Gamble as I climbed out of my car and strode toward the open bay door of a garage attached to a decent split-level apartment complex.

She was here, somewhere in this building. I couldn't wait to see her again.

But as I approached the opening, I caught sight of some guy standing inside the garage, his back to me and his hands on his hips. It wasn't Mason, that was for damn sure. I was about to call out some kind of greeting to him, make sure he wasn't some creeper lurking around when he said, "Holy shit, you got fat."

That's when I spotted Eva in the garage, trying to pull something out of an open chest freezer. Her ass was pointed out at us, which didn't look fat at all to me. Hell, I couldn't even tell she was pregnant until she popped upright and spun to face the other visitor.

Her face instantly drained of color as she said, "Oh my God. *Alec*?"

Shit.

I ducked out of the doorway and grabbed onto Noel when he tried to pass me to walk into the garage. Then I yanked him down next to me while I crouched to my knees.

I have no idea why I wanted to hide while she had a talk with Alec, but meeting her baby daddy was not high on my priority list. I wanted to race in there and remove his balls from his nut sac in the most painful way ever, which I doubted Tinker Bell would appreciate.

This was none of my damn business. That was not my woman, and that fucking douche probably meant way more to her than I ever would.

That's what I kept repeating to myself, anyway. I had to hum in my head to give her some privacy and not listen in, though.

When Alec stepped too close to her, I almost lost it. Gamble had to grab my arm because he must've known I was about to go ape-shit.

"Don't," he warned in my ear. "This is their fight, man. They obviously have issues to work out. If you get involved and break your parole, you'll land right back in jail."

Yeah, but if Eva was in trouble, parole was the last thing I'd be worried about.

I watched her face closely. She wasn't putting out any anxious or frightened vibes. She seemed to be used to arguing with him this way. But I hated how he grabbed her and moved in close. If Gamble hadn't yanked me back again, I would've intervened.

Why the hell hadn't I just intervened?

12

I was going to see him again! Any minute now.

I'd been a flurry of anxiety all day. Ever since Reese told me Mason had invited Pick over to look at her new car, I hadn't been able to calm myself down. It was pathetic really. I should've been deciding what I was going to do with my life after Skylar was born, or looking for places to live, or researching parenting tips, or finding a job. Anything. Instead, my mind kept lobbing back to his tattooed arms, the one on his neck, and oh, I'd noticed one on his chest when all those horny women had ripped off his shirt in the bar.

God bless horny women.

Pick Ryan possessed one fine naked chest. Definitely a Jake Gyllenhaal lookalike, with a freaking nipple ring. His muscles had been packed into a set of wide shoulders and a tapered frame that led down to the slimmest waist ever. It had been impossible to contain the drool when he'd playfully scolded the women for undressing him during the auction. His smile, added to those pecs and his Mohawk plus the tattoos, had been too much to take. I'd melted into his arms the moment he'd forced that dance on me.

And his singing voice. Oh, my. The guy could actually carry a tune.

Humming "Baby Love" under my breath, I opened the door to Reese and Mason's garage. Since they lived in a split-level duplex, there were quite a few steps to climb down to reach the cement floor. I'd come out here in the guise of looking for a bag of frozen peas in the chest freezer that was kept in the garage, claiming peas sounded good to make with the meal I was cooking for supper. But in truth, I was watching for *him*.

He could be here any minute now.

Typical male Mason hadn't set any specific timetable with him. Being guys, they'd only said Saturday night. Well, there was a lot of time to cover during a single Saturday night. I needed to know exactly when he'd make it. I was going crazy without a precise countdown to wait by.

I don't know why I was craving him so much. It wasn't like getting a man was anywhere on my to-do list, plus he was the last kind of person I should choose—if I *were* on the market. And let's not forget he was *married*, which I seemed to keep forgetting, damn it. Besides, I had no idea what I'd say to him when he arrived, or . . . damn it, why was he taking so long?

"*My baby love. I need you, oh, how I need you,*" I sang the words under my breath as I pulled up the freezer door. There wasn't much piled inside, so it wasn't hard to spot the peas. But it *was* impossible to reach them with my baby bump in the way. I tried turning so I could bend down sideways but didn't have any success with that either.

Not ready to give up, I tried the other side and was able to reach in a little farther until the tips of my fingers barely grazed the cold bag. Frozen air wafted up and coated my bare skin. The baby doll top I'd put on had thick straps but no sleeves, so the skin on my arms prickled instantly with goose bumps, which made my breasts bead from the chill.

I'd dressed for Pick. It was stupid, I know. I was seven and half months pregnant, not exactly the most glamorous time of my life. He was married—*why* I had to keep reminding myself of that was just plain scary. And we came from completely different worlds. My father would've stroked out if he'd ever seen me with a tatted-up, metal-faced guy like Pick.

Okay, so that would've been a plus—anything to kill off the old bastard—but even *I* hadn't been able to go that far. That type had always intimidated me, as if they were tough enough to chew me up and spit me out without a second glance, as if they saw me as nothing but a spoiled rich bitch.

But Pick had completely smothered my fears and reservation in that regard. He'd never intimidated me. And he'd never treated me as a spoiled, rich anything. He looked right past types, stigmas, and prejudices and made it easy for me to do the same.

He was still forbidden though. Having Reese paint my toenails for me earlier this evening because I could no longer reach them, just to impress him, was wrong.

Leaning into the freezer a little more this time, I pressed my belly against the opening of the lid, making Skylar jump at the pressure.

"Sorry, kiddo." I patted my belly, hoping I hadn't hurt her. Time to call on Reese for help with pea-from-freezer extraction.

"Holy shit, you got fat."

At the familiar voice, I whirled around and gasped. A chaotic buzzing filled my head as I stared at the sight before me. It didn't seem possible that my ex from Florida, nine *hundred* miles away, was standing in Mason and Reese's garage. But there he was, gaping in horror at my stomach.

I blinked twice. Then shook my head to deny it. "Oh my God," I finally found the air to gasp. "*Alec*? What're you doing here?" I looked behind him to make sure my parents or anyone else from home hadn't come with him, but he was alone, thank God. The last words we'd ever shouted at each other had been pretty final. I couldn't think up one more thing he'd need to say to me for closure. "How did you even find me?"

Slipping one hand into a pocket of his pressed khakis, he strolled closer, his lip curling into a mocking sneer as he looked me up and down. "Mason told me you were here."

Next item on my to-do list: murder Reese's interfering boyfriend.

Stopping in front of me, Alec let out a breath and shook his head as if disappointed. In me! "I talked to your parents, Eva—"

"Oh, well, you know what?" I snorted and held up a hand to stop him, knowing he still wanted me to do what he'd been demanding the last time we'd spoken. "I talked to my parents too, and I know exactly what their position is. I wouldn't be here in BFE Illinois, sponging off my cousin, if they hadn't kicked me out because I refused to get an abortion. And since I'm still here, *Alec*, I guess that means I haven't changed my mind. So, sorry for your wasted trip, but you came for nothing. You can turn around and go right back to Florida."

Alec gritted his teeth, his expression showing all the frustration he was experiencing. I didn't care; he wasn't going to tell me what to do with my baby. He'd given up his right to make a decision the moment he'd called me a cheating whore after I told him I was pregnant.

But then his face went blank.

"You're really going to play this out, aren't you? Fine, I'm willing to play. What do you want, E.?"

When he caught my arm in a hard, vise-like grip, my warning signals shot sky-high. Alec had never been physically abusive before. But something wasn't right about him today.

Men who found themselves on the edge of desperation usually acted out in terrible ways. I'd learned that the hard way from my father. Well, today Alec looked eerily desperate.

Knowing I had to handle this carefully, even though his presence was ticking me off big time, I tried to take his entire reason to feel desperate away from him.

"This isn't a power play for me to get a pretty toy, Alec," I assured. "The only thing I want is my child."

"Bullshit!" He jabbed his finger accusingly in my direction. "What happened to the girl I met who said kids gave her the willies?"

"You knocked her up," I shot back, fury rising inside me. "So I guess I'm just going to have to learn to adjust."

"Jesus Christ," Alec shouted inside the garage, making me narrow my eyes and set my hand on my hip. "Why can't you just take care of this?"

"I am! I'm going to stay here and take care of my baby, like a mother should."

"A mother? Oh my God." He let out a degrading laugh. "Are you even listening to yourself? This is not you. You're not mother material, Eva. You're a fucking spoiled, rich cunt."

Ouch. That one hurt. I was a single, nineteen-year-old child with no job, no home, and I was about to bring an innocent little human into the world and be totally responsible for her. Sudden dizziness made me sway on my feet. Poor Skylar seemed royally screwed and she wasn't even born yet. With a douchebag for a father and a spoiled, rich cunt for a mother, my baby didn't stand a chance.

But I was still determined give her one. No matter what anyone thought, I would love my girl and I'd find a way to be a damn good mother, if it was the last thing I did.

I squared my shoulders. "Just because I didn't plan on this ever happening, doesn't mean I'm going to brush it aside like a minor inconvenience. I'm keeping my child."

Alec sneered as if he knew a secret. "Well, I can't allow you to do that."

I tried to tug my arm away from him. "Why not? I'm not asking you to do anything. In fact, I don't even *want* you involved."

Alec jerked me closer. "How stupid do you think I am? I know you'll get the law on your side, and you'll fucking bleed everything from me. You could hold this over me for the rest of my life, suck me dry with some bullshit child support, make me pay for all kinds of shit I want nothing to do with. And I refuse to let you get away with it."

"Alec . . . " I gave a long, tired sigh and even rolled my eyes as dramatically as I could, even though my heart was racing. For some irrational reason, I thought letting him see my fear would cause him to pounce. "Believe me." *Please, please believe me.* "I will not do that to you. I don't want anything from you. Actually, if I never saw you again, I would be overwhelmed with joy. I'll even sign a piece of paper saying so."

"See, now." Alec shook his head and laughed softly. "I'm having trouble believing that. I know you, remember? I know what a conniving, manipulative bitch you are. And I refuse to let you continue this."

"Well, I've changed." I huffed out a sound of aggravation when I tried to tug my arm free of his grip and he wouldn't release me. "People can change, you know. Now *let me go.*"

"Not until you agree to get rid of it."

Was he on crack? It was way too late for an abortion, even if I'd been on board with the idea. I sniffed and lifted my chin. "Never."

"Then you leave me no other choice."

Oh, shit. I realized I'd made a big mistake by standing up to him, and even egging his temper on, a split second before he shoved me against the wall.

As my back cracked against sheetrock and then my head banged into it, fear seized me. He clutched me by the throat until I was screaming and screaming, and just screaming for all I was worth, hoping I was loud enough to get Mason and Reese's attention.

He was going to try to hurt my baby. I didn't feel the pain at first; I was too scared for Skylar and what Alec was trying to do to her. But then he punched me in the stomach.

I think I kept screaming. I'm not sure. The sound echoed through my ears as I tried to curl my arms around myself and protect my daughter. But he held me by the neck, pinning me in place, loose enough that I could continue to scream, yet tight enough I couldn't get away. I could barely breathe, let alone shield my stomach. My legs flailed, but the splitting feeling inside me was so severe it was hard to concentrate on much of anything past each gushing slice.

Just as abruptly as he attacked, Alec stopped. The pressure on my throat vanished, and I crumpled to the floor. I couldn't stop myself, couldn't catch my fall, could barely gasp for air. It was as if I had no control over my own limbs. I landed with a jarring thud, which hurt even more. But at least the assault was over.

I thought maybe Alec had come to his senses and backed off.

But then he said, "What the—" just before an *oof* and the thud of something cracking against bone echoed throughout the garage. A choked groan followed.

"You just messed with the wrong girl, pal," someone growled, his voice pissed and male.

From inside my shell of agony, muted sounds of fists against flesh followed, along with shouting and threats. I knew someone was defending me, but at the moment I didn't care. I was too busy trying not to die on the floor. Tears spilled down my cheeks as I cradled my stomach.

Skylar wasn't moving. She always wiggled around or jumped when something startled her.

Why wasn't she moving?

"No," I croaked and rested my cheek on the floor, squeezing my eyes tight as my abdomen felt like it was exploding and tearing apart from the inside.

More shouting filled the garage. I think I finally heard Mason's voice join the melee, but suddenly Reese was with me, her hand on my shoulder and her panicked voice in my ear. "E.? Eva! Can you hear me?"

I tried to nod, or answer, or even blink, but all I could manage was a pained gasp when another round of horror constricted my abdomen.

"E.?" Reese tried again, her voice trembling. "What happened? Are you okay? Oh my God. Mason. She's hurt bad."

The agony-filled wave passed, leaving a low, aching throb. I drew in a breath and tried to talk again. "I think I'm bleeding." My cramped fingers somehow managed to uncurl enough for me to try to look down between my legs, because I could feel a trickle. I wanted to make sure it wasn't blood, but I couldn't see past the baby bump.

Another lightning bolt of pain arched across my belly. I curled in around my baby.

"*No!* No, no, no." One of the male voices turned hoarse as he crouched down beside me. I thought it was Mason until he croaked, "Tinker Bell?" and then I realized it was Pick.

As warm, tender arms enfolded me, I opened my lashes and looked up into a pair of devastated brown eyes. "Pick?"

He scooped me against his chest. He'd finally made it. Just in time.

He kissed my forehead. "Hey, beautiful. You want to take a ride with me? I got a real fast car, and we can get you taken care of in no time."

For a moment, I was confused. Why was he talking about cars and rides when it felt as if everything inside me was splitting apart and my baby was in trouble? But then I understood what he meant. Hospital.

That's when I knew it was bad. Maybe if he'd sounded as cool and collected as I'd always heard him, I could've stayed calm. But he sounded scared, so I got scared.

What if . . . what if Skylar didn't . . . make it? What if Alec had succeeded in . . . ?

Too horrific.

I sobbed out a moan and buried my face in Pick's shirt, my fingers clutching fistfuls. I was so grateful he was here with me.

"It hurts," I told him. It wouldn't hurt so bad if Skylar was okay, would it? Something had to be wrong.

Something was wrong with my baby.

"I know, baby. I know." Crooning, Pick pulled me closer and stood.

Nausea filled me as another band of pain tightened around my abdomen. I tried the breathing technique I'd used when my father had brutalized me. Long, even breaths. But I couldn't seem to calm down enough to stop the fast, shallow pants. I thought I was going to vomit when I was suddenly sky-born and lifted off the ground. Oh, God. Vertigo made my head swim and my stomach convulse.

"Well?" Pick's voice barked. No clue who he was talking to. "Let's get her to the hospital."

I checked out for a minute, refusing to think about anything but his smell clouding my nose. It was hard to think anyway. So I let his scent, which reminded me of coconut tanning oil, make me miss the only thing from Florida that actually made me feel at home. A nice, warm sunny day. The beach. Sand and the soft spray of a wet ocean.

Pressed up against this man who smelled like my favorite kind of sunny day lulled me. I was home again.

People were talking around me, but I didn't really register what they were saying. To focus on words would be to focus on the pain and on what might be happening to the baby inside me.

I clenched my eyes shut and curled deeper into Pick. At that moment, he was the only thing in my universe.

"Hey, it's going to be okay," he murmured into my ear, his voice finally strong with confidence and reassurance.

I clung to that reassurance.

He jostled me enough to let me know we were sliding into a car, then I was nestled on his lap and his arms readjusted to hold me close. I couldn't stop squeezing the front of his shirt. Occasional starts of pain would breach my consciousness, but I was good at blocking unpleasant things. I'd done it for years.

So I shoved them right back out. I absolutely refused to acknowledge that anything bad could happen to Skylar.

It wasn't until we veered sharply around a corner that another shock of pain startled me out of my safe place.

"Easy," Pick barked at whoever was driving.

"Damn, man," a male voice I didn't readily recognize shot back. "I'm trying here. Your car's got more power than I'm used to."

I whimpered and Pick's lips instantly hovered over my ear, his breath warm and soothing. "We're getting you there, Tink. Just a little bit longer."

"My baby," I managed to rasp.

"She's okay. She's going to be just fine. Nothing is going to happen to that precious little angel. I promise you."

"How . . . ?" There was no way he could make such a promise.

"She's fine. I've seen her," he whispered, before choking back what might've been a sob. "And she's beautiful. Absolutely perfect. She's got your amazing blue eyes and the sweetest little cherub face, kind of shaped like a heart. And her hair's dark with the slightest curl. She has a cowlick in her bangs, right here." He pressed his lips to a spot on the right side of my forehead, just at my hairline, where I did not have a cowlick. "Her bottom lip's fuller than the top, and her nose turns up slightly at the end, just like yours."

If he'd used all my features to describe her, I would've had a harder time believing him. But the mention of a cowlick and dark hair—so unlike me—made me envision the child he described until she became a living, breathing creature again. She was alive, and she'd stay that way.

This time, instead of blocking the pain, I embraced it. Still clutching Pick's shirt with one hand, I gripped my belly with the other. "I'm not going to lose her," I promised him.

"No, you're not," he said. "You're going to fight for this little girl, and she's going to make it. You both are."

13

-PICK RYAN-

As a frantic E.R. staff wheeled Eva away on a stretcher, I collapsed onto the nearest bench I saw and pressed my back to the wall, closing my eyes. Unable to hold her any longer, my hands began to shake, so I gripped the edge of the bench for dear life.

Reese paced by me as she chattered on her phone, talking a million miles a minute to a dozen different people. Noel, who'd driven us to the hospital, was lingering nearby, and Mason, who'd stayed back at the apartment to take care of the guy I'd damn-near killed for touching my Tinker Bell, was still absent.

All the while, I couldn't stop feeling the wetness of Eva's blood soak through my shirt.

What the fuck had I been thinking?

I'd stood outside that garage, listened in on her conversation with her ex, and I'd done nothing. *Nothing!*

It didn't matter that Noel had kept telling me not to

intervene; it was none of my business. I'd felt the violence oozing off him. I'd known he was a hair trigger away from unleashing it on her.

Why the hell hadn't I just walked into the garage, made my presence known, and diffused some of the anger? She could've still gotten her big, closure conversation with him while I was standing right there, openly listening to everything.

But shit, I'd let Gamble talk me into thinking it was best to let her have this moment on her own. And that bastard had gotten in way too many punches before I'd been able to reach him.

Pinning him to the wall by the throat, jacking him in the face with a wrench, and kicking him in the balls hadn't been nearly enough before Gamble had managed to pull me off him. I still regretted inviting that bastard to come with me tonight. He might be all torn up over losing his woman, but his helping to convince me to stay back might've just lost me mine.

I gulped and tried not to freak out.

No, we weren't going to lose Eva tonight. She was going to be okay. The baby was going to be okay. Everyone was going to be okay, except maybe her baby daddy. I kind of hoped he died.

But there'd been so much blood coming from her. I choked out a sound and surged to my feet to pace.

"Hey, man." Gamble grabbed my shoulder as I passed him, but I shrugged him off and sent him a death glare.

He obligingly lifted his hands away from me, but kept talking. "You okay? Let me see your hands."

"They're fine." I'd barely gotten two punches into Alec Worthington. Everything on my body was perfectly fine. He should be worried about Eva.

Fuming, I stepped closer to him, needing to unload some of my anger and fear. "Why the fuck did you keep pulling me back? Why—?" When I realized accusing him would solve nothing and only make me regret my words later, I whirled away and stalked off.

Feeling lost, I roamed the halls, staring blindly at framed pictures of stupid pink flowers on the walls. I didn't stop walking until I found myself in the opening of the hospital chapel.

It was eerily quiet inside, the lights were dimmed, and a creepy-looking Madonna statue tipped her head to the side and clasped her hands to her bosom as she sent me a sympathetic stare. I'd never stepped foot inside a church before, but I did now, needing something. Anything.

I sat down in the last pew in the back and stared at the statue, who kept staring back.

I knew I shouldn't feel so shredded about this. I'd known Eva for what, two weeks? She wasn't the girl I'd been dreaming about for ten years. She was a perfect stranger, and if she or her child didn't make it through the night, it wouldn't be the end of my life. But convincing myself of that was impossible.

I didn't want her to die. I didn't want that little baby who'd kicked my hand through her belly to die. I wanted to look into her eyes again and let her fix me up with another Mohawk. I just wanted more time with her.

Glancing up at the worried Madonna, I sent her a respectful nod. "Thanks," I said, and slipped out of the chapel. It wasn't until I was walking by the closed gift shop and saw the stuffed pig Skylar had been holding in my glimpse that I really calmed down. It was like a sign, telling me she was going to be okay. She still had a pig waiting for her love.

My cell phone rang as I headed back toward the waiting room.

With a sigh, I answered, "Tristy, I can't talk right now."

"He won't stop crying," she shouted, totally frantic. "I don't know what to do."

Torn between needing to stay and find out what had happened to Eva and needing to help Tristy and Fighter, I gnashed my teeth. I could hear him wailing through the phone.

"Did you check his diaper?"

"I just fucking changed it."

With a sigh, I ran my hand over my hair. "And you fed him?"

She growled at me. "Yes! I'm not a fucking moron."

A bit my tongue to keep from responding to that. "Tris, I can't come home right now. Someone got hurt; I'm at the hospital. Why don't you actually trying taking him out of his swing and holding him."

She called me a dirty name but stopped talking for a moment because, as I suspect, he'd been in his swing and she was finally pulling him out. His screams almost immediately tempered.

"Isn't it crazy how well that works," I murmured into the phone, my voice acidic.

"You don't have to be a dick about it," she grumbled before adding, "He's still kind of fussy."

"Okay, fine. Put the phone to his ear."

"What?"

"Let him hear my voice."

"That's stupid."

"Will you just shut up and try it? It's soothed him before."

"Fine." A second later, I heard heavy breathing and a scuffle against the speaker before he cooed. I smiled. "Hey, kiddo. I hear you're giving your mom a hard time. Think you could try calming down for her until I can get home? I swear, I'll rock you in the chair twice as long as I usually do when I get back."

"Fuck, it's actually working," I heard Tristy's voice in the background. "Keep talking."

So I started singing to him. Halfway through "Kryptonite" by 3 Doors Down, I saw Noel rush around the corner. When he spotted me, he started waving wildly.

They must've gotten word on Eva and the baby.

"I gotta go," I said, cutting into my own song.

"It's okay," Tris said. "He's fallen asleep."

"Good." I hung up on her and sprinted around the corner to follow Noel.

" . . . and there was significant enough trauma to the uterus to cause a placental abruption," a doctor was telling Reese and Mason, who must've showed up while I was trying not to freak the hell out. He wrapped his arms around Reese and pulled her close as the doctor kept talking.

I had no clue what a placental abruption was, but it

169

didn't sound good. Instantly nauseous, I slumped back onto the bench I'd sat on before to rest my elbows on my knees and bury my face into my hands.

I'd promised her the baby would be okay. I'd described Skylar to her and given her my word of honor, but—

"We had to do an emergency cesarean section. The good news was the placenta was low in the uterus when it abrupted. That's why there was so much external blood loss, but it cut down on the internal bleeding and everything was successful when the baby was delivered."

I lifted my face in surprise just as Reese yelped, "You mean, the baby's *alive*?"

With a slow nod, the doctor confirmed it. "She's up in NICU, but you'll have to consult her pediatrician for the infant's update."

Reese slumped down next to me, tears glistening in her eyes. "Oh, God. Oh, thank God." Then she blurted out a happy laugh. "They both made it. They both—wait. They *both* made it? Right? Eva's okay, too?"

The air in my lungs stalled when the doctor hesitated. I gulped and wanted to vomit all over the floor. No, this couldn't be happening. I'd just met her. After all this time of waiting for her, I meet her two times and she *dies*? No. No way in hell.

"A case of shock affected her kidney," the doctor finally admitted. "She's showing signs of diffuse cortical necrosis, so we've put her on dialysis. But her status is holding steady."

Again, no clue what any of that meant. All I really heard was steady, and to me, that said *still alive*.

Alive was good. It was frigging amazing. Tink was alive.

Reese hugged herself, and her voice shook as she asked, "Can we see her? Either of them?"

"I'm sure you can look at the baby through the window in the maternity ward, but I'll have to send a nurse out when the mother is stable enough for visitors."

We all nodded in understanding, and the doctor left. Noel took off not long after that, having heard all the important stuff. But I wasn't going anywhere until I got an eyeful of both girls. I needed visual proof they were okay.

I followed Reese and Mason up to the maternity ward and then to a window, where they opened the blinds to let us see Skylar.

Lying in the incubator, a little red human had a respiratory tube plugged into her mouth while I.V. lines and monitor patches on her chest made her look like she was on the brink of death.

I sucked in a hard breath. Next to me, Reese whimpered and covered her mouth with both hands. "She's so tiny. How could something so tiny possibly manage to survive?"

I swayed, a little dizzy with worry. Reese was right. She was so small and frail. What if Skylar still didn't make it?

Trying not to panic, I closed my eyes and rested my forehead against the glass.

Mason placed a hand on my shoulder and squeezed. "Hey, Alec and I made a deal. He's not going to tell anyone what you did to him . . . not if he doesn't want us telling the authorities what he did to Eva. So, you don't have to worry about getting into trouble or anything. Okay?"

Getting into trouble because of that douche had been the very last thing I'd been worrying about. Going to jail for trying to kill him over what he'd done to Eva would've been an honor.

I pointed into the window, feeling bitter. "So then, he gets away without even a slap on the hand for doing *this*?"

"Trust me, man. You messed him up pretty good. I'm almost positive he'll be spitting and pissing blood for quite a while."

It wasn't enough. Not nearly enough, but I said, "Good."

They didn't let us in to see Eva for another hour. Reese and I camped outside the window and watched Skylar most of that time. The nurses checked her vitals frequently, and a few times she'd squirm a little, but mostly, the little princess was pretty quiet.

Tinker Bell was probably pissed as hell because she couldn't see her.

And that's exactly the first thing she asked about when we entered her room.

"Have you seen her?"

I froze in the doorway. She was yellow and swollen, so fucking swollen. Her eyes, face, and neck were puffed out to ridiculous proportions and it seemed hard for her to see. All sorts of tubes and machines were hooked up to her, keeping her going.

Panic clawed at my throat, but I swallowed it down and silently followed Reese, though I stopped at the end of the bed, unable to move closer.

Reese grasped Eva's hand and grinned. "She's so small, E. Like a miniature, perfectly-shaped little human with a head full of dark hair . . . like me."

Tears trickled down Eva's puffy cheeks while she smiled. "Does she? She's okay then? They keep telling me so, but I can't go see her. I can't—"

"Shh." Reese leaned down and kissed Eva's forehead. "You'll have the rest of your life with her. Just lay back and relax so you can heal."

Her cousin's words seemed to reach her because she calmed down after that. Mason hung back with me, watching them with worried eyes. When he caught my gaze, he gulped down a guilty-looking cringe. "I feel like such a piece of shit right now," he murmured under his breath. "I told that idiot where she was. I swear to God, I had no idea he'd do this. I thought he was going to step up and finally help out."

Glad I wasn't the only one carrying around a shit-bag of guilt, I clasped his shoulder. "At least you didn't wait around until he was actually punching her in the stomach before breaking into their talk."

Mason opened his mouth to respond, but Eva suddenly said, "Is that Pick I hear?"

I turned to her. I wanted to get down on my knees and beg her forgiveness. I wanted to show her how much it hurt to see her like this, how scared I was for both her and her daughter. But I choked. "Of course, it's me."

I moved toward her and gently took the swollen,

needle-stuck hand as she held it out to me. Shit, her grip was weak. "You did good, Tink. That little girl is so damn cute." I leaned down and kissed her cheek.

Turning my way, she brushed the side of her face against mine. "Thank you. Thank you so much for being there tonight. You saved both me and my little girl."

A trembling breath shuddered from my lungs. I pressed my forehead to hers and finally let some of my feelings slip. "I almost got you killed, is what I did. I listened to you guys talk, and I didn't step in. Not until it was too fucking late. I am so, so sorry I let him that close to you."

A hand touched my hair. I closed my eyes.

"Listen to me, Patrick Jason Ryan. You *are* my hero, and you have nothing to apologize for."

She must've sensed I didn't believe her because she tightened her grip. "You are. You're my hero."

"I'm still sorry," I whispered, unable to combat the guilt.

"I'm not." She shook her head and sent me a trembling smile. If you hadn't come over tonight, I'd be dead right now. My daughter would be dead right now. Why can't you understand that?"

I opened my lashes and met her gaze. Maybe this was the reason I'd had those glimpses. If I hadn't seen her in my head, I wouldn't have been fascinated with her for the past ten years, ergo I wouldn't have been so eager to visit Mason's house tonight. And if I hadn't come over, no one would've been here to stop her ex from killing her. Leaning in, I kissed our entwined hands, so very grateful she was still alive.

"I'll never let anything bad ever happen to you again. I swear it."

It was a promise I meant from the bottom of my soul.

14

-EVA MERCER-

From that day forward, my life changed completely.

As soon as I could walk and the nurses allowed me to leave my hospital bed, I shuffled like a stoop-shouldered old woman to the NICU to sit with Skylar. She was the most beautiful thing I'd ever seen. But looking at her scared the crap out of me. She was so little, so breakable and delicate. How was I supposed to protect her and care for her? I knew absolutely nothing about any of this.

It didn't seem to matter how many parenting articles I'd read, nothing had prepared me for this. This was real.

A nurse entered while I was sitting in the rocking chair, my arm resting inside the hand hole of the incubator to softly pet her miniature fingers.

"Sweetie, you probably need to head back to your room and get some rest now. You've been here quite a while. We don't want you to have a setback."

I barely even looked at her as I studied the little

cowlick in my baby's hairline. How the hell had Pick gotten that right?

Maybe I'd just imagined the description he'd given me of her. There were a lot of fuzzy spots in my memories of the night she was born.

"I'm okay." I didn't want to leave her yet. I didn't think it was possible to love something so much. My chest felt completely full. I could've sat in that chair and just watched her sleep and breathe for the rest of my life.

"Does she need a blanket?" I asked when her tiny frame shuddered in her sleep as if she were shivering. "She looks cold."

The nurse's lips pinched with irritation. "She's fine. But you really need to get back to your own room. They said you just got off dialysis yesterday. You don't want to overdo it."

I nodded as if agreeing, but answered, "Just a little bit longer."

With a grumble, she spun away and stalked off. When I heard the phrase, " . . . typical single teen mother. Thinks she knows everything . . . " I turned and stared after her, watching the extra twenty pounds of weight on her waistline shift back and forth as she marched off in an angry huff.

I don't know why I let her comment get to me. Maybe it was leftover pregnancy hormones swimming through my veins, the start of some baby blues, or normal insecurity issues of a typical new nineteen-year-old mom. But tears immediately filled my eyes. I turned back to my child, small and helpless, fighting for her life, and the floodgate opened even more.

What the hell did I think I was doing?

I'd gone into this with my usual fake confidence, thinking *sure* I could raise a kid. Millions of women popped out babies every year. Why would I have a problem with it? And look, I'd almost gotten Skylar killed.

I sobbed even harder, my chest heaving. I had to pull my hand free of Skylar's incubator and bury my face in both my palms to muffle the gut-wrenching sounds so I wouldn't wake her.

She was here, like this, because I was unfit, because—

"Hey," a cheerful voice interrupted my pity party. "Well, looks who's up and out of bed already."

He sounded so relieved and happy. I turned to look up at Pick. He stood in the doorway with the biggest grin and a pink gift bag dangling from his hand. When he saw my face, his smile dropped flat.

"What's wrong? *Skylar?*" He dropped the bag as he hurried to the incubator.

The worry on his face warmed my heart and helped calm my tears. "No, she's okay. Getting better every day."

A heavy sigh escaped him as he set his hand on the clear plastic separating him from my daughter. "Thank God."

I blinked, still in awe over how worried he'd been. "How did you get back here?" They hadn't even allowed Reese into the NICU. She still had to look at Skylar through the window in the hall.

"Being a flirt comes in handy sometimes." He finally turned to me and winked. "The nurses love me." His grin was brief though. His worry returned almost immediately as he reached down to pluck me out of the chair. "Now what're all these tears about? You're looking better, by the way. The yellow skin and swollen face scared the shit out of me."

I didn't realize he was going to sit me in his lap until he was already settling me into place. I felt even younger, and stupider than I had when I'd started my crying jag. A silly little girl needing to sit on a nice comforting lap to get over herself.

"I don't know," I mumbled, wiping the drops off my cheeks and feeling lame. "I'm just so . . . overwhelmed." *Along with scared, worried, lost, unsure*—ugh! What had happened to the cocky Eva Mercer I'd been a year ago? I'd take a nice, big dose of her right now.

Pick chuckled and kissed my forehead, stirring up a nest of butterflies in my stomach. Or maybe it was the staples in the C-section cut that created such a sensation, except I really couldn't feel much in that area. Awesome drugs and all.

Unable to help myself I plunked my head onto his

nice, wide comforting shoulder. I mean, he was offering it. I couldn't resist. And it felt good, so amazingly good to let someone hold me for a minute.

"I'm sorry," I started, sniffing up the end of my tears. "Just ignore me. I—"

"No, I will not ignore you. I will never ignore you. You have every reason in the world to have a freak-out moment. Fuck, you just gave birth. That alone would put enough strain on anyone's emotions. Tristy cried for three weeks straight after Julian was born."

I'm sure if he'd looked at me in that second, he would've seen a frown line appear between my eyes. I really didn't want to hear about his wife right now, not when I was snuggled on his lap, letting him comfort me and wishing things from him that he could never give. But I guess it didn't bother me enough to slide off him. It would take the Jaws of Life to get me off Patrick Ryan's lap.

I ran my finger over a tattoo of a cat face on his forearm as he kept talking.

"But look at what else you've had piled on top of that. I don't know all of it, but what I do know seems like a lot of shit. It'd certainly break me down if I were in your shoes." He kissed my temple this time. "You don't have to be brave and strong all the time, Tink."

My lips fluttered with amusement. "You're never going to get over that nickname, are you? A girl wears Tinker Bell on her shirt one time—"

"Embrace it." He grinned before nuzzling his nose against my temple. "Not everyone can pull off the Tink image."

My smile bloomed wider. Petting the cat's ears, I asked, "Does this one mean anything? The cat tattoo?"

He glanced down. "Of course. They all mean something. I don't get random images tattooed on my skin for no reason at all."

He sounded defensive enough for me to glance up. "Then why do you?"

With a shrug, he glanced at the cat face. "I grew up in foster care from birth to eighteen. I didn't stay at the same place but a couple years each, if that long. And you learn young that the rules change from house to house. You don't always get to bring much with you wherever you go next. And you don't always get to keep what you bring. Forget photos or sentimental knickknacks. It's just you and the skin on your back. So if I ever wanted to keep a memory of anything, I just—"

"Tattooed it into your skin," I finished for him. Studying him in a new light, I glanced back at the cat. "Was that cat your first pet?"

"Only pet," he corrected with a grin in his voice. "Actually, it wasn't really a pet at all. It was just some mangy alley cat. A stray that came by our place. I snuck out some food to it, and it kept coming back. After a while, it let me pet it while it was eating. It never let anyone else in the neighborhood come near it."

I smiled, liking that story. "What'd you name him?"

He sent me an irritated look. "He was a wild stray. You don't name strays."

Something in his narrowed brown eyes made me nudge him lightly with my elbow. "Whatever. You so named him. Now spill."

With a sigh, he leaned his head back and stared up at the ceiling before mumbling, "It's stupid."

That only made me like him more. "I don't care. Tell me."

"Shakespeare," he said, rolling his eyes. "I named him Shakespeare."

Aww. There I went, liking him even more. I touched his chin, loving the way his rough jaw scraped against my fingers. I wanted to touch the metal hoops in his lip next, but managed to restrain myself. "You were a daydreamer, weren't you?"

His voice was dry and still full of irritation as he grumbled, "If you knew how many fights I've gotten into over the years, you wouldn't think that."

"Bet I would. I've seen why you get into fights. It's frankly shocking I don't see a hero cape inked anywhere on here." I scrolled my fingertips up toward his elbow. "I can only imagine how many other damsels in distress you've saved over the years."

"Ha ha," he muttered.

I grinned. "My daughter and I have our lives to thank you for, Patrick. I'm not just going to forget that."

He stared at me, and something thunked heavily into my stomach. My breasts tingled and I seriously don't think it was my milk coming in.

"Why do you call me Patrick so much?" he whispered.

"Because it's your name," I whispered back, not even daring to breathe. The glaze in his eyes told me he wanted to kiss me. And, *oh hell,* I wanted to kiss him back.

But he glanced away toward Skylar.

"Only social workers and teachers ever called me Patrick."

The moment was growing too deep. Remembering I was sitting on a married guy's lap, I refrained from pushing the issue. I didn't ask whether or not he liked me calling him that. Instead, I focused on another tattoo of a plant. "What about this one? What does this stand for?"

"My favorite foster mother. She liked to garden."

We went through the list, from his wrist to his shoulder, going over the meaning behind each tattoo. I sighed wistfully after he explained the one symbolizing the first car engine he rebuilt from the ground up. I liked knowing what mattered most to him.

"I'd like to get a tattoo someday," I said thoughtfully, knowing exactly what mattered most to me as I gazed at my daughter.

"You will." Pick traced his finger delicately along the bare patch of skin behind my left ear. "Right here. You're going to get my name."

I rolled my eyes, fighting back a smile because I knew I shouldn't encourage his flirtatious attitude. "Always so sure of yourself, aren't you?"

He grinned. "Of course. I don't say shit I don't mean."

He sounded awfully serious about that. But I shook my head and finally let a smile seep out. Resting my head back on his shoulder, I continued to outline the pictures on his arm with my fingernail. "Your wife would probably kill me if she knew I was letting you hold me like this."

"Nah." He leaned in and buried his nose in my hair. As I listened to him inhale deeply, something tight and foreign wrapped around my stomach. "She's not like that."

Well, maybe she should be, because I wasn't feeling friendly companionship for him just now. Experiencing something so much deeper, I opened my mouth to argue. Accepting, non-jealous wife or not, this was still wrong. He belonged to someone else. I shouldn't let him keep coming to my rescue. It might not mean so much to him, but to me, it meant way more than I knew it should.

"In any case," I said, letting the issue drop so he wouldn't know just how much I was crushing on him. "I really appreciate you being here and talking me off my crying jag. You always know when to show up at just the right time to save me."

His arms tightened, and I knew he was thinking about what Alec had done.

I touched his face. "I'm serious, Patrick. Look at me."

He lifted his face, and I wanted to press my mouth to his so bad. "You did everything right that night. Now stop worrying about it."

Shaking his head, he gave me a small smile. "Right after you stop reading my mind, woman. It's too sexy."

I opened my mouth to tell him he found the strangest things sexy, but the nurse who'd made me cry returned. An irritated line deepened between her eyes before she focused on Pick's face. And just like that, her cheeks flushed with pleasure.

"Oh, my lands. I didn't think I'd ever get to see your gorgeous tush again, Mr. Pick."

Pick grinned at her. "Hey, Charlotte. Have you been taking good care of my two girls, here?"

She glanced at me, looking slightly guilty before turning back to him. "I had no idea they were yours, but of course we have. Now come here and give me some sugar."

When she leaned past me, Pick dutifully kissed her on the cheek. Pulling back with a happy glow, Charlotte ducked her head from the room and called into the nurses' station. Within moments, the entire room was crowded with women crawling all over him, demanding hugs and kisses. He gently slid me off his lap and placed me back into the chair so he could oblige them, telling Whitney he liked her new hairstyle, and Megs that she looked as if she'd lost too much weight. In return, they pawed at him, cooed, and asked how Julian was doing.

Julian, right. That must be how they knew him. He had to have been here when his wife gave birth.

Another round of envy bit me in the ass as I watched him become the center of all my nurses' attention. He pulled out his phone to show off pictures of his son, and I shook my head in wonder. The man certainly knew how to work a roomful of women.

When he caught my eye, he winked and pointed as he asked the ladies, "My Tink's not giving you any trouble, is she? I know how sassy she can be."

The nurses rushed to assure him I was a perfect patient, aside from the fact I needed more rest.

After that, he took it upon himself to personally escort me to my room for a nap. I touched Skylar's fingers in farewell, hoping I'd soon be able to kiss her forehead, or cheek, or tiny little toes, or actually hold her in my arms. Then Pick took my hand and walked me back to my room. Once he tucked me back into bed where everyone seemed to want me, he pulled up his gift bag. The stuffed pink pig he brought for Skylar was perfect. I thanked him and held it to my chest long after he had to leave, saying he'd already stayed way past his lunch break.

The nurses were much nicer to me after that. One eyed the pig I was clutching and smiled knowingly. "From Pick?" she guessed.

I nodded, cuddling the stuffed animal to my chin.

"So, how long have you known our favorite daddy?"

"Oh," I smiled up at her. "Not long. My cousin Mason works with him at the Forbidden Nightclub."

The nurse nodded. "Well, he's a one of a kind, that's for sure. I think every single nurse fell in love with him when he was here for that Tristy gal. He was amazing with her baby. Patient, good-natured. A real natural."

I smiled softly, faltering when I realized she'd said

'her' baby, not 'his' baby. Strange. "I bet he was. I haven't met Julian yet. Just seen a picture Pick showed me."

The nurse clucked her tongue. "He was so proud of that kid. Damn shame it wasn't his."

I blinked. "Wait, what? What do you mean *not his*?" Oh my God. There was no other meaning for such a phrase. But that would have to mean . . . "Holy shit. Does Pick know?"

With a snort and roll of her eyes, the nurse checked the level of water in my pitcher. "Honey, that baby came out blacker than I am. Ain't no way that baby can be his. And *everybody* knew it."

I drew in a sharp breath. "Oh . . . wow. I . . . I just assumed the mom was . . . I can't believe his wife cheated on him."

"Wife?" the nurse squawked, pausing as she plunked the pitcher down. "No, don't you dare tell me he went on to marry that girl." She shook her head sadly. "Worst patient I ever had. I tell you what," she leaned in closer and lowered her voice. "You didn't hear this from me, but *no one* liked her. Mm-hmm. She was a bitch with a capital *B*. And I don't even curse." To prove herself right, she lifted her gaze to the ceiling, and murmured, "Forgive me, Father," as she pulled a crucifix from her under her blouse and kissed it.

My mouth fell open. My biggest worry had been that his wife would be sweet, gorgeous, and awesome. But learning she wasn't as grand as I'd feared was almost worse. I didn't want to learn he was strapped to a bitch who'd fucking cheated on him.

My poor, poor Patrick. I wanted to scratch her eyes out.

"Did he know the baby wasn't his before it was born?" I asked, my voice just as low as the nurse's.

She straightened, slapping playfully at my hand. "Well, of course. He and that girl never had *that* kind of relationship, if you know what I mean. They were more like brother and sister. I think he said they'd been in the same foster home once." She rolled her eyes. "He's been looking out for her for years. And if they got married, it's *only* because of her baby."

My chest suddenly felt tight and I wanted to cry. A guy like Pick—who'd beaten up Alec because he'd tried to kill my baby, who'd taken on the care of an infant he knew wasn't his, who'd held me in his arms to comfort me—deserved a true love match, a wife who adored him.

My crush on him grew even stronger. If only I'd known him the night I'd met Alec "the Bastard" Worthington. But even if I had, I probably still would've gone after Alec, because I'd been stupid and prejudiced. All I would've seen in Pick were his bad-boy tattoos and non-branded clothes. I would've labeled him a sleazy loser. But Alec was the true loser, and Pick was the sweetest, most honorable man I'd ever met.

15

As soon as she could breathe, eat, and stay warm on her own, Skylar was discharged from the hospital. She was twenty days old when I was finally able to take her home.

I'd only had to stay for a week myself. After my kidneys decided to function on their own again, they'd kicked me out two days later. It was the hardest thing in the world to leave the hospital without my baby, my little girl who'd been with me for the past seven and half months. So, usually I just stuck around there all day, annoying the nurses with every question under the sun. I think they were patient with me only because they knew I was Pick's friend.

For Skylar's situation, her doctor didn't foresee any long-term problems. He warned me she'd probably have some delays in developments, maybe a little trouble in school. But physically, she was fine.

That first night with her home was rough, and not because Skylar was fussy. In fact, she was a dream come true compared to some of the new-baby horror stories I'd read. I actually had to wake her a few times for her scheduled feedings. What made it rough was that I couldn't stop worrying. I popped out of bed to check on her every time she moved or breathed a little too loudly.

Before the night was over, I shifted her crib until it was squished against my bed, so she was no longer all the way across the room from me. I could only fall asleep when I slid my hand through the crib's slats and rested my fingers on her. If I hadn't feared I might roll over and accidentally suffocate her, I would've kept her in bed with me.

Morning came before I knew it, and I woke to what I swore was the sound of Pick's laughter. At first, I thought it was part of the lovely dream I was having. He was holding Skylar, telling her what a princess she was, right before she passed gas.

He threw his head back and laughed. I thought he'd add something like, *"Princess of Gas,"* but instead he said, "Christ, Lowe. I can't believe you actually bought this piece of shit."

My lashes fluttered open, and my bedroom at Reese's duplex came into focus. Daylight bounced off the pale walls, telling me it was no longer five in the morning, which was the last time I'd been awake with Skylar. The curtains shifted, letting in a warm spring breeze because I'd left the window open all night. The light gust dusted my cheeks, making me smile.

These past few hours were the most sleep I'd had all night. My body ached and I needed to take my pain meds, plus my milk-logged breasts were on fire and hard as stones. I was in the worst physical condition of my life, and yet I couldn't remember feeling so content.

Then I heard Pick's voice again. "I'm frankly surprised the thing is still running. Have you looked at this engine?"

I bolted upright in bed. Oh my God! Pick *was* here, right outside my window.

Oh my God times two. That hurt. Oh, hell . . . *Ouch*.

185

That really hurt.

Wrapping my arm around my middle as white-hot pain slashed across my healing C-section incision, I gasped and tried to breathe through the waves of agony. But, wow. Sitting up too fast after you'd had your gut cut open did not feel good. It didn't help that my abdomen was still bruised from where Alec had punched me, but this . . . this had come straight from that stapled-together line.

"I wasn't there when Reese bought it." Mason's voice floated in through the window behind Pick's. "It was sitting in the drive by the time I got home from class."

"Want me to help you beat the hell out of the asshole who sold it to her?"

I smiled softly. It should probably bother me that Pick was so ready to use his fists, but that very trait about him had saved me and my child's life. I couldn't help but cherish it instead.

"God, no," Mason muttered. "I've seen how you beat the hell out of people. I'll pass. Just see if you can get this thing safe enough to drive."

"You got it. Hey, do you want—"

But Pick didn't get to finish the question, because another voice broke in, this one loud and obnoxious. "Yo, mother fuckers! Wuz up?"

Hearing the newcomer made me tilt my head in curiosity. Whoever it was sounded vaguely familiar.

Mason obviously wasn't expecting more company, because he said, "What the hell are *you* guys doing here?" I guessed more than one person had just walked up the driveway to visit him.

"I heard Pick got a golden invitation to your house and I was feeling left out."

"I'm only here because Ten was my ride to football this morning," another voice chimed in. "We started summer practice today, so I was dragged along without consent. Don't worry; I'll be out of your hair soon. My girl's going to swing by and pick me up in a few minutes."

"I'm sorry," a third voice interrupted. "Ten told me we were hanging at your place today, so I followed him. I didn't know we weren't invited."

"It's okay," Mason answered. "I don't mind you other two being here."

"Hey!" Ten yelped, clearly offended, which only made Mason laugh.

"Yo, Gamble," Pick called, his voice more muted than it'd been before. "Hand me that wrench by your feet, will you?"

"You're not going to jack some guy in the face with it, like you did last time we were here, are you?"

Wow, had he actually hit Alec in the face with a wrench? Even though I winced over how much that must've hurt my ex, an uncontrollable grin spread across my face. I hope Pick had left a scar; Alec had always been so proud of his pretty face.

"Funny," Pick muttered. "Bastard had it coming. Hey, I heard you got your girl back. I haven't worked much with you lately to offer you a congrats."

"Thanks," Noel said, sounding pretty proud of himself. "Though I have no idea why she took me back; I lost her her job and then basically saddled the responsibility of three kids on her when I took my siblings away from my mom. But I'm not looking a gift horse in the mouth. She's here and I'm appreciating her for as long as she decides to stay with me."

"Yeah, I heard about your brothers and sister moving in with you, too. That sucks, man."

"Actually, it doesn't. I'm less worried about them now, plus they're in a better place. It's better for all of us . . . except maybe Aspen, who's taking it upon herself to get them settled in and enrolled in school here. She's been such a godsend."

"Hey, whose beer?" Ten butted back into the conversation.

"Mine," Pick answered, his voice muffled as if he'd just slid back under Reese's car.

I heard the pop and fizz of a can opening. "Damn, you have cheap taste." Then he paused before sighing in refreshment as if he'd just guzzled half the can.

"If you're going to help yourself..." Pick's voice was dry, "then keep your damn trap shut about the label."

"Hey, I wasn't complaining. I dig cheap beer. And talking about cheap, you remember the chick who came into the bar to see you the other night? You gave her some cash and sent her on her way."

"Yeah," Pick said suspiciously. "What about her?"

"*That* was one cheap, easy broad. I'm telling you, all I bought her was a snow cone and she went down on me right there in the parking lot. Then she followed me home and screwed me every which way 'til Monday."

"You . . . " Pick didn't seem to know what to say to that. Then he finally asked, "You didn't give her any drugs, did you?"

"What?" Ten's voice was full of clueless confusion. "No! I don't do drugs. Why would you even ask that? Wait, is that why she was at Forbidden to see you? Oh, dude. Are you a *drug dealer*?"

"Oh, Jesus. Really? If I was the one giving her money, why would *I* be the drug dealer?"

"Shit. So *she's* a drug dealer?"

"No. Damn. Just . . . shut up. Neither of us deal drugs."

"Then why did you bring up drugs? And why were you giving her money? Who the fuck is she?" Ten was beginning to sound alarmed.

"I brought up drugs because she used to be a crack whore. I was making sure you didn't give her anything. And *I* gave her money because she's my wife."

I slapped my hand over my mouth as it dropped open in shock. But, wow. I hadn't expected that answer. Neither had any of the guys, apparently. A pregnant pause floated through the window before Ten exploded. "I fucked your *wife*?"

Then Mason, Gamble, and Quinn shouted together. "You're *married*?"

"Oh, shit." Ten's voice sounded hollow. "I knew you had a kid, but since when are you married? How the hell can you be married? You're like the biggest man-whore I know."

"I'm not the biggest man-whore you know." Pick sounded insulted. "*You're* the biggest man-whore you know. All you see is me driving drunk girls home from the bar every other night. I don't actually sleep with any of them. What kind of ass takes advantage of an inebriated lady?"

"I don't know," Gamble murmured thoughtfully. "Some of them are pretty persuasive. They can get hard to resist."

"Literally." Ten snorted at the pun.

"You're cracking jokes, Ten?" Mason asked. "Really? Right after learning you cuckolded poor Pick?"

"No," Pick was quick to reassure. "Tris and I don't have that kind of marriage. I mean, I've certainly never gone there with her. She's more like a sister to me. I'm just helping her out with insurance until she and her kid get back on their feet."

"So, the kid's not yours either?" Ten asked.

"Not . . . technically. But I'm probably going to be the only dad he'll ever know, so it doesn't really matter who donated the sperm to make him."

"And you've never fucked her? Ever? So, I still haven't had any of your leftovers."

Wow, was that what worried him most? I sniffed. That Ten guy was a piece of work.

"No." Pick's answer sounded a lot more good-natured than my own would have been. "She and I have never . . . and will never. Frankly, I'm shocked even *you* wanted her. She's not exactly . . . "

"Dude, I'll fuck anything with tits who'll willingly spread her legs for me. I don't care what she looks like. And shame on you for caring so much about appearance. It's a wonder all the ladies go so ga-ga over you, you prejudiced prick."

Pick made an aggravated sound. "Hey, fuck you. I wasn't talking about her *appearance*, dumb ass. I was going to say she's not very nice."

"*Oh*. That. Well . . . " A grin laced Ten's tone. "You screw a dazed smile onto a girl's face and the bitch comes. Get it? It *comes* right out of her."

"Okay, okay. Enough talk about sleeping with Pick's wife already," Gamble scolded. "Damn, Ten." He must've turned to Mason next because he said, "Lowe, change the subject. What's been going on with you? How're you and your old lady after that cougar came by the bar?"

I held my breath because I hadn't even thought of Mrs. Garrison since Mason and Reese had gotten engaged. I'd been a little preoccupied with my new piece of heaven on earth. Checking on her, I leaned over to watch her sleep in her crib, and wow . . . She was just so precious.

"She let me put a ring on her finger," Mason was saying outside, "so I'd say we're doing fine."

The pride in his voice made me smile. It was just so nice to know how much he loved Reese. I liked seeing her happy. Reaching out, I stroked Skylar's soft cheek. She stirred and began to wake. Since it was past time to feed her anyway, I leaned over the railing and pulled her into my arms before opening my shirt to give her some breakfast.

Gamble's stunned voice floated into the room. "You're getting married? Holy shit, guys. I was only out of the loop for a couple weeks. I knew Ten was moving in with Hamilton since I left him homeless so I could move in with my girl. But Pick's married with a kid, Lowe's engaged, and Ten's turned to sleeping with married women? Shit. Pretty soon you'll be telling me Hamilton here's lost his v-card." After a moment of silence, Gamble exploded, "Holy shit! Hamilton lost his *v-card*?"

When a round of chuckles answered him, Gamble joined in. "Well, congratulations, bud. What'd you think?"

"What'd he think?" Ten's incredulous voice snorted. "The guy had sex for the first time. She could've been the lousiest lay on earth; if he came, he liked it!"

"She wasn't lousy." Hamilton sounded offended, which made me smile. It was nice to hear a guy defend a girl instead of trash talking her to his friends.

"Oh, yeah?" Ten sounded intrigued. "She climb on top of you and take control or let you think you were in charge?"

"Hey, easy. Lay off the kid," Pick scolded. "He doesn't have to give details."

"What the hell ever. I want to know everything. When, where, how long, which positions. How many times you made her come."

"I don't—" Quinn started, only to cut himself off abruptly.

"Well, spit it out," Ten demanded. "Don't leave us hanging now. You didn't what?"

I could almost feel poor Quinn blushing from all the way inside the house. His voice was more of a mumble when he finally admitted, "I don't know if I actually made her . . . I mean, how do you know?"

Silence greeted his question. Finally, Ten said in a scandalized, horrified kind of voice, "You didn't make her come?"

More silence. Then, "I don't know."

"Trust me, Ham. You'd *know*," Gamble said.

"But . . . how?"

Ten snickered. "Did she scream your name, claw your back, chant, *'ohmigod, ohmigod, ohmigod, harder faster. Right there, Quinn. Fuuuuuuck me!'*"

"Which is proof the ladies obvious fake it with you," Mason said dryly.

"Hey, fuck you, man. How do *you* know when it happens then, oh great and mighty Lowe, king of all sex gods?"

"You can feel it," Mason shot back. "That sweet little muscle contracts around your junk right about the time her eyes roll into her back of her head and her back arches up and her thighs clamp around you."

I gagged a little, not wanting to think about him—or Reese—in that way. Startled by my reaction, Skylar broke away from my nipple and seemed confused. I was so busy trying to help her latch back on, I almost missed it when Pick answered, "He's right. You can definitely feel it milking your dick."

Immediately, I went hot all over, imagining him that way. With me. God . . . I thought it was the pregnancy hormones that made me horny for him. But I wasn't pregnant anymore, so I should've been over this by now.

"Yep," Gamble added with a single affirmative as the conversation continued.

Ten snorted. "Whatever. You can't feel that shit."

"Maybe you're not big enough to feel it then." Mason

snickered.

"Oh, look who's bragging about his size today?" Ten sounded suddenly put out.

As if to save him from feeling deficient, Quinn quickly said, "I don't think she came, then. How do I—" Once again, he cut himself off, but everyone, me included, knew exactly what he was asking.

"Sounds like you need to put your tongue to work." Pick's suggestion made me realize I'd grown wet. How freaking embarrassing. Just his voice and the word *tongue* aroused me.

"Huh?" Quinn was obviously confused.

Pick clarified. "You. Need. To. Lick. Her."

"Lick her?"

"Oh my God." I envisioned Pick spinning to glance incredulously at the other three guys with his hands in the air. "Is he serious?"

"He was sheltered," Ten explained. "Raised by his grandma."

"Oh . . . well, then. Hell yeah, *lick* that girl. Behind the ear, down the neck, between the breasts, all over her nipples, right up in her pussy, down her—"

"Right up in her . . . *what?*"

I slapped my hand over my mouth to keep from laughing aloud over Quinn's horrified tone.

"Especially there," Gamble added, and I found myself nodding in agreement.

Right behind my ears, down my neck, and all over my breasts were already burning as if they'd just physically experienced Pick's verbal assault. But between my legs burned the hottest; it could handle Pick's tongue quite nicely.

"Spreading jelly on it and licking that off works well, too."

I grimaced. Oh, no, no, no. That was something I never wanted to know about Mason. Eww. I hoped to God he wasn't talking about something he'd done with Reese. I'd never be able to eat a PB&J from our kitchen again.

"Damn, Lowe. Getting creative over there."

"I'm definitely going to have to try that on Aspen."

I slapped my hand over my mouth to keep from laughing aloud. Wow. I had no idea guys actually had these kinds of discussions with each other.

"So, you seriously lick . . . there? And she doesn't mind?"

"Mind? Why would she mind? Chicks fucking love that shit. I get requests for it all the time. *Ten, baby, it's your turn to go down on me tonight.*"

"But—"

"Sounds like you still need to learn the parts of a woman," Pick said. "Next time you guys are together, don't be afraid to explore. She won't mind. If you're touching, licking, kissing, and nibbling on every little place you go, she'll actually appreciate it. Trust me. Get down there at eye level with everything and just . . . look around. Test it out with your tongue. She'll let you know what she does and doesn't like."

"Loudly," Noel added.

I sighed a little, wishing I'd met Pick years ago. He sounded like a very considerate, thorough lover. I doubt he'd even let me zone out and try to escape to my safe, numb place. I bet he'd be able to show me what good, pure, honest sex was supposed to be like.

Regret burned my throat because I'd never had that, never enjoyed an intimate moment with a guy.

"I'd listen to Pick. The man knows what he's talking about."

"What the hell?" Pick answered. "Did I just get a compliment from *Ten*? Are you okay? Oh shit, are you dying?"

"Shut up."

Pick's chuckle warmed me from the inside out, just as Gamble spoke up. "Shh. Woman alert. Lowe's old lady is walking up the drive."

The men instantly settled down. A few seconds later, Mason called, "Hey, Sweet Pea." I could picture him snagging her around the waist and pulling her down onto his lap.

"Been grocery shopping, huh?" Ten asked. "Run out of jelly again?"

My mouth fell open, hoping to God Reese had no clue

what he meant. But when she said, "What is he talking about?" a little too sharply, I just knew she'd caught on and was sending Mason the evil eye for sharing too much with his friends.

He must've put on the perfect innocent face, because after he answered, "I have no idea," Reese dropped the subject. I envisioned her popping off his lap with a refreshed smile and carrying her bags of groceries toward the back door. "Where's Eva?" she asked, and yep, her voice sounded a lot closer to where the door was.

"Haven't seen her yet this morning," Mason answered. "She must still be in bed. I know I would be. I swear that baby was up every hour."

I rolled my eyes. It'd been every two hours, not one. That had been the recommended feeding schedule the nurses had given me.

"Why don't you go see if she's up yet?" Pick said. "And drag her out here. I haven't had my Tinker Bell fix for the day yet."

I instantly smiled. He wanted to see me. That was so—

I bit my lip to kill the grin. Bad Eva. I had to stop thinking about him this way, even though his wife was like a sister to him and he'd only married her for insurance purposes. This was the worst time for me to develop honest feelings for a guy. I had baggage, issues, and trouble stamped all over me. And despite how obvious it was that Pick didn't mind wading through that kind of crap for a woman since he'd married an ex-crack whore just to help her out, I still didn't want to pile any of *my* crap on him.

He was too amazing to deal with the likes of me.

"Sure. I'll check on her," Reese was telling him. "Hey, are you guys staying for lunch? I could make Mason fire up the grill."

"Say what?" Mason started while Ten hooted. "Free food? Hell, yes. Count me in."

"Thanks, but my family's going to pick me up soon," Gamble said, to which Reese answered, "They can stay too. We'll make a party of it. The more, the merrier."

"Well, okay then. Count me in, too."

"I could eat," Quinn added.

"And I'm not letting you say no, Mr. Ryan. After the way you saved my E., I'd feed you every day for the rest of my life."

"I actually can't stay long. Saturday is always my morning with my kid. I'm already missing out on some daddy time."

"Okay, no problem," Reese said, but she didn't sound convinced.

"I still want to see Eva and Skylar before I go, though," he called just as I heard the back door to the garage open.

Since Skylar was done eating, I climbed off the bed and carried her toward the kitchen, burping her as I went.

"There you are!" Reese cheered as I strolled into the room. She set two overflowing bags on the table before turning to me and snatching Skylar from my arms. "I was just coming to check on you."

"I know. I heard. My window was open, and oh my God . . . " I leaned in, lowering my voice. "The things men will talk about when they don't think a woman's listening. They make us think it's all cars, and sports, and sex with them. Well, I mean, there was plenty of sex talk but—"

Reese gasped and stopped patting Skylar's back to grab my arm. "I knew it! Mason spilled about the jelly, didn't he?"

I bit my lip, but my expression gave me away.

Her mouth fell open. "I am so going to kill him."

I stole Skylar back before she really did turn homicidal. "I don't think he meant to let it slip, if that's any consolation. They were giving tips to Quinn because he'd just slept with his first girl and—"

"What? Wow. Quinn was a virgin? But he's so hot."

"I know! Apparently he was raised by his grandma and didn't even know about going down on a girl. Plus, he's like super shy."

"Holy shit, E." Reese pulled back and shook her head. "How the hell long did you listen to those guys?"

"Oh, they were a fountain of juicy gossip."

I settled Skylar into the bouncer on the table and helped Reese prepare our impromptu picnic. I was telling her how Gamble and his teacher girlfriend were back together when the back door opened and Mason popped into the kitchen.

"Hey, babe," he told Reese as he swooped in behind her to draw his arms around her waist and kissed the side of her neck. "The grill's fired up and ready to go, and Noel's family just showed up." A strange expression crossed his face before he added, "They agreed to stay for lunch, which brings the head count up to eleven and one beautiful little baby." He released Reese to turn to Skylar, pull her out of her chair, and rub his nose into her belly. "Hello, little girl."

It still shocked me how affectionate he was with her, and how willing he was to hold her. As he cradled her and cooed to her, I glanced Reese's way. She'd pressed her lips together tight and was holding both hands to her heart as she watched him with this love-struck grin on her face. When she caught me watching her, she fanned her face with a hand and mouthed the words, *"Isn't he amazing?"*

I rolled my eyes, but grinned, because yeah, she'd found herself an amazing man.

"Mind if I take her outside and show her off to the guys?" Mason asked, glancing at me. "I think Pick's about to chew his arm off if he doesn't see one of you soon."

There was just no way I could deny him such a wish, so I waved him on. But at the door he paused, and turned back to Reese. "Oh, and Dr. Kavanagh's here. She and Noel are back together."

"Oh, I know. Eva was just—" Realizing she was about to give away the source of her gossip, Reese clamped her lips shut and then over-exaggerated big time as she burst out a fake gasp. "Really? Wow, that's great. I like her."

"Yeah, but Noel warned us not to call her Dr. Kavanagh. He didn't want to weird her out and remind her how we used to be her students."

"Sure. Sure. Wait? What *is* her first name?"

16

Reese and I whipped up a fine spur-of-the-moment backyard barbeque, if I do say so myself.

Aspen—never to be referred to as Dr. Kavanagh again—and Noel's sister Caroline found their way into the kitchen at one point. They helped us out a lot, and we had our own round of juicy gossip, talking about all the guys while veggies were chopped and hamburger patties were formed. Skylar remained the main attraction of the day and went from outside, to inside, to outside again as more people than I could count passed her around, taking their turn at holding her.

By the time I finally left the kitchen, carrying Reese's legendary potato salad into the garage, a table and chairs had been set up, spilling out into the front drive. Pick shut the hood to Reese's car and was describing to Mason everything he'd fixed, while Ten and two younger boys were making fun of how uncomfortable Noel looked

197

holding Skylar.

"Don't listen to them," I told Gamble as I scooped my baby from his arms. "You're doing just fine." I turned away, looking for a place to sit, only to find Pick's gaze on me.

"So you really were inside," he murmured, strolling forward. "I was beginning to wonder when you were ever going to make an appearance."

My heart fluttered in my chest as he grinned down at Skylar.

"Reese has been working my ass off in the kitchen. But I think we just about have everything ready. Have you already taken your turn holding Skylar?"

"Not yet." He lifted his hands to show me how black and greasy his palms were. "Lowe's been working *my* ass off out here. I'm going to go clean up and come steal her from you, though."

I nodded, unable to stop smiling at him. I hadn't seen him since his last visit to my hospital room to deliver Skylar's stuffed pig. That had been way too long ago. Just gazing into his warm, brown eyes refreshed something inside me.

He paused a moment as if he wanted to say more. Then he shook his head, smiled, and turned away. I watched him disappear into the back door, and let out a little sigh, already wanting him to return.

Shaking such strange thoughts from my head, I made my way to the chairs set up out in the driveway where Mason was flipping burgers on the grill. I found the nearest open seat and sank down, holding Skylar to my chest.

I guess I should've known better than to sit by Ten, though.

He sent me a chin bob and wiggled his eyebrows. "How's that breastfeeding coming along?"

Oh, good Lord. Really? I sent him my best dry stare. "About as well as your ability to sleep with married women, it appears."

"Oh, snap. That was low." He scowled at me before glancing around and lowering his voice. "How do you know about that, anyway?"

I tipped my head to the front of the house. "Window to my bedroom's open."

Ten's face actually reddened as he sank lower in his chair. "Not cool."

The back door opened again, and I forgot about Ten as I glanced over. But it wasn't Pick who emerged. Reese was the first to come outside, hauling an armful of hamburger buns and paper plates. Aspen was behind her, carrying the vegetable tray. Caroline came next, toting a basket of ketchup, mustard, relish, and other condiments. And then, finally, Pick drew up the rear, his tattooed arms loaded down with pop bottles, cups, and bags of potato chips.

"Pick," Reese called over her shoulder to him. "Why don't you just call your family and ask if they want to come to lunch too?"

Next to me, Ten muttered under his breath. "Shit, no. *Say no, say no, say no.*"

Pick gnawed on his lip before casting me a quick glance. Then he shrugged. "Okay."

Ten groaned and sank even lower.

Even though I knew Pick's marriage wasn't a love match and he'd never slept with his wife, I wasn't sure how to feel about meeting her. I *did* want to meet Julian. But Tristy? Not so much. She had his last name, his beloved time, and so much of his attention. I couldn't help but be jealous of her.

After a minute of pressing his phone to his ear, a worried look crossed his face. "Hmm. She's not home."

"Oh, thank God," Ten whispered.

"So, they won't miss you if you stayed for lunch?" Reese pressed, batting her lashes hopefully.

"Yeah. I guess." But he still looked uneasy. "It's just strange. She doesn't usually like to take the baby out. I wonder where they went."

Across the driveway, Noel's two younger brothers were trying to teach Quinn how to whistle.

"You have to curl your tongue like this," instructed the oldest brother, whose name I think was Brandt.

Noel chuckled. "Okay, leave him alone. His poor tongue already has enough to worry about."

I glanced at Ten, waiting for him to jump in with his own crude comment. But he was too busy concentrating on kicking the toe of his shoe into the ground.

I frowned and jabbed my elbow his way.

He looked up and scowled at me. "What?"

I lifted a hand. "Aren't you going to say something to that?"

"Huh?" He glanced around, obviously clueless.

"Oh my God. Noel left that *wide open* for you to say something completely offensive. Hell, even *I* had something dirty swimming through my head. What is *up* with you?"

If anything, he frowned even harder, clearly irritated by my question. "Nothing. I'm fine."

Hmm. Something had definitely changed since more people had arrived to the party. Thinking maybe he had a thing for Noel's professor girlfriend, I glanced toward Aspen, but she was busy helping Colton heap some food onto a Styrofoam plate. That's when I caught site of Caroline darting a quick glance between us. When she caught my eye, she flushed and quickly averted her gaze. Her cheeks were still red when I lifted my eyebrows and turned back to Ten, only to find his attention on her.

Interesting. Very interesting.

I leaned closed to him. "That sister of Noel's is stunningly beautiful, isn't she?"

He snapped his gaze away from Caroline and blinked at me. "What?"

"She just has that delicate, classic look about her. Don't you think? And I love that hair. I swear, it's an even lighter blonde than mine."

He continued to scowl, his eyes only narrowing as if suddenly suspicious. "What's your point?"

I shrugged and sent him an innocent little smile. "I have no point whatsoever." Skylar squirmed in my arms, so I looked down to check on her.

As I was resituating her to hopefully make her more comfortable, Ten leaned in to whisper, "If you're thinking what I think you're thinking, then stop. Right now."

I turned to study the seriousness on his face. He

definitely wasn't kidding around, which only gave more credence to my suspicions.

"Hey, E.," Reese called across the drive. "You want me to hold Sky while you get your lunch or do you just want to sit there and flirt with Ten for the rest of the afternoon?"

When everyone at the party paused to glance between Ten and me, my cheeks heated. I could kill my cousin for that question. But Reese just smirked at me and winked.

"We were *not* flirting," Ten stated a little too adamantly.

I lifted an eyebrow at him. "Excuse me? Are you saying I'm not flirt-worthy? You know, I am almost already down to my pre-pregnancy weight, and my breasts are like twice the size they usually are. Any other heterosexual man on earth would totally hit on this right now."

"Tink, you are the most flirt-worthy girl I know," Pick spoke up, striding over with his arms open. "Here. I'll hold Skylar while you get yourself something to eat. Then come back and sit by me. I'd be happy to hit on you."

God, could anyone honestly be so thoughtful, sweet, flirty, and too hot for his own tattoos? Pick Ryan was too good to be true.

When I didn't answer soon enough, he lifted his hands to show me his palms. "Don't worry; I got all the car grease scrubbed off."

I smiled. Yep, he was definitely the perfect guy. But I shook my head at his offer. "That's okay. You haven't eaten yet, either. You go ahead."

"Woman, you better take my offer. That little girl there's going to turn hungry soon, and you'll get busy feeding her. Might as well eat while you have the chance."

"Oh, all right." Since he made such a good point, I stood and transferred my baby into his arms. It was obvious he was used to infants; the transaction went effortlessly. He grinned down at Skylar.

"Well, hello there, little precious. I've been dying to get my hands on you all morning." After he lifted her just enough to stamp a kiss to her forehead, he glanced at me with the same fond smile. "Go. Eat."

So, I did. I ended up in line behind Caroline. When she looked at me with a hesitant smile, as if she wanted to say something but was unsure about it, I leaned in toward her. "I recommend the potato salad. Reese makes a kick ass potato salad."

"Okay. Thanks." Her smile was shy but pleasant. She really was stunningly beautiful. But the dark hollows under her eyes told me something was haunting her. She scooped up a modest portion of Reese's salad, gaining my approval.

"How old is your baby?" she asked.

I bloomed with pride. "Three weeks today. She was a preemie so I didn't get to bring her home from the hospital until yesterday."

More shadows filled Caroline's eyes, but she gave me a sad smile. "She's adorable."

"Thank you. I think so too."

A small cry rent the air, and I immediately spun toward the sound. But Pick was already holding up a hand as he cradled Skylar in the other arm. "We're good," he called. "Ten just looked at her. That mug'll make any girl cry."

I arched an eyebrow at Ten. He lifted his hands in surrender. "I didn't even touch her."

"I think it was his awful breath," Pick offered casually. He jiggled Skylar lightly. She'd already calmed down and seemed fine again.

"Stop breathing on my baby, asshole," I hollered, making Caroline laugh, only to cover her mouth and blush.

"Hey!" Ten scowled. "What is this? Rag-on-Ten Day?"

"No, that's every day," Noel shot back.

Ten sliced him a dirty look, but didn't volley back an insult.

I returned to my seat between him and Pick with a plateful of food, where Pick was studying Skylar's face so intently I wondered if he was going to burst into tears.

"She okay?" I asked, sitting next to him. I didn't realize just how close he'd drawn his chair to mine until my hip brushed his as I sat down. A thrill of arousal streaked up the insides of my thighs.

He looked up, and the sadness remained in his eyes, but his lips lit with a panty-dropping grin. I had to blow out a breath to cool myself before offering him a smile in return.

"Yeah," he murmured. "We're great. I got the prettiest little girl right here in my arms, and she's soaking up every compliment I feed her. Life doesn't get much better than this." Then he looked back at Skylar. After seeing the tenderness and affection in his gaze, that was it, I was a total goner.

This man could have me any way he wanted me.

When he glanced up at me again, our gazes locked. I wasn't too sure what was happening here—traveling between us through a single stare—but it was big enough to crowd into my chest until I almost couldn't breathe.

"That potato salad sure looks good." He severed the contact and glanced down at my plate to, I swear, purposely kill our moment.

"Oh, here." I blinked myself back to reality. "Want a taste?" I hadn't realized quite what I'd offered him until I lifted the forkful to his mouth and he slid his lips around the sample. My gaze caught his as I slowly pulled the fork free. We stared blatantly while he chewed.

This thing between us was just too intense.

Once he swallowed, he licked his tongue over his bottom lip and around his lip rings. I nearly whimpered. "Mmm. That *is* good."

I nodded robotically. "Want another?"

Please. Please. Please.

His lips spread into a slow, sensual smile. "As if I could say no to you."

So I gave him another bite of potato salad, and the experience was just as jolting at the first time. Then I made the moment even more intimate by giving myself a bite. His eyes heated as he watched the fork disappear into my mouth.

"Pickle," I asked, lifting a dill spear next.

He nodded. "Hell, yeah."

So I let him rip off a sliver of pickle from my fingers.

When a wet drop fell from his lip and landed on Skylar's forehead, I laughed. "Oops."

I grabbed a napkin and reached out to wipe her clean, but Pick was already lifting her to his mouth. He lapped up the splatter with his tongue.

My mouth fell open. "Did you just *lick* my daughter?"

Oh, crap. The mention of licking made me think of everything the guys had said earlier. When my face instantly heated, Pick winked. "Only because I'm not allowed to lick you."

I sucked in a breath, unable to believe he would actually say that.

Ten groaned. "Jesus, guys. Get a room already. There are kids present. And I'm trying to eat over here."

Pick and I exchanged a look before he tipped his head Ten's way. "What's his problem?"

I shrugged. "I think he's jealous. I let you hold Skylar."

Ten snorted. "Like I want to hold your damn kid."

"Hey!" I spun to deliver him a nasty glare. "Watch your mouth around my daughter, fuck face."

Ten gaped at me a second before he leaned past me to send Pick an incredulous glance as if he expected Pick to rein me in. "She's got a fucking mouth on her."

Pick grinned. "Isn't it great?"

While Ten snorted in disagreement, Pick bumped his knee into mine. I looked up at him, and he leaned closer. "Good one, Tink."

Across the way, I overheard Reese say to Caroline, "So Aspen said you graduate from high school next Sunday."

I lifted my eyebrows and nudged Ten with my elbow. "Oh, she's still in *high school*, huh. The plot thickens."

"Shut. Up," he muttered and nudged me back. Hard. Right in the stomach, way too close to my C-section incision.

Instantly dropping my plate full of food, splattering potato salad, pickles, and hamburger everywhere, I sucked in a breath and doubled over, clutching my belly. White-hot flames of pain licked up my abdomen.

"Oh, shit." Ten popped to his feet, clutching my

elbow. "I'm sorry. I'm so sorry."

"Tink?" Pick was there half a second later. For a breath, he was the only thing I could focus on. I leaned into him and clutched his shirt, burying my face in his neck as he swooped me up and tucked one arm under my knees with the other around my back.

When my ears stopped ringing, the first thing I heard was Mason's angry shout. "What the hell is your problem, Ten? She just gave birth three *weeks* ago and her gut is held together by *staples*."

"Not to mention that's where her asshole baby daddy hit her, sending her into premature labor," Noel added, his tone just as sharp and angry.

Pick pressed his cheek to my temple. "Eva? Talk to me. Say something, baby."

My knuckles were still white from holding onto his shirt so hard. But I managed to gasp, "I'm okay."

"Is she okay?" Reese asked, her voice coming closer.

I held my thumb up with my free hand but couldn't unclench my eyelids. "Where's Skylar?"

"Quinn's holding her," Pick said.

"Wasn't he sitting all the way across the driveway?"

"Yep. Kid moves fast when he needs to." Lifting his face away from mine, he asked, "Where's her room? I'm going to lay her down."

"It's this way. Follow me," Reese instructed just as someone else asked, "Should we take her to the hospital?"

Pick took charge as he carried me inside. "Let's see if she broke anything open first."

Though my stomach felt as if it had been cut apart without anesthesia, I was glad to be back in his arms and inhaling his intoxicating coconut scent. He was laying me down on my mattress way too soon for my liking. Without him right there against me, I curled into a ball and tucked my knees up toward my chest as I cradled my inflamed stomach.

I heard enough voices to realize just about everyone at the picnic was cramming into my room, trying to get a peek at me.

"Is she okay?" Ten asked, right before Pick growled.

"Get the fuck out of here."

"Okay, that's enough," Aspen instructed, her voice brooking no room for argument. "Why doesn't every guy get out? We need to make sure she didn't re-open her incision."

"Wait," I gasped at the last second, reaching out my hand blindly. "Pick."

He was there immediately, kneeling next to me. "I'm here, Tink."

I pulled him closer and he came without any kind of resistance, his brown eyes swirling with anger and concern. The anger was what worried me.

"Promise me you won't kill Ten. It's my fault he—"

"It was *not* your fucking fault."

"I was egging him on and elbowed him first."

"Well, he should've used his damn brain. And even *if* you were perfectly healthy, no way in hell should he have elbowed back that hard. Fucking idiot."

I grasped his chin in my hand. "Patrick."

He growled out his irritation but gave a terse nod. "Fine." Then he leaned in and pressed his lips to my forehead for a long twenty seconds. Just before he moved away, he brushed his tongue out and tasted my skin. Then he smoothed my hair with his fingers. "You better be okay."

"I'll be fine." The pain was already subsiding. Everyone had made a much bigger deal about my injury than they'd needed to.

Once Pick was gone, Reese shut the door after him. She, Aspen, and Caroline remained.

"Let's see what we have here." As Aspen neared the bed, I tried to sit up.

"Dr. Kav . . . " *Crap*, forgot I was supposed to use her first name.

"It's just Aspen," she said, smiling slightly. "And I'm not really a doctor, doctor."

I nodded, a move that made me wince. "Sorry."

"Quite all right. Do you feel comfortable with letting us see your . . . ?" She motioned vaguely toward my lap.

I gave a small laugh. "A room full of complete strangers got up close and personal with my *hoo-ha* when I gave birth. I think I'm okay with it."

"E.'s not exactly shy. Or modest." Reese sat on the mattress next to me and took my hand.

"Geez. Streak topless across a beach *once* and you suddenly get labeled indecent." I rolled my eyes and squeezed her hand back.

"Actually," Reese argued with a grin. "I think it was you laughing and screaming *'Look at my titties'* that cinched the whole indecent label for you."

When Aspen and Caroline exchanged scandalized glances, I sighed. "In my defense, I was really drunk at the time."

"Oh." They seemed to understand that, which made me wonder what both of them had done in drunken episodes.

I sank back on my pillow as Aspen slowly peeled down my yoga pants to reveal my stomach. Caroline inched in closer, biting her lip. Reese leaned in to look too. I closed my eyes, hoping for the best but fearing the worst.

Aspen's surprised "Oh!" had my lashes flying open.

"Oh, God. What?"

She smiled up at me with complete reassurance. "I didn't realize your staples were already out."

I nodded. "They took them out last week."

"I guess I haven't updated Mason recently with all of Eva's medical issues," Reese added. "He was just a little behind on the times when he said they were still there."

"Well, it seems to be healing . . . okay. I mean, I'm not a *doctor*-doctor, but nothing's broken open and there's no blood or redness or puffiness. Just some greenish looking bruises that look a few weeks old."

That would be where Alec had punched me.

Aspen bit her lip. "Want me to poke on it to see if there's any extra tenderness?" Her fingers were slowly inching toward my abdomen, but she was cringing as if she'd rather have her wisdom teeth removed.

I smiled. "I'll do it." After reaching down, I prodded my bikini line. Aside from the usual, I felt okay. I pulled my pants back up to where they usually rested. "I think I'm good."

When I went to sit up, all three girls reached out to keep me down.

"Maybe you should just rest for a while," Reese suggested.

I opened my mouth to tell them I was fine, but a commotion outside the door caught our attention.

I'd barely sat up and slid my feet to the floor by the time Aspen, Caroline, and Reese had thrown open the door and rushed from my room. Pick was shouting something, Ten was shouting back, and both Mason and Noel were shouting for them to calm down. I huffed out a breath and rolled my eyes.

Boys.

"Pick," I scolded before I'd even reached the doorway. I found Mason holding him back by the arms while Noel was setting his hand against Ten's chest to keep him away. Ten had a very distinct red mark on his cheek.

"What?" Pick said, shrugging off Mason so he could come to me. "He's still breathing."

I sighed. "You seriously just couldn't help yourself, could you?"

"If someone hurts you, I'm going to hurt them back. That's all there is to it."

The sincerity and emotion in his eyes made me gulp with longing.

If only.

I shook my head. "Well, I'm fine, so you can leave him alone. And just where is my baby while all you guys feel the need to brawl?"

"Right here," Quinn spoke up. He stepped from the corner where he'd been shielding the bundle in his arms from all the testosterone surging through the room. He looked extra huge with a preemie in his arms, but he carried her with the upmost care as he brought her to me and handed her over.

"She's been asleep the whole time." His voice was hushed as if he were afraid to wake her, even after the yelling match that had ensued between the other guys.

I smiled up at him. "Thank you, Quinn."

"It was my pleasure." He blushed and stepped back, sending a worried glance Pick's way, as if afraid he'd get into trouble for standing too close to me.

Pick ignored him as he set his hand lightly on my back and steered me back into my room. "Let's get you two ladies settled into bed."

I tried to tell him I was fine, but he wouldn't hear anything of it. The frustrated man wasn't satisfied until he had me reclining on my mattress with Skylar cradled to my chest. And even then, he sat on the edge of the bed next to me, looking forlorn as he watched us.

When he drew in a deep breath as he slowly reached out and ran his hand lightly over Skylar's dark hair, my heart broke for him, even though I had no idea why he was so sad.

"Hey." I set my hand on his thigh. "What's wrong?"

He grabbed my fingers and squeezed. "Nothing. I..." He shook his head and blew out another breath. "I really need to get going. Tris still isn't answering her phone. I can't believe she'd have Julian out this long. She's not..." He shook his head again. "It's just not like her."

I nodded as if I understood, even though I understood nothing. "Why didn't you ever tell me about you and her?" I blurted out.

He hesitated and refused to meet my gaze. "What do you mean?"

"You don't have a real marriage."

He lifted his face and cringed, looking apologetic. "Trust me, it's real. I have a license signed by a judge to prove it."

"But it's not *real*, real. You don't love her. You don't have sex with her. You've never had sex with her. And Julian's not yours."

"How . . . ?" He cocked his head to the side, suddenly suspicious. "How'd you learn all that?"

I let out an exaggerated sigh. "It doesn't matter how. It matters that you never bothered to tell me any of it yourself. Why didn't you think I deserved to know? I thought we were at least friends. And you knew I always felt guilty about the way we . . . interacted."

"Eva . . . " He glanced away, torment creasing his face as he ran his fingers through his hair. When he came back to face me, he gave a heavy sigh. "We *are* friends."

"Then . . . " I shook my head, confused and hurt. "Why?"

He opened his mouth. "I . . . I like you," he admitted as if it were some kind of great confession.

"Okay," I said slowly. "Wouldn't that mean you should feel more comfortable sharing those kinds of facts with me, then?"

He lifted his hand, as if to tell me he was having trouble explaining. "I . . . I mean, if I wasn't tied down to her right now . . . if I wasn't . . . " He groaned and shoved his fingers through his hair again. "I would want to be *more* than just your friend."

"Oh." I gulped. *Oh, wow.*

He watched me intently, regret in his dark brown eyes. "I can't annul the marriage. She's an awful mother. I feel sick about even admitting that out loud, but it's true, and I feel even worse every time I have to leave Julian alone with her. I never know if she's going to skip feeding him or not change his diaper or just leave him in his swing all day. That's why I'm itching to get home right now. What if . . . anything could be happening. If I stop this marriage, I will have no rights to him whatsoever. I basically don't now, but it's better than nothing." His eyes reddened around the edges as he pushed off the bed and cleared his throat. "I need to get home."

He was at the door before I collected my scattered thoughts enough to say, "Pick."

He stopped but kept his back to me, his head bowed.

"I understand," I said softly.

He glanced at me, looking almost sick with regret. Then his gaze flickered longingly over Skylar. "Take care of yourself, Tinker Bell."

And then he was gone.

17

-EVA MERCER-

On Sunday evening, Reese and I gave Skylar her first sponge bath at the kitchen table. We were *oohing* and *ahhing* over every tiny finger and toe when Mason got a call on his cell phone.

"Shit," he muttered to the caller. "Yeah, I can take on tomorrow night. I'm already working Wednesday and Thursday. Can you handle Friday? Good. I promised Reese a date night."

When he hung up and rubbed his tired face, Reese straightened to shoot him a curious glance. "What's going on?"

Mason glanced uneasily at me before saying, "That was Noel. Pick's babysitter has chicken pox, or her kids do or . . . someone. I don't know. They're all contagious for the next two weeks, so he has to stay home with his boy until he finds someone he can trust to watch him."

I frowned. "What about his wife?"

It was *her* son. Why was *he* looking for babysitters? And why wasn't she taking off from her own job to watch him?

"She, uh, she left," Mason mumbled, ducking his chin as he answered.

"What?" I plopped down into at chair at the table and gaped.

He blew out a breath. "Yeah. He came home from the picnic at our house to find her gone."

"Oh my God," Reese gasped. "And she left her baby there? *Alone?*"

I felt sick to my stomach. Pick had tried more than once to call home that day with no answer. Julian had probably been alone the entire time. "I wonder how long he was there by himself. Jesus, he's only four months old."

Mason shook his head. "I have no idea how long he was alone. And I'm pretty sure Pick doesn't even want to think about it. Gamble said he sounded pretty upset."

"I bet." I set my hand over my heart, and checked on my own kid, still wrapped up in her towel as she tried to kick it off.

I felt like crap. Pick had been here, talking to me, caring for me, while his stepson was being abandoned by his own mother. He probably never wanted to see me again.

Even as I had that thought, though, I blurted, "I'll babysit."

I'd make this up to him. Somehow.

-PICK RYAN-

I was still in a state of shock, anger, and heartbreak when someone knocked on my door early Monday morning. Even though Tris could definitely improve on her mothering skills, I hadn't thought she would actually do this. It still haunted me to remember how I'd found Fighter screaming in his swing, beating his fists in the air, his face red with anguish as I'd come through the doorway and found him home alone.

So many things could've happened to him. Just thinking about them made me physically sick to my stomach. My hands were shaking from fear. If I ever saw Tristy again, I was honestly afraid of what I might do to her. But how could she do this to *him*? Her own child.

With my fingers curled into fists as I strode to the door, I half-hoped it wasn't Tris because I was scared of what I'd say, and I half-hoped it was her so I could say exactly what I wanted to. I'd been loath to put Fighter down these past few days, so he was slung over my shoulder as he napped.

I opened the door and jerked back in surprise when Reese grinned up at me. She held out her hand. "Cell phone please."

"Wha . . . ?" Confused, I wrinkled my brow and dug my phone out of my back pocket, without thought. "What're *you* doing here?" I was so dumbstruck, I handed the phone over, not even asking her what she planned to do with it.

"Pass-code," she ordered.

With a sigh, I took it from her and got her into the phone before handing it back.

"Thank you." Focusing her attention on the screen, she punched some numbers into the phonebook. "Here's my cell. Call me when you're done with her, and I'll come pick her up immediately. Oh, and please take care of my girl. She's not only my favorite cousin, she's my best friend, too."

I took the phone when she handed it back to me. Shaking my head and not catching on at all, I said, "Huh?"

That's when a panting Eva came up behind her, lugging Skylar in a huge-ass car seat with a diaper bag thrown over her shoulder.

Reese was instantly forgotten. I blinked repeatedly to make sure I was seeing what I was seeing. "Tink?"

She smiled, and my entire chest lit up with warmth.

"Mason said you needed a babysitter." She gave a breathless explanation. "So . . . here I am."

"You . . . ?" I shook my head in confusion, even though she'd just made it perfectly clear why she was here. "What?"

This couldn't happen, because if she stepped into my home, I'd never want to leave. Eva used the car seat as a cattle prod, plowing forward and forcing me to shift aside. Yep, I was going to have to call in and quit my job. Both jobs. I could become a professional couch potato and just drool every time she walked past. This was my new life goal.

"Okay, bye, E. Love ya." From behind me, someone in the hallway made kissy sounds. I have no idea who it was. No one else in my universe currently existed, except maybe Julian and Skylar.

But Eva leaned past me to smile at that other, annoying person, and blow her a kiss. "Love you, too. Thanks for the ride."

Her ride must've departed soon thereafter because Eva arched me an amused glance. "Are you going to shut the door?"

"Huh?"

"Go take a shower and get ready for work, Patrick." Her voice was dry, yet amused. "You don't want to be late."

"Work?" I echoed. I thought we'd already decided my new job was to ogle her.

Turning away, she set Skylar's carrier on the floor and slung this fancy looking purse thing with Skylar's name stitched across the side next to it. Then she went to unbuckle her baby. The entire time she was bent over, my gaze was fixated on her ass. And the only reason I could believe she'd been pregnant not quite a month ago was because I'd seen it with my own eyes.

Instead of taking her baby from the seat, she straightened and caught me staring. "Goodness gracious. You can check out my ass later. It's not going anywhere. Now scoot." She reached forward and began to ease Fighter out of my arms.

It was a testament of how crazy I was about her that I didn't snap her fingers off for trying to touch him. But after Saturday, I had some major attachment issues, yet another reason I couldn't go to work today. Leaving Julian just felt wrong. I really needed to sit there and hold him while I ogled the babysitter.

And then Tinker Bell made it even worse by immediately cooing as soon as she got him in her arms. "Oh my God. He's so cute. Look at those perfect cheekbones. He's going to be a model someday."

Julian stirred and opened his eyes. I tensed, ready to snag him back, because Eva was a stranger and would probably scare him. But he merely blinked at her a few times.

She grinned and kissed him on the nose. "Hey there, handsome. You're even more adorable when you open those big chocolate brown eyes. Yes, you are. My name is Eva. Some people call me E." She slid a grin my way. "Or Tinker Bell." Turning her attention back to my boy, she kept talking to him, explaining how he was going to hang out with her and Skylar today and they were going to have loads of fun.

I just kept staring. Tinker Bell was talking to him; Tristy would claim he couldn't respond, except that's exactly what he did. He responded by breaking out one his famous grins and making her melt.

"Aww." Glancing up at me, she said, "I think I just fell in love."

I was very nearly tempted to say, "So did I," but that was just stupid.

Wasn't it? Shit, having her here, watching my kid, was too dangerous for my peace of mind.

Eva sent me an odd frown as if she knew exactly what I was thinking. I shifted uncomfortably.

"What are you still doing, gawking at us?" she said. "Go! I'm on the clock and getting paid for this. You might want to do the same so you can afford me."

Finally, I grinned and shook my head. "I owe you . . . big time."

With a roll of her eyes, she waved me off. "I think you already paid me back the night you saved my daughter's life."

I had to work through my lunch break. It sucked ass.

All morning, I itched to get home and check on Julian. See Eva. Snuggle Skylar. My attention stayed more on the clock than under the hood of whatever car I was fixing. Then some rich douchebag in a fancy suit showed up with a flat tire. We weren't exactly a tire repair or replacement shop, but the only thing my boss saw was green flashing, so yeah, I was called in to fix the Bentley's tire. Not sure what a damn Bentley was doing in our neighborhood, but whatever.

Someone else must've thought he didn't belong either, because a knife-slash had given him the flat. It definitely wasn't an accidental blowout.

The prick owner stood over me the whole time, arms folded over his chest as he scrutinized every little thing I did and sneered at all my tattoos, but at least he didn't offer a critique. When I handed him the ticket to go in and pay, telling him he was all set up, he finally smiled, all his wrinkles puckering around a thin, white scar slashed high across his left cheekbone. But it wasn't a friendly smile. His eyes spelled out his true thoughts. They looked down on me and all my tattoos and piercings, telling me what a piece of shit they thought I was.

Rich people.

I'd love to see him try to make it in this neighborhood. Sometimes, to survive, you had to blend in and adapt, project an image of intimidation so sick motherfuckers would leave you alone.

Besides, I liked my badass appearance, though I'm sure this look would never let me fit into the country club scene where Eva had been raised. Remembering she was in my apartment, surrounded by my low-class things, I dialed her up.

"Hey," I said as soon as she answered the phone, the melody of her voice making my pulse skyrocket.

"Hey!" She sounded upbeat and awake. Watching two kids all day didn't seem to have worn her out yet.

"What's going on?"

"Just checking in. I was going to stop by on my lunch break, but we had a car come in at the last second." I stepped away from the Bentley as the rich suit strolled from the cashier's desk and pulled his keys from his pocket. His gaze was on me as he opened his door, so I sent him a respectful nod. "Have a good one."

His return smile was a little too knowing for my taste, so I kept watching him as he slid into his ride.

"We're doing great here," Eva told me as I stared. "Julian just had his lunch and went down for a nap, so Skylar got bored and nodded off too. I don't know how I coordinated getting them both to sleep at the same time, but I even impressed myself."

I smiled. "I'm not at all surprised; I knew you'd be that good. Sounds like you got it under control. I know he can be a handful at times." Tristy claimed he cried nonstop.

"Well, I haven't seen proof of it yet. This little man is a complete sweetheart. He hasn't cried once and boy, does he love to smile."

My face stretched as my own smile grew. "Yes, he does."

"Though I'm learning a big difference between the genders when it comes to diaper changing. That was a. . . wet learning experience."

My eyes went wide. "Oh, shit. Did he piss on you?"

"A little bit, yeah." Her laugh was full, letting me know she wasn't upset at all. "I hope you don't mind that I used your dryer."

My head filled with images of her sauntering around my apartment topless while her shirt dried.

Oh, hell. Instant wood at work. Not good.

"No," I croaked, my voice hoarse and jeans way too tight. "Not at all. I'm sorry he got you. I guess I should've warned you he might do that. After I open his diaper, I usually only lift it up just enough to let the air hit him and he can do his thing before I unwrap him completely."

"What a good tip. Thank you. I will definitely keep that in mind for tomorrow."

"Tomorrow?" I echoed stupidly, while my heart raced faster.

"Well, yeah. I thought your normal sitter was going to be contagious for a good two weeks."

I went dizzy. Eva Mercer was going to be in my apartment, watching my kid every day . . . for *two weeks*? How was I going to survive that, always knowing she was there, caring for my child, walking through my rooms, sitting on my furniture, drying her pissed-on shirts in my dryer? I was itching enough to get off work now so I could rush home and just bask in her presence. But two weeks of this luxury? God, I could overdose on such a rush.

"Oh, hey. Quick question before you go."

Go? I'd been planning on dragging this phone conversation out as long as possible. "What's that?" I asked.

"He's four months old now, right?"

"Yeah."

"That's what I thought. So I borrowed your laptop and looked up a few sites so there wasn't anything huge I was missing about caring for that age. And it said four months is an okay time to introduce them to a couple of solid foods. But I didn't see any in the cabinets, so—"

"Wow, I hadn't even thought of that yet. But yeah, I'll make sure to pick up some the next time I go grocery shopping. What do I get for him?"

"They said it's okay to wait a couple more months, but he seems to chew a lot, so I thought maybe . . . I know, I'm overstepping my bounds. Sorry, I—"

"No! That's . . . actually, I'm glad you brought it up because I have no clue what he really needs. I've pretty much been faking it for the past four months. Any advice you have is appreciated."

"In that case, you can start weaning him on baby rice. I think he could use this diaper cream I have for Sky, too. It's got the best recommendations, and Julian's poor little tushy seems to be recovering from a nasty rash."

I couldn't tell her that was because his mother had never changed him and many times he'd gone most of the day without a fresh diaper. It was humiliating enough, knowing my kid was going through that and that I couldn't be there to keep him constantly changed, but listening to Eva point out the obvious only ratcheted up the shame.

Sad as it was to admit, it was a godsend that Tristy had left. He was finally getting some real care.

Five o'clock couldn't come soon enough. I punched my timecard and sped home. As I unlocked and opened the front door to my apartment, a baby's laughter startled my ears.

Frozen in the doorway, I watched Eva—her back to me—as she sat cross-legged on a blanket on the floor and leaned over Julian. Flat on his back, he kicked his legs and flapped his arms, giggling uncontrollably up at her while she made raspberry sounds.

When she paused, he stopped smiling, stopped kicking and stared up at her with a serious expression. But then she started again and even swished her blonde hair in his face, making him laugh and kick again.

Next to him on the other half of the blanket, little Skylar was sprawled on her stomach as she tried to lift her head off the floor, her miniature little noggin wobbling from the effort it took.

The three of them together like that was the most amazing thing I'd ever seen.

I stood in the doorway, unable to do anything but stare at this woman charming my little boy. In that moment, I loved her. I loved her so damn hard my entire chest ached. Tears might've even gathered in my eyes because the whole thing made me so damn emotional.

But fuck, she was making my kid laugh. How could I not love her?

I didn't care who she was, how many years I'd dreamed about meeting her, wondering what she'd be like in real life, I loved this woman right here on my floor for what she was in this very moment.

Sensing my presence, Eva finally looked up and

glanced over her shoulder. She yelped in surprise before setting a hand over her heart and laughing.

"Hey, look who's home." Picking up Fighter, she cradled him close so their cheeks smashed together. Then she took his hand and helped him wave at me. "Hi, Daddy. How was work?"

I sniffed up my emotions and stepped into the apartment, feeling almost disconnected from my body because I was so completely submerged in this moment. I never wanted it to end. I wanted to frame it and hang it on the ceiling over my bed, so I could look up and relive it again and again, every night for the rest of my life before I went to sleep.

After the front door shut behind me, I stepped closer and slid down onto the floor to sit at the edge of the blanket with my back propped against the couch. "Work was good, but I doubt I had as much fun as you guys seem to be having."

"We've been having a blast," Eva reported, grinning as she pressed her lips all over Fighter's face. The lucky little bastard. He soaked it up, too, smiling and half closing his eyes, then grabbing fistfuls of her hair and pulling.

"Hey, buddy. No pulling." I reached forward to help untangle the mess.

"He's okay." Eva laughed as we both worked to free her silky pale strands. "He definitely loves to grab onto things."

I loved that she knew what he loved already . . . after a single day of watching him.

When Skylar squawked, frustrated with being unable to lift her head, I scooped her up and pressed her cheek to my nose so I could inhale her clean, fresh baby scent. "Hey, kiddo. Was that your way of getting my attention? You got it, babe."

"I don't think she's forgotten that you still owe her a dance," Eva said, her eyes sparkling as she watched us cuddle.

"That's right. I do owe her a dance, don't I?" I settled Skylar into the crook of my arm and got to my feet so I could hum George Strait's "Baby Blue" into her hair and sway her around the living room.

Noticing how pleased Eva seemed about watching us together, I winked down at her and then motioned to the blanket. "I'm surprised you guys are on the floor. It's got to be filthy." I couldn't remember the last time I'd cleaned it. Maybe not since Fighter was born. I'd been taking on as many overtime hours as I could scrounge up to pay for all the bills that had come with his birth. So I was usually too busy with laundry, dishes, or bathroom work to worry about spiffing up the front room.

"Funny thing about that," Eva told me with a sly smile. "I found this thing in the closet over there. I think it's called a vacuum. It cleaned the floor right up."

"You vacuumed?" My head whipped around to take in the entire front room. I'd been so centered on the three of them playing as if they were a real family I hadn't been able to see anything else. But, shit, not only were there vacuum lines on the floor, but everything had been tidied, the coffee table and end tables cleared off, possibly even dusted. The lap blanket Tristy used to curl under was folded and draped over the back of the sofa, and the couch pillows were straightened and fluffed.

"You cleaned." The wonder in my voice only made her roll her eyes.

"These two really enjoyed their beauty sleep today, so I had a lot of spare time on my hands."

"Yeah, but . . . " I turned back to her, shaking my head. "You didn't have to do all this, Tink. I mean," I splayed out my hand, overwhelmed, "Just being here for Julian . . . God, you have no idea how much I appreciate you coming over today and watching him. You completely saved my ass."

The compliment made her glow. I'd flirted with her numerous times and flat-out told her she was gorgeous. But *thanking* her seemed to have an even better effect. She just looked so satisfied. In her element. The pleased glow on her cheeks made her more beautiful than she already was.

A high-pitched beeping from the kitchen interrupted the moment, making me frown. What the hell was that? For a second, I thought it might be a smoke alarm. But

Eva bolted upright, taking Julian with her. "Oh! Your supper's ready."

Supper? My mouth fell open. "You cooked?" *She cooked?*

"Don't get too excited. It's just a frozen pizza. You seriously have nothing in your cabinets, Patrick. I'm thinking you need to leave a little cash with me tomorrow, so I can go grocery shopping for you. Julian's almost out of diapers, too. I'd have given him some of Skylar's but, compared to her . . . " She paused to set her hand over the little boy's ear so he couldn't hear. Then she whispered, "He has a huge ass."

I laughed. "Compared to this little doll, I think *everyone* has a huge ass. But yeah, if you want to go grocery shopping, I'd be more than happy to fund it." I'd be happy to kiss the ground she walked on.

But cleaning? Cooking? Grocery shopping? I was beginning to wonder if there was some rare disease I could somehow inflict on the Rojas family, that way Eva could be the temporary babysitter forever.

"Here, can you hold him for me?"

I blinked because that was usually the question I asked Tristy. "Yeah. Of course." After transferring Skylar to one arm, I opened the other for Julian. Eva grinned at the three of us after she handed him over. Then she sauntered off, her hips swaying with a natural rhythm that made my mouth water.

I wanted every little part of this woman that ever existed. Needing to trail after her, I followed, bringing the kiddos with me.

18

-PICK RYAN-

Eva talked me into going to work that evening at the club. So I did, and that sucked ass too, because I couldn't let a pair of drunk girls drive home on their own, which made me run even later than usual. After I dropped them off at their front door, I realized how potently it left my poor Barracuda smelling like fruity perfume. So I took the long way home with the windows down to air it out.

I didn't want Eva smelling them and thinking something had happened that hadn't when I had to take her back to Mason's. But when I finally returned to my apartment at damn near three in the morning, she was dead asleep in *my* bed, with both babies tucked around her. I spent a moment just watching them, loving the sight of them together. This was supposed to be my family. My happily ever after. And she should've been my wife.

My chest swelled with longing and a thirsty kind of

need, but also with joy because they were really here, for however long I had them.

I planned to relish every second.

Backing away, I tiptoed to the living room and texted Reese to tell her Eva was asleep. I'd drive her home in the morning. Then I flopped onto the couch, pulled the lap blanket onto my shoulders, and passed out.

Hours later, I woke to Eva tapping me on the shoulder. "Why didn't you wake me when you got home?"

I tried to tell her I hadn't wanted to disturb any of them and that I'd already called Reese, but I'm not sure if she understood much through my tired slurring, until she answered, "Well, thanks for letting us get our rest, but Skylar and I can take the couch now. I didn't mean to fall asleep and steal your bed."

I waved her off. "It's okay. Go back and stay there for the rest of the night."

She frowned. "I'm not kicking you out of you own bed, Patrick."

"Damn." I let out a dreamy sigh and grinned up at her as I rolled onto my back. "It still sounds hot when you call me that, even when I'm half dead asleep." With a yawn, I curled back onto my side, facing away from her. "Please, God, don't make me get up and move right now. Can't 'member when I last had this much sleep."

She was quiet for a minute before saying, "You're right. I'm sorry for pestering you. Go back to sleep, Patrick."

I smiled at the address and then sighed when she lightly ruffled my hair. I loved the feel of her fingers against my scalp. About to sink back into peaceful oblivion, I bolted upright when a thought occurred to me.

"Shit! Is Fighter awake?" I hadn't gotten up with him yet, and usually I did once or twice a night.

"No, I just fed him, changed him, and put him back down."

I rubbed my face. Why did I feel so crusty? "You didn't have to do that, Tink. I'm home, I could've gotten up." I was a little chagrined that I had slept right through his crying.

Eva merely rolled her eyes. "Don't worry about it. Seriously. I was already up with Skylar."

"Thank you," I said, meaning it from the bottom of my heart. "I owe you."

She shook her head as if amused by me and strolled down the hall toward my bedroom . . . to sleep in my bed. I groaned and collapsed back on the couch. With as much wood as I was sporting, it'd be a while before I got back to sleep now.

In the morning, I got out of the shower to peek into my bedroom, my towel wrapped around my waist. Eva wasn't in bed and neither was Skylar. I heard rumblings in the kitchen so I dropped the towel and dug through my underwear drawer for something clean. Once I was dressed, I carried my socks into the kitchen, which for some reason was where I put them on each morning. When I reached the entrance, I was surprised to find Eva pouring two bowls of cereal.

From the back, she looked good first thing in the morning, her clothes wrinkled and molded to her curves and her hair pulled up into a fashionable yet sloppy knot with these tempting little stray tendrils hanging down and teasing the back of her kissable neck. I knew she'd look twice as amazing when she turned around. I was so tempted to come up behind her, wrap myself around her and kiss the tops of her shoulders. My arms ached because I restrained them from acting on the impulse.

She turned around, and I saw she had Skylar cradled in one arm. "'Morning," she said brightly, though lavender bruises of sleeplessness underlined her eyes.

I yawned and ran my hand through my wet hair. "'Morning." After I padded barefoot across the kitchen to the table, I plopped into a chair and pulled on my socks. Though I'd gotten more sleep than usual since I hadn't needed to pace the floor with Julian at all, I felt stiff and sore from bunking on the couch.

I jumped when Eva set one of the bowls of cereal in front of me. About to tell her she hadn't needed to do that, because it seemed to be my catch phrase these past twenty-four hours, I paused, wondering if she was getting sick of me constantly repeating it. So I settled for a sincere, "Thanks."

She sat across from me and rocked Skylar in her arms as she ate with one hand. "So how many days do you work from nine in the morning until two the next morning?" she asked between bites.

I smiled through my munching, amazed by how well she multitasked. When a drop of milked dripped down her chin, making her scramble with both hands full to wipe it up, I smiled even wider and leaned over to mop it up for her.

"A couple," I answered, licking the droplet of milk off my thumb. I worked that much most weekdays, actually.

She shook her head, staring at my thumb as I pulled it away from my tongue. "I don't know how you do it without tumbling dead from exhaustion."

I motioned to her with my spoon before I took a big bite. "You just worked the same hours as I did yesterday. More, actually. How're you still going?"

She shook her head to disagree. "But I had plenty of down time."

I snorted. "When? When you were watching not just mine, but your own kid, cleaning my house or cooking me supper? Oh, and don't think I didn't notice you gave Fighter a bath last night. He smelled all clean and fresh when I leaned in to kiss his head just now."

"Okay, fine," she relented on a sigh. "I'm secretly Wonder Woman. I just hid my bracelets, tiara, and lasso in Skylar's diaper bag so you wouldn't find out."

I grinned. "Wonder Woman was always my favorite superhero."

"And I'm sure her breast size, tiny waist, and incredible thighs had nothing to do with it either."

I snorted out a laugh and nearly choked on the last of the milk I was drinking from my bowl. "You know me too well." Rising to my feet, I went to rinse it in the sink, only to realize how freaking spotless the sink was. Not only had she done dishes, she'd scrubbed the sink as well.

Shaking my head and thinking she really must be Wonder Woman, I turned to say, "I can drive you back to Lowe's whenever you're ready."

She looked up in surprise. "Aren't I watching Julian again today?"

I drew in a quick, pleased breath. "You were serious about that?"

"Of course." She frowned as if I was crazy for asking. "You still need help watching him, don't you?"

"Yeah, but . . . " I shrugged, suddenly self-conscious. "I was kind of an asshole to you the last time we saw each other. I don't get why you're being so amazing and helping me like this."

She shook her head, her confusion blatant. "How were you an asshole to me?"

I glanced away, ashamed. "I basically told you I didn't want you knowing I didn't have a real marriage because I didn't want you tempting me into something I knew you could very easily tempt me into doing. And then I walked out on you and never talked to you again."

"Okay, first of all, that was three days ago, not decades like you're making it sound. And your hands were full, Pick. That's totally understandable. Besides, you weren't obligated to ever talk to me again, though not calling when your wife left you hanging with a four-month-old to take care of by yourself stung a little. I thought we'd become friends. Why didn't you think I'd help you watch him?"

"I . . . " I gave a small laugh. "Actually, the idea didn't even occur to me. I'm not used to asking anyone for help. Usually, it's the other way around and people come to me when they need something."

"Then it sounds as if you need new friends. If you never get anything in return from them, they're not your friends. They're just people who use you." Before I could respond to her statement, she continued, "And besides, I totally understand why you didn't tell me about the true nature of your wedding vows. I only had to spend five minutes with Julian to know how amazing he is and how much he needs you in his life. I would never do anything to jeopardize that." A line between her brows formed. "How is that going to work out, anyway? Now that she's gone. I mean, it's okay for you to keep him, right?"

"I don't know," I confessed quietly as I leaned against the kitchen counter to wipe the exhaustion from my eyes. "But I'm certainly not going to call up a social worker to see if it's fine. No way in hell am I doing anything that might land him in the foster care system."

Her eyes softened with sympathy. "You had a pretty bad experience with foster care, didn't you?"

I shrugged and glanced down into my cleaned cereal bowl before I cleared my throat and set it on the counter. "Some places were okay. Others were fucking hell. It's all a crapshoot. Most of those people take on kids for the money. They don't care what happens to you as long as they keep getting a check. You never feel like you belong. Anywhere." When a cry came from my bedroom, I glanced toward the sound. "Julian doesn't deserve that. Not when he's got me."

I left her in the kitchen to go get my boy out of his crib. When I pulled him to my chest and kissed his head, he burrowed into me, grabbing a handful of my shirt.

Eva and Skylar appeared in the doorway. When Tink smiled at me, her gaze soft and understanding, something in my chest screwed in tight. It hurt even more, knowing she completely understood why I couldn't pursue the attraction between us.

"You sure you don't need to go back to your place to get anything this morning? Change of clothes, stuff for Skylar?"

She shook her head. "Already got it covered. Reese is on her summer break from college and she doesn't have to watch Mason's sister today. She can bring me anything I need. Besides she'll need to give me a ride to the grocery store."

My eyebrow shot up. "You were serious about that too?"

"Hell, yes. I'll starve if I don't get more food in your cabinets soon."

"You can take my car if you need to go anywhere. The garage where I work is only about twelve blocks from here."

She shuddered as if that was a horrible idea. "I kicked you out of your own bed last night. I'm not taking your ride too. Especially in this heat."

"Yeah, but you looked really hot all curled up in my sheets, so that was more of a bonus for me."

She sighed and rolled her eyes. "There it is. I was wondering where that flirty side of you had gone this morning."

I winked. "It just needed a little time to wake up and kick in."

"I don't know," she murmured, eyeing me as if she suddenly thought I was shifty. "You were telling me my voice sounded hot last night when I called you Patrick, and you were half out of it then."

"I did? Hmm, I must be better than I thought."

She laughed and laid Skylar in the crib. "You better get to work already, *Rico Suave*. Or you're going to be late."

"I'm always late. My boss would probably drop dead from shock if I actually showed up on time."

When she turned to me, I was tempted to lay Julian down too, so I could scoop Eva up and just tackle her onto the bed and have my sexy way with her.

"Well, Wonder Woman Eva is on the scene today," she said, completely oblivious to my lusty thoughts. "So you don't *have* to be late. Now give me that beautiful boy so I can spoil him rotten."

Sold. I handed Fighter over and waited until she had him settled in her arms before I leaned in to kiss my kid one last time and told him to be good for Tinker Bell. Then, I snuck to the bed to skim my fingers gently over Skylar's forehead. She'd fallen asleep, so I whispered, "Take care, princess."

When I straightened, Eva met my gaze, her awesome blue eyes expectant.

It felt wrong not to give her a special goodbye too. So, I said, "Thank you," before pressing my lips to her forehead. I lingered for longer than I should have. But she didn't push me away. She gazed up at me when I pulled back, and her eyes mirrored all the yearning I felt deep within my chest.

Turning away before I gave into temptation, I strode from the room.

After I left the apartment, the strangest fullness swirled in my chest. I was sure I could damn near float off ground and drift in my contentment. I could do anything. Because it felt as if I'd just wished my family goodbye for the day.

It was the dirtiest tease ever; I knew that. When Eva returned to Mason and Reese, I was probably going to feel more empty than I'd felt before she'd come into my life. But I refused to regret her presence, because it felt too good to have her here now.

-EVA MERCER-

Reese was more than willing to help me out. "I know you've only been gone a day, but I already miss you. I had to do a load of my *own* laundry this morning. And I actually had to *cook* last night. It was awful."

I laughed. "Oh, now I see why you hadn't kicked me out yet."

"I know. Not everyone has a free live-in maid. Seriously, E., I never realized how much you did around our place since you came to stay with us. But Mason and I definitely noticed it after Sky was born and you were stuck in the hospital. You do realize you didn't have to take over all the cooking and housework just because we took you in, right?"

I shrugged, unable to tell her how strongly I'd felt the need to pay her back somehow. "I actually enjoyed it. I never got to do that kind of stuff when I was growing up. We always had people to cook and clean for us, and my mother made such menial tasks sound like they were beneath us."

"God, it's crazy how different our mothers are when they were raised by the same parents."

Reese braked at the entrance to the first grocery store

we came across in Pick's neighborhood. Yikes, was that a prostitute hanging around just outside the entrance? When a beat up car stopped along the curb beside her, the passenger side window rolled down and the driver waved some cash at her. She hobbled forward in her tight skirt and heels and hopped into the passenger's seat. Reese and I we exchanged similar, wary glances.

"Anyway," she said as she pulled right back out of the exit and started toward the grocer we used closer to her apartment. "My mom always made me clean my room and do my own laundry once I turned sixteen. Then I had supper night and one Saturday morning breakfast a month."

Reese had no idea how well she had it by getting Aunt Andrea for her mom, and not mine. But I couldn't tell her just how fortunate she was. So I kept my trap shut and glanced back to check on both babies. They were so cute, all bundled up in their car seats, side by side. Julian looked like a hulking gorilla next to petite little Skylar, and she looked pasty pale next to his nice mocha skin tone. They made the perfect contrast, and I felt grateful to have them both with me for as long as Julian would be under my care. I already knew I was going to miss him like crazy when Pick no longer needed me.

Shopping with Reese and two infants was quite an experience. We needed two carts to carry around both kids, and I swear Reese had to *ooh* and *ahh* over every brand of kids' cereal and ice cream; she was such a five-year-old at heart sometimes, but I loved that about her.

I had checked Pick's cabinets before leaving for the store to see what exactly he needed; I swear, the list would've been shorter if I'd written down what he didn't need instead. The man had *nothing*. But he'd left a butt-load of cash with me, more than Mason and Reese had to grocery shop with. So we might've gotten a little carried away.

One thing was for sure, Pick wouldn't be able to

complain about an un-stocked pantry any time soon, and Julian now had a good month's worth of diapers. Reese had to impulse buy a sucker at the checkout line. The cherry scent it emitted as soon as she unwrapped it and started in before she'd even purchased it induced me into tossing my own sucker onto the pile of groceries.

She was such a bad influence.

On the way back to Pick's apartment, the babies slept in their car seats while Reese and I sat up front, working our way through our lollipops.

At one stoplight, she popped hers free of her mouth to waggle her brows at me. "So how was spending the night with Pick?"

I rolled my eyes and pointed my sucker at her threateningly. "Don't start with me. He's married."

"So? His wife *left* him."

"He's still married to her, and he's not going to change that any time soon. I already told you why he needs to stay married."

She had to mumble around her lollipop when she stuck it back into her mouth. "Yeah, I still don't understand why that's keeping you from claiming him. It's obvious to everyone you two are completely into each other."

"Because he's *married*, Ree Ree." How many times did I have to repeat that?

"Yeah, but it's not like a real marriage. They've never even kissed."

I sighed. "But he's still connected in some way to another woman. How would you feel if Mason married *me* just to give Sky and I some insurance?"

Reese instantly frowned. "That's different."

I lifted my eyebrows. "Oh, is it? How?"

"Because . . . because Mason and I are already engaged."

"So?" I lifted my arms, needing more of a reason than that. "What if Pick and I started something and decided *we* wanted to get engaged too? Then what? He can't divorce her."

"Okay, fine. You have a point." She rolled her eyes before mumbling, "I just wanted you to have a happily ever after, like I found."

Well, so did I. But Reese and I were two totally different people, and I had a feeling I'd never end up with any of the gifts she'd been given. I just didn't deserve that, even though I'd already received the most precious bundle of all, still snoozing beside Julian in the back seat.

Reese left the issue alone after that, thank goodness. She ended up sticking around the rest of the afternoon to help me put groceries away and play with the babies.

She booted up Pharrell's "Happy" on her iPhone and danced Julian around the kitchen while Skylar napped in the bouncer and I finished the hamburger helper I was cooking. Pick made it home from the garage in the middle of our supper-fixing party.

"Hey, little man, guess who's home?" Reese smiled at Pick before letting out a low, appreciative whistle. "Yowza. You know, all you Forbidden boys look fine in those tight black T-shirts you have to wear to the club, but this greasy, fresh from the auto shop look is even better on you. Yummy."

Pick arched me a shocked glance. "Did Lowe's woman just hit on me?"

"What?" Reese asked, clueless. "I can appreciate the aesthetic appeal of male beauty whenever I see it. Mason doesn't care if I look; he knows no one else can compare to him. But seriously, I'm going to have to buy this getup for him too, so we can play Naughty Mechanic sometime."

"Wow." Pick shook his head, stunned. "You are the complete opposite of your boyfriend, aren't you?"

Reese scowled. "What do you mean?"

"At work, that boy avoids women like the plague, never checks them out, and he never shares details about you two . . . I mean, other than the jelly thing."

Reese gasped, turning a bright tomato red. "I am so going to kill him for that. Now if you two will excuse me, I need to go home and . . . punish my man, probably with a nice strawberry or grape." She touched her chin thoughtfully. "Though he does have an affinity for peach jam."

233

While Pick burst out laughing, I rolled my eyes. "Okay, enough. Cut that kind of talk out. Not in front of my children, please."

Reese arched an eyebrow. "Your *children*?"

I flushed hard, and met Pick's grinning gaze before frowning at my cousin. "*The* children. *Grr.* Just . . . quit correcting my grammar. Go home and spank your boyfriend with flavored jelly already."

Reese tossed back her head and laughed before turning to Pick and handing Julian over. "Yours, I believe."

"Thank you." He took the boy into his arms. "And thanks for keeping Tinker Bell company today."

"No, thank *you* for fixing up my engine," Reese shot back with a small curtsy. "It runs like a whole new car."

He sighed, disagreeing. "It's still a piece of shit, so let me know if anything ever sounds strange or acts funny, especially if you're going to keep driving *my* children all over kingdom come in it."

Reese glanced back at me and made a pleasantly shocked face before mouthing the words, *"He's a keeper."* Then, she turned back to Pick and patted his cheek indulgently. "Will do, boss. I assume E. will be playing sleepover again since I checked Mason's work schedule and already know you'll be working at the club tonight."

Pick glanced at me but turned back to answer Reese before waiting for my reply. "Sounds like a plan."

Reese winked. "Take care of my girls for me, then."

She skipped up on her tiptoes and slapped a quick kiss to his cheek, right where she'd just patted it. Then she waved goodbye to me. "Toodles, Tinker Bell. Love ya."

I rolled my eyes. "Bye, Sweet Pea. Love you too."

After Reese had floated out of the room and we heard the front door open and shut, Pick lifted his eyebrows. "Wow. Is she always so . . . "

I laughed. "Yes. Yes, she is. But I love her to death. She's the only person I know I can trust implicitly."

His smile faded as his eyes turned warm and caring. "You can trust me too, you know. I would never let anything bad happen to you."

Even though I knew his claim couldn't possibly be supported in the real world, it was nice to hear him say it so adamantly.

"Well, you *are* my hero," I said, making the claim sound flippant as I tossed my hair over my shoulder. "I wouldn't expect anything less from you."

I loved knowing I could make such bold, arrogant claims, and he knew I wasn't actually serious.

He grinned and motioned toward the table that was already set with his mismatched plates and silverware, pulling out a chair for me to sit. "My lady?"

"Why, thank you." Since Julian could sit up fairly well in the high chair Pick had bought off Mrs. Rojas, I placed him in that and buckled him up. After making sure Skylar was still sleeping in the bouncer, I sat in my chair and Pick tucked me in.

He moaned and closed his eyes after he took his first bite. "I'm going to get fat if you keep feeding me like this." His voice was muffled through a mouthful of noodles.

I snorted and waved a hand, waiting until I swallowed to say, "Oh, please. I heated up frozen pizza, poured a bowl of cereal, and stirred together a skillet dinner. That's definitely not gourmet cooking. If anything, such measly meals will slim you down."

"Trust me. These have been three more meals than anyone has cooked for me in years."

I didn't like knowing that no one had ever really taken care of him. He was the special type of man who should be pampered. And I was really getting into this pampering shit. My mother would be appalled if she saw me now, but I actually loved being a homemaker.

I think the mom life completed me.

19

-PICK RYAN-

That night, I came home from work to find Eva curled up on the couch asleep.

"Oh, hell, no." This was not going to fly with me.

If she was going to stay the night in my apartment, I didn't want her anywhere but in my bed. So I scooped her up and carried her back to my room. She stirred along the way.

"Pick?" I loved her sleepy, blurry voice, especially when she was saying my name. "What're you doing?"

"You are *not* sleeping on that couch."

She curled more fully into me and rested her cheek on my shoulder. "Well, neither should you."

I shook my head. "My place, my rules. No sexy new mother is allowed to sleep in anything but a bed."

Neither of us mentioned the extra bed in Tristy's room, and she had to know it was there. She'd passed the opened doorway to get to my room I don't know how many times.

I guess we'd silently agreed it was off limits. But it felt wrong for her to sleep where Tris had slept. It felt as if Tristy had soiled the mattress and made it too dirty for the likes of my Tinker Bell.

As we entered my bedroom, I saw that both babies were asleep in the crib. I had to smile. They could've been brother and sister. It was as if this was how things were meant to be.

Eva didn't resist when I laid her on the mattress, but she did grab my shirt when I tried to straighten. "You stay too. This bed will hold us both, and I'm far and away from being a modest, maidenly virgin. Plus, I trust you."

The *I-trust-you* part won me over. Blood surged through my veins, hot and thick. My skin prickled, suddenly extra sensitive. I was going to sleep beside my Tinker Bell.

Oh, fuck. She was going to be right next to me, all night long.

My arousal thrummed painfully hard, but I nodded in agreement because no way was I turning this down. Then I held my breath, irrationally afraid she'd come to her senses if I breathed wrong. If she knew how much the very idea of lying beside her turned me on, she'd probably freak.

"Just . . . uh, just let me just change, and I'll be right back."

She was already fast asleep again by the time I returned, wearing a hole-ridden t-shirt and a pair of sweatpants. She'd scooted to the outside edge, probably so she could take the side closest to the kids, which meant I had to crawl over her to reach the inside of the bed that I had pressed against the wall.

"Night, Tink," I told her softly before kissing the crown of her head.

"Mmph," was her only reply.

I smiled, killed the lights and crawled in with her. The blonde silken tresses of her hair, illuminated by the nightlight that was plugged in by the crib, looked like spun gold. I wanted to reach out and touch it, run my fingers through it, and bring it to my nose to smell. But I was a good boy and kept my hands off the woman I'd been dreaming about for the past decade. She was inches away, safe and secure, and so damn beautiful. Our children were sleeping only a few feet from us. Life was pretty damn spectacular.

I fell asleep with a smile on my face. And again, I slept right through Julian waking up in the middle of the night.

The next night, Eva stayed over again, and she slept in my bed. Again. And once again, I crawled under the sheets with her after I got home from working at the club.

But unlike the two nights before, I woke to suckling sounds in the early hours.

"Julian?" I mumbled, rolling over to face her.

"He's already gone back to sleep," she answered. "I'm up with Skylar now."

Shit, she didn't need to get up this many times. "Need me to do anything?"

"Nope. Got it covered." And she did; she'd thrown a blanket over her shoulder, covering all the action.

My squinted eyes suddenly weren't so squinted with sleep anymore. "Are you breastfeeding?"

"Mm-hmm."

I sighed and reclosed my eyes. "That is so hot. Breast-feeding mothers kick ass. If I wasn't this tired, I'd be incredibly turned on right now."

Screw it; I was already growing wood.

She laughed softly. "Go back to bed, Patrick."

I smiled. "Call me that again."

"Patrick." She teased my hair with her fingers.

Damn. "Yep, I'm having a serious wet about this dream tonight."

Then I fell back asleep to her amazing laughter.

-EVA MERCER-

By the beginning of the fourth day of playing Nanny Mercer, I was exhausted, and yet strangely invigorated. I just felt good. Good about myself, about what I was doing for Pick and Julian, about how I was spending my days. Just plain good about everything.

The fatigue was beginning to get to me, though. Today, I was going to sleep whenever the kids did. That's all there was to it. Besides, I'd mostly caught up with all the housework, even though Pick kept insisting I didn't have to do so much. I felt better being in a cleaner place, plus I wanted to help him out since he worked himself like a dog. And I had to admit, I loved all the appreciation I saw in his eyes every time he came home to a hot meal or freshly washed sheets.

Oh, God. I sounded like June Cleaver.

I'd always made fun of those women who didn't work, who stayed home like the obedient little housewife, barefoot and pregnant, and always sweating over a hot stove. But after being that woman for the past three days, I knew I would never make fun of her again.

This kind of life took some serious girl power. It was no cushy job; it was more like slave labor. I was so freaking tired, sometimes my eyelids hurt from keeping them pried open. I don't care how much Pick was paying, no dollar amount would ever compensate. Except, I already felt compensated. I went to bed each night with this awesome feeling, knowing I'd accomplished something. I'd set a plan of how to tackle all my duties, and I reached every goal, every day.

I'd honestly never felt as good about myself as I did now.

It was this emotion—this love I was cultivating for the babies I nurtured as well as the man who kept looking at me as if I could do no wrong—that made it all worth it. Even when Julian woke up earlier than usual, right after I'd been up with Skylar for the past two hours because the girl just wouldn't go back to sleep, I felt quenched.

Popping out of bed before he could wake Skylar

again, I snagged him from his crib and turned back to the cozy nest I'd shared with Pick two nights in a row. But Pick wasn't there. I paused and cocked my head until I heard the shower running from the single bathroom down the hall.

Wow, I hadn't even stirred when his alarm went off.

After settling Julian and myself back on the bed, I propped some pillows behind my back so I could sit comfortably, and then I pushed up my nightshirt to unsnap my bra.

"Are you hungry, little guy?" I asked as I cradled him into position and drew his face up to my nipple.

I didn't realize what I'd just done until he began to suck. The strength of his pulls was a lot stronger than Skylar's. It snapped me right out of my foggy, half-asleep daze. With a gasp, I bolted upright, suddenly fully awake.

"Oh, shit." I was breastfeeding Julian.

This had to be wrong. He wasn't mine, and I was only watching him for a couple days.

What Pick would say if he knew?

Julian didn't seem to mind, though. The kid kept drinking while his chubby little fingers rested possessively against the side of my breast.

Instantly, something inside me softened. I stroked his head, letting him have his fill. Wet nursing was no new thing; it should be okay. And Skylar certainly wouldn't go without. The preemie rarely drank much; there was more than enough to go around. And everyone said breast milk was so much better for a child than formula. Plus, if they both ate this way, I wouldn't have to get up so much in the middle of the night, shuffle to the kitchen, warm a bottle, carry it back to bed . . . *yada, yada, yada.*

When I realized I was rationalizing why I shouldn't stop, I flushed. The God's honest truth was I liked taking care of him this way. I liked the bond, and I loved this baby.

Down the hall, the bathroom door opened. I sucked in a breath. Oh, *crappity,* crap, crap. Footsteps in the hall urged me to grab a nearby blanket and toss it over my shoulder, completely covering which baby I was feeding. *Do, to-do, to-do*, went the whistling in my head, *nothing going on here.*

Pick appeared in the doorway, wearing nothing but a towel. My mouth dried up and I forgot what I was trying to hide from him.

He jerked to a halt when he saw me. "Oh. You're awake."

I was a too busy staring to answer him. Yeah, I was definitely awake now.

He motioned toward his dresser. "I forgot to bring my clothes into the bathroom with me."

When he entered and crossed the room to pull open the top drawer, I waved him on. "Trust me, I don't mind." *Really.*

"In that case." He tossed me a wink over his shoulder and dropped the towel.

My mouth fell open. Oh, sweet mercy. Naked Pick Ryan looked amazing from the back. His tush was tight and sculpted to perfection, and his spine muscles looked all sleek and shiny, wet from the shower. My gaze swept up and down, then up and down again. He really did only tattoo his arms and neck, didn't he? Oh, and his heart. I remembered seeing a peek of that one at Forbidden during the auction, but I hadn't been close enough to see what had been special enough to place it directly over his heart.

I forgot all about tattoos when he bent to pull on a pair of boxers. I caught the barest glimpse of a shadow from his junk hanging down in the front and had to press my legs together tight. He didn't turn around until he had on a pair of jeans and was zipping up the fly.

"Hey, you got a little drool." He wiped the corner of his own mouth. "Right there."

I begin to lift my fingers to wipe up the mess before I realized he was teasing. Eyes narrowing, I muttered, "Shut up," and I stuck my tongue out at him. Then I laughed at my own silliness. As my gaze caught on the single tattoo over his heart, I couldn't stand the curiosity. "You never did tell me what that one meant," I said, hitching my chin toward it.

He froze, with one of those hand-caught-in-the-cookie-jar expressions. Then he briefly skated his fingers over it as if he wanted to hide it. Shrugging, he yanked on a white undershirt. "Just a list of names," he said and grabbed a fresh work shirt from his closet before buttoning it up.

Holy crap, he was so hiding something. I couldn't let this drop. "I caught a glimpse of it at the club on auction night. But I've never gotten close enough to see the details. Whose names are on it?"

Ha! A direct question. Let's see him evade this answer.

"Just . . . " He focused his attention on straightening non-existent wrinkles on his shirt. "Names."

I wasn't deterred. "Of important people?"

"Mm-hmm."

"Is this in any way related to the reason why my birthday is the passcode to your cell phone? Because, you know, you refused to talk about that too."

He lifted his face to frown at me. But he said absolutely nothing.

"Fine." I flung out a hand. "Go ahead and shut me out. *Again.*" I lifted my chin in an airy, pretentious way. "It's fine. I mean, I thought we were becoming friends and talked about everything. But don't worry. I get it. You know the worst possible thing there is to know about me, but I don't need to know anything about you at all."

His shoulders deflated and his expression turned bleak. "Don't be that way, Tink. I—"

"I'm kidding!" I broke in with a roll of my eyes and forced laugh.

Okay, fine. It did twinge a little that he didn't feel comfortable enough to share something with me, but seriously—

"You don't have to tell me anything you don't want to. I understand. I really do. And I'm sorry for teasing you about it. I didn't mean to make you take me so seriously."

He drew out what I hoped was a relieved breath, but something on his face told me he wasn't quite reassured. I opened my mouth to go on and keep apologizing for making him feel guilty when a rustling from the crib caught our attention.

Pick was quick to check it out. "I'll get him," he offered, only to stop short when he looked down at the baby inside. He hesitantly drew Skylar from the bed and turned to me. When his gaze dropped and fixated on the lump where Julian was still having his breakfast, I knew I'd been caught.

"Eva . . ." he said slowly. "Are you . . . feeding Julian?"

"Um . . . " The guilt on my face totally gave me away.

His eyes shot open wide. "Holy shit."

"I'm sorry. I'm so sorry." I immediately pulled Julian away from my chest and covered myself. "I was half asleep and just so used to taking care of Skylar this way. I didn't realize what I was doing until he was already latched on . . . " I faltered when Pick's eyes widened at that description. "But he took to it so naturally and seemed happy, I didn't want to disturb him."

He seemed kind of fussy now, though, since I'd interrupted him mid-meal. But I swung him over my shoulder and began to pat his back quickly and nervously. My gaze sought Pick, trying to gauge his reaction, but he looked more surprised than anything.

"Oh, God. You think I'm gross and disgusting, don't you?"

"I think . . . " He shook his head as if he had no idea what he thought. Then he uttered, "I think you're feeding my kid from your . . . your . . . "

"It's supposed to be much more nutritious this way." I motioned vaguely at my boobs. "This milk is packed with disease-fighting . . . stuff, you know, to help protect him. I read all about. He'd get a much healthier, safer diet from me. Besides, Skylar never eats enough. I usually have to pump out the extra to keep my boobs from hurting. And why the heck are you looking at me like that?"

He grinned, and I knew everything would be okay. "Sorry, I just . . . " He shook his head. "This has to be the hottest conversation I've ever had with you. Please . . . continue talking about your breasts."

"Oh my God." I rolled my eyes toward the ceiling. "Pick, this is serious. Do you have a problem with what I did, or not?"

He jiggled Skylar in his arms, swaying her back and forth to keep her happy. "Why would I have a problem with it? You just listed a million reasons why it's better for him."

"Because . . . I don't know. He's not mine. Surely *someone* would have a problem with it . . . for some reason."

"Well, they're not here in this room, so fuck them."

"But . . . " I closed my eyes and held Julian just a little bit tighter. "What if . . . what if attachment issues come from this . . . or something?" *Like they already had.*

Pick sat on the edge of the mattress next to my hip. "Tink, you are the best thing that's ever happened to that kid. I don't care if he only has one day left with you or twenty, you just keep doing whatever you're doing until you have to go, and I will forever worship the ground you walk on. Because a little slice of heaven is better than none at all. I will gladly deal with attachment issues if they crop up. Got it?"

A smile lit my face. "Got it."

But, wow, this man was too good to be true. He always knew the exact right thing to say to make me feel better. Was it any wonder I'd been able to sleep next to him all night without a single qualm?

I'd never been able to fall asleep next to any guy; too many lingering childhood traumas prevented it. But there had been no reservations about urging Pick to crawl into bed with me. Sure, I could argue that I'd been half-asleep and too tired to care. But honestly, I just felt that completely and utterly safe with him. I felt protected, and I knew if he ever touched me, it'd be because I wanted it, and I he'd make sure I enjoyed it.

"Here, trade me," I told him, holding up Julian as Skylar began to complain. "She's gotta be hungry too."

He readily complied, setting my daughter in my free arm. After we switched off, and I tucked Skylar under my nursing blanket, Pick narrowed his eyes at a happy, babbling Julian.

"Oh, don't you smile at me with that milky grin, you lucky shit. There's no need to rub in it. I know where that mouth's been."

"Pick!" I rolled my eyes.

He sent me an innocent glance. "What? He's clearly rubbing it in."

"You are such a guy."

"Hell, yeah, I'm a guy. What'd you expect me to be?"

His smile was slow and seductive, which reminded me I'd just seen his taut naked tushy. I didn't know how I was going to handle living with him for another week and half. Keeping my hands off him while I slept next to him every night was already a challenge, but now that I'd seen what the goods looked like under his clothes, the challenge had just ramped itself up into mission impossible.

"I'm going to make myself a bowl of cereal. You want one?" he asked.

Tickled he thought to ask and was willing to serve me, I smiled. Oh, yeah. Reese had been right. This one was a keeper.

If only he was available to keep.

I shook my head. "No, thanks. I'll grab a banana later."

His eyebrows shot up. "Banana? We have bananas?"

Before I was even able to answer, he was gone, shooting from the room like a rocket. Seconds later, I heard, *"Holy shit!"*

He pounded back down the hall until he reappeared with a pile of food loaded down on Julian's lap as he carried the poor boy like a human bowl. "Eva, there's . . . there's food freaking everywhere. And fruit. I love fruit."

I laughed, glad I had remembered that detail when I'd gone shopping. "I know. I bought it, remember? With your money?"

"But." He strode to the bed with his loot and let the heap tumble off Julian's lap and onto the mattress beside me. "There's apples, and oranges, and what the fuck is this?" He took a bite before moaning. "I don't care. It tastes amazing."

"Didn't you see everything I bought last night—or the night before—when you were in the kitchen, eating supper . . . and breakfast?"

"No." He shook his head as he settled next to me on the bed, placing Julian between us. Then he started a picnic with the food, letting Julian gnaw briefly on his nectarine before he stole it back. "I was too busy eating, and staring at you, and running off to my next job in between getting hit on by your cousin to notice much else."

"Oh, she was *not* hitting on you."

"Whatever." He shrugged. "You know, you keep treating me this good, I may never let you leave."

I couldn't say what I was really feeling, which was, *who said I* wanted *to leave?* But I definitely thought it. I think we were going to have to worry about me suffering more from attachment issues than Julian would.

20

So the week progressed. And then a couple more days. I lived on a daily high where no one could bring me down, no matter what they did or said. I'd always been good at rolling with the flow and taking things in stride, but now I actually smiled through it all. Life was just amazing.

I didn't care if I woke up every morning with a raging hard-on that not even yanking off in the shower could calm. I woke up next to *her*. The smell of lilacs on my sheets, her hand resting next to my pillow only inches from my face, accidently spooning with her on some nights. Yeah, I had no complaints.

"So, how're things working out with Eva?" Mason asked one night, just before we opened the club, where I'd actually arrived on time to work . . . for the eighth stretch in a row.

He must've realized I was thinking about Tink,

because his knowing smirk made me scowl.

"Oh, it's just . . . you know . . . awful." I gave an exaggerated roll of my eyes. "Supper's waiting on me every night when I get home from the garage. My apartment's spotless. The laundry's always folded and put away. My kid's happier and healthier than he's ever been, and this drop-dead gorgeous woman parades around in front of me nonstop, wearing ass-hugging yoga pants. It just, yeah, totally sucks."

Mason chuckled. "I didn't realize exactly how much E. did around our place too, until she was gone. Strangely, we kind of miss her."

I frowned, ready to tell him he couldn't have her back. She was *mine*.

"I didn't know she was going to actually *move in* with you while she watched your kid, though," he added. Narrowing my eyes, I studied him, trying to figure out what he was really saying. He shrugged. "I know you work some long hours, but there were a few nights in there you didn't work late at Forbidden."

Eva and I had always managed to fill those nights with reasons for her to stick around until it was basically too late to drive her to Mason and Reese's. Once we'd borrowed a couple strollers for the kids and took a walk down by the nearest park. On another night, we'd cooked spaghetti together and ended up talking afterward until almost midnight.

But Mason's blatant comment made me realize what I'd been doing. I'd been playing house with my dream girl, using her on borrowed time, and relishing every damn minute of it. I didn't like his questions, though. They threatened my paradise.

"What're you getting at, Lowe?"

He lifted his hands and laughed uneasily. "Hey, I'm not complaining. I finally have Reese to myself, and that rocks. I'm just . . . concerned. You two slipped into this domestic little . . . whatever it is, way too easily. What's going to happen when you get your regular sitter back? You just going to send her home to us without a backward glance? Or what if your wife returns? Where does Eva fit in this?"

I shook my head. "My wife's not—" I stopped short, telling myself he was right. What I was doing with Eva was selfish, and it couldn't last. I groaned and glanced away. "So, what're you saying I should do?"

Mason shrugged. "Hell, I have no idea what you should do. I'm just saying don't hurt her. Keep her, send her back, whatever. But if you hurt her, you'll upset Reese. And *that* will piss me off."

I nodded, a little miffed he was more concerned about affecting Reese than Tinker Bell. But Reese was his girlfriend, so I guess it made sense.

"I get that." I nodded. "And I'll talk to Tink about it. Make sure she's getting what she wants from this."

Mason was silent after that, seeming satisfied by my answer.

But I never did talk to Eva. I was too afraid she might say she wanted to leave once this was over, or maybe that she was counting down the days to break free . . . just as Tristy had done.

It was bound to happen. Thirteen days after Tinker Bell came to watch my kid, the chicken pox passed from my neighbor's apartment, and they were no longer contagious threats.

That night at dinner, Eva waited until we were seated at the table—Julian slapping at the top of his high chair and Skylar nestled over her shoulder—before she said, "So, Mrs. Rojas called today . . . "

The baked potato I was chewing caught in my throat. Why the hell had Mrs. Rojas called the landline too, when she'd also called my cell phone? I'd been trying to forget or at least put off responding to the conversation I'd had with her for as long as possible. Like maybe another week or so. A decade perhaps.

Eva glanced up at me, her gaze seeking, trying to read me. "I guess they're all healthy, and you finally have your regular sitter back."

I nodded and reached for my glass of iced tea, unable

to say a thing. But iced fucking tea. The woman even made iced tea. How the hell was I supposed to just let her go?

Fine. Iced tea had nothing to do with it. Even if she'd never once cleaned or cooked a damn thing, I still want her to stay.

"Skylar and I packed our things this afternoon," she added, stabbing me right through the chest with her casual announcement. "After the supper dishes are cleaned, we can call Reese to come pick us up."

"No!" When Eva blinked in surprise, my face heated. "I mean . . . " *Shit.* I ran my hand through my hair. "You don't have to call her. Fighter and I can drive you guys over."

"Oh." Her shoulders fell half an inch, and I swear I saw disappointment in her eyes. It lit a fire of hope inside me. I opened my mouth to ask her to stay, but then she grinned and added, "That'd be great. Thanks."

Damn it. What the hell had I been thinking? I couldn't keep her forever.

Skylar saved my mortified ass by picking that moment to spit up, and Julian helped by throwing his chew toy over the side of the high chair and crying for someone to fetch it. But that was only a temporary distraction. After Eva and I worked side by side to clean the dishes, she brushed her palms over her hips and turned to me with a tense, expectant smile.

"Well . . . " she said.

"I'll, uh . . . " I blew out a breath. "I can carry your things down to the Barracuda."

Her blue eyes were soft and appreciative. "Okay. Thank you."

I nodded, stalled a minute, and then turned and headed from the kitchen. It only took me three trips to get everything she'd accumulated over the past few weeks piled into the trunk, which meant, after only three brief trips to my car and back, it was time to take her home.

We were both quiet as we bundled up the kids. I picked up both Julian's and Skylar's carrier, one in each hand. Eva slung her purse over her shoulder and slowly glanced around the front room as if bidding it farewell. Then she lifted her shoulders and asked, "Ready?"

I couldn't answer so I turned toward the exit. Tink got the door for me and led the way down the stairs, and then she opened the main entrance for me as well. I wanted to blurt out, *"We work so well together, it seems like a damn shame to end this so soon,"* but I swallowed the urge.

Once the four of us were buckled in, I fumbled for the keys. There was a moment of silence before I could start the engine in which Julian screwed up his face and began to whine, tossing his arms as if prepared for a royal tantrum.

"Hey, it's okay, little man." Though she was technically no longer my babysitter, Eva undid her seatbelt and leaned over the seat to check on him, finding him a toy to latch onto and chew.

I glanced over and watched her sooth him. "I think this is his way of telling you he doesn't want you to go."

Eva sent me a sharp look and abruptly turned around, settling herself forward again. I bit my lip, gnawing on the rings at the corner, and stabbed my key into the ignition.

When I didn't turn the engine on and just stared straight ahead out the front windshield, Eva cleared her throat.

"Um . . . Pick?"

"Hmm?" I shifted my attention to her.

She crinkled her eyebrows. "Why aren't we going?"

"Oh." I looked down at my hand still resting on the key. But I just couldn't turn it.

Fuck. It was confession time. "I guess it's my turn to balk." I drew in a heaving breath and added, "Because this is my way of telling you *I* don't want you to go."

Then I held in the breath I'd just gulped down, creating a pocket of distress in my gullet as I waited for her response.

"You want me to stay?" She sounded hopeful as her eyes lit up. Or maybe I was the hopeful one, trying to project it onto her. Yeah, that had to be it.

"Ignore me," I mumbled, reaching for the key again.

"I'm being stupid."

But she snaked her hand out and covered my fingers, stopping me from starting the car. "I want to stay, too," she said, her admission so low I almost didn't hear it.

I straightened and twisted my entire torso to face her fully. "You do?"

Nodding, she yanked her hand from mine and began to wring all ten fingers at her waist. "I mean, Julian's going to need a babysitter anyway, whether it's me or Mrs. Rojas. And if you pay us the same, then I don't see why it'd make any difference if I—"

"Stay," I said simply.

Eva bit her lip. Her chest rose as she took a deep breath. And then she nodded. "Okay."

-EVA MERCER-

This was crazy. Insane. Completely foolish. I'd pretty much just agreed to move in with a guy I'd never even kissed after only having known him for a few months.

We never did clarify how long I had agreed to stay. I'm not sure if that made the situation better or worse. Maybe he only wanted me another month or two. Maybe forever.

I hoped forever, though oh God, I shouldn't be hoping that, should I?

What if his wife came home? What if he started dating? What if . . . ?

"Do you need to call Reese and let her know you're not coming back?" he asked, carrying both kids again as he followed me back up the stairs to his apartment. "She was expecting you tonight, wasn't she?"

I bit my lip but didn't turn to let him see my sudden unease. "Yeah, I guess I should." I pulled my key from my purse. As I was unlocking the door, I realized I should've given the key back already since I'd been planning on leaving.

God, I had subconsciously known all along I wouldn't

be going anywhere tonight, hadn't I?

"Do you want to use my cell phone? Her number's already in the phonebook."

"Okay." But I didn't want to call Reese. I already knew what she'd say. She'd turn into my conscience and tell me what a terrible, awful, stupid idea this was. And then, what if she somehow convinced me not to do it? I didn't want her to convince me not to do this. I wanted to stay with Pick and Julian.

Pick set down the two carriers and fished his phone from his pocket. As he extended it to me, he sought my gaze with his own. When I realized he was trying to read me and see if I wanted to change my mind, my decision to stay cemented itself further. He wanted me here, but he'd never do anything to force my hand. That's why I didn't want to leave, because he wanted me to be my own person and make my own decisions.

I took the phone and entered my birthday to get into the home screen, which reminded me he had secrets he was keeping. Damn, maybe I was acting too rashly. I didn't know much about him.

But the phone was already ringing in my ear, and I still wanted to stay. My instincts trusted this man; they rarely trusted anyone.

My gut churned. Pick was getting the kids free of their carriers, so I turned away and hurried down the hall to our room.

When my cousin answered, a cold sweat poured over me.

"Hey," I answered. "I, uh, I guess I won't be coming back tonight after all."

Reese didn't sound suspicious at all. "Really? What happened now? The neighbors contract malaria?"

I didn't laugh along with her. "No. No." I shook my head and nervously started playing with my hair, winding tendrils around my finger and letting them corkscrew free. "The Rojas are all healthy now. Pick and I just . . . we decided I might as well just stay on, you know, for the foreseeable future, as . . . as his permanent babysitter."

When my cousin didn't answer, I squeezed my eyes

253

closed and clenched my teeth.

"The *foreseeable* future?" she echoed.

"Yeah." I shrugged, making it sound like no big deal. "You know, just play each day by ear. He needs a babysitter anyway, and I still need a job. It just . . . it works well for us this way. And you and Mason get to keep your love nest undisturbed."

"Right." Reese drew out the word. "Because this is *all* about Mason and me."

Her scathing tone made me scowl. I opened my mouth to tell her I *did* want her and Mason to get some freedom from me—even if that wasn't the main reason— but Reese exploded.

"Seriously, *what're you doing, E.*? You're the one who convinced me why the two of you can't be together. So, why are you torturing yourself like this? You're going to end up falling for him, and then his wife's going to come home, and you'll be thrown out on your ass, homeless, jobless, and freaking heartbroken."

I sighed and closed my eyes, not about to tell her part of her prediction was too late. I'd already fallen for him.

"It's not like that," I argued. "We've never even kissed."

Reese snorted. "I was far and gone in love with Mason before he ever put his lips anywhere near mine. Love doesn't start with kissing or sex, it starts with feelings. And you and Pick . . . *gah*, you can't tell me there aren't feelings there."

I closed my eyes and sighed. "I can't leave, Ree Ree. I just . . . I can't. I know you don't understand that, but—"

"No, sweetie. I understand it perfectly, and that's why I'm worried. But I also want you to be happy, and I've never seen you as happy as you are with him. I'm going to keep worrying, though, because I love you."

My heart melted when I realized she meant her words. It was still so strange and amazing to me that anyone gave a shit about me. "And I love you too, but—"

"No *buts*. I understand. I'm just leery. And now that I've voiced my concerns, I'll shut up. Just remember, I'll always be here if you need me. I can at least promise you won't go homeless."

"Thank you." I bit my lip. Knowing she had my best interests at heart but was still suspicious made me second-guess myself. "You know," I said slowly. "Just to be on the safe side, maybe I won't take *all* my stuff from your place quite yet."

"Smart thinking."

After I hung up, her words echoed through my head. I walked slowly from the hallway back to the living room, where Pick was pacing the floor with Skylar. He turned to me abruptly, his gaze anxious.

"Well?"

"Well what?" Damn, he knew I was waffling.

"Did she talk you out of staying?"

The scales tipped in his favor again, and a glow lit me up from the inside as I shook my head. He'd been so worried about me leaving. It felt nice to be this wanted. Correction: if felt nice to know *he* wanted me.

"No. She didn't."

His stare narrowed. "You talk *yourself* out it?"

"Not yet." After strolling the rest of the way to him, I braced my hands on his forearms and leaned in to kiss Skylar's head. While my lips were still pressed against her soft skin, my gaze met his. Heat coiled inside me when I realized we were only inches apart.

His brown eyes were watchful, wary, and yet filled with their own brand of desire. "So, we're really doing this, then?"

I pulled back slowly and nodded. "Yeah. We're really doing this."

Relief hissed from his lungs, and a slow smile spread. "Good."

-PICK RYAN-

Eva had reassured me, but we still stayed quiet for the rest of the evening. After putting the kids to bed, we curled up on the couch together and found a sitcom to watch. I wrapped my arm around her shoulders and she rested her cheek on my chest.

At bedtime, we still didn't talk much as we readied ourselves for the night. A nervous tension thrummed through my bones. I turned off the light and waited until she climbed onto the mattress before I followed her under the sheets. And finally, I drew out the edgy breath I'd been holding, a little more certain she was really going to stay.

The nightlight by the crib brightened the room just enough to put a romantic glow on the atmosphere. Eva and I lay on our sides, facing each other, our hands tucked under our cheeks. We studied one another for a while without speaking. I wondered what she was thinking, but I was too afraid to ask, so I let my lashes flutter closed.

Almost immediately, I could feel her mind start to whirl, and my guts knotted right back up as worry pierced me. If she called off our new arrangement, I didn't know how I'd survive it.

"Pick?"

Damn it.

I opened my eyes warily. "Yeah?"

Concern coated her gaze. "Is this wrong?"

I shook my head, trying not to lose it. "Why would it be wrong? It's no different than what we've been doing for the past two weeks."

She shrugged and bit her lip. "But I was only here because you needed help. Now . . . now I'm here because . . . I *want* to be."

Wow. Just hearing her say that warmed me up all over. I swallowed noisily, trying not to reach out and just yank her against me. "I still need help. Julian still needs a sitter."

"But it's different now. Can't you feel it? Me deciding to stay . . . it changed things."

Reaching out slowly, I caught her hand and squeezed her fingers. "Yeah, I feel it," I admitted. "But I still don't want you to go."

"I don't want to go either." Even as she said that, though, she slid her hand out from under mine, putting emotional distance between us.

Fuck, I hated emotional distance.

Confusion filled her eyes. "I know in my gut this is wrong, but I think I found my niche in life by being here. I mean, is it lame that I actually *like* being a home-maker? That I like watching kids? They're just . . . It's fulfilling to watch them learn every little thing, like how to reach out their hand to grab a hold of something. I like . . . it feels so satisfying when I manage to get them to stop crying after they've been upset. I like feeding them and cleaning them and dressing them. They're just these perfect miniature little people who have no clue how to be people yet. When I bring them down off a big cry, it's as if my super power just kicked in. I feel . . . rejuven-ated."

I shook my head, my brow crinkling with confusion. "Why would that be lame? I think it's amazing."

She flushed and picked at a corner seam on her pillowcase. "I don't know. I just . . . where I grew up, domestic women who stayed at home, taking care of the house and watching the kids, were always looked down upon. If you wanted to get anywhere in the world, you went off to college and got a *real* job, so you could pay someone else to watch your kids if you ever had any. But being here these past few weeks, actually doing this . . . it's hard work. It takes effort, patience, perseverance, and more freaking energy than I ever thought I possess-ed. And yet, at the end of every day, I feel more fulfilled, more . . . I don't know . . . just satisfied with my life and myself than I'd ever felt before."

I reached out and covered her hand again, halting her nervous plucking. "I think what you're doing with those two children is just as important if not *more* important than any 'real' job with a time card and W2 could ever be. That other kind of life would be fine, if that's what you wanted. But you don't have to be something splashy and important to the world, not when you're the entire world to Skylar and Julian."

I shook my head. "I never had a mother. She aban-doned me in the hospital where I was born. She didn't even name me. A couple of nurses dubbed me after their husbands. That's why I have three first names." Bringing her hand to my mouth, I kissed her palm reverently. "You have no idea what I would've given to have a mother as attentive as you are, someone my entire life revolved around. You make a difference, and it's a huge one. There's nothing silly or inconsequential about it."

Tears filled her eyes. "Boy, do you have a way with words, Patrick Jason Ryan."

"I do, don't I?" I smiled softly and reached out to flick a tear off her cheek.

She sniffed and brushed at her cheek too. "Is it bad of me to say I hope your wife never comes back?"

I blew out a long breath before whispering my own awful confession. "I hope she doesn't either."

Eva shifted, moving to the edge of her pillow and closing the gap between us. Instant heat flooded me. The erection I always had when lying in bed with her went raging hard. I let go of her hand to fist my fingers into the mattress and keep myself from touching her.

"Tink . . . " I started, but saying that name felt wrong in this moment. Tinker Bell was a fantasy, a dream of a woman I'd never met, someone I wanted to come and save me from my fucked up life. Eva was a reality and so much better than a few glimpses I'd had when I was fourteen. So I added, "Eva . . . "

My voice was a lot more hesitant and leery than the rest of me. I wanted her to move closer. I wanted her against me, on top of me, under me, all over me. But there seemed to be all kinds of reasons why it was a bad idea.

"I just want to kiss you," she said, her eyes full of hope.

I squeezed mine shut, so fucking tempted; it wouldn't take much to tip me over the edge. "Baby, you know this can't go anywhere."

"I know." She shifted even closer, then lifted her hand and set it against my cheek. "But I still want to anyway. Just once."

I crumbled. "Just once?" Slipping my trembling fingers around to the back of her neck, I tipped her face up, even as my other hand curled around her waist and drew her against me. "You'll have to be the one to stop when you've had your fill, because . . . " I shook my head. *I sure as hell wouldn't be able to.*

"I will." She nodded and drove me insane when she licked her lips in anticipation. Goddamn, this might kill me.

Don't do it, a small, rational part of my head screamed. But I totally didn't listen to that guy.

I dipped my face down and stopped a breath from contact, letting the anticipation build in that tiny pocket of air between us until it damn near crackled with electricity. Eva whimpered and strained against me, her impatience snapping when she closed the gap and pressed her mouth to mine.

My fingers tightened in her hair at the base of her neck, not letting her get any closer. I'd waited ten years for this; no fucking way was I rushing it. Except her soft body sliding against mine made it difficult to restrain myself.

Her fingers fisted around the cloth of my shirt, right over my heart where her name was imprinted on my chest and into my very soul. I increased the pressure against her lips bit by bit, letting us both experience every little nuance of each other. Her mouth was soft and supple, giving into mine with exactly the right heat and pressure. And when her breath came from between them, mixing with mine, I groaned. She tasted like . . . I don't even know, but it tasted like home.

She clutched my shoulder with one hand and let go of my shirt with her other to bury her fingers in my hair. I shifted closer until her breasts flattened against me, and my arousal dug into her hip.

Clutching my hair with more fervor when I applied more pressure to her mouth, she canted her hips and undulated slowly, hypnotically. My palm slid down to her ass to help her grind. By the time our mouths opened and our tongues touched, we were pawing at each other, going as far as we could with our clothes on and our hands staying outside the cloth.

But shit, damn, fuck, I swear I had an orgasm without actually shooting my load when her tongue slid against mine and rolled around it. My muscles seized and my hips slammed up. Rolling her onto her back, I climbed above her and nestled my legs between hers as our mouths fucked the shit out of each other. Lacing our fingers together, I pulled her hands over her head and kissed her senseless, lips smashed, tongues diving, hearts pounding, teeth clashing.

Jesus, it was everything.

I bit her bottom lip and her hips bumped up against my aching cock.

"Pick," she gasped, tightening her grip on my hands. "I need . . . I need . . . "

"I know, baby. I'm on it."

But when my hand slid down over her hip and along her thigh, headed toward the sweetness between her legs, my son decided to wake up.

"You've gotta be kidding me," I growled, lifting my face.

Under me, Eva snickered. "Wow, he's more effective than a chastity belt."

I whimpered and rolled onto my back beside her, flinging my arm over my face and trying to control my raging hormones. But Eva continued to snicker.

I turned my face to scowl at her. "There is absolutely nothing funny about this."

Which only made her laugh harder.

Women.

When she sat up to get out of bed, I caught her arm. "I'll get him for you." I needed a reason to get out of this bed and hopefully cool down.

She beamed her appreciation, and her smile was so beautiful I was tempted to dive back on top of her. But I filled my cheeks with air and turned away. Scowling at the kid, I picked him up and carried him back to the bed, where Eva reached out with open arms to take over. After I climbed back over her to settle in, I groaned bitterly as Eva opened her shirt and plucked out a bare breast, with the biggest, brightest berry-red nipple attached to the end before she hid it inside Fighter's mouth.

"You cock-blocking little shit," I muttered. "You couldn't have had a dirty diaper to help me cool down, could you? Oh, no. You had to be hungry so I could see *that* . . . " I waved my hand irritably at Eva's exposed breast. "And only get amped up even more. Thanks a lot, pal."

Cracking up over my lecture, Eva covered her mouth and shook her head. "Leave the poor boy alone. He's just making sure I work for my money."

My shoulders slumped. Being reminded she was here for a job I paid her to do killed my mood more than anything. I watched miserably as she fed Julian.

"You really are my employee, aren't you?"

Her eyes widened as she realized what that meant. "Don't," she scolded. "I know what you're thinking and you did nothing wrong. I *begged* you to kiss me."

"No, I kissed you because I wanted to more than I wanted my next breath, even though I should've pushed down my selfish wants and said no." I pulled at my hair, wanting to give myself a black eye. "What the hell was I thinking? I will not do this to you. I won't start something that can't go anywhere. That's not fair to you. At all."

She opened her mouth, but then closed it and nodded silently before finally adding, "I understand."

I squeezed my eyes closed. Hearing her say that should've relieved me of my worries, but it only made me feel shittier, guiltier, and achier. And it made me love her even more.

Turning my face her way, I opened my eyes and forced a smile, trying not to focus on her exposed breasts. "It was an amazing kiss, though, wasn't it?"

Her smiled bloomed, which finally eased some of my troubles. "Yes. Yes, it was. You're right. A little slice of heaven is better than none at all."

Damn straight.

21

-EVA MERCER-

Another week passed. Things between Pick and I should've smoothed out and fallen into a nice, platonic routine.

Well, shoulda, coulda, woulda.

After we—or maybe it was just he—decided we weren't going to be anything more than friends, the sexual tension between us grew thicker.

One morning, I made sure I was awake when he got out of the shower because he never remembered to take clothes with him to change into. And he made sure to drop his towel and give me a show, like he always did. When he glanced my way at one point, giving me a side profile of him, I bit my lip and slid my hand under the sheet as if I was going to touch myself.

His gaze heated and his cock grew out from his body as if on command. I stared at it as I arched up my back and sucked in a breath.

"Fuck," he choked out.

Grabbing his junk, he rushed from the room. The bathroom door slammed a second later and I heard the shower come back on. I laughed, but then let out a little moan when I got to thinking about what he was doing in there, touching himself and sliding his warm hand up and down his thick, wet, slick—

So, yeah . . . I went ahead and touched myself for real. I finished about the same time he did because he cautiously poked his head into the room when I was still coming down off my high.

"Are you done fucking teasing me yet?"

I grinned and nodded. "Please enter."

"Jesus." He shook his head and strode naked to the dresser. "If only you'd said that *before* I took a second shower." When I snickered, he shook his head. "That was really low."

I couldn't feel guilty, though, because I felt too good. "But don't you feel a lot better now?"

He speared me with a glare as he jerked his jeans on. "I'd feel better if I could've done that *inside* you."

Even though I was completely satiated, my body heated again. "Maybe someday," I said.

His gaze flooded with misery, but he nodded. "Yeah. Maybe."

That night, he was beyond restless when he got home from the garage. He played with the babies while I finished supper, but he kept popping into the kitchen and checking on me, asking if he could help with anything.

"You *are* helping." I threw my hands into the air, flabbergasted with his antsy behavior. "You're watching the kids. Now go. You're driving me insane with your pacing and fidgeting."

"I'm not fidgeting," he muttered but left me with a moment of peace.

He didn't have to work at Forbidden, so we'd be together for the rest of the night. That might've been why he was so on edge. I began to worry I'd upset him this morning. Maybe he was going to kick me out because he just couldn't handle the way I had teased him. He'd already made it clear he wouldn't touch me again. My playful temptation could've come across as not so playful to him.

Julian turned into a little butt after supper, throwing things and crying when we didn't pick them up for him fast enough. Since Skylar wasn't causing any problems, I dumped her off with Pick and focused my attention on the boy, wondering what was up with the guys in this apartment. But I guess the little boy only wanted to hog all my attention because as soon as it was just him and me, he settled down and went right to sleep. Pick carried a sleeping Skylar in a few seconds later.

But with the kiddos down for a while, that just left the two of us.

I silently followed him into the living room, but he didn't sit. He paced from one side of the room to the other.

Leaning against the hallway entrance, I watched him, knowing this was probably it. He was going to give me my walking papers, except I wouldn't go down gently. I set my hand on my hip and lifted an eyebrow. "What is *wrong* with you tonight? Sit down before you wear a hole through the carpet."

He glanced at me, his gaze intense, but then he followed my order and perched himself on the edge of the couch where he wrung his hands together between his spread knees. He was so masculine and beautiful. Regret speared through me. I was going to miss him.

"I'm getting an annulment," he blurted out, jerking me from my doldrums.

My gaze shot from his tightly clasped hands to his nearly panicked expression. "What?"

He nodded, letting me know I'd heard him correctly. "And I'm asking Tristy if I can adopt Julian."

The breath left my lungs. I shook my head. "I . . . okay." *Don't freak out.* Just because this was the very best thing he could say to me right now, there had to be a catch. Somewhere. I took another small breath to calm down. "Um, do you think she'll agree to that?"

He lifted his hands in a slight shrug. "I don't see why not. She's been gone this long and hasn't checked in on him once."

I stepped fully into the living room, letting my hope grow. "But what if she says no?"

"Then . . . nothing. Nothing changes at all. I have no rights to him now as it is. If social services came in here tonight, they'd take him away. I've looked it up online and read everything I could find. Being his stepparent in this state means nothing. I am illegally harboring that child. So, remaining married to Tristy isn't accomplishing anything either. That finally struck me today. The only thing it's doing is keeping me from you."

I gulped. "So you're doing this because of me?" *Oh my God! Yes, yes, yes!*

He surged to his feet and went back to pacing. "I'm not being fair to you, Tink. I keep thinking about what you said the first night you decided to stay on and how you were worried about us being wrong. The last thing I ever want to do is make you worry about anything. But you have it right. Kissing you, wanting you, just being here with you while I'm legally bound to another woman . . . that's not what I should be doing. I don't want to belong to her in any way when my heart is *yours*."

"Oh." The word puffed from my lips in a stunned gasp. "Oh my God." I pressed my palm to my chest, hoping that could help slow the thumping of my heart, but it didn't help at all. My blood raced with ecstasy.

Moving my fingers up to my mouth as tears filled my eyes, I let out a nervous, scared, thrilled laugh. But, oh my God. Pick *loved* me. He'd just proclaimed his love in the sweetest, most romantic way ever.

"Then we're totally asking her." I shifted toward him a step and then stopped. "It can't hurt to ask, right?"

He took a step toward me, only to stop as well. Eagerness and uncertainty filled his brown eyes. "Can't hurt at all."

"Do you know how to find her?" I moved another step closer and he countered by doing the same.

"Not physically, but I have an idea of how to get in contact with her. If she's still logged into her Facebook account on the laptop she left behind, I could message her."

Overwhelmed by the realization that we might actually end up together after all, I darted around him to the couch to sit and soak this in just as he started to reach for me. Covering my face with my hands, I focused on taking deep breaths.

"Tink?" He sat next to me, sounding worried. "Baby, what's wrong? Do you not want—?"

"Yes!" I dropped my hands to face him. "I do. I want it . . . so much."

He took my hands and rubbed his thumb over my knuckles. "Then what's wrong?"

"I just . . . " I shook my head, not sure where to start. So I blurted, "Reese was the first person I ever really loved, like, I actually care more about her than I do myself. I only want to see her happy."

"Okay." He nodded, following along with me so far and letting me know he was willing to listen.

"And then, I guess, in a lukewarm cousinly way, I love Mason too . . . because he's so good to Reese and he let me move in with them when he hated me."

That one made him scowl, so I rushed to add, "And I love Skylar. Almost as soon as I knew she existed, she wormed her way into my heart." I waved a hand. "I mean, after I was finished freaking out because I'd just found out I was going to have a baby. But yeah, I fell for her pretty much immediately. "

Pick smiled and tightened his fingers around mine.

"I love Julian too," I told him, "from, like, the first day I met him."

Drawing my hands to his mouth, Pick kissed my knuckles. "Thank you."

I nodded. "So, all this . . . *love* . . . it's really only happened within the last year. You'd think I'd be overwhelmed from it, right? I mean, I go from basically caring about no one but myself, and not even really about myself either, to completely loving four people. But I'm not overwhelmed. Not at all. In fact, I feel as if I have so much more room, because . . . " I looked up and met his beautiful brown gaze. "I love you, too."

His face filled with a dazed kind of shock and joy. Then he whispered, "Tinker Bell," before catching me by the back of the neck and hauling me against him.

Our mouths collided. I inhaled him as his lips crashed against mine. But even that wasn't enough. Not nearly enough. My fingers fumbled to grasp him, digging into the flesh at the back of his neck and over his shoulders, afraid to slow down because I needed to feel every inch of him before I lost my chance.

He was just as desperate, pulling me close, right up onto his lap. I straddled him and slid forward until I could feel his erection through his jeans as it ground against my core.

I'd never felt this carnal and delicious, as if my entire body had just become a vessel for pure pleasure. Or maybe that was Pick's feeling channeling into me, because I'd also never felt this connected to another human being before. He was me, and I was him, and we were just this beautiful twisted mass of all our hopes and dreams coming together and exploding into a dizzying array of euphoria.

"Please tell me I'm not dreaming," he broke away from my mouth to gasp, right before kissing his way down my throat and into the collar of my shirt.

"Stop reading my mind," I said and then bit his earlobe. "This feel like a dream to you?"

He groaned and threw his head back, "Fuck, yes. My favorite kind of dream."

I chuckled and decided to do to his neck what he'd done to mine. I licked my way over the tattoo of a tree root and then grew curious about the ink on his heart. Plus I wanted him shirtless.

"This is in my way."

"Then by all means." Pick was quick to grab the cloth at the back of his shirt and yank it over his head.

My vision went a little bit fuzzy at all that fine, tanned, toned naked flesh before me. I wanted all of it at once. Greedy, my fingers reached and immediately skimmed over the smooth, hard planes of his perfect canvas. And that nipple ring . . . *ooh*. I was going to have some fun with that. As Pick caught the hem of my shirt and started tugging it up, I finally focused on his one chest tattoo.

And that's pretty much when everything went to hell.

"What the . . . ?"

I pulled back so fast I started to tumble off his lap.

"Tink?" Pick caught me, but I batted his hand away as I scurried to the other end of the couch, unable to stop gaping in horror at the words inscribed on his chest.

"What's wrong, baby?"

He started to crawl toward me, his concern thick and wild. But I held up a hand to ward him off.

"You . . . your chest . . . names."

His eyes flared. "Oh, shit. I forgot." Slapping his hand over the mark, he closed his eyes and shook his head, cursing under his breath as he bowed his face.

"You forgot *what*?" I screeched. "That the name you call me is tattooed to your chest? That my *daughter's* name is . . . Oh my God. What the fuck is going on?"

His lashes parted. His eyes begged me to calm down even as he lifted his hands in a placating gesture. "Promise me you won't freak out."

Oh, that ship had sailed, buddy. "But you . . . you . . . Oh. My. God. That's not fresh ink, Pick. That's . . . This tattoo is old. It's like *years* old."

His brown eyes filled with worry as his gaze darted around my face. "Yeah."

"How the hell can you have my daughter's name tattooed to your heart for years when she's only a few months old? And Julian . . . and oh my God. *Tinker Bell?* There's another Tinker Bell in your life? All three names listed together like that is a mighty big coincidence. That *cannot* be a coincidence. The only name *not* freaking me out right now is Chloe, but I still hate her because she was obviously important to you."

"No, don't . . . I will tell you everything. I swear, Eva. But it's a . . . " He shook his head and blew out a breath. "It's a pretty crazy story, so please try to listen until the end. Okay?"

I folded my arms over my chest, and I'm sure he could tell just how upset I was. I'd pinched my mouth with displeasure and put up all kinds of walls to block him because I knew, I just *knew,* whatever he had to say was going to hurt. He had that panicked, apologetic look on his face as if he knew he'd fucked up big time. No bastard looked that way unless they knew they were about to majorly upset a woman's life.

When he just kept watching me, looking frightened, I rolled my eyes. "Okay." I waved my hand for him to start talking already.

"All right." He blew out a long breath and closed his eyes before saying, "Ten years ago, on November twentieth, Tristy tried to kill herself."

I shivered at the mention of my birthday, remembering how he had the date set as his cell phone's passcode, which only confused me more. Why the hell would a suicide attempt be such a noteworthy date? But I was a good girl and let him keep talking about how he visited the witch who'd upset Tristy, hoping to get revenge, and how he got stuck in some ankle trap she'd set up in her yard. He even hiked up his pant leg to show me the scars around the base of his foot. Then he started talking about glimpses, wedding dances, and immaculate backyards. I just stared at him, unable to—yeah, I was too dazed to say much of anything.

But in no way could I envision him as the freaky, weird kind of guy into witchcraft.

When he was done talking, he blew out another breath and said, "Well?"

I shook my head, stunned. "So, you had this *glimpse* thing when you were fourteen where saw me? You saw us get married and have three children together named Julian, Skylar, and Chloe?"

He nodded slowly. "Yeah. Well, basically. I mean, I thought they were my biological kids. They called me dad, and I . . . I felt like their father. I don't know how to describe it, exactly. It was just so real, like I was really living it, feeling it, tasting it. You smelled like lilacs, even then."

I lifted my hands to stop him because this was getting overwhelming. "Okay, just . . . slow down."

I think he was afraid to slow down, though, afraid I'd call him insane and leave his crazy ass. He kept talking. "Everything, I mean *everything*, has matched up so far. I was so pissed at Tristy for naming her kid Julian. But he's turning into my son, isn't he? And Skylar? How the hell could I predict you would name her that? Or that you'd be wearing Tinker Bell on your shirt the first night I met you? And that damn pink pig."

He motioned toward the stuffed animal I had sitting in the swing because we rarely used the swing anymore. "She was holding it in my vision, and then I saw it sitting in the hospital gift shop window the night she was born. That's not just a coincidence."

I covered my mouth with my hands as tears filled my eyes. "And you knew she'd have dark hair and a cowlick."

He nodded. "And in my vision, we dance to 'Baby Love' at our wedding reception, which just so happened to be the first song you played on the jukebox that night."

I couldn't listen to anymore. I popped to my feet and lit out of the living room as quick as I could.

22

-PICK RYAN-

I was almost too scared to go check, but I walked down the hall toward our bedroom, anyway. I just knew she'd be in there, packing all her things, scooping up Skylar and preparing to leave me.

When I reached the doorway, though, all she was doing was standing at the crib and looking down at the babies sleeping together. Sensing me, she said, without turning around, "You just had to wait until I fell in love with him before you told me, didn't you?"

Julian. She wasn't going to leave then, but not because of her feelings for me. She was only staying for my son. Pain slashed through my stomach. I leaned my forearm against the doorjamb and then pressed my face into it.

"I understand why you're unsettled and shocked. The entire thing is fucking unbelievable. That's why I didn't know how to tell you. I knew you wouldn't believe me.

You'd think I was insane, or delusional, or I don't know what."

She turned slowly. Tears had filled her eyes but they weren't falling. "Oh, I believe you."

I bit my knuckle, hating how far away from her I felt, how hard she was blocking me out. "Then why are you so mad?"

Her blue eyes flared with anger. Jabbing her finger toward the front of the apartment, she hissed so as not to wake the kids, "Because you just stood out there and told me you *loved* me, you asshole. But you don't love *me*. You love some woman you've made me up to be for the past ten years."

"Tink," I started, warning in my voice. I pushed away from the door and stepped toward her.

She held up her hand. "No. Don't you dare call me that. Don't *ever* call me that again. I am not your Tinker Bell. I'm Eva Mercer. That fucking Tink is the one you love, the woman you've built me up to be in your head. Not me."

"Bullshit," I growled as I caught her face hard in my hands. "I don't even know that woman. I saw her for thirty seconds ten fucking years ago. All I know is that I felt happy with her. Happier than I'd ever felt before. It was that feeling of peace, contentment, and satisfaction that I've been searching for. But *you*, Eva Mercer, are the one I fell for. *You* were the one who came to my home to save my ass and watch my little boy. *You* were the one I found sitting on the floor, playing with him and making him laugh. And it's *your* beautiful caring heart that makes me so eager to race home from work each night so I can feel your soft, warm body curl up next to me in bed. So don't ever fucking tell me how I feel about you again. I know exactly how I feel. If you don't want me to call you that name again, fine. Done. But it is *this* person . . . " I placed my palm against her chest and pressed in. "*This* is the woman I love."

Her tears spilled down her cheeks. "But you probably never would've paid attention to me if it wasn't for *her*."

I shook my head, trying to clear it. It seemed incredibly strange to me that she was jealous of herself, that she could separate Tinker Bell from Eva. To me, they were one and the same, but I also understood exactly where she coming from.

"You know what," I said, throwing my hands in the air, defeated. "You're right. I probably wouldn't have."

When her face contorted with devastation, I leaned forward and gently kissed the corner of her mouth before brushing my fingers over her cheek. "You're not exactly the type of woman I usually go for, and I saw that Alec prick who fathered Skylar. I know perfectly well I'm not your type, either. So I'm going to be eternally grateful those glimpses made me pay attention to you. I never would've gotten to know you as well as I have or learned what an amazing woman you are otherwise."

She sniffed and shook her head even as she leaned toward me. "I think those glimpses are blinding you to what a vain, pretentious, selfish bitch I am."

"Shut up," I whispered and kissed her, harder this time. "No one bashes the woman I love." I slid my fingers down her cheeks to cradle her neck. "I've never been as happy as I've been since you stepped foot inside this apartment."

She caught my elbows, her eyes earnest. "I haven't either."

I pressed my forehead to hers. "Then what're we fighting about?"

"Are we fighting?" Her fingers trailed up to my shoulders.

I skimmed my lips over her jaw. "I think so. It feels like I'm trying to talk you into staying."

With a relenting sigh, she wrapped her arms around me and hugged me before nipping my jaw with her teeth. "You know I won't leave. You had me at 'bullshit.'"

I smiled and then groaned when her mouth started traveling south, down my throat. Lifting my chin to let her do whatever she liked, I swallowed when she licked her way over my pulse. Her fingers smoothed along my shoulder and down my back.

I arched a brow. "So I've been blathering like an idiot about how much I love you because . . . ?"

She made a humming sound in the back of her throat,

which sent an alarming rush through me and had me harder than I already was. "Because I like listening to you blather about how much you love me."

I chuckled. "Evil woman. I'm going to have to punish you for that."

Backing her toward the bed, I let her keep kissing my neck as relief flooded me. She wasn't leaving. I probably should've stepped away and slowed the pace, not pressured her into more right after my big revelation, but her fingers were slipping down the front of my chest toward my throbbing cock.

"A spanking?" she guessed, lifting her gaze enough to slash me with a curious glance.

I shook my head, picked her up by the hips, and laid her back on the bed. Standing above her, I watched her stretch out on my sheets, looking eager and delectable.

"First," I said, bending just enough to slip off her socks. "I'm going to torture you by touching and licking you all over until you're writhing and cursing me for more." I unbuttoned the top clasp of her blue jeans and licked my lips. "And then I'm going to lick you and touch you even longer."

"Oh, God." She arched her hips and lifted them to help me when I hooked my fingers in the waistline and drew the jeans down her legs, but I paused when I reached her knees.

Keeping her legs trapped in the denim confines, I leaned in and pressed my mouth to her mound, right through her pristine pink panties. With a gasp, she bucked up and grabbed two fistfuls of my hair. I nipped lightly at her hipbone, then I used the tip of my nose to cruise my way up along her ribs, bunching up her shirt as I went.

"Here," I murmured when it caught on the swell of her breasts, "let me help you take this off."

When I had her down to her bra and panties with her pants still clinging around her knees, I skimmed some kisses around her lace-covered breasts. Crawling above her and bracing my weight on my forearms, I framed either side of her face.

"Hi," I said, grinning down at her.

She grinned back and touched my face. "Hi, yourself. I don't think you got my jeans all the way off yet."

I winked. "For now, they're right where I want them." Leaning in close to her ear, I whispered, "It's all part of your torture."

She shivered, and I kissed her. Our mouths melted together. Her lips opened under mine, and my tongue skimmed alongside hers. Under me, her body rose up, trying to rub against mine, so I lowered my hips to hers, and she whimpered, digging her fingers into my hair.

My erection ground into her, and she broke away from my mouth to gasp for breath over my shoulder.

"Oh, my. I never . . . this never . . . "

My teeth caught her ear and tugged, making her shudder and tighten her grip on my ass as she wound her arms around me. "Never what?"

She shook her head. "I don't know. I just . . . I'm not used to feeling this much. It's . . . it's . . . "

"Perfection," I finished for her.

"Yeah."

She attacked my mouth, kissing me hard, licking inside and clawing at me with her eager hands. She latched onto my lip rings with her teeth and tugged lightly.

I growled and pushed my hips deeper into hers.

"I'm beginning to see how torturous having my jeans there is. I want to wrap my legs around you so bad right now."

Me and her both. I was tempted to rip them off, as well as the rest of her clothing. But I wanted this to last.

"I wonder what it'd be like to kiss you if you had a tongue ring?" she said as she touched my eyebrow hoop.

"I'll get one tomorrow," I panted right before tangling my tongue with hers again.

We kissed forever.

Growing restless, Eva arched against me, trying to wrestle free of her jeans. "Pick, please . . . "

I couldn't take anymore, so I ripped them off and tossed them over my shoulder.

"Oh, thank God."

She immediately moved to wrap my waist with her

thighs, but I caught her hip.

"Not yet."

She groaned. "Patrick."

I smiled. "That's what I like to hear, baby. Say my name in that sexy voice."

"Pat . . . " Her head fell back as I began to kiss my way back down her body, " . . . *trick*."

I lingered around her pretty bra, buried my nose into her cleavage and inhaled her heavenly lilac scent. Then I moved on again, licking and nibbling my way down, worshipping every inch. When I reached her belly button, I dipped my tongue inside, then grasped her panties with my teeth and peeled them off. She tensed in anticipation, making me smile when she began to pet my head encouragingly. But I paused when I came across her bright red C-section scar.

I kissed my way across it before lifting my face and caressing her hip. "Your doctor has cleared you for this, right?"

She nodded, but it looked like she was holding her breath. "Yeah. Like a month ago."

Curious what had her suddenly uptight, I kept watching her as I kissed the scar again, right above her pubic line.

"You okay?" I asked.

She nodded but couldn't seem to calm down. So I crawled back up her body until we were eye to eye.

"What's up?" My question was gentle, but it still made her gnash her teeth as if upset with herself.

"I just . . . " She shook her head and gave a small laugh. "I'm getting nervous, I guess. I mean, you and I have never . . . you know . . . before. And it's all so intense and overwhelming and—"

"Hey." I cupped her cheek and pressed our foreheads together. "Don't worry. Nothing has to happen."

That seemed to distress her more, though. "But I want it to—"

I kissed her silent. Then I rested my brow back against hers, feeling so lucky to be here with her. I'd already gotten more than I'd ever thought possible from her; anything else would be gravy. "How about this? We don't think about what could come next. Don't think ahead at all. Just enjoy what *is* happening."

Her blue eyes softened with adoration. "You are the wisest man I've ever known."

"Damn straight." I kissed her again.

Her limbs relaxed under mine. Then her body melted into me and her breathing picked up. When kissing left us weak and breathless, her legs shifted restlessly. I slipped my fingers between her thighs. She gasped and tightened, but her hands clung to me, trying to draw me closer.

Dipping inside her, I shuddered and closed my eyes.

"Ah, fuck. You feel so good. So hot and wet. I want to taste this." She strained against me, her eyes squeezed shut as she threw her head back and grasped my shoulders hard.

"O...okay."

I grinned. Well, okay, then.

Eva whimpered as I lowered myself. She moaned her pleasure when I licked her, soaking my tongue with a heavenly musky flavor. My fingers continued to pump the tight warm hollow as my tongue massaged her clit, my mouth watering for more.

"Oh . . . oh . . . " She was already so close. Her arousal vibrated through me and her fragrant excitement amped me up. I wanted to bury myself deep inside that wet heat. But I wanted to feel her release against my mouth first.

"Come for me, Eva," I commanded just before I bit her sensitive little nub and pushed two fingers deep. She went crazy, pulling my hair from the roots and squeezing her thighs around my ears as she cried out a strong orgasm. I relished every second and groaned with defeat when two little voices woke from the crib.

"Damn it." I buried my face into Eva's stomach while she came down from her high. "We're moving that crib into the other room *tomorrow*."

Under me she laughed. How she could always laugh at a time like this, I'll never know. There was absolutely nothing amusing about blue balls.

"Promises, promises," she said as she squirmed out from under me to see to the kids.

I grumpily sat up and crossed my arms over my chest. She brought Julian to me because she claimed he was dry. After I took him, and she busied herself with changing Skylar's diaper, I held my son up so that we were facing eye to eye. "We need to have words, young man. You can't keep doing this. Waking up before Daddy gets his boom-boom is just not cool."

"Boom-boom?" Eva asked, her eyes twinkling as she brought Skylar to bed with us.

I shrugged. "Well, what do you want me to call it?"

"Actually, I would prefer that you not talk about sex with him at all."

"Hey, he needs to have that talk someday."

She snorted out a laugh and started to feed Skylar, which destroyed how much my body had just calmed down. My dick came right back to life. I couldn't stop staring at her luscious huge breasts on display. I might've even whimpered a little. But damn, this was so unfair.

Eva caught my crazy-eyed, desperate stare, and pity filled her gaze.

"Are you okay?"

"Hmm?" I gave her a drunk little grin as I openly kept watching. "I'm amazing," I said. "I just had the best snack of my life. Why?"

She rolled her eyes, but slid her gaze to the hard bulge still protruding from my jeans. "You didn't get anything from it, though."

I snorted. "The hell if I didn't. That was fucking awesome." I reached out and stroked Skylar's hair. "I don't think I have any condoms anyway, so . . . " I shrugged and grinned at her before giving my attention to Fighter while he tried to grab ahold of the tattoo on my chest.

"I could still do something for you," she offered, which yeah, spiked my pecker's interest immediately. "After they go back to sleep . . . "

I kissed Fighter's hair, not caring so much what happened to me. Making Eva come had been worth the pair of blue balls that followed.

"Maybe," I told her.

I actually meant to wait up and collect on what she'd offered, but I ended up falling asleep before she was finished with the babies. I stirred when Eva ran her fingers through my hair and kissed my cheek, but I only had enough energy to pull her into my arms and press her back into my chest as I mumbled, "Sleep."

We had the rest of our lives to finish what we'd started. With an annulment on the horizon and Julian's adoption to start, it was a life I looked forward to.

23

I had to work late at Forbidden for the rest of the week. Any free time I saw Eva, she was either passed out asleep or had her hands full of kids.

But whenever our gazes met across the room, the sparks arcing between us grew almost toxic. She'd smile and bite her lip and tuck her hair behind her ear before glancing away with a heated flush. Then I'd chuckle at her obvious anticipation of the next time we could be alone together, and I'd have to bite the inside of *my* mouth to hold in my own groan of anticipation.

The next free evening I didn't have to work was Friday. Call me presumptuous or too hopeful for my own good, but Thursday night I stocked the drawer of my nightstand after stopping by a convenience store on the way home from Forbidden.

When I checked the mail slot on my lunch break on Friday, the official letter I received had me even more anxious for alone time with my woman. I wanted to thank Eva for how amazing she'd been these last few months, though I already knew I'd never be able to show enough appreciation for everything she'd done for Julian and I. I still wanted to try, though, so I called Reese with my plans.

"Hey, it's Pick," I said when she answered.

Her return greeting sounded leery. "Hi, Pick. Everything . . . okay?" Then came the worry. "Eva? Skylar—"

"They're fine. Doing great."

"Oh." Reese's guarded tone returned. "Then . . . what's up?"

"I want to take her out," I rushed the words. "You know, just out of the apartment for a night. To . . . maybe a nice dinner or something. Pay her back for how much she's helped me and Julian. I don't know what we would've done without her. The babysitting money I give her is nothing compared to what I really owe her. So I was thinking something extra . . . a night out, away from the kids, would be better than nothing. It'd be a start."

Reese paused before responding to my big, long explanation, and I chewed on my lip rings, thinking she'd come up with a perfectly logical reason why my idea was ridiculous. But instead, she said, "That's so sweet. What a good idea."

"Really?" *Thank God.* "So, you'll babysit?"

"What?" The adoration dropped from her voice. "You mean, both babies? Together?"

My eyebrows wrinkled. Why did she make that sound so unreasonable? "Yeah. Would that be a problem?"

"No. Well . . . I just . . . I'm not Eva. She makes taking on two babies at once look easy. But me? One teeny tiny, kid, okay. I could swing that. I think. But two of them, so close to the same age, so young. What if I—"

"You'll do fine. Lowe's not working tonight either, is he? Make him come along to help. And you have my cell phone number. You could call anytime."

"Oh, good idea. I hadn't thought of dragging Mason along. Okay, then. What time?"

Whew. Mission accomplished. Mind switching gears, I said, "Uh . . . I get off work at the garage at five. So . . .

maybe five-thirty? That'd give me a minute to clean up."

"*Pff.* You boys and your minute clean-up jobs. It's just not fair. Takes us women a good hour to prepare for a special evening out."

I grinned. "Yeah, but we guys don't look nearly as nice as you ladies do after all the preparation you put in, so I'm saying it's time well spent."

"Mm-hmm. No wonder E.'s so sweet on you. You do have a way with the compliments. But anyway, I'll bring something nice for her to wear. She'd be pissed if she knew I was in on her surprise date, and I let her go out with old rags on."

"It's not a date," I was quick to correct. "No, just dinner—"

"And dancing," Reese cut in. "And maybe a moon-lit stroll on the beach. A little messing around over the clothes and—"

"Okay, smart ass. Enough." I rolled my eyes. "But we're not going to *call* it that. Unless she wants to."

"Whatever you say, boss. I'll arrive for babysitting duty at seventeen hundred hours, sharp. Affirmative?"

I hung up, shaking my head. Lowe definitely had his hands full with that one.

-EVA MERCER-

I seriously dug being Nanny Mercer. I was proud of the routine I finally had down, because it hadn't been easy to perfect.

Typically, I was up at seven with Skylar, the morning bird. About the time she went down for her early morning nap, Julian would finally open his bleary little eyes. He'd help me around the apartment; there was always something for us to clean or fix. By the time lunch rolled around, Skylar was awake again. Feeding both of them took some serious energy. One of them would always get cranky if I placed too much attention on the other. But then they gave me a break when they took their afternoon nap together. And that's when I'd nap, too, or squeeze in a quick shower.

It was about time for them both to wake from their afternoon siesta when a knock came on Pick's front door. I had answered the phone for him over the past few weeks, fielding off telemarketers, but no one had come knocking before.

I checked the peephole, except whoever stood on the other side was too close and I could only make out the top side of a gray head of hair. Wondering if it was some relative of Pick's, momentarily forgetting he'd been in foster care because he had no relatives, I unbolted all the locks and eased open the door.

I had it cracked about a foot when the caller finally turned and smiled pleasantly at me. "Hello, Eva."

I gasped. "Oh my God." When I tried to slam the door shut, he jutted out his foot and wedged a glossy black loafer into the jamb.

"Now, sweetheart. That's no way to greet your father."

"You're not my fucking father." When he just smiled his evil smile, I whimpered. Breathing hard, I tried to concentrate, calm myself so I could rationalize my way out of this. "What do you want?"

"I want you to open the door and let me come inside like a big, grown-up girl before we garner the attention of all your neighbors."

"How about you just leave me the hell alone instead?"

He made a *tsking* sound with his tongue and shook his head. "You owe me more than that."

My jaw fell open. "Like hell."

His eyes hardened, but his smile remained calm and pleasant, which always meant I needed to be on my guard the most. "You're still on our insurance plan, you know. How do you think you paid for that hospital bill of yours?"

Oh, God. I hadn't even thought of that. I was such a stupid, stupid girl. I'd been so sure I'd severed all ties with Bradshaw and Madeline Mercer. But I'd missed one of the biggest cords.

"Or were you planning on reimbursing me?" Shaw

went on. "With your *babysitting* salary? Three weeks in NICU's not cheap, you know."

Giving up the pressure I was applying to the door, I regretfully stepped back and let him enter Pick's apartment. He passed over the threshold, looking ridiculously out of place in his slick, Gucci suit. After sending a dismissive glance over the front room, he smoothed his hand over his blazer and turned to me.

I folded my arms over my chest and glared. "Do you accept payments?"

Here came the evil, calculating smile I was so used to. "Why, yes, I do. But not in monetary form."

When his gaze settled over my milk-laden breasts I couldn't keep completely hidden under my arms, I snorted. "You're still a disgusting old lecher, aren't you?"

With a sigh, he shook his head sadly, clearly disappointed in me. "And here I'd come to thank you for the gift you sent me."

"Gift?" I frowned, instantly suspicious.

"What? Don't you remember sending Patricia Garrison my way a couple months back?"

Oh, shit. My eyes flew open wide. I had no idea the rapist of Mason would actually follow my advice and approach my father. This was not good. Two evil people like that, teaming up—

"I very much appreciated the toy, sweetheart. But I'm afraid I may have broken her."

"You . . . ?" Dear God almighty, what had he done to Mrs. Garrison? Wait. I didn't care. If she was broken—whatever that meant—hopefully she was out of the way forever.

"Some ladies just can't take a little rough treatment. They certainly don't make women as hearty as you and your mother every day. Eventually, the others always give up the fight and let me have my way. But not you. Never you. I still remember the way you'd glare up at me with all that fire and spirit in your eyes and your chin held high after I bent you over—"

"*Please* don't tell me you're here just to reminisce because I'd rather vomit all over your pretty new shoes." In fact, I just might anyway. But hell, if I'd known being defiant when he'd molested me had only turned him on more, I would've curled up into a ball and cowered like I'd always wanted to.

My skin was cold and my nerves were strung out. I didn't know what I'd do if one of the babies woke up. I did not want this monster anywhere near Skylar or Julian.

"What the hell do you want from me?"

"I want you to come home, of course."

I snorted. "You're delusional. I'm never stepping foot in that place again."

He spread his arms and laughed. "You'd rather stay *here*? With the metal-faced, tattooed idiot? Really, Eva? I don't buy that."

It made my stomach churn all the harder to realize he knew who Pick was. He probably knew every secret Pick had and how to hurt him. Oh, God. What had I gotten my sweet, innocent, metal-faced, tattooed boy into?

Lifting my chin, I sneered, "Pick Ryan is a hundred times the man you could ever be."

My statement only amused him. Then it struck me how he liked it when I was bold and defiant. I instantly stepped back, scowling.

"Why do you even want me? *You* kicked me out remember? Because of Skylar? And what about *her*? Or are you still planning on trying to make me get rid of her?"

Good luck with that, old man.

He merely shrugged. "Your mother and I decided you can keep the child. At least it comes from good Worthington stock. But it turns out having a missing daughter is much more unseemly than one who gives birth young and out of wedlock. So, you're allowed to return. We'll just set you up in the room over the garage where Reese stayed, so the crying won't bother us."

"So gracious of you," I sneered. "But I respectfully decline your offer. Thank you." Then I nodded my chin toward the exit. "You may go now."

His chuckle was still amused. "Come now, darling. You can't tell me you don't miss your old lifestyle."

I shook my head. "Not even a little."

"I'll raise your allowance. Double it, even."

"Fuck. You."

"God, I've missed your dirty mouth." When he reached for me, I squeaked and jumped back.

"What're you doing? *Get out!*"

He prowled after me, his eyes crazed with arousal. "No one fights back like you do, Eva. I crave the way you claw and bite."

Oh, God. Oh, God. Oh, God. I was so sure I'd escaped him for good, that I'd never have to endure another one of his visits again.

That it was happening here—in the place where I'd laughed, and loved, and felt more at home than I'd ever felt anywhere—was even more traumatic.

"You'll have to hump my cold dead body before you ever touch me again. Because I will fight you until one of us is dead."

"Great." His eyes gleamed with sadistic pleasure. "That's just the way I like it. It's no wonder I can never control my urges around you."

When he lunged, I skipped to the side, and then took off running. As I entered the hall, I realized I was leading him straight to the babies. I'd hoped to reach a room and slam the door in his face, hole myself up and lock him out until Pick came home. But it was too risky, so I veered into the kitchen instead.

I was going to have to give him what he wanted. I was going to have to fight.

-PICK RYAN-

Reese must've been looking forward to this evening just as much as I was. She was already at my place, waiting outside the front of the building with Mason when I made it home from work.

"You're early," I said as I approached, breathless and antsy.

She bounced forward with a smile and a gray garment

bag folded over her arm. "Hey, I was a good girl and stayed out here until you got home so I couldn't ruin the surprise. But seriously, E. may want to primp. This is the first night she's been out since Skylar was born. I have three outfits for her to choose from, and a couple pairs of shoes."

I shook my head and glanced at Mason whose arms were piled down with shoe boxes. "Chicks."

He sent me a dry look over the top of them. "Oh, you don't have to tell me."

Reese sniffed as she followed me into the lobby. "I'm going to ignore your masculine comments because I'm awesome like that," Then she bumped her hip into mine. "So, where're you taking her? You know her favorite is Italian, right?"

I smiled, because I did know. "I was thinking of Luigi's down on the Plaza."

Reese clapped and sent me an approving grin. "Perfect. She'll love that." She chattered all the way up the steps to the third floor, telling me how she wanted to do Eva's hair and how she'd downloaded the perfect song onto her iPhone to dance to with Julian.

"I can't wait until Skylar's old enough for me to play with her hair. I am going to buy her so many bows and barrettes."

I paused to unlock my front door, only to frown when I found it already unlocked. "Huh. That's strange." I pushed it open. The first thing I heard was both Fighter and Skylar crying down the hall in our room.

A chill raced down my spine. I hadn't come home to a crying baby since the day Tristy had taken off and abandoned Julian. Jesus. Eva wouldn't have left and deserted my babies.

Would she?

I started for the hallway when I heard her scream.

"Pic—" The shriek was cut short before something clanged to the floor in the kitchen and the sounds of struggling followed.

"*Eva.*" I bolted in that direction and skidded to the opening.

The sight before me was what nightmares were made

of. Some dead bastard—because I was going to kill him—wearing a fucking three-piece suit was struggling with her and fighting for possession of a chopping knife as he pinned her against the refrigerator. Tears streaked down her face, where one side was bruised and swelling from her forehead down to her cheek. The neckline of her shirt was torn and claw marks had been raked across her neck.

Launching myself forward, I grabbed the old fucker's wrist and wrenched it, satisfied when I heard a snap and he cried out. As the blade dropped from his broken hand, I hauled him off Eva and spun him away, shoving him into the cabinets and making the back of his head crack against wood.

While he was still dazed from that blow, I landed another into his face and then one into his gut, only to realize he'd undone his belt and the top button of his pants.

"Oh, fucker. You are dead."

After another punch, his blood flew, but hands and arms wrapped around me and yanked me back. Mason and Eva's voices buzzed in my ears. I resisted, but when a sobbing Eva wormed her way between me and the guy I was trying to kill, plastering herself to my front, it was impossible to fight around her without hurting her.

Mason backed me against the far wall, but I could still see the bastard as he shook his head, then cupped his face and wiped blood from his nose. I recognized him. The rich douche from the shop who'd come in with a flat tire on his Bentley. For some reason, that pissed me off even more. Made me think he'd targeted Eva specifically.

So I tried to surge forward to get back at him, but Eva was desperate to keep me away.

"Please," she begged. "No, Pick, no. You can't. You have no idea what he's capable of. He could destroy you. Please." She buried her face in my neck, her tears wetting my skin.

Shock made me suck in a breath. I couldn't believe she actually knew this creep. "Who the fuck is he?"

"Her father," Reese answered me from the kitchen doorway where she stood pale-faced and frozen, gaping at her uncle from a pile of spilled shoe boxes littering the floor around her feet and the garment bag she clutched to her chest.

24

-PICK RYAN-

At the sound of his niece's voice, the Bentley prick spun toward Reese.

Her gaze dipped to his open belt. "Uncle *Shaw*?" With a sob, she dropped the garment bag and covered her mouth with both hands as she backed up a step.

I looked down at Eva just as she glanced up at me. The loss in her eyes explained everything, all the sorrow, shame, and regret. Her expression told me exactly who'd been brutalizing her for years.

"Oh, fuck," I whispered.

Her eyes widened. "Pick." She placed her sweet fingers on my cheeks, keeping my focus on her and no one else. "Please, don't."

I vibrated from my rage. I wanted to rip apart the monster who'd terrorized my Tinker Bell.

But fuck. Her own *father*? I fisted my hands and squeezed my eyes closed, trying to obey her pleas. It seemed vital to her that I not pound him into nothing, but God, I wanted to so bad. I even had to jiggle my knee to alleviate some of the aggression thrumming through me.

"Reese, you saw nothing," the dick was saying, his voice making me twitch, craving to charge him. "I could destroy you, got that? If you say anything to anyone, I'll destroy you *and* your little prostitute boyfriend over there."

Reese gasped and went sheet-white while Mason flinched against me. Eva kept staring at me, begging with her gaze, asking me to stay calm. I pressed my forehead to hers and attempted to focus on nothing but her.

But her fucker of a father had to point at me next. "And *you*. You'll pay for putting your dirty, greased-stained, orphaned hands on me."

I probably should've been shocked he knew so much about me. But I was more eager to beat him to a pulp. "Bring it," I said. I would love to—

"No," Eva moaned. She clutched me tighter and pressed her cheek to my chest.

A growl worked up my throat. Damn it. Why didn't she want me to hurt him for her?

Somehow barely respecting her wishes, I kept staring at her father without losing it. Not sure how I accomplished that, but I impressed myself with my own ability to tether in my emotions, even though I could still hear my kids down the hall, wailing for us.

"Get the fuck out of my house," I snarled.

Her father narrowed his eyes. Fucker didn't like being told what to do, did he? Too bad. This was my domain right here.

Finally, his lips twitched as if amused. When his gaze shifted to Eva, I wanted to pluck his eyeballs from his head for even daring to look at her.

"I'll go," he murmured. "For now." Then he turned on his heel.

Reese stood in his path. Realizing he needed by her to get out, she leapt out of his way with a gasp and darted toward us, tripping over spilled shoes in her haste. Mason let go of me to snatch her up and pull her against him. Free of Lowe's restraining hands, I wrapped both my arms around Eva, kissing her hair and breathing in her scent.

As soon as we heard the front door close at his departure, she wiggled out of my arms, and took off down the hall toward our bedroom. When the babies quieted a few seconds later, I finally couldn't contain my aggression a second longer.

I reared back my arm and punched the refrigerator. Twice. The burst of pain that came as I split my knuckles open actually felt good and relieving.

"Oh my God," Reese moaned, pulling away from Mason to pace in a tight circle. She buried her fingers in her hair as she tried to grasp what had just happened. "That was . . . oh my God. Her own father . . . *Uncle Shaw* was . . . he was trying to . . . "

When she looked to Mason and me as if seeking help, I looked away and gritted my teeth.

"You knew," she realized, staring at me hard. Her mouth fell open. "You . . . but . . . " She shook her head. "When did he . . . how long . . . why did she never tell me?"

"Sweet Pea," Mason started, sympathy ruling his tone.

But Reese held up her hand, warding him off as she stared at me. "Pick?"

"What?" I snapped back, scowling at her. "What do you want me to say?"

"I want you to say I'm wrong," she cried. "Tell me I did not see my uncle just try to rape my cousin. Oh my God. My cousin. My best friend. My—" Tears filled her eyes. "Holy shit, that wasn't the first time either, was it? Holy . . . oh . . . God. I think I'm going to be sick." She cradled her stomach as her tears fell harder. "How could you know that and not say anything? He came to our apartment, looking for her. He came to me and I . . . I *told* him where she was. I never would've done that if I'd . . . if . . . *Mason.*" Turning to her man, she hurried to him.

He wrapped his arms around her, kissing her hair and murmuring, "It's okay, baby. It's okay."

Pushing back enough to gape at him, she squawked, "Okay? How is this *okay*? He . . . he . . . to *Eva*."

Mason didn't have an answer, so he just pulled her against him tighter and forced her to bury her face against his chest.

As I watched her knuckles go white from how tightly she clutched his shirt, I tried to reassure her. "I didn't know," I said. "Not *who*, anyway. Not until just now."

She sniffed and wiped her nose with the back of her hand. "But you knew someone had . . . ?" When she couldn't finish the question, I nodded. Confusion clouded her expression. "Why would she tell you and not me?"

"She didn't tell me. I figured it out."

"Oh, great." Reese threw her hands into the air with disgust, almost taking Mason's eye out in the process. "So I was just too stupid to realize it myself?"

Spinning away from us, she raced from the room.

"Reese," I growled. "Don't—" When she didn't listen to me, I shot Mason a glower. "Will you stop her? Tink doesn't need a big inquisition right now."

He cursed under his breath but hurried after his girlfriend.

Alone in the kitchen, I took a moment to clear my head. I bent at the waist and blew out a long, hard breath. But raised voices—okay, fine, just Reese's voice—coming from the bedroom compelled me to head that way.

"Does Aunt Mads know?" Reese was demanding as I paused at the doorway and watched Eva sitting on the bed, her arms full of both Skylar and Julian as she rocked them comfortingly back and forth. They clutched onto her for dear life, but I noticed she was clutching onto them just as much. It made my guts tighten, knowing I hadn't been here to save them from this scare. Then my jealousy spiked because she was seeking comfort from them, not me.

Damn it. Why hadn't I taken off work a few minutes early?

"We should tell her," Reese was encouraging, bobbing her head vigorously. "We'll call her right now."

She pulled out her phone before Eva murmured, "Ree Ree, stop. She knows."

"What?" Reese yelled.

"Shh. Don't raise your voice. The babies are still spooked." She glanced accusingly at me before turning back to her cousin. "What're you doing here anyway?"

Reese was too agitated to answer, mumbling, "How could she know this and not . . . how could she stay with him and . . . oh my God." She clutched her face as her eyes went wide. "She's as evil as he is. I can't believe there's that kind of evil in my bloodline."

Answering Eva's question for her, I told Tinker Bell, "They were here to babysit. I was going to take you out tonight. Give you a break from the rug rats."

Her gaze slid my way and she blinked as if trying to keep herself from crying. Finally, she glanced away and her voice rasped. "Thank you. That's . . . sweet, but I don't . . . I don't really feel like going out tonight."

I pressed my back to the doorframe, bumping my spine against it harder than I needed to, seeking more nips of pain to keep my anger in check. I was still so tempted to race from the apartment and hunt down her father.

"How long has this been going on?" Reese demanded.

Eva shook her head. "You don't want to know the answer to that."

Shoulders curling in around herself, Reese started crying all over again. "I can't believe this is happening. I can't . . . why didn't you ever tell me?"

"Because I knew you'd react this way." When Eva's voice went sharp with agitation, the babies responded, whimpering fitfully.

I pushed away from the doorway and went to them. "Give me Skylar."

Eva didn't seem to want to at first, but when she realized she couldn't soothe both kids at once, she finally relented. I took the little girl into my arms and held her close to my face, closing my eyes and making a silent promise that nothing and no one would ever do to her what had been done to her mother. Not over my cold dead body.

Watching me as I settled next to Eva on the bed so she could still be close to her daughter, Reese's eyes lit with horror. "Oh, shit. She's not . . . *He's* not Skylar's father, is he? Uncle Shaw?"

"No," Eva instantly answered. "Alec is her father. Not that he's a much better candidate."

"Are you su—"

"I'm positive, Ree Ree. I was sixteen the last time Bradshaw . . . caught me unaware."

Reese gagged and slapped her hand over her mouth. Then she surged forward to sit on the bed and throw her arms around Eva. Sobbing and unable to stop apologizing, she made a mess all over Fighter and Tink. "I'm so sorry, E. If only I knew, I'd . . . I'd have been there for you. I would've driven to Florida and stole you away from that house. Jesus, I can't believe even Aunt Mads..." She shook her head and bawled some more.

I glanced toward Mason who was silent and solemn. Leaning against the wall, he watched the cousins hug with sad empathy as if he understood Eva's plight. It reminded me of that cougar's visit to the bar, and the word Eva's father had called him. *Prostitute.*

When he caught me studying him, he glanced away guiltily, his throat working while he swallowed.

Reese wanted to stay; she clung close to Eva. But Eva kept shooing her off. "I really just want to be alone with the babies right now. I . . . I just need some space."

Her cousin finally peeled herself away, but I could tell from her face that she didn't want to leave. She gave Eva one last hug, and Mason shocked the shit out of me when he stepped forward to hug Eva too.

"This explains a lot," he said as he pulled away.

Eva smiled sadly. "I guess you and I share more similarities than you ever thought, huh?"

He didn't answer, just solemnly took Reese's hand and led her from the apartment.

After the door closed behind them, I caught Eva's gaze. "You're crazy if you think *I'm* leaving you alone in this apartment right now."

I didn't mean to be rude, but I had to put that out there. No fucking way was I leaving her alone.

She smiled softly and rested her cheek on top of Julian's head. "I don't want you to go. I just couldn't say that in front of Reese. Might hurt her feelings if she knew I wanted you here and not her."

My gaze pierced hers. Even though I knew her reasoning probably had nothing to do with who she cared for more, my chest filled with a crazy kind of pride. But I had to guess, "Because you knew I wouldn't ask questions?"

She bit her lip and dropped her gaze before nodding.

I nodded too. Didn't matter why she wanted me, I was just glad she did. I stood and put Skylar in the crib. Then I took Julian from her and put him down too. They were both still awake, but they'd settled enough to lie contently by themselves for a minute.

Turning back to Eva, I held out a hand. "Let's get you cleaned up."

She frowned in confusion before looking down and seeing how torn her shirt was. Dried blood clung to her skin from a scrape on her arm and the backs of her hands bore more marks. Nodding, she took my fingers.

I led her into the bathroom and had her sit on the edge of the sink. Then I wetted a washcloth and dabbed at the cut on her lip first. After cleaning the scratch on her shoulder, hands, and along her neck where her torn top revealed the deepest marks, I leaned in to kiss the worst cut before gently applying a bandage.

She sucked in a breath and looked up at me. "You're being extremely cool about all this."

I snorted out an amused laugh. "You're the one who told me to simmer down."

"So you really don't feel as calm as you're acting?"

I shook my head and studied the bruise forming on her forehead. "Not even a little."

"Well, you put on a good show."

"Thanks." Reaching around to the back of her skull where her father had cracked it against the refrigerator, I winced. There was a decent-sized goose egg back there, but at least the skin hadn't broken open.

"What about you?" I finally asked, studying her eyes for signs of dilated pupils. "You okay?"

"Oh, you know . . . " She shrugged and lifted a nonchalant hand. "Reese, the one person on earth I never wanted to find out about all this, just found out, so . . . no. No, I'm not okay at all." Her chin trembled and she bit her lip to stop it.

I nodded, completely understanding. She was putting on just as good a show as I was. "So . . . your dad, huh?"

Glancing away, she sniffed. "He's not really my dad. The night he found out from my mom that I actually belonged to someone else was the first night he, you know, visited my room."

I swallowed the bile that rose in my throat and blew out a hard breath through my nose.

Shaking my head, I said, "I don't care if he was blood or not, he was still your father." Still a sick, disgusting motherfucker.

Her face fell and her shoulders shrank in around her body as she hugged herself. "I know." Her voice was so small and her expression so defeated. This was not my strong, sassy Tinker Bell.

I hated what that bastard had done to her and was still doing to her.

My breathing picked up. I lifted my hands to my head and buried my fingers in my hair as I coasted right back onto the edge of uncontrollable fury.

"Fuck, Eva. I can't handle this, knowing what happened to you and not being able to do anything about it because it's already over and done. I want to hurt him. I want to hunt him down and hurt him so bad. If I could just get my hands around his neck . . . " I lifted my fingers, all ten of them tensed and curled, eager to constrict.

Eva caught them and lifted them to her mouth. "Just breathe," she instructed as she kissed the dried blood on my knuckles.

"I can't," I bit out. "All I can do is see him pinning you in the kitchen and—"

She kissed me.

Her mouth against mine. It was . . . yeah. Everything. I closed my eyes and sank into her, cupping her face and lifting her chin so our lips aligned perfectly. It might've

297

been dry and closed-mouth, but it was still a perfect kiss and tugged up all these feelings I had for her from the bottom of my soul.

"Better?" she asked as she slowly pulled away.

I kept my eyes closed, reliving that kiss in my head as I swayed forward. "Um, I don't think so. Maybe you should try kissing me some more."

Puffing out a light laugh, she rested her cheek against my neck and hugged me.

I stroked her hair, and pulled her closer as the urge to protect her flared hotter. "If I ever find him near you again, I'll kill him. I won't be able to help it."

"Pick, I was serious when I said he could destroy you. He'll learn all your weaknesses and find a way to use them against you."

Remembering how he already knew I was an orphan, I didn't doubt her. He was probably a very powerful shithead. But the knowledge didn't scare me. I pressed my lips to Eva's temple. "You're my only weakness."

She sighed as if she knew she wasn't getting through to me enough to intimidate me, not until Julian and Skylar started crying from the bedroom. Then she pulled back and looked up at me with a steady, probing gaze. "You sure about that?"

My eyes widened as my chest caved in around my heart with instant dread. "He wouldn't. They're only babies."

Her laugh was bitter. "What? A man who started raping his daughter when she was twelve? Oh, I think he would. He uses every available resource he can against his enemies to take them down and get what he wants. Even innocent little babies."

I closed my eyes and gritted my teeth. "*Twelve*?" I whispered, bowing my head. "You were only twelve? Jesus, Tink. That's not information that's going to stop me from going out right now and finding him to rip his worthless head right off his shoulders."

"He could make you lose Julian." She snapped her fingers. "Just like that."

My eyes flashed open. When I looked up, she studied me a moment longer before the stark, raving intimidation set in. Blowing out a breath, I slumped onto the closed lid of the toilet and buried my face in my hands. "Fuck me." I felt sick, nauseated. My head pounded as if someone was whacking a mallet against it. I swear I could even hear—

I lifted my face to realize someone really was knocking, but not on my head. On the front door. Hard.

Oh, if that fucker was back, he was dead. He couldn't use Julian against me if he was dead.

But the muted call that came from outside the apartment said, "Police. Open up."

Shit. Didn't that just figure?

Eva jerked in surprise, her eyes going wide. "What the hell?"

She obviously wasn't used to growing up in the same kind of neighborhood as I was.

Hissing a curse under my breath, I pushed to my feet. "Neighbors must've called the cops again."

Her eyes only grew wider. "Again?"

I let out a weary sigh, and smoothed my hand over her hair before kissing the bruise on her forehead. "Check on the kids. I'll take care of the police."

She nodded and moved from the bathroom. I started down the hall, wishing the night had gone how I'd initially planned it. We'd probably be getting served our meal right about now, the soft glow of candlelight setting the mood as a server refilled our glasses.

But nope, we were stuck dealing with this instead.

Reality sucked ass.

"So, what is it tonight?" The cop who'd arrested me asked as soon as I opened the door. His partner, who'd given me the 'friendly' warning last time followed him inside as I silently stepped aside for them.

"I thought I warned you what would happen if we had to keep coming here, Mr. Ryan." He looked disappointed, which bothered me more than his pissy partner's degrading sneer.

I opened my mouth to answer, but Eva exited the hall, carrying both babies. They took one look at her with the bruise swelling on her face and her blouse still torn, and that was it for me.

Pissy Cop grabbed my wrist and lifted my hand to check out my knuckles. They were still roughed up from punching Eva's dad and then the refrigerator. He sighed knowingly before he twisted his grip and spun me around until my back was to him. After capturing my other arm and holding them together, he whipped his handcuffs off his duty belt.

Fuck.

"Oh my God." Lurching forward, Eva rushed toward us. "What're you doing?"

When the nicer officer stepped into her path with his hands up to block her, she stumbled to a stop and met my gaze over his shoulder, her shock and confusion making my throat tighten with remorse. What kind of shitty life had I pulled her into by bringing her here to take care of my son?

"They think I hit you," I explained.

She snorted. "That's insane." Turning back to the good cop, she batted her long beautiful eyelashes. "Sir, you're making a huge mistake. Pick would never, *ever* hurt me, or any woman."

The cop hooking me up snickered. "That why he already has a record for assault and battery?"

Eva's mouth worked, but she didn't have a ready comeback. Her big blue eyes, registered confusion and veered my way before she turned back to the good cop. "If he was arrested due to a fight, then it was in defense of himself or someone else, but my guess would be someone else. I *know* this man." She jabbed her chin in my direction. "And he is the furthest thing from a woman beater as you'll ever meet."

"So, you're saying he didn't do *that* to you?"

When the cop pointed out her scratches and bruises, she faltered as if just remembering what had happened to her. A groan left her.

The cop holding me in custody lifted my mangled knuckles and added, "Think before you perjure yourself, lady."

She narrowed her eyes at him and then lifted her chin self-righteously. "Like I *said*, Pick only gets into fights to defend someone. So I hope you'll excuse him for hitting the man who forced his way into our apartment and was trying to . . . " She paused and had to swallow before shakily adding, "rape me. Pick was my *hero*, not my tormentor. He saved me."

"Someone broke in, huh?" Pissy Cop asked, totally not buying it.

She must not have liked his tone of voice because she snapped, "That's what I just said, isn't it?"

"Tink," I warned. She'd get hooked up too if she wasn't careful. "Easy, babe."

She spun toward me, her heated blue eyes flashing. "What? He's being a total dick. Why the hell are they arresting you when *we're* the victims here?"

"If someone broke into your home, then why didn't you call us instead of leaving it to complaining neighbors?"

"And why isn't there sign of forced entry?" Pissy Cop motioned toward the opened door of the apartment.

Eva's gaze dropped to the perfectly intact doorjamb. Her eyes glazed with horror. My gut twisted, pissed these fuckers were making her relive what had happened.

"We were busy trying to calm the babies after Pick threw him out. You showed up before we had a chance. Thanks for your quick response time, by the way."

Neither cop cared for her dry appreciation. "And the doorjamb?" Pissy Cop prodded.

Across the hall, the neighbor's door cracked open a few inches. "He wore a fancy suit," a timid voice from inside said.

The good cop stepped toward the hallway. "What was that?"

"The guy who showed up wore a real nice suit. He knocked on the door and she opened it for him."

I ground my teeth, wishing to hell the snoopy neighbor would shut the fuck up.

But the witness's account kept flooding across the hall. "She told him to leave and tried to shut the door in his face, but he stuck out his foot, stopping her, and finally got his way inside."

I drew in a sharp breath. "That son of a bitch," I muttered, wanting to find Eva's father all over again.

And kill him at least three or four times.

"He was only in there a few minutes. Something banged against the wall once and there was shouting inside. Then this one came home." A finger appeared from the crack, pointing at me. "He had a couple with him. They all went inside. More shouting and banging followed. Then the fancy guy limped out, holding his side with one arm and his pants up with the other hand because they were unbuttoned. The other couple left a few minutes later. They looked upset."

Suddenly believers, the cops turned to Eva. "Did you know who he was?"

She hesitated before shaking her head. Then her gaze slid to me, her eyes begging me to back her up. "I'd never seen him before in my life."

"He had an old scar slashed across his cheek," I said helpfully.

Eva shifted the babies in her arms as if they were growing heavy, but her attention was focused on me.

"Anything else?" The good cop asked, tugging a notepad from his front pocket.

I shrugged, holding Eva's stare. "Like the neighbor said, he was in a fancy suit. I didn't notice much else, except he was white, mid-fifties, gray hair. Frankly, I wasn't paying much attention to detail because I was busy trying to rein in my temper enough to not kill him for touching her."

"Pick saved my life tonight." Eva shivered and kissed the top of Julian's head before she snuggled her cheek against Skylar's. "And maybe the lives of my babies, too. That guy just . . . he had a crazy look in his eyes."

From there on, we were deemed innocent. The cops asked a few more questions. I let Eva answer. And she rushed to me as soon as they took the handcuffs off. I lifted Fighter from one of her arms, and hugged the four of us together.

Pissy Cop left first. The other lingered a second longer, his gaze on Eva before he glanced at me. "Traded up, huh?"

My lips twitched as I looked at Eva. "Hell yeah, I did. And the other one left her kid with me, so I got the best of both worlds."

The cop chuckled and started from the apartment. "Don't forget to call if that guy shows up again."

"Will do." After I shut the door behind him, I rested my back against it, blew out a breath, and met Eva's gaze.

"Well, shit," she said, rocking Skylar in her arms. "That was definitely a first for me."

I have no idea why I thought that was funny, but I threw my head back and laughed.

25

-EVA MERCER-

We didn't get the kids to bed until almost an hour after their usual bedtime. I caught Pick watching me a lot, as if he were waiting for that moment when I'd finally let the stress from the entire evening get to me and I'd fall apart. But I managed to hold it together.

When we finally slid under the covers, facing each other in the glow of the nightlight, I tucked my hands under my face and studied him across the bed as he did the same, examining me right back.

I'd been so sure the next time he had a night off, we'd finally get in some physical yumminess . . . but alas, my father had completely smothered that idea. Pick looked too scared to even touch me, which made me wonder how I'd ever gotten a kiss out of him in the bathroom earlier.

A soft smile lit his face. "What're you thinking?"

I smiled back. "I was thinking how sweet it was of you

to get a babysitter for us tonight so we could go out."

He sighed. "Yeah, well, I'm sorry that fell through. I guess that's what I get for making plans."

I reached out to stoke his cheek. Then I straightened the ring in his eyebrow. "It was the thought that impressed me."

He continued to watch me as I groomed him, combing out unruly strands of his hair next.

"We were actually going to celebrate," he said. "I received a letter in the mail today. My annulment was finalized."

I drew in a surprised gasp. "Really? So you're a single man again?"

He nodded but an odd look flooded his features. I could almost swear it was guilt. "I know it was pretty presumptuous of me to take you out on the very day I was no longer married. I'm sorry. It didn't—"

Suddenly, I realized what he felt so bad about. "Patrick Jason Ryan," I murmured in a teasing scold as I sat up. "Were you planning on getting laid tonight?"

Before he could stop me, I flung open the nightstand to find a new box of condoms inside.

Pick jerked upright, looking even guiltier than before. "Eva—"

I pulled the box free and studied it. "Aww, and you even got *ribbed for her pleasure*. How considerate."

That didn't seem to soothe his remorse, though. "I didn't mean to—"

I leaned in to kiss him, shutting him up. He tasted of surprise and the apple he'd eaten before coming to bed. I opened my mouth to taste more. The very tip of his tongue touched the very tip of mine and he groaned, starting to lean in before he yanked himself back.

"We probably shouldn't," he said, though his breathing was already thin and fast. "Not after what happened tonight."

But I caught his hand. "Do you know what he said to me once? He said it didn't matter how many other boys I had, I'd never be able to wipe away his touch. He'd stained me forever."

Pick's face turned purple with fury. "Mother fucker,"

he gritted out right before he pulled me close and pressed his forehead to mine. "He was lying, baby. You are not stained. Not at all."

I hooked my hand around the back of his neck, my gaze pleading. "But he made me believe him. I never . . . *enjoyed* an intimacy with any guy. Not until you. I just zoned out and pretty much erased every encounter from my head. When I'm with you, though, you make me feel everything. I'm beautiful, loved, and clean. I need you to make me feel that way right now. I need you to prove that bastard wrong."

When I pressed the condom box into his hand, he closed his eyes and groaned. "I love you so much." His fingers trembled as he touched my cheek.

"And I love you, Patrick. Now make me your Tinker Bell."

He opened his eyes, and the confusion on his face told me he wasn't sure how to respond since I'd ordered him to never call me that again.

"You called me Tink tonight when the cops were here," I said. "And before that in the bathroom."

"I . . . " He gulped and shook his head. "I'm sorry. I just . . . it slipped out." He closed his eyes briefly before flashing me a regretful cringe. "It won't happen again. I swear."

I shook my head. "No, it was fine. It was wonderful, actually. I've missed it." Scooting closer to him, I ran my fingers over his face, across his lip rings and down the tattoo of tree roots on his neck—roots because he'd always wanted a family and a place to belong.

Knowing *I* was his roots and his place to belong, I felt complete.

"I didn't realize the night that I learned about Tinker Bell how much of an honor it is to be her. Because I didn't understand it wouldn't just be a dream come true for you; it's a dream come true for me too. You have given me things I never even knew I needed or wanted, but they've ended up being the most precious things I've ever had. My job, this family . . . " I gestured toward the crib. "A love that completes me. All of this is because of you. Honestly, I can only think of one more thing I need from you, and my life will be perfect."

When my hand trailed down his naked chest, paused over his heart tattoo, and then continued lower, he caught my wrist gently.

"If we actually do this tonight, I'm going to stop paying you for being the nanny. Because that would just be weird. You'd be more like a . . . "

When he couldn't seem to come up with an appropriate term, I grinned. "More like a stay-at-home wife?"

His eyes flared. "Would that freak you out?"

It would probably freak Reese out if she knew about it. She'd say I was crazy, we were moving too fast, I needed to slow down and think about this. But I already knew it was the perfect solution for us.

"I am absolutely not freaked out at all. Now . . . " I caught the top of his pajama pants and began to peel them down. "Can we move on toward the main entertainment of the evening, or are you going to hold out on me forever?"

He blew out a breath and shuddered when I pulled his hard, swollen flesh into my palm. His eyes fell shut as he growled his appreciation.

"Are you absolutely positive you want to do this?" he asked, his voice tense, his restraint nearly shattered.

I flickered with sudden uncertainly, but only because his continued resistance bothered me. "Only if you're okay with having a girl who grew up being molested by her dad."

He sucked in a sharp breath and rolled toward me, dislodging my grip from him. "That has nothing to do with this. You are not dirty, Tink. Not at all. *He's* the filthy one. I'm just afraid you're trying to rush this to prove something you totally do not have to prove."

I smiled at his adamant proclamation, even more certain than ever about what I wanted from him. Curling my hands around his shoulders, I leaned in to kiss my favorite tattoo. "You just called me Tink." Lifting my face to whisper in his ear, I said, "Do it again." Then I licked his nipple ring before catching it between my teeth.

"Damn it," he growled, rolling me onto my back and hovering over me. Then he rasped, "Tinker Bell," in an achy soft voice as he cupped my cheek and gazed into my eyes. "My Tinker Bell. My soul mate."

He kissed me, closed-mouthed, his lips gentle and perfect. Then he rocked his erection against my thigh, and things got even better.

He peeled my shirt up; I peeled his pants down. He cupped my weighted breasts through my maternity bra, and I shuddered under his intense attention.

"Fuck me, I want to suck on them so bad." He swirled an index finger around my nipple, and though I could barely feel it through all the padding, they still hardened. "When the kids are done with them, they're going to be mine. You got that? I'm going to spend an entire day with my mouth on nothing but these beauties."

I whimpered and arched my back, wanting his mouth on them now. "Stop teasing and put your mouth on *something* before I combust."

"Mmm. Bossy. I like it." He leaned in to nibble at my ribcage, just under my bra line.

I grabbed his thick hair. "You're still teasing."

"And you're still bossing." Glancing up at me, he winked. "Relax, Tink. I got this." After flashing me a mischievous grin, he peeled off my panties and buried his face between my legs, but he inhaled a deep breath, smelling me, before he actually started to lick.

At the first touch of his tongue, I arched my back, gasping from the shock of pleasure. I couldn't tell what he was doing different, but it felt better than ever. I grabbed onto a handful of sheets under me. He spread my legs apart, making room for himself. Then he licked a little lower. My eyes flared with surprise as my core tightened with naughty, greedy pleasure. But then he moved up again, before I could come. His tongue flickered over my clit, and something unexpected and hard nudged it as he pushed a finger deep inside me. I began to quiver and moan, already that close.

He covered my mouth with his hand right before those clit-teasing fingers abandoned my aching channel. "Shh," he warned. "We never did move the crib. If you wake them up again tonight, we'll never make it to the best part."

I didn't like that. I wanted to verbalize how good this felt, loudly. Unable to control myself, I bit his finger.

With a curse, he yanked his bitten digit away from my teeth and deserted my pussy to climb his way up my body. "Damn it, woman. If you're going to be a biter, I guess I'll have to mute you some other way. Wrap your teeth around this." He kissed me long and hard, his tongue muffling whatever noises I made next as it spiked deep.

When I felt a clink of metal, I yanked back. "Wha. . .?"

He wiggled his eyebrows and stuck out his tongue to show me his newest piercing. "Surprise. Got it the day after you said something."

Oh, mother of God. I grabbed two handfuls of his face and yanked him back to me, playing with his tongue ring until he had to pull back and cool off, panting hard and eyeing me as if he couldn't believe I was really there.

Spotting the condom box beside us, he ripped it open. I felt obligated to help him put it on, and suddenly he was the one making all the noise with a deep groan as I rolled latex over his long, quivering, steel length.

"Okay, so I guess we both need to be muffled," he said before kissing me and fitting his hips between my thighs. I felt the head of his cock greet my opening. I was so wet and aching, I arched into it.

He caught my hip, steadying me. "This'll change everything," he broke away from my mouth to say. "Once I'm inside you, you're mine, I'm yours, and we are together. There will be no friendship and mild dating. It's going to be all or nothing."

I gazed up into his eyes. "Then make me your all."

His eyes heated. "You always were." Then he pushed inside me.

Neither of us had our mouths muffled. Slight mistake. We gasped in unison, sharing our shock as we gaped into each other's eyes, stunned by the force of our pleasure.

"Oh, damn," he breathed, looking thunderstruck. "There it is. This is that feeling I've been searching for."

From the crib, one of the babies stirred. Pick cursed under his breath and froze inside me. "No, no, no," he whispered, as he leaned his face in to bury it by my neck.

"Please, no."

Someone must've heard his prayer because both babies stayed asleep. We sighed in relief.

"We're seriously moving that crib," he growled. "Tomorrow."

I chuckled, to which he kissed me quiet. Then he pulled his hips back, only to thrust inside me again. I had to bite his lip to keep from crying out. His shook with silent laughter. I swatted his ass in reprimand for laughing at me, only to curse when the slap of my palm against flesh made way too loud of a crack in the quiet room. The shuddering of Pick's chest only increased.

"It's like we're trying not to get caught by our parents," he whispered in my ear. "Except in reverse."

This was definitely a first for me. Laughing and having fun in the middle of mind-blowing sex. But the rush of happy endorphins only seemed to make everything feel better when he moved deeper. I wound my legs around his hips to hold him there longer.

"You make me so happy," I murmured in awe.

"That's the plan, Tink." He kissed my neck and slid his hand up my thigh, before cupping my ass.

God, that felt . . . wow. Oh, yeah. Right there. I started to moan again, which got us both to laughing and groaning together, which made us kiss to hush ourselves. I loved every second. I loved the feel of his warm skin sliding against mine, and his hard flesh buried inside me; his mouth against mine as our tongues dueled for more, and his brown eyes sparkling when he met my gaze and grinned.

The craving inside me kept rising until I couldn't even remember giggling with him only seconds before because now I was clutching him and trying to keep from coming too soon. I wanted it to last, just a little longer, except my body started to tighten and quake. He kissed me harder and thrust faster. We held hands and squeezed our fingers tightly together as we both crested euphoria.

26

Two weeks passed.

Pick had been dead serious about no longer paying for my babysitting services. Instead, he set me up with a new cell phone on his plan and found an old car for me to drive around. It ran a hell of a lot better than Reese's. We really were like a married couple, and I'm sure if we'd had the opportunity, Pick and I would've turned into a pair of humping bunnies to boot.

It just figured I'd learn to like sex, right after I became a mom and never had the time for it. What was worse, Skylar got a fever, which scared the crap out of me. After two doctors' visits, and half a dozen different opinions from nurses and other mothers, we finally decided she had a sore throat.

Quarantining her away from Julian was almost impossible, but it did give Pick a reason to set up the crib in the other bedroom so Sky and I could camp out in there while he and Julian stayed in our room.

I never knew having a sick kid would be so utterly frightening. Every cough from my daughter made me frantic with worry. I was so glad to have Pick by my side through it all. His unwavering support sometimes made my chest tight with the overwhelming love he brought me.

But seriously, it'd been three days since I'd last had my wicked way with him, and that was way too long for my liking. Tonight, I didn't care how late he got home from the bar, I was going to stay up and jump his sexy bones so I could go wild animal on him, because I was most definitely in heat.

It was close to the kiddos' bedtime, and we were finishing up my new nightly yoga routine. I was giving both Skylar and Julian some tummy time so they were perfecting the reverse corpse pose and I was in the downward dog when a key in the lock made me yelp, startled.

I knew it was way too early to be Pick, so my mind immediately tracked to my father. The door was halfway open before I realized whoever it was had a key. Ergo, not Bradshaw Mercer, thank God. I started to wonder why Pick was home already when a rough-looking redhead entered.

"Whoa!" I popped to my feet, ready to drag the trespasser into the hall by her scraggly scarlet mop. Instead, she jerked to a stop when she saw me and narrowed her eyes as if I was the one who didn't belong.

"Who the hell are *you*?"

I blinked. Hey, wasn't I supposed to be the one asking that? And how did a complete stranger have a key to our apartment? Why was she coming inside as if she owned the place?

"Who're *you*?" I shot back.

"I'm Tristy. I *live* here."

My mouth fell open. Oh, hell. That was not what I was expecting to hear at all. But . . . wow.

This was Pick's wife? I mean, ex-wife. Annulled wife? Whatever.

My first jealous, selfish thought was that I was so

much prettier. But that was wrong. Wrong, wrong, wrong. I couldn't help it, though.

"Where's Pick?" When she glanced around only to settle her gaze on Julian, I stepped protectively in front of him. Ugly or not, her looking at my little boy was not cool. A spurt of panic shot through me when I realized he really wasn't my little boy, was he? He was *hers*.

Oh crap. This just got real.

Pasting on a bright smile, and totally sucking up, I said, "Hi, I'm Eva. The babysitter."

Her gaze sprang back to me. Then it narrowed.

So I nodded encouragingly. "Julian is such a sweetheart. He's been the perfect little ang—"

Her derisive snort cut me off. "You're the *babysitter*, my ass. I know who you really are." When she took an intimidating step toward me, I lifted my eyebrows. If she thought to threaten me, she better watch out. I didn't take well to threats. "You're the fucking reason my husband got an annulment. *You're* why he wants to take my baby from me and adopt him for himself. So the two of you can have your perfect little family together . . . with *my* kid?"

Well, when she put it that way, she kind of made it sound bad. Except we wanted it because we *loved* Julian. She obviously did not. She hadn't even asked about him or tried to hold him since barging through the doorway; she was too busy being a bitch.

Setting my hand in my hip, I got my attitude on and sent her an arch glare. If she wanted to play the conversation this way, I would so go there with her. I was foaming at the mouth to let my inner overprotective momma come out to verbally bitch slap this piece of work.

"*Take* your baby?" I repeated. With a dark laugh, I stepped right up into her face. "Lady, you're the one who abandoned him here in the first place. You left him alone in a house with no adult supervision whatsoever. The place could've caught fire, he could've fallen and died, been beaten to death by some . . . burglar who'd found his way in. *Anything*. But did you consider that? No. You were too busy being a fucking nasty heartless cow."

Okay, maybe I was going a little overboard, but I was too mad to think rationally. "You don't have a baby. You do not *deserve* this baby."

Yeah, I felt all good and jazzed about telling her off and saying what I'd been dying to say to her for weeks. I felt like bouncing on my toes and cracking my neck to the side like some kind of boxer preparing for a big match. I was about to go off on my Pick tangent next—telling her how shitty she'd treated him—when her face turned purple.

"That's it. I don't know who the fuck you think you are, but I gave birth to that kid. And I'm getting him away from you."

"What?" Oh, shit. That wasn't supposed to happen. "No. Wait." When she moved around me toward him, I stepped into her path and grabbed her arm. "You can't do that."

A sick nausea swirled up my nostrils until tears sprang to my eyes.

Tristy yanked her arm out of my hold and pushed me aside. As I stumbled back, she jerked him up roughly. He started crying instantly.

I leapt in front of the door and barred it with my body. "Wait, wait, wait. I'm sorry. Let's just talk this out."

"Get out of my way, bitch." Her eyes were wild. I wasn't sure she was sober. I gulped and called upon every nerve in my body to calm myself. But, oh my God, I'd never heard Julian cry like that before. It made Skylar start to cry too, and I already knew tears were pouring down my own cheeks. I just wanted scoop both my babies up and kick this piece of trash out of my home.

"Just take a breath and think about this. Think about what you're doing to Pick."

She blinked, swayed by his name. So I kept pressing that point. "He has stood by your side your entire life. He has always helped you whenever you've needed help, and you know he always will."

Her eyes were filling with tears now, too. "Oh, is *that* why he wanted the annulment, then? Why he wants to adopt Julian? To *help* me? You and that bastard must be pretty cozy if he's told you so much about me. I think he's doing this just so he can keep *fucking* you."

I ground my teeth, upset she could twist what Pick and I had into something so perverted. But I had to settle down and think of Julian. "You're wrong. Pick *is* thinking about you. He understands you need your freedom, and he's trying to give it to you. He wants to take care of your baby for you. You left him here for that reason, right? Because you knew Pick was the best person for him. And look, he's taken care of him, hasn't he?"

I motioned to Julian, but he was wailing so hard, I don't think I made a very good point. I continued begging, "The least you can do is wait here and talk to him. You owe him that much." Then, when Pick got here, he'd talk her out of taking our little boy away. I had every confidence in him. What I didn't have confidence in was myself and my ability to keep Tristy here that long.

Both children kept crying. If I went for Skylar, I knew Tristy would escape out the door, so I tried for him. I held out my arms tentatively. "Do you want me to hold him? I can get him to stop crying."

"Get the fuck back." She scurried away from me and shot me a glare. "Don't touch me."

I curled my arms back to myself. They felt empty without him.

"Okay. Let me call Pick, then. I'll call Pick, and you guys can talk." He could fix this. He knew how to deal with irrational women, this one specifically. He could get Julian back.

Indecision crossed her face. But after a moment, she gave a jerky nod. "Okay . . . okay."

It felt like the biggest gamble of my life, stepping away from the door, but I did it, my legs shaking the entire way. I scooped up Skylar, held her close and sat next to the landline phone. Three finger-shaking attempts later, I was shot straight to Pick's voice mail. My stomach roiled with unease. I left a message, and tried the club next. No answer. So I tried Mason, hoping he might be working tonight too.

Another no-*fucking*-answer.

Next, I rang Reese. She picked up in four rings.

"Please," I sobbed. "I need you."

-PICK RYAN-

It was long, dragging, obnoxiously loud night at Forbidden. Hamilton had the bar with me. He worked with quiet efficiency, so we easily filled our orders. The loud music from the jukebox, and the women dancing with all the men chasing after them was starting to give me a headache. Same damn thing every night. I just wanted to get home to my Tinker Bell and curl up around her, and maybe finally get inside her again. It'd been too long since we'd last done that. Skylar was feeling better, so maybe—

When I saw a familiar face weaving through the crowd, looking intent to worm her way through, I frowned and moved toward Reese just as she reached the bar.

"What're you doing here? Lowe's not working tonight."

"I know." Her blue eyes were large and bright as she grabbed my arm hard. "You need to get home. Right now. Mason's on his way to fill in for you."

The urgency in her voice, the fear in her eyes—I barely waved Quinn off before I was leaping over the bar and sprinting toward the exit.

I made it home in record time. I didn't realize Reese had followed me until I found her at my heels, pounding up the stairs to my apartment.

I shoved the door open as soon as I reached it. Eva paced inside the living room, clutching Skylar to her chest. For a moment, I was relieved to find her unharmed. Then I noticed how heavily she cried in great, heaving sobs. Her eyes were swollen and red, her hair a mess, her face as pale as chalk.

"What's wrong?" I crossed to her and clutched her shoulders in my hands, prepared to kill whoever had upset her. Had Skylar taken a turn for the worst? Or her father—

"He's gone," she wailed. "Oh, God. Oh, God."

"Who . . . ?" I glanced around, realizing Julian wasn't anywhere in the front room. When I turned back, the devastation on her face made my skin prickle with a new kind of horror. "Where's Fighter?"

Squeezing her eyes closed, she choked on a sob and bent forward, crying even harder. "She took him. She came in here and just . . . she took him."

"What? Who?" I shook her, needing her to focus. "Damn it, Tink. What the hell happened?"

"Tristy. She took him."

My fingers tightened reflectively. For a second, I was too scared to speak. Then I roared, "And you just *let* her?"

She yanked out of my hold and glared up at me, her tears making her blue eyes glitter with an ethereal kind of fury. "Yes, Pick, I just stepped aside and blithely let her stroll in here and take him out without a single word of protest. Fuck you! Of course, I didn't just *let* her."

She turned away and sought comfort from Reese, who immediately gathered both her and Skylar in a hug. It hurt to watch her seek solace from somebody else, making me realize how harsh I'd been.

Cursing fluidly, I clutched my hair and squeezed my eyes closed. I knew I should apologize, but Julian was gone and I couldn't get past that.

"What happened?"

Since my voice was calmer, she straightened from Reese's shoulder and pushed the tears out of her eyes. "The neighbors called the cops. She and I had yelled at each other and—"

"Yeah, yeah." I waved my hand, irritated. I knew how easy it was to get the police to our place. "What did they do?"

She shook her head, blindly. "They let her take him. What do you think they did? She's his *mother*. I had no legal right to keep him here. I even told them I'd never met her before in my life and had no proof she was really his mother. But then she supplied proof. I tried to tell them she'd left him months ago; she was unfit. Then they asked about you. I told them you were working, but I couldn't get a hold of you . . . I tried everything. I'm so sorry, Pick." She turned back to Reese, weeping solidly. "I'm so sorry."

"It's—" I wanted to tell her it was okay. I even reached out to touch her back, but I ended up pulling my hand away so I could rub my face instead, unable to get past the fact that my son was out there, with a druggie, doing God knows what. "Jesus. I gotta find them. I gotta . . . " I spun in a circle trying to think. I glanced at the girls, and met Reese's gaze, her eyes brimming with concern. "I'm gonna go find them."

I was out the door and running for the stairs before I fully collected my next breath.

-EVA MERCER-

For the first half hour, I was utterly inconsolable. Reese just held me and let me cry. She tried to take Skylar from me, but I couldn't part with another child tonight. So I made myself calm down enough to let Skylar find some rest in my arms. And that's when I started blubbering.

"It's all my fault. If only I hadn't smarted back to her. Me and my fucking big trap. I pissed her off, and she took my baby. Oh, God. Pick is never going to forgive me." I closed my eyes and tried not to pass out. "What if she hurts Julian? What if she leaves him somewhere else and—"

"Shh." Reese stroked my hair. "Don't even go there, sweetie. Don't let yourself think about that."

"But—"

"No. It's late. You're exhausted. Your daughter is exhausted. Let's get you into bed."

She tried to draw me to my feet from the couch, but I resisted. "No, I can't." I shook my head emphatically. No way could I go back to the room I had shared with Pick for the past few months. "I can't stay here. Take me home."

Reese bit her lip. "Are you sure?"

I nodded. "He must hate me right now."

"I doubt he—"

"*I lost his son, Reese.*" My chin bunched as a fresh wave of tears fell. "Please. Just take me home." Even though her apartment didn't feel like home at all. *This* was my home.

Reese granted me my wish, and drove me to her duplex. She pried a sleeping Skylar from my arms and laid her gently in the crib. Then she tugged me to my bed and lay down with me. I rested my cheek on her shoulder and stared straight ahead, numb and cold.

At some point, Mason came home from work. Appearing in the doorway, he gazed in at us.

"She okay?"

"Not yet." Reese waved him away and went back to stroking my hair.

"Do you think Pick will find him?" I asked, staring at the far wall.

"I think he'll keep looking until he does."

I closed my eyes. Yes, he would. That thought comforted me as I replayed my last few seconds with Julian. I hadn't even been able to kiss him goodbye. When the police officer finally agreed to let Tristy take him, she'd tried walking out the door without his car seat or his diaper bag. I'd stopped her and piled them on her, every diaper I had, and all the powdered formula he hadn't drank from in over a month, bottles, blankets, everything I could think of, hoping to overwhelm her into giving in and letting him stay. But the cops' presence spooked her too much. She'd strapped everything over her shoulders and ran.

I would never forget the last words she'd said before taking my son away.

After glancing me up and down with a degrading sneer, she'd hissed, "I just want you to know he'll never really love you. You're not his Tinker Bell."

I hadn't been able to resist snorting. "Oh, but I *am* his Tinker Bell."

But, was I really? I'd lost his son, and that probably

destroyed any love he'd ever felt for me. How could he ever forgive me for this? I sure as hell wouldn't be able to forgive myself.

27

-PICK RYAN-

Sore, drained, and scared out of my mind, I let myself back into my apartment in the wee hours of the morning. Without Fighter. I had looked in every crack house and heroine den I could think of, trying to find Tristy. I'd never been in tight with that crowd, but I'd stumbled across a few old acquaintances who knew her, and they'd given me a couple ideas where she might be. But every single lead was a dead end.

I had no idea where Julian was or what was happening to him. Thinking about him being hurt, scared, or alone messed with my head too much; I tried to keep those thoughts out, even though they kept crowding back in and nearly sending me into a panic.

I contacted every hospital, asking for either Tristy or him. I'd called every old friend of hers I could think of, asking them to pass along a message. But not even fucking Quick Shot had seen her in the last twenty-four hours.

I'd bombarded her Facebook page. I'd driven around for hours, and even stopped by the police station. I didn't know what else to try. I figured the next move was Tristy's, but I couldn't accept that. I couldn't wait for her to grow tired of him again. She probably wouldn't last long, not by herself like she was. She'd bring him back. Eventually. But even five minutes away from him was too excruciatingly long for me.

God, this hurt.

Needing my Tinker Bell to help ease my broken heart, I stumbled back to my bedroom only to find it empty.

"Oh . . . fuck."

She'd been hysterical, and I hadn't comforted her. Recalling the way she'd begged me to forgive her ripped through my chest. But I'd told her it was okay, hadn't I? Shit, I couldn't remember what I'd said. I'd been too frantic to find my boy. One thing I knew, though, was that I couldn't sleep in my bed without her.

I found myself knocking on Mason Lowe's door at four-thirty in the morning. It took him over a minute to pull it open, but when he saw me, he heaved out a big sigh, shook his head, and moved aside without saying a word. I stepped inside, and he followed me back to Eva's room.

I went straight to her bed and touched her shoulder, rolling her onto her back, only to realize this woman had dark hair. Next to Reese, another form stirred and the hall light made her gorgeous blonde locks glisten. Bypassing Lowe's woman, I reached for Eva and pulled her into my arms. Her lashes fluttered. When she was awake enough to focus on my face, she clutched my arm.

"Did you find him?"

I drew in a breath. "Not yet."

From the bed, Reese rose and hurried to collect Skylar from her cradle. I didn't even have to ask her, she simply bundled the sleeping infant into her car seat and then gathered up the diaper bag for us. After she nodded at me, letting me know she'd follow with the kid, I carried Eva from the room and out to my car. She didn't protest, which was good, because I didn't have any fight left inside me.

When we made it home, we put Skylar in the crib. She looked extra small in there by herself. Then we went to the front room and sat on the couch to wait. Pressed up against her and holding her hand, I squeezed Eva's fingers.

"Thank you for fighting for him," I finally said.

She didn't answer, just leaned her cheek on my shoulder and quietly cried, waiting through the rest of the night with me.

Two days passed. The two longest days of my life.

I didn't work, rarely ate, and only slept in spurts because I'd always jerk awake with a new idea of where I could look for Tristy. But she was never anywhere I searched. Reports came back to me from people who'd seen her with a baby, but I always just missed them by the time I got there.

At the beginning of the third day, my cell phone rang at two in the morning. I was instantly awake to answer the unlisted number. Next to me, Eva bolted upright and flipped on the bedside lamp, her eyes wide and alert.

"Hello?" I rushed out. *Please be Tristy, please be Tristy, please—*

"P-Pick?" Tristy's hoarse voice sounded scared and uncertain, but it made me sob out my relief.

"Oh God. Oh, thank God. Tris, where are you? Is Julian okay?"

"Julian?" she sneered after a loud sniff. "All you care about is *Julian*, isn't it? You used to ask if *I* was okay."

"Christ, Tristy. You abandoned him here, *your own son*. You fucking left him with me to take care of. So I did. Can you blame me for growing to love him? For worrying about him? Why did you take him?"

"Because he's mine! Why shouldn't I take him back? He's my kid. You annulled our marriage."

"I annulled the marriage because you took off. Now, where are you? I'll come to you, and we can talk, face to face." When she didn't answer, I closed my eyes and gritted my teeth. "Tris, please. You scared the shit out of me. These last few days, not knowing where you were, not knowing what was happening to him, they've been the worst few days of my life. Just . . . talk to me. Please . . . Tell me where you are."

"I don't believe you," she said in a hoarse voice. "See, I don't believe that's why you stopped our marriage at all."

"What?" I shook my head, utterly confused. "You're not making any sense. Why are you doing this? Where are you? Why did you leave without even talking to me first?"

"Because of that blonde slut you had in your apartment, that's why."

My gaze shot to Tink. She chewed on a thumbnail as she watched me, her blue eyes wide with worry. "What?" she mouthed.

I shook my head and returned my attention to Tris. "What about her?" I asked cautiously.

"Who was she? And why was she taking care of my son?"

"She was taking care of your son that you abandoned because she's the babysitter."

Eva sat up straighter, her thumb dropping from her mouth as she realized she was being brought into the conversation.

"I thought Mrs. Rojas was watching him."

"The Rojas got sick. I had to hire someone else. Why should this upset you? Are you saying you suddenly care what happens to him, after you fucking left him alone? It was hours before I found him that day. Jesus, Tristy, how could you do that? He's not alone now, is he? Is he there with you? Is he okay?"

"He's fine," she muttered dismissively, "and I still think you're lying. I think she's a hell of a lot more than just the babysitter."

I hissed out a curse and rubbed at a spot on the center of my forehead that was beginning to ache. "Why are we even talking about this? Are you telling me you fucking took Julian away from me because of Eva?"

Eva gasped and set her hand against her heart. Tears immediately welled in her eyes. I reached out and grabbed her fingers hard, letting her know she'd done absolutely nothing wrong.

"She told me she was your Tinker Bell."

Except maybe that.

Damn it. I squeezed my eyes closed.

I didn't let go of Eva's hand though. All she'd done was tell Tris the truth. I couldn't fault her for that. Tristy would've just come up with some other reason to overreact. She always did.

"Yeah," I said, letting go of Eva so I could climb off the bed and pace the room. "Yes, she is. So what? How does that affect anything? You left."

She sniffed. "So, it's true, then? You found her. You really found the girl that witch told you was your one true love?"

My throat went dry. Why I hated talking about this with Tristy, I don't know why, but I did. I detested it.

With a nod, I gave the rusty answer. "Yes. I did."

Her sniffles turned into full-fledged sobs. "So, it's all going to come true. You're going to go off and live with her in your perfect little happily ever after in your perfect fucking house with the green lawn. And I'm going to die, young and alone."

"Damn it, you're not going to die young and alone. Not when I'm here for you. I've always been here for you. You're the oldest friend I have, and I will take care of you and Julian no matter what. Just tell me where you are, and I'll come take care of you."

She didn't hear anything I said, though. "I always thought you'd grow to love me . . . the way you loved her. I thought . . . I thought we'd stay married, and you'd finally realize how much we belong together. We've already been through everything. We know each other inside and out. How could she fucking come along and take you away from me?"

"Tristy, please don't do this. You need help. Just . . . let me come help you."

"I don't want to be your fucking charity case anymore. I want . . . I want you to look at me and just . . .

love me already."

"I do," I said, my voice going hoarse and my entire chest tightening with fear. I didn't want to lie to her, but I absolutely could not say anything to cause her to hang up without telling me where she was. "Do you think I'd put up with so much shit from you all these years if I didn't love you at all? Who was always there after he raped you? Who carried you into the bathroom and washed you up? Who beat up anyone who ever hurt you? Who took you in when you were three months pregnant? Who made every fucking effort to help you get over your addiction? How can you even think I don't love you?" Just because I would never love her the way she wanted me to, didn't mean I didn't care.

I glanced at Eva, wondering what she was thinking as I expressed my feelings to another woman. Tears poured down her face, making me feel like shit. Glancing away because I couldn't handle watching her cry, I held out my hand and was rewarded when she took my fingers, squeezing supportively.

"I love you, Tris," I said, swallowing down the acid in my throat as I spoke the words, all the while pulling Eva close and burying my face in her neck. "Now, please . . . please, please just tell me how to get to you."

"I . . . " She paused to cough. "I'm in an abandoned underpass by the train station."

"Okay, good. Good. I'll be right there. Don't go anywhere. I'll be right there." It took everything I had not to ask about Julian again, but I didn't want to do anything else to upset her and cause her to leave before I arrived.

"Hurry," she slurred. "I'm getting tired."

"I will. I'll be right there." I hung up and immediately whirled to Eva. "I'm sorry."

She blinked, looking startled. "For what? You got her to tell you where she was."

Yes, yes, I had. And it'd taken out a chunk of my soul to do it.

Yanking open my dresser drawer, I pulled out the first shirt I saw. "But I hated that I had to . . . that I had to say all that . . . in front of you."

Eva reached forward, her fingers trembling as she helped me dress. "Pick, we don't have time for this. I understand. Just . . . bring back our boy."

I paused and looked at her. "You know you can't come." It wasn't a question, but a startled revelation. I had assumed she'd fight to go with me. She'd try to call Mrs. Rojas or Reese over to watch Skylar so she could be right there when I saw Julian again. But that couldn't happen. It'd only set Tristy off, and Eva knew it as much as I did.

Finding some jeans for me, she bent in front of me and held them open for me to step into. More love and respect surged inside me. Setting my hand on her head, I put my first foot into the denim and then the second.

"I love you so much, Tink."

She yanked the jeans up my legs. "I know." Her voice was a little breathless as she rushed to zip me. "I love you too." Her smile trembled and tears still welled, but when she looked at me, that was all I needed—her gaze on me.

"I gotta go."

She nodded, but when I started to turn away to fetch my shoes, she grabbed my shirt and yanked me back. "Wait." When I met her gaze, she captured my face in her hands. "You're the best man I've ever met, Patrick Ryan. Thank you for choosing me."

I kissed her hard. "I'll always choose you."

It took me twenty minutes to make it to the train station, but finding the overpass Tristy had been talking about was another matter entirely. There were so many railway lines and viaducts I didn't even know where to start. Parking at the station, I started at the closest, jogging to it on foot and calling out Tristy's name. I rustled up a homeless bum, but it wasn't Tristy or Julian. He began to snap at me until he took in my metal and tattoos. Then he backed off and left me alone.

I tried the next overpass, winded by the time I reached it. Still no luck. Working in a circle around the train depot, I kept searching.

About an hour into my hunt, I heard police sirens.

My stomach knotted into one big painful bundle as a bad feeling hit me hard. I tore off in that direction, because it came within a half mile from the train station.

They already had barricades up and were blocking off a crowd by the time I made it there. Breathing hard from my sprint, I nudged my way to the front where a cop was commanding everyone to clear out.

When I heard a baby crying up where all the red and blue lights were flashing, I panicked. It sounded like Julian's wail. Hurdling one of the police lines, I started that way but a cop shouted at me.

"Hey!" He grabbed my arm.

"I think that's my baby." I pointed and slowed a little but I kept walking in the direction of all the commotions of cop cars and ambulances. "My wife took off a couple days ago with my son, and I think she's somewhere around here. I have to see if that's my baby."

"Okay, fine. All right, kid. Just calm down. You stay here, and I'll find out if that's your son." He pointed at me warningly, but as soon as he turned away to stride off, I followed him. Another police officer noticed us approaching. When I caught his eye, his widened, and we both recognized each other at the same moment.

The nicer cop who'd been at my apartment for all the complaints pointed in my direction. "Hey, there's the father."

Oh, God.

Realizing I'd found Julian, I surged forward, scanning frantically. "Where is he? Is he okay?"

"Right here," someone answered. I turned to find a male cop, standing at the opened doors of an ambulance, trying to hold a hysterical Julian. The blanket wrapped around him was shredded and dirty enough it could've been dragged on the ground for the past three days. But what caused tears to prick my eyes was the dirt smeared all over my son and the swollen, bruised cuts slashed across his forehead.

"Oh, fuck." My knees buckled once, but I kept running until I was with him and taking him out of the other man's hands. "My boy. My little boy."

I turned him to press his chest against mine as he liked to be held best when he was upset, and I immediately started cooing in his ear. "It's okay, buddy. I'm here. I'm here now. It's okay, Julian. My little Fighter."

I started singing "Kryptonite." He grabbed onto my shirt and buried his face in my neck. My tears kept flowing as he settled. But he'd been so upset, little tremors from hyperventilating occasionally shot through him as he gasped for air. Through it all, he refused to let go of me. And I refused to let go of him.

"It's okay," I repeated when I could sing no more. I kept my voice calm, even though the rest of me grew more and more furious. Kissing the side of his head, I petted his hair, and then rested my cheek against him before glancing at the cop who'd been holding him. "How could she do this to him? Where the fuck is she?"

The man's eyes filled with sympathy and regret. "I'm sorry, sir. But your wife overdosed. She didn't make it."

-EVA MERCER-

Pick was gone six hours. He only called once to let me know he had Julian, and that our son was okay. They were on their way home from the hospital where the police had demanded a checkup.

The mention of a hospital and the police freaked me out. Pick's voice had shaken so hard, though, and sounded so frantic, I didn't question him. If he was on his way home, I figured I'd get my answers soon enough. And I did as soon as he opened the door. I saw Julian's swollen, scratched face and lost it.

"Oh my God. My little boy." I snatched him from Pick's arms and moaned as I pressed him against me, breathing in the unfamiliar smells that were wafting from him. I held him tight as he buried his face into my neck, grabbing handfuls of my hair like he always did—

which only made me cry harder.

"How could she do this to him?" I demanded, whirling to face Pick over Julian's shoulder. "Where the fuck is that crazy bitch?" I was determined to claw her face off.

Pick stared at me, his expression hollow and eyes red-rimmed from crying. His voice was hoarse when he said, "She's dead."

My mouth fell open. I waited for him to explain, but he just trudged past me like a tired, old man. He started toward the couch before he caught sight of Skylar sleeping in the bouncer. Scooping her up, he pulled her close as he sat down with her and buried his nose in her hair.

When he finally looked up at me, the dazed expression in his eyes told me he was in shock. Without a word, I sat next to him, and the four of us huddled together, just sitting there.

Though I was by no means ready to let him go, I knew Julian needed lots of rest, so at some point, I reluctantly rose and carried him to the crib. Pick followed me with a still sleeping Skylar and nestled her next to Julian.

I delicately touched the scrapes on his face and once again felt the rage welling. Setting my knuckles to my mouth, I wished Tristy were well on her way to hell.

Pick caught my hand, startling me. When I looked up, the darkness in his eyes shocked me. He looked savage. Turning away, he started for the doorway, drawing me out of the nursery with him.

I had no idea what was going through his head. His son had finally been returned, yet he had to be pissed about what'd been done to Julian. On the other hand, his oldest friend had just died, even though she probably wasn't his favorite person at the moment. His head had to be all over the place.

Touching his back, I asked, "Are you okay?"

He didn't answer, just kept his back to me as he

quietly shut the door so as not to disturb the children. Then he spun to me and pushed me against the wall. His mouth was on mine and his tongue was inside me before I even knew what was happening.

Heat lightning exploded out the ends of my toes. Instantly aroused, I wrapped my arms around him as he lifted me up again the wall. I tried to follow suit with my legs but he stopped me so he could grapple with my pants and shove them down, along with my underwear.

Then he grasped my bare thigh and hooked it around his hips. He sank his teeth into one of my breasts through my blouse, and I squirmed against him, wanting all my clothes out of the way so he could bite whatever he wanted.

"I need you so much right now," he panted as he opened his jeans and slid a condom on. I gaped at how hard and hungry he was.

The man was desperate, and he proved it by thrusting into me, rough and fast. The shock of his ravenous penetration made me cry out. Just as needy for him, I moved with him, arching into his next deep pump. His mouth ravished mine as he pinned me to the wall and took me without mercy.

"Yes," I said, biting his ear and clenching around him when he hit a spot that had my toes curling.

"Eva . . . " He groaned, breaking off to breathe into my mouth as his hips bucked in a ceaseless rhythm, pounding faster until I was clutching fistfuls of his hair and we were both crying out. He released into me hard, using my body to heal himself, and I was honored to alleviate his pain.

When his entire frame sagged against me and he buried his face in my neck, I knew he'd just worked through some of whatever was haunting him.

"I love you so much," he murmured, his voice slurred and sleepy.

I kissed his cheek and brushed his hair off his forehead. "I love you too."

"I don't know what I'd do right now without you."

"Well . . . " I bit my lip, wanting to make him smile. "To begin with, you probably would've had to jack off."

His lips fluttered into a half-smile as he lifted his face. "And it wouldn't have felt nearly this good."

He scooped me up into his arms and carried me toward our room. Once we were nestled under the blankets, he spooned himself behind me and wrapped his arms around my waist before setting his chin on my shoulder.

"I'm serious, Eva. Without you, I have no idea how my life would've turned out. If I hadn't had that vision of you and wanted you with every fiber of my being, I probably would've followed the same path as Tristy and gotten sucked into drugs. Or I would've done what my other friend Harvey did, and joined a gang. He was shot and killed in a drive-by when he was sixteen."

I kissed his jaw. "I'm so sorry for all your loss."

He mumbled something incoherent as if he didn't want to think about that. Then he began to pet my side. "You know how you keep saying I was your hero and I saved you when I beat up your ex and your dad? That's bullshit. You're *my* hero. Meeting you in those glimpses saved me. It made me want to be a good person so I could deserve you when I finally found you. And now that you're here, holding me and letting me love you when I just want to implode from the inside out . . . " He buried his face in my hair and inhaled deeply. "You don't even know what your mere presence does to me. You're my sanity."

I reached around behind me to comb his hair with my fingers. "You're mine too. There's nowhere else in the world I'd rather be."

"Don't ever leave me," he demanded in a broken voice.

I smiled, thinking my next words were the easiest promise I'd ever make. "I won't."

28

-PICK RYAN-

They buried Tristy on a Saturday morning.

No one attended the graveside service except Tink and me. We brought Fighter along, so he could pay his last respects to his biological mother, but the windy day kept taking his breath, so Eva carried him to the car, and I was left alone to say goodbye to my oldest companion.

I knew I should've mourned her loss, but mostly I just felt relieved. She didn't have to suffer anymore, and I didn't have to worry about her anymore.

"That witch was wrong," I told her as I tossed a handful of dirt into the hole on her casket. "You didn't die alone. You had your beautiful little boy with you. I can't think of any better company in the world than that. I swear, Tris, I will bring him up right and teach him to love the memory of you."

Then I turned away to join my family at the car.

I made love to Eva that night slowly, worshiping

every dip and curve of her body. She held me afterward, stroking her fingers over my heart tattoo, and I kissed her hair. I knew I should be happy. We were finally together without breaking any marital vows. But uncertainties continued to plague me.

What would happen to Julian when the state finally realized I wasn't any kind of legal guardian to him? How much longer did we have with him? And what about Eva's father?

She'd expressed her concern about him more than once, but I'd told her everything would be okay. What could he really do to us? Her uneasiness made me antsy, though. She knew the douche bag a hell of a lot better than I did. If she felt certain he'd try to get back at us for the way I'd kicked his ass, then I couldn't discount the idea either.

Unfortunately, the next day, one of my worry-filled questions was answered.

When the boss's daughter Jessie called all the Forbidden employees in for a Sunday afternoon meeting while the place was still closed, I hoped to God she was going to announce that her dad was ready to return to work and take over running the place again. Gamble had pretty much taken charge since the owner had been out of commission, and I hated having Gamble boss me around.

I arrived about ten minutes before the conference. All the other bartenders, plus most of the waitresses, as well as the two cooks, had already arrived and were loitering around the back of the club by the bar.

Needing my fellow bartenders to lift my mood, I bumped my arm into Quinn's elbow when I approached him from behind.

I nodded my chin at him and grinned as he turned to acknowledge me. "How's that tongue of yours doing, kid?"

He flushed. "Good."

Next to him, Ten laughed and jabbed Quinn in the belly teasingly. "Aww, look at that humble little grin, while I know for a fact his girl can't keep her hands off him. Always begging to stay the night, unable to stop kissing him. He's turned her into a fucking nympho."

"And he keeps saying she can't stay over." Quinn scowled at his new roommate. "But I don't care if *he* brings women in overnight. It's not fair."

"Hey, life's not fair," Ten said, completely unrepentant about refusing Quinn more time with his girl.

"Maybe you should tell him he can't have any women over until he agrees to let your—"

"Save it," Ten cut in, scowling at me for putting in my two cents worth. "I don't care if he bars them from my bedroom; I'll just take them somewhere else to fuck . . . like he's going to keep doing with Cora."

"See," Quinn told me. "He won't budge on the issue at all."

When I noticed Ten shift uncomfortably behind Quinn's back, I decided Ten probably had a damn good reason for saying no, and I had a bad feeling it'd leave me pissed at him. But I didn't get to think about it much because Jessie strolled out from the back hall.

"Everyone here?" she asked. "Good." Before waiting to hear that a handful of waitresses hadn't arrived yet, she kept talking. "Dad got an offer to sell this place, and he took it. Meet your new boss."

Just like that, she dropped the big news. No easing into it, no foreplay to soften us up and tell us what good workers we'd been to her family. Just . . . boom. New boss.

What the hell?

Gasps and questions flew around me as my jaw fell open. But damn, I hadn't expected *this* to happen. I glanced at the other guys, and they returned the same puzzled glances before Mason glanced over and his eyes went wide.

"Oh, shit," he whispered.

I turned and froze.

Bradshaw Mercer strolled out of the hallway behind Jessie, looking as rich, polished, and pristine as ever. When his gaze met mine, his smile grew.

"Good afternoon, everyone." He nodded pleasantly, breaking his gaze with me before looking at all the others as if he were some kind of honorable businessman.

My eyes narrowed. I still wanted to hurt him. Bad. Even more so now than ever. But if he thought he could control me by buying the bar where I worked, he better try to come up with a better strategy. I would drop this place so fast . . . Except I had Eva, Julian, and Skylar to think about. I wouldn't be able to support them on just the garage salary alone. What if I couldn't find another job somewhere else? What if—?

Damn, he was good, I'd give him that.

"My name is Shaw, and yes, I'm technically your new boss, although I've already hired an assistant to run the day to day management. You'll be receiving all your instructions directly from her." Stepping aside, he swept out his hand to the figure who I suddenly noticed waiting in the shadows behind him. "Patricia? Would you care to introduce yourself?"

When Mrs. Garrison stepped into the light, my jaw dropped. Quinn, Noel, Ten, and I instantly glanced toward Mason.

Gray eyes swirling with murder, he threw up his hands. "I quit."

But as soon as he turned away, our new supervisor smirked after him, her eyes gleaming with triumph. "Not so fast, Mr. Lowe. If you quit, I'll relieve these four gentlemen here from their duties right along with you."

My stomach dropped as Mason ground to a halt. He turned back slowly and glared at her before swerving his tortured gaze to us guys. His eyes begged us to let him go, while ours begged him not to get us fired.

"Fuck it," Ten was the first to answer. "If you need to break out of here, then go. I can find a new job."

Noel closed his eyes and muttered, "Shit." We all knew he couldn't lose his income. He was living with a woman who was still looking for work, and now he had three siblings to take care of on top of that.

"I . . . I just signed a six-month lease on my apartment," Quinn said in a small voice. "But I . . . oh, man. I understand if you have to . . . Whatever you need to do, Mason. It's okay."

Mason glanced at me. He knew exactly who I had to support, and he knew who *he* had to support. Gritting his teeth in a snarl, he turned back to Mrs. Garrison and glared at her. He was going to stay.

She smiled smugly. "That's what I thought."

She started talking to the crowd as a whole, explaining a bunch of bullshit no one cared about. As she blathered on, detailing her new duties as our direct supervisor, I slid my gaze back to Eva's father. He was watching me—a small, smug smile twitching around his mouth.

I'm not sure what his game was, if he was doing this to get revenge because I'd hit him, or if he wanted to draw his daughter away from me, but I was used to being the underdog, the one always forced to bow to superiors. He had another thing coming if he thought this was going to spook me.

Mason was spooked though. He vibrated as he glowered at Mrs. Garrison. It seemed like a lifetime ago that she'd come into Forbidden and tried to convince him she was pregnant with his baby. God, so much had happened since then.

Eva had happened.

Eva, the woman I couldn't lose, no matter what.

My stomach churned with unease.

Mrs. Garrison dismissed us a few minutes later, reminding us our new work policies would soon show up on the board in the break room. Mason didn't move, so Ten, Noel, Quinn, and I stuck around too, backing him up for . . . whatever he may need.

With a pleasant smile, Mrs. Garrison sauntered toward us.

"Why are you doing this?" he demanded, his voice low and deadly. "And how'd you get hooked up with *him*?" His gaze sought Eva's father before he turned back to her.

She grinned. "What? Are you jealous, darling?"

"Hardly. I just wanted to give him my congratulations in case he's the one who put those bruises on your neck."

Her eyes turned dark and troubled as her fingers found her throat, where I spotted dark fingerprints I hadn't noticed before.

If he'd done anything like that to Eva when he'd molested her, I'd—fuck, I couldn't kill my boss. I would go to jail.

But, oh man, it'd be worth it.

Leaning closer to Mrs. Garrison, Mason lowered his voice. "Too bad I didn't know you were into that before. *I* wouldn't have stopped squeezing."

"Hmm." She blinked repeatedly, her eyes flickering out all her troubled thoughts. Ignoring him, she turned to Quinn. "Well, don't you have a pretty face? What's your name, handsome?"

When she reached out to touch Quinn's cheek, Mason slapped her hand away. "Don't touch him."

She lifted her brows, pleasure spreading across her face. "My, my, you really *are* jealous today. Do you know how much that turns me on?"

While the rest of us dropped our jaws in shock, Mason sniffed and spun to us, dismissing her. "Mess with her at your own risk, but be forewarned. She's a lying, manipulative, blackmailing bitch."

"Dude," Noel said, shaking his head. "I think we've already figured that out."

Mason nodded and strode from the building. Mrs. Garrison huffed as she stared after him. When she glanced at the rest of us, we all lurched away. Even Ten, who usually didn't know any better. Frowning even harder, she whirled away and marched off toward the office, breezing past Eva's father who had just waylaid one of the waitresses by catching her arm and sending her a friendly smile.

"Was it just me," Ten murmured to Noel, Quinn, and I. "Or was that meeting totally fucked up?"

I kept watching Mercer as he slid alongside the girl, whispering intimately, and dread coiled hard in my belly. Great, here was yet another reason I couldn't leave Forbidden. I didn't want any of the waitresses to get tangled in his web.

"Tansy!" I yelled, lifting my chin and beckoning her to me when she glanced over. All the waitresses knew I was their protector. They trusted me. So, when I called her away from that prick bastard, she sent me a relieved smile and deserted him, hurrying to me without question.

Glaring Mercer down, I curled my arm around Tansy's waist and lowered my mouth to her ear. "Do not trust that snake. He's a fucking rapist. Do you hear me?" She shivered and looked up at me with wide, brown eyes. When she nodded, I nodded too. "Don't *ever* let yourself get caught alone with him. And warn all the other girls too. I don't care what he says to any of you, *no one* talks to him alone. Got it?"

"Okay, Pick." She leaned up and kissed my cheek. "And thank you. I thought I felt a strange vibe from him, but I tried to ignore it."

"Don't ignore those vibes, honey. They keep you safe."

"No, *you* keep us safe, Pick. Ever since you saved me from that customer who followed me out to my car and Mandy from the guy who cornered her alone by the bathrooms, there's no one in this building I trust more than you. And if you say he's bad news, consider all of us waitresses forewarned."

I nodded, glad she'd spread the word. Now I just had to figure out how to keep Tinker Bell and my children safe.

29

-EVA MERCER-

Mason text bombed me before Pick even made it home from his meeting. It was still strange to get an incoming message on my new phone. I wasn't at all the social butterfly I'd been back in Florida. But what my soon-to-be cousin-in-law wrote was even more bizarre.

"Your father is evil incarnate."

I snorted. That was the understatement of the century. *"What has he done now?"* Dread seized me. *"Is Reese okay?"*

"NO ONE is okay with that asshole still alive. He bought Forbidden."

I frowned, not sure what he meant. *"What?"*

"The bar where your boyfriend and I both work. He BOUGHT IT. HE OWNS IT. HE FUCKING OWNS US!"

Shaking my head, I stamped out a quick reply. *"That makes no sense."*

"You seriously didn't know? What is he planning to

do to us? I don't like this."

"Of course I didn't know, you idiot. But I'll find out what he wants." Though I already knew.

"Good. Oh hey. Don't tell Reese about this yet. I don't want her to freak."

Oh, but he had no qualms about freaking *me* out. Thanks, buddy.

Pick walked in the front door, then. His eyes were hooded, but he sent me a warm smile. "There's my reason for getting up every morning." He swept toward me and kissed me sweetly.

If I hadn't just talked to Mason, I wouldn't have known anything was bothering him. He didn't let me in on any of his troubles, so I assumed he didn't want to worry me any more than Mason wanted to worry Reese.

Stupid boys. Sweet, caring, amazing but definitely stupid boys.

"How was your meeting?" I asked directly.

His eyebrows shot up. "Unexpected. Our boss sold the bar to some rich guy from out of town." Well, at least he didn't lie. But he certainly wasn't telling me the entire truth, either.

"Oh, yeah?" Hey, if he refused to tell me what he knew, I wasn't going to tell him what I knew. That way, we didn't have to worry each other.

Pick nodded, not meeting my gaze. "He's already hired someone else to run the place for him too."

My phone dinged, telling me I had another text. Pick let me check the message while he greeted the babies who were both chewing on toys together on the floor.

"Oh yeah," Mason added. *"And he put Garrison in charge. She said if I quit, she'll fire Pick and all the other guys too."*

My gut tightened and cold coated my skin. Hands shaking, I typed back, *"Pick just got home."* Maybe that would shut Mason up for a while, because I couldn't take any more distressing news. I needed some time to think about this.

"Okay, good," he wrote back. *"He can tell you the rest."*

But Pick told me nothing, which let me know he was

just as terrified as I was.

We took the kids to the park for the rest of the day. Like Pick, I pretended nothing was wrong or that our happy little bubble wasn't about to pop in the loudest way possible. When we returned to the apartment, I told him I had to run an errand to the grocery story because I had a surprise for supper. Which was about as true as what he'd told me about his meeting.

I left him with both kids, and strode out to my car, the car he'd looked over so thoroughly before buying, making sure it was sound enough for me to drive. I didn't burst into tears until I'd started the engine and was on the road to the store.

My father probably knew everything about Pick by now, where he worked, what he drove, that he had no rights to Julian. If I didn't do what Bradshaw wanted, he'd find a way to get Julian taken away from Pick. He'd destroy the man I loved. I knew that for a fact. Julian would probably get thrown into foster care, and Pick's biggest fear would come true.

I knew how to stop the monster, though. As soon as I went home with him and gave him the façade of a perfect happy family so he could continue to show the public what an outstanding man he was while he kept being a depraved bastard behind the scenes, he'd leave Pick and Julian alone.

The only way to keep them together was to give my father what he wanted. The idea made my hands shake and my stomach clench. But I was going to do what I had to do.

I'd stopped crying by the time I'd reached the store, thank goodness. On autopilot, I pushed a shopping cart down the aisles, picking up the ingredients for chicken parmesan, Pick's favorite dish. Then I wheeled past the bedding section to browse.

Pick had detailed to me every one of his glimpses. If I was going to break my promise to him and end up leaving him the next day to go back with my father, then I could at least make one of his visions come true tonight.

We had a late supper, waiting until the kids were asleep before we ate. He put them to bed while I cooked. The meal I prepared pleased him. His eyes lit as soon as he strolled into the kitchen and saw his favorite. Shaking his head, he grinned at me as he pulled out my chair for me to sit. "You spoil me more than I deserve."

I could never spoil him enough. A hitch in my chest caused me to glance away. I could spend the rest of my life cooking him his favorite supper every night, and it still wouldn't be enough.

If only I had the rest of my life to show him that.

Too observant for his own good, he touched my chin. "Hey." His gaze softened into a confused frown as it traveled over my face. "You okay? You seem extra quiet tonight."

I nuzzled my cheek into his hand and then hugged him around the legs, resting my chin on his abs so I could look up at him. "How can you even ask that?" I murmured, smoothing my hand over his taut ass. "I'm here with you. My life is perfect."

He chuckled and leaned in to kiss my hair. "You keep touching me like that and you might get lucky tonight, woman."

"Mmm. Sounds nice. But what if I touch you here." I smoothed my fingers around to feel how hard he'd already grown.

He sucked in a breath. "Food now, or later?"

"Later," I said.

He groaned, his brown eyes swirling with need. "God, I love you."

Sweeping me off my feet, he carried me to our room, where tonight, I was going to be as loud as I could possibly be.

He set me down gently on top of the main comforter,

but I shook my head. "I want it between the sheets."

Pick's eyes squinted with suspicion but he complied, ripping the blankets back to reveal the final surprise I had in store for him.

He lurched back when he saw it, as if it were a snake waiting to strike instead of brand new sheets. "What the hell?"

It hadn't been easy keeping them from him since he'd been home all day. I'd had to hide them under a pile of socks in the clothes basket to get them washed and ready. Then I'd piled both kids on him in the living room to keep him preoccupied while I'd made up the bed.

"Fuck me," he breathed.

I stood up and bit my lip, not sure if he was scared of the bed, or just in that much awe. I shifted nervously. "You never mentioned what color they were."

"This . . . " His voice croaked off before he cleared his throat and pointed to the sheets. "This color," he said. "Exactly this same pale blue color. Oh my God." He turned to me, looking dazed. "You . . . "

For some reason I was still nervous. "They're not silk. You said silk. But they didn't have genuine silk sheets at the store, so I had to settle for a microfiber blend."

Pick stepped toward the bed and hesitantly reached out to run his trembling fingers over the mattress. Yanking his hand back to his chest, he turned to me, still looking awestruck. "No, this is right. This is exactly how they felt. Christ, I can't believe you found the exact same sheets from my . . . " He shook his head, still flabbergasted. "You are the most amazing woman ever."

Suddenly, I was no longer nervous. Feeling on top of the world, I sauntered toward him and caught the hem of his shirt. "So, Mr. Ryan," I murmured, lifting the cloth up above his perfect abs and chest. "Our babies are in bed for the night, and we have this room all to ourselves. Are you ready to make a glimpse come true?"

"Oh my God. Yes." He caught me by the waist and flung me onto the bed.

I laughed as I bounced. Ripping his shirt the rest of the way off, Pick rushed to shuck his jeans next. The entire time, his hungry gaze never left mine.

Just as famished for him, I lifted my hips off the mattress and peeled off my own clothes. He paused at the nightstand for protection before crawling on top of me. Sitting on his knees naked above me with his legs imprisoning my hips, he gazed down at me as he rolled the condom on. Watching the plump wet head disappear inside the latex before he stroked himself, he teased me by letting the massive column bob out in front of him directly above my face so I had a very intimate view of the show he put on. Further up his body, his nipple ring glistened in the overhead light.

Heat and moisture pooled between my legs. I clamped my thighs together, not ready to be quite so aroused. I wanted to draw our last night out for as long as possible.

But Pick, Mr. Super Lover, had other ideas. He caught my thighs and drew them apart, gazing at me spread open and throbbing before him. "You are the most beautiful woman I've ever known. Inside and out." The love in his eyes was so profound I could feel it swelling in my own chest and between my legs.

Dipping his face, he feasted. Shocked by how good it felt, even though I knew what to expect, I jerked under his mouth, pulsing and needy. His tongue ring gave me no mercy. He barely pressed a finger inside me before my womb constricted and my body exploded. I cried out in anger because I so wasn't ready for it to be over yet, but also in passion because it felt so freaking perfect.

"Wow, you're responsive tonight." Pick grinned as he lifted his face. It was one of those self-satisfied, smug grins, and I loved putting it there.

I reached up, grasped his face, and jerked him down to me. This kiss was warm and carnal, yet laced with more adoration than I'd ever felt for anyone. Tasting myself on his tongue, I moaned and clutched him desperately, needing to feel him deep and full inside me.

"I need . . . I need . . . "

"I know," he soothed, lowering his hips to mine. "I've got you, babe."

His penetration was slow and so torturously amazing, I started to come again before he'd even gotten all the way inside. Realizing what I was doing his eyes widened with shock. "Fuck, Eva." He surged the rest of the way in, letting me pulse around him.

Waiting until I was finished, he blew out a breath, then pulled his face away to show me his stunned expression. "Did you take some kind of aphrodisiac?"

Sweat beaded to my brow as I tried to catch my breath. "You're my only drug," I panted. "I just . . . I want you so much."

"I'm right here. There's no rush. You have me for the rest of the night." Moving his hips, he kissed my cheek and whispered, "For the rest of our lives."

I closed my eyes and bit my lip. *If only.*

As he kept sliding in and out, flexing his hips and hitting me just right every time, it didn't take long for my body to coil back up with arousal. "You're going to come a third time, aren't you?" he teased, his eyes all bright and proud.

"Shut up." I slapped his butt and then groaned at how the erotic sound made me even more sensitized. "No one likes a braggart."

His mouth lowered to my ear. "Oh, but I think you like this one . . . quite a bit."

Then he groaned and trembled on top of me when I tightened my inner muscles around him. "Minx," he muttered, working faster now.

Loving it most when he was ground all the way in, I grabbed his ass and dug my nails in, trying to hold him there. My inner muscles quivered in delight. Pick slid his fingers into my hair and I opened my lashes to find his attention of my face. Our eyes met, and I didn't have to ask to know how this felt to him.

"Tinker Bell," he said, except what I heard was, *"I love you."*

I sighed in dazed wonder, knowing that no matter where my life led me from here, I would always cherish this incredible man. Smiling up at him, I had to say, "I love you."

He shuddered and his eyes went unfocused as his cock swelled inside me. And that was it; I came for a third time, throwing back my head and pushing my breasts up against his chest. He groaned, his muscles coiling taut before he thrust deep and held himself there, releasing his love.

Afterward, we panted together as he collapsed on top of me like a heavy, limp anvil. I hugged him close, relishing these quiet moments of perfection. Then I couldn't help but ask, "So, how close did we come?"

He laughed, knowing I was talking about his glimpse, and shook his head. "Every fucking detail was spot on."

I sighed, satisfied. "Good."

He pulled back to gaze at me. "It's going to be fine now, Eva. No matter what happens next. Everything's going to be fine. I know it."

I nodded, glad I'd accomplished my job of giving him such peace of mind, because I *was* going to make sure everything was fine—for him and everyone else I loved.

30

-EVA MERCER-

The next day, I waited until after Pick left for his job at the garage. I kissed him at the door, trying not to let on that it might be the very last kiss I ever gave him, and yet I was also trying to get as much out of it as possible.

And then he was gone.

I blew out a shaky breath, commanding myself not to cry. It was time to dig out Bitch Eva and get my attitude back on. Dropping the babies off with Reese, I gave her the excuse that I wanted to get my hair cut and styled. She bought the entire story, happy to help me watch my munchkins.

Mason wasn't so taken in, though. He caught my arm at the door before I left and leaned in close to whisper, "What're you *really* doing, E.?"

I patted his cheek with a grin. "Don't you worry about it. I'm going to take care of everything. All you need to concern yourself with is making my best friend insanely

348

happy, remember."

But he shook his head, his eyes narrowing. "No, really. What're you doing? Do I need to come with you?"

I sighed in exasperation and finally got him to simmer down. "No, you do not need to come with me. Nothing bad is going to happen."

I was just going to sell my soul to the devil.

My hands shook as I entered Forbidden twenty minutes later. It wouldn't open for business for a good eight hours, but all the lights inside the empty club were on and one of my father's favorite melodies played from the jukebox, making my skin crawl.

Uncertainties rose as Pick's voice filled my head along with everything he'd say if he knew what I was doing: *"What are you thinking, Tink? Turn around and walk out of there right now. This plan isn't going to work. Think about your babies. They need their mother. Think about me. I need you. I'll come after you wherever you go."*

But I couldn't think of anything else I could do to save them. So I strode purposefully down the hall until I reached the door that said *Manager* on it. When I pushed it open without knocking, the first thing I saw was Quinn with his back pressed hard to the wall. He was tipping his head away from Mrs. Garrison as she leaned into him, reaching for his face.

I sniffed. "Bitch, you're pathetic."

She jumped and whirled around. Quinn immediately snaked out from between her and the wall. He hurried to my side, looking relieved that I'd saved him.

"Well, well, well," Mrs. Garrison murmured, glaring at me. "If it isn't daddy's special girl. Didn't he ever teach you to knock?"

I lifted my chin and crossed my arms over my chest. "Of course not. He taught me to do whatever the hell I wanted."

From the opened office door behind me, a familiar

laugh haunted my ears and made my heart drum hard and fast against my chest. "That's my girl," Bradshaw murmured approvingly.

I turned and lifted an eyebrow, edging closer to Quinn without meaning to. "You wanted my attention," I said to the bastard. "You have it. Here I am."

"Yes, here you are." Eyeing me appreciatively, he moved into the office. His gaze flickered to Mrs. Garrison, and then Quinn. "Leave us."

Mrs. Garrison huffed in disapproval but started for the exit.

Quinn didn't budge. He glanced at me, his gaze apprehensive. "Pick warned all the waitresses to never get caught alone with him. He'd never forgive me if I left right now."

I wasn't sure which man I should be more proud of: Pick, for looking out for all the ladies he worked with, or Quinn for standing firmly by my side.

I touched his arm. "It's okay. He's my dad."

Quinn's eyes flared with horror. "W-w-well if Pick said that after actually *knowing* who he is, I'm definitely not leaving you alone with him. Just . . . just pretend I'm not here."

After reaching into his pocket, he unwound a cord of ear buds from a cell phone and plugged them in. Then he leaned against the wall, giving me as much privacy with Shaw as he would allow.

I smiled at him, actually grateful he wasn't going to let me face my greatest fear alone. "I guess he's staying," I said.

Mrs. Garrison huffed. "Well, if he's staying, then I'm staying."

"That's fine." I glanced at my father, snickering because this had probably spoiled half of his nefarious plans. "I don't mind an audience."

He growled out his displeasure and moved to sit at his desk, probably hoping the flawless leather throne gave him an air of superiority.

"I'm ready to deal," I told him, not waiting for him to take control of the conversation.

A slow, creepy smile spread over his face. "Is that so?

I had a feeling you'd change your mind."

I nodded. "If you want me to go back with you, then sign the deed of this place over to Pick. Right now."

He lifted an eyebrow. "And you'll come back with me? Just like that?"

"I have a few more stipulations."

His eyes narrowed slightly. "Like what?"

"My daughter doesn't come with me. She stays here with Reese. And you never have anything to do with either of them, nor do you let them have any contact with me."

I bit the inside of my lip hard to keep my chin from quivering and my eyes from tearing. But that had been the hardest thing to let go of. My Skylar. It went against every instinct inside me to leave my baby behind. But no way would I let her grow up anywhere near him. And the only way to get her out of his life for good was to sacrifice myself. This would be best for *both* of my babies. Reese and Pick, and even Mason, would take care of them, and love them exactly how I wanted them to be loved. And none of them would ever have to worry about Bradshaw or Garrison again. They'd be free to live the rest of their lives in peace.

"Hmm," he murmured, stapling his fingers as he studied me. "I wasn't expecting that one. I thought you'd grown rather fond of your brat, but fine, I'll gladly allow that condition." His lips quirked smugly. "Next?"

"Fire that bitch you hired to torment Mason. And keep her away from him."

Bradshaw shot an amused glance toward Mrs. Garrison. "She won't go willingly, but I'll enjoy pulling her away. Anything else?"

"Yes. Make sure Pick keeps his son."

My father lifted his eyebrows. "I'm afraid I don't know what you're talking about."

I snorted. "Bullshit. You know everything there is to know about him. And you know what Julian means to him."

"*Oh*, you're referring to the little crack whore's baby. *That* son. Yes, I'm fully aware he could lose the child if I made one small phone call to Social Services. It's a shame, really. I doubt any foster parent would care for the kid as much as your young man has. Though I'd never allow such a character to remain associated with my daughter, he does seem to be a good father."

He was the best father ever.

God, I was going to miss Pick, Skylar, Julian, Reese, damn, even Mason. But I'd do this. For a chance to keep them safe, I'd do this in a heartbeat.

"Then help him *remain* a good father."

Bradshaw chuckled and rocked back in his chair. "Really, darling. I don't see how I could do that."

"I don't care how you do it. Falsify a birth certificate with his name on it. Create adoption records. Don't tell me you can't do it. I *know* better."

"Okay, fine. You're right. I can do such a thing." His chest bowed out, showing me how proud he was of his illegal powers.

I rolled my eyes. "Then do it."

"And you'll come back?"

When I nodded, Quinn made a sound from his perch on the wall. I glanced at him, but he seemed preoccupied with whatever he was doing on his phone.

Mrs. Garrison laughed out a harsh sound. "Oh, please. Tell me you're not serious about meeting all her silly little conditions."

My father glanced at her. "I'm dead serious, Patricia. This is exactly why I came here."

Garrison sniffed, only to have her face leach of color when she seemed to realize just how serious he was. "No," she whispered. "Bradshaw, please don't do this." Hurrying to him, she fell to her knees in front of his chair and ran her hands up his thighs toward his lap.

He caught her wrists and pulled her claws away from him, clucking his tongue. "Really, Patricia. Don't be so unseemly. Besides, you're not that good of a fuck to sway me on this."

After he pushed her aside, openly dismissing her, he unfolded what I guessed was the deed to the club. Waving his pen, he grinned. "You know, I assumed you'd ask to have the club put into your own name. But I guess your heart is softer than I ever took it for. That's . . .

disappointing. Nevertheless, it doesn't matter to me who it goes to. Getting you back under my roof is all that matters."

As he signed away the nightclub to Pick, Mrs. Garrison clutched her hair and screamed. "No! You can't do this. You made me a promise. I let you do all that shit to me. What about *Mason*?"

Bradshaw sighed and rolled his eyes as if extremely tired of her theatrics. "You were a means to an end, Patricia. And I don't give a shit about your little prostitute. My daughter wants you to stay away from him, so you're going to stay away from him."

"But—"

"You're dismissed," he cut in, glaring at her. "Get out."

Screeching out an inhuman shriek, Garrison tore across the room toward her purse.

I had no idea what she was after until she opened the top clasp and yanked out a gun.

I opened my mouth to scream. Bradshaw opened his mouth to yell. Quinn pushed away from the wall, his eyes wide with horror. And Mrs. Garrison lifted the barrel, pointing it at my father's head.

"No one tells me what to do, you son of a bitch."

"*No*," he bellowed just before she pulled the trigger.

Watching his head explode imprinted itself in my retinas. It was something I'd never be able to un-see. Mrs. Garrison whirled to me, her eyes crazed and livid. She raised the gun in my direction, and my life flashed before my eyes. Pick, Skylar, Julian, Reese. They were finally free.

But shit, I didn't want to die.

Two-hundred and forty pounds of football player tackled me from the side, driving me to the floor as the gun went off. I screamed and landed hard, cracking my head against cold tile with Quinn piling on top of me. As he tightened his arms around me, shielding me from head to toe, my ears rang, my head swam, and my vision went fuzzy.

Just as Quinn went dead weight, a voice yelled, "Patricia!"

Though I was still seeing stars and couldn't focus properly, I saw a blurry image of Mrs. Garrison over Quinn's shoulder as she whirled toward the doorway of the office.

"Mason?" she gasped, her voice stunned as her gun aimed his way.

"Jesus, Patricia. What did you just do?"

He'd ducked back into the hallway but stayed right outside the door with his back pressed to the wall. I could see the corner of his shoulder from where I lay.

"I . . . I . . . he made me. He was taking you away from me again. Taking me away from this bar. I worked so hard to get him to buy this place and let me manage it. I let him . . . I let him do so much to me. And now he just wants to take it all away. Take *you* away? Just like that? No fucking way."

"But you just *shot* someone. Are you *insane*?"

"I was so tired of waiting. I missed you." Mrs. Garrison's chin trembled and tears filled her eyes. "You don't know what he did to me. Oh God, Mason. The things he made me do so I could get to you . . . "

Mason's answer was dry and unimpressed. "Were they anything like the things you made *me* do with *you*? Yeah, excuse me if I don't feel sorry for you."

Mrs. Garrison's mouth worked in shock. "That . . . that's not the same thing. You *liked* what we did." When he didn't answer, she let out a noisy, wet sob. "Didn't you?"

"Why don't you put the gun down, and then come out here to talk to me?"

"Why don't you answer my fucking question?" Mrs. Garrison screamed and stomped her feet.

On top of me, Quinn's weight seemed to grow heavier. When I felt something wet trickle over my arm, I looked up into his face, but his eyes were closed. Oh, shit. Not Quinn.

Turning my gaze toward Mason, he shifted just enough so I could see his face. He met my gaze as he answered Mrs. Garrison. "No. I didn't like it."

"Yes!" She wailed, stomping her feet some more and dancing around like the whack job she was. "You did too.

You *loved* it. You loved it as much as I did."

At the desk, Bradshaw remained slumped backward in his chair with more than I'd ever wanted to see of his insides splattered on the wall behind him.

I closed my eyes and shuddered, holding Quinn a little tighter and hoping he was okay. A surreal sense of shock blanketed me, making everything fuzzy and dreamlike, even Mrs. Garrison's ranting as she sobbed, "You loved it, and you love me."

Mason's voice was steady as he said, "I love Reese."

"No!"

I'm not sure what he was trying to accomplish, but if he wanted to agitate her and send her into an even crazier, raving fit, he was totally succeeding. I kind of wondered if Mason was on a suicide mission, trying to get us all killed. But at least I'd be able to tell Reese later on how he never wavered from his feelings for her, not even to patronize a cracked, wild woman.

That was, if I survived long enough to see Reese again.

When police sirens rang from outside, Mrs. Garrison freaked. "Oh, God. Oh, God. Oh, God." She pointed the gun toward Bradshaw, but he was already long gone. Shuffling with indecision, she glanced my way, but I think she only saw Quinn's prone form slumped on top of me and the blood pooling under us. "Oh, God," she moaned. "What do I do?"

"Patricia," Mason said calmly. "It's over. Just . . . put the gun down."

She didn't. She lifted it to her face, stuck the barrel in her mouth, and pulled the trigger.

Mason rushed to Quinn and me and knelt beside us. "E.? Are you okay?"

"I told you not to follow me," I grumbled.

"Right. Like I ever listen to you." With a snort, he shook his head, only to suck in a breath as he turned his attention to Quinn. "Is he . . . ?"

"No, he's alive." I stroked my rescuer's hair. "I can feel his breath on my neck."

"Oh, thank God." Grasping Quinn's shoulder, Mason gritted his teeth as he rolled the brick mass off me. "Damn, he's solid muscle, isn't he? Freaking football players."

I sucked in air as soon as Quinn was off me. Wow, it felt good to breathe again. As Mason gently settled our friend onto his back beside me, I sat up and crawled toward them.

"There's a lot of blood." When I looked down, I realized it was smeared all over me, as well as his left side.

"Yeah." Mason gulped bleakly, and lifted Quinn's arm to find the source of the wound. "Here. She hit him in the arm."

I ripped off the outer shirt I was wearing until I was down to a bloodstained camisole. When I applied it with some pressure to Quinn's arm, he sucked in a breath.

Long dark eyelashes fluttered before he shook his head and opened his eyes. He focused on me first, and then turned his head slightly to take in Mason before he turned back to me. "What happened?"

"You refused to leave me alone in the office with my father, you sweet, noble idiot," I told him.

"And you got a little shot because of it," Mason added.

"Really?" Quinn frowned as he tried to sit up. "I don't feel shot. Nothing hurts." When I motioned to the bloody wound on his arm that I was pressing my shirt into, he sucked in a breath, and his face immediately drained of color. "Okay, now I feel it."

His voice grew faint, and he swayed.

Mason caught his shoulder, steadying him. "Whoa, there. Maybe you should lie back down before you faint again."

Horror flooded Quinn's expression. "I *fainted*? Oh, man. You're not going to tell Ten that, are you? He'd never let me live it down."

I snorted out a shocked laugh, even though the sound wavered at the end into an odd kind of sob. "Yeah, I think I can manage to avoid mentioning that and focusing more on the part where you *dived* in front of a speeding bullet to save my life."

Quinn nodded, not catching my amusement. "Thanks. I'm sorry I passed out on you. How mortifying." His eyes were so sincere; I shot Mason a disbelieving glance. But seriously, had this guy just apologized to me after risking his own life to save mine?

"I think she'll find a way to forgive you, man." Mason's lips tightened as he tried to hide his own smile.

"Good." Quinn sat up again, only to spot the bodies of my father and Mrs. Garrison across the room. "Oh," he said, his eyes widening as he went from white to green. "Are they . . . ?"

"Yeah." I bit my lip, refusing to look at them. My stomach protested and I covered my mouth. "Let's get out of this room."

"Good idea."

Mason and I helped Quinn to his feet. He still looked woozy, but he could stand without any help.

As soon as we cleared the office, a shout from the front of the club told us the police had arrived. Mason called back, telling them we were coming out.

I don't know how much time passed after that, but the three of us clung together as we were questioned about what had happened and a paramedic looked at Quinn's arm. The poor guy was even more embarrassed about passing out when he realized the bullet had barely grazed his bicep. It was so minor a wound that the EMT decided to patch the scratch up right there at the bar without even taking him to the hospital.

Flesh wound or not, I still thought he was beyond brave, and I told him so as I smacked a grateful kiss to his cheek. Then I just kind of lingered close to him, feeling safe with him beside me.

When he flushed bashfully and ducked his face, the officer nodded in his direction. "Now what were you doing here again, Mr. Hamilton?"

I didn't know it was possible for Quinn's face to turn even redder, but it did. Glancing quickly at Mason, he mumbled, "Mrs. Garrison called me in early before my shift tonight. She said she needed some crates moved.

But . . . that's not what she really wanted." After clearing his throat, he continued. "When Eva showed up to talk to, er . . . Mr. Mercer, I stayed with her because I didn't trust him. While I was on my phone, pretending to listen to music, I texted her boyfriend, Pick, telling him what was happening."

"You texted Pick?" I sat up straighter and glanced around the club, looking for him.

Quinn nodded, wincing as if apologizing to me for his trickery. "I had no idea Mrs. Garrison would pull a gun like that, but my gut told me something wasn't right. So I followed my instincts."

"Thank goodness you did," the officer said. He didn't have many questions after that, and he wandered away to get more information from the office.

I glanced at the two men flanking me, glad they were there. If not for their presence, I'd probably be a freaking, irrational, hysterical mess.

I blew out a breath, needing some comedic relief. "You know, this is the second time I've been shot at within a year. This shit's getting old."

Mason snorted and shook his head. "Yeah, well, it's the second time I've had to get a gun away from the person who shot at you."

I snorted right back, not impressed by his dinky problems, but I lifted my finger as a thought occurred. "Oh, by the way, you totally suck as a negotiator."

He threw his hands in the air, sending me an incredulous scowl. "What did you want me to say to her, that I loved her back?"

"Yeah," I retorted. "The woman had a gun, numb nuts. She could've so easily shot at you for telling her you loved Reese. Oh, shit. Have you called Reese?"

"Yes." He rolled his eyes. "She's freaking out because she's stuck watching your kids and can't come be with us."

"Poor girl." I patted his arm, and studied him a second longer when I felt his muscles tremble under my touch. He was still pretty shaken over everything. But then, he wasn't the only one. "Are you okay?"

He glanced at me with his eyebrows raised. "Sure.

Why? No one shot at *me*."

What a liar.

"Well . . . " I motioned down the hall toward the office. "Your rapist is finally dead." That had to mean something.

He shook his head as if he didn't want to think about what had happened back there, but then he glanced at me. "So is yours."

I gulped. "Yeah." Oh, God. I didn't want to go there either. "I guess that means you're in about as much shock as I'm in right now, huh?"

"Basically." He took my hand and squeezed my fingers in companionship, letting me know everything would be okay, eventually.

Quinn glanced between us, his eyes wide. "I should probably pretend I never heard any of that, huh?"

I thought I'd be horrified to realize yet another person knew my deep, dirty, dark secret, but honestly, it didn't matter anymore. Pick had pulled me from all the horrors that had haunted me, and now I could find a way to deal with it.

But thinking about Pick made me crave him even more. If Quinn had texted him an SOS, why the hell hadn't he come? I needed his—

And then, as if my cravings had drawn him there, I heard him shout my name. At the entrance of the club, he was being waylaid by a group of police officers holding him back and telling him he couldn't enter. When he spotted me, he shouted my name again and tried even harder to break through the barricade.

I hopped off the stool and hurried to him. "It's okay. He's here for me."

A leery copy shot me a look but finally let Pick in.

He almost broke a rib he crushed me against him so hard.

"Oh, baby. *Shit*. Are you okay? I've been freaking out so bad since I read that text." Spotting the blood on me, he paled. "Why're you bleeding? Where're you hurt? Did he touch you? What happened?"

"I'm okay. It's not my blood. I'm okay." I hugged him back, definitely feeling better because I was finally where

I wanted to be most in the world. In his arms.

And yet now that I had him where I need him most, all the emotions I'd been bottling up spilled out. Clutching him tighter, I buried my face in his neck, breathed in drudges of his soothing coconut smell, and cried.

"That's it," he murmured, cupping the back of my head and rocking me. "Let it out, baby. Just let it all out."

He had no idea why I was crying, or what I'd just survived. He just knew I needed to release all the fear, horror, shock, and distress that was crowding its way through my system.

I have no idea how long he held me there until my tears dried up, but I was dizzy from how hard I'd sobbed, and my head ached. I pulled back to look up at him, and he kissed my cheek, then wiped my face dry with his palms.

"What took you so long to get here?" I said.

He shook his head, looking dazed. "A social worker showed up at the garage to talk to me."

Oh, shit. And here, I'd barely scratched through the surface of the numb shock of what had happened in the office. This shoved another cold wash of dread through me. "Julian?" I whispered, clutching his arm.

Thank God he was with Reese. No officials would know where he was; they wouldn't be able to steal him away. Maybe Pick and I could sneak over to Mason's place and run off together with the babies, somewhere no social worker would ever find us.

Pick nodded, but he didn't look worried. "Before she died, Tristy wrote on a napkin that she wanted to give me guardianship of him. The state is taking that into account as well as a statement from one of the police officers who saw me taking care of him. They're going to put it under review, but she thinks I have an honest-to-God chance of being able to adopt him."

"Oh my God," I screeched and flung myself at him for another hug. "That's so amazing."

"I know." He began to pet my hair. "Hamilton's text came in while she was talking to me. I didn't read it until after she'd left. And then . . . fuck, Tink. I have never been so scared in my life." Clutching my face in his hands, he stared at me hard before growling, "How could you be so stupid?"

I blinked, not expecting that question. "What?"

"You want to know why I didn't tell you about him buying this place? Because I knew you'd try to pull this. Well, no. No fucking way. If you left, I would've come after you and I would've kept looking until I found you. You made me a promise. You said you'd never leave. And I swear to God, you're going to keep that promise."

I nodded, and my lips trembled. "Okay."

He frowned at my easy acceptance. "Okay?"

"Okay, I will keep my promise. I'll stay with you forever."

His shoulders relaxed. "Yes, you will," he murmured before kissing me hard and pressing his forehead to mine. "God, I love you so much."

Crap, I thought I was done with my tears for a while, but more crept down my cheeks. "I love you more,"

"Not even possible." He shuddered and just held me. When I heard a sniff, I lifted my face to find how red his eyes were.

"Oh, baby. It's okay." I smoothed my fingers over his face and kissed his cheeks. "It's all over now."

He just shook his head and squeezed his eyes closed. "I don't like almost losing you."

"Well, you don't ever have to worry about him trying to take me away again."

Pick blew out a breath before glancing around. "Where is the bastard anyway? Have they already taken him into custody?"

"Um . . . " I had no idea how to even start to tell him what had happened.

"Who owns this place?" One of the detectives asked, breaking into my thoughts.

"Oh!" I pointed to Pick. Yeah, I had a lot more to tell him than I'd initially thought. "Right here."

Pick glanced at me. "What?"

"There's a deed with your name on it in the office."

He shook his head, still confused. "I'm not following."

Yeah, there was plenty left to tell him. And there were

a whole new batch of problems for me to work through. But at least this time around, I knew I had people who loved me and were willing to help me heal. To me, that meant I had everything.

PICK'S EPILOGUE

Some days I was grateful to Eva for the deal she'd made with her dad. As the new owner of Forbidden, I only had one job instead of two. Cleaning up all the mess after the shooting had taken up so much time, I'd had to quit my position at the garage, which was fine because now that things were beginning to settle back into place, I could be with my family more.

Other things were better as well. Tink and I had found a bigger apartment in a better neighborhood, closer to Reese and Mason. And not just a bigger apartment, but a three-bedroom apartment so Julian and Skylar each had their own space and their own cribs, away from our room. We could be as loud as we wanted to be.

Though I think the kiddos missed sleeping together because sometimes Tink and I still couldn't get them to settle down at night until they were snuggled up next to each other.

We'd also hired a lawyer to help us adopt Julian. The state had allowed us to keep him as foster parents after we'd gone through a couple classes. But he still wasn't ours for good.

But most of the time I was grinding my teeth in frustration for all the hassle Eva had put me through by making that deal with her dad. I had so much more responsibility now; it was crazy. Sitting in my office—which had been completely redesigned and moved to another room in the past few months after the murder-suicide—I was trying to figure out schedules and fix an incorrect order plus fill out all these freaking legal forms I didn't even know existed until I became a club owner when a knock on my door had me lifting my head.

It was a Thursday, so I had to hurry because I still didn't have a new bartender to replace me to help on ladies' night. I'd already lost the two I *had* hired, because neither of those had worked out. So, I was stuck working the floor every Thursday.

The guy I found lingering in my doorway looked youngish with waves of dark hair and bright grass-green eyes.

"I'm looking for . . . Pick?" he said as if he were sure he had my name wrong.

I nodded. "That's me. How can I help you?"

Shifting his weight from foot to foot and appearing nervous, he held out his hand when I stood up and approached him.

"Sir, I'm Asher Hart. And I—"

"Have we met before?" I frowned as I moved closer. He looked so damn familiar.

He faltered, even more antsy as he blinked. "No. I don't think so."

"Hmm." I studied him harder as he went on.

"Anyway, my buddies and I just started this band. We're kind of heavy metal with a folksy twist and call ourselves Non-Castrato. I think we'd really fit in with the Forbidden crowd."

I arched an eyebrow, making my brow ring pull a little. "Oh, you would, would you?"

We'd never had a live band before, didn't even have a deejay or an area appropriated for music. But the seed he planted was already making my head spin with a sudden flurry of ideas.

"Yeah," he went on, looking excited. "You guys have been getting really popular lately. Just imagine what holding a few gigs for local groups would do for you." Then he added, "We could play for free."

I grinned and shook my head. This kid was quite the salesman. But still . . . "I'm sorry, Hart, but I haven't even considered bringing bands in here. I'm still trying to find another bartender right now."

"I could bartend," he said helpfully, his eyes full of hope. Then he shrugged, and his lips lit with a rueful grin. "I mean, if we're not going to be paid to play, I'd have to make money somehow. On the nights we're not singing, I can mix drinks."

His enthusiasm warmed me, but I only sat back down in my big-ass boss chair and folded my hands together under my chin as I studied him. "You must not have a woman."

The question seemed to catch him off guard. "Uh, no. Why?"

"You just promised all your nights to me. That's not going to leave a lot of time for anything else."

A slow grin spread across his face. "Are you saying I'm hired?"

"Of course you're hired," a new voice answered from the doorway. Eva swept into the room, looking so amazing she damn near glowed. Going to Hart, she took both his hands and beamed up at him. "I think the idea is wonderful. We could do so much if we put up a stage and sound system. And with your enthusiasm, I already know exactly who to put in charge of that. Welcome to Forbidden."

When she went to hug him, I bristled and pushed to my feet. I wasn't upset because she was barging in here, making decisions. Aside from watching our kids, she doubled as my partner in running the business. In fact, she usually took care of filling out all the legal forms I hated, though I was still trying to learn how to deal with them, anyway.

No, I was upset because Asher Hart seemed a little bit too enthusiastic about hugging her back. His eyes looked glazed when she pulled away and grinned at him.

Taking her hand, I pulled her to my side and wrapped a propriety hand around her waist. "She's taken, by the way."

Hart glanced between the two of us. "I kind of figured that out when I spotted your name tattooed on her."

"What?" Startled by his declaration, I twisted back to Tink and caught her chin before turning her face until I could see behind her ear. When fresh, black ink stared back, spelling out my name, I sucked in a breath. "Shit, you really did it."

She winked up at me. "I didn't want any of your glimpses not to come true."

I grinned and kissed her hard and long.

Remembering we had company, I glanced up to find Hart watching us in amusement. "So, when can I start?" he asked.

"Tonight." I was starting to tell him every new bartender needed to get broken in on a ladies' night, when I suddenly realized where I'd seen him before. The tat behind Eva's ear brought the glimpse back into my mind. Hart was the deejay who was going to play at my wedding reception.

Realizing he would have a bigger role in my future than I'd first realized, I smiled at him. "Yeah, I think you're going to fit in just fine. Wear at tight, black T-shirt and jeans and show up before six when we open."

A grin spread across Hart's face. "Will do, boss."

After he disappeared from my office, the woman with her arms wrapped around my waist gazed up at me with absolute adoration. "So I'm guessing you're not pissed at me for hiring him on the spot. I just felt a good vibe from him."

I leaned down to rub my nose along hers. "Don't worry. I got the same vibe. We definitely have us a new Forbidden boy."

"And he's definitely hot enough to fit in," she answered, her unique blue eyes gleaming with mischief.

I narrowed mine. "Oh, you think he was hot, huh? That why you were so eager to hug him?"

She laughed, spilling out that sound I loved most in the world. "No, I hugged him so you'd turn all jealous and caveman and pull me away from him."

"You are one devious woman," I murmured. "Is that the only reason you came in today? To make me prove how crazy I am about you? I thought you were staying home with the babies."

"I was but . . . " She yanked open her purse and pulled out an official-looking envelope. "This came in the mail, so I dropped the kids off with Reese and came straight here."

My stomach roiled with instant unease. We'd gotten too many official letters lately. After her father's death, his will had stipulated Eva get a nice chunk of his inheritance that she was forced to share with her newly widowed mother. But her mother had been fighting for more of the money, so she'd hired a lawyer, to which we'd had to put our new lawyer to more work to fight back.

Eva had said she didn't want any of her father's money, but I thought he owed it to her, and more. For Skylar, Julian, and our future Chloe, she'd decided to keep it.

"It's from social services," she said, surprising me.

I hadn't thought we'd get word back about Julian quite so fast. A new worry gnawed at my gut as she stuck her finger in the slit and opened the letter. Tightening my arms around her, I held my breath as she quickly scanned the single page.

Her eyes lifted to mine, sober and unsmiling. I almost started sobbing right then. We hadn't been granted the adoption, had we? We were going to lose him.

Then tears prickled her eyes. "They said yes. Oh my God. They said yes. We can adopt him."

"What?"

"We can really keep him." Hugging me, laughing and crying at the same time, Eva began to jump up and down and screech her excitement.

"Oh, shit." In a split second, I was crying with her,

tears of joy streaming down my face.

Hauling her up off the ground, I spun my woman in a circle as I sobbed into her neck. As we held onto each other tightly, I wondered why this moment hadn't been in any of my glimpses. I didn't know if I'd ever felt quite this happy and relieved before.

But I guess Madam LeFrey hadn't wanted me to see too much. Damn witch had made me sweat it out. Which only made me appreciate the moment more.

"I love you so much," I told Eva, kissing my way up her neck to her mouth.

She found my lips and kissed me back. "I love you too."

"Before we adopt him, though, you have to do me one favor."

"Anything," she promised, only to pause and give me a leery eye. "Wait. What do I have to do?"

I winked. "Marry me."

EVA'S EPILOGUE

"Are you sure you're ready for this?"

I smiled over at my husband as he turned into the long lane of our driveway. Trees in the front yard cast a nice shady shadow before revealing our four-bedroom ranch-style home. "Why are you so worried? I don't see how this time is any different than the last."

He sent me a dry look. "The *twins* didn't exist the last time you came from the hospital after giving birth." He said *twins* as if he actually meant evil, demon spawn.

I laughed and shook my head. "I'm sure they didn't destroy the house that bad."

Pick snorted. "Reese is probably trying to peel them off the ceiling right now. I'm telling you, letting her and Mason watch our kids while you were at the hospital was a bad idea. Who knows what kind of habits their insane twins have already taught our perfect little angels."

"My God. You're getting dramatic in your old age,

369

Patrick."

But he did have a point.

The two-year-old Lowe children could be quite a terror. They went full-speed all day long, curious about everything and always eager to play.

We heard the commotion from inside as soon as Pick killed the engine and opened the car door.

Glancing at me with gritted teeth, he muttered, "Still think I'm overreacting?"

I rolled my eyes. "I'm sure Reese will pay for anything they broke."

"Lovely." He slid from the car and pulled open the back door to carefully pull out our two-day-old sleeping son. Pausing to stare, his face immediately softened. "Damn, he's perfect."

I hurried around the car to trail my fingers up his back. "Because he looks just like his daddy."

Pick winked at me as he tugged the carrier free. "Be careful, Tink. Or I'll be ready to start making baby number five."

I moaned. "I think four's enough."

"Oh, come on. We don't even have a basketball team yet." When I shot him a glare, he laughed.

It still irked Pick that he'd never had a glimpse of baby number four. After Chloe had been born, he was so sure that was all the kids we'd have. But then I'd gotten pregnant again, and honestly, it tickled me pink that he'd been so stunned. The first few years of our marriage had been grossly unfair. He'd known every big thing that was ever going to happen. He'd known Chloe was going to be a girl, he'd known this would be our home from the moment we'd taken a tour and stepped into the backyard. But now he was just as clueless about the future as I was. And it felt good to finally know as much as he did.

The door to the house opened before we reached it.

"Hold the baby! Hold the baby!" hollered a small blur I knew to be Gracen, Thing One of the terrible Lowe duo. "Baby."

Pick caught Reese's son around the waist with one arm as he continued to carry the new baby in his carrier with the other.

"Not on your life, pal," he told Gracen.

When the toddler began to kick his feet, Pick thrust him at his mother when she too hurried outside, smiling wide. "Here. Control your child."

"Oh, did he get out?" Reese swept the boy up high into her arms and made him squeal with laughter.

"Hold baby," Gracen demanded.

Reese laughed and kissed his nose. "Me first, squirt."

Julian was the first to tackle us when we came through the door. "Mom! You're home. No one told us you were home already. Are you okay?"

"I'm wonderful." I hugged him to my waist and ruffled his dark curls. "Glad to be home with you again. How are things . . . here?"

Wow, there really was something unidentifiable and blue dripping from our ceiling.

He looked up at me and grinned, his dark eyes warm with adoration. "We were going to make you a special supper."

"And clean," Reese added ruefully.

I glanced around the front room, only for my jaw to fall open. Behind me, Pick murmured, "Oh dear God. Did a bomb go off in here?"

"Nope. Only three two-year-olds and two eight-year-olds," Reese answered.

"I did *not* make any of this mess," Skylar announced as she went to Pick to get a look at her newest little sibling. "Oh, my goodness," she murmured, her eyes wide with awe. "He's so small."

Pick ruffled her hair and pulled her against his side. "Trust me; you were a lot smaller than this when you were born."

"No way." Her eyes were wide and she leaned in to get a closer look.

Mason appeared in the doorway from the kitchen hall, his arms full of Chloe. My youngest daughter was a major uncle's girl and clung to poor Mason whenever he was around. Spotting me, she grinned and pointed. "Mama." But she seemed satisfied to stay right where she was.

"Where's Thing Two?" Pick asked, glancing around suspiciously for Miss Isabella, the second twin. She made Gracen seem mild when she was around.

"Asleep," Mason answered. Then he hitched his chin toward the carrier. "What do you have there, Pick?"

Pick glanced at me and grinned, and I felt so full of love, surrounded by my favorite people on earth. Lifting his son, Pick announced, "Everyone, meet Patrick Mason Ryan."

- THE END -

UP NEXT
MARCH 2015

WITH EVERY HEARTBEAT
QUINN'S STORY

Shy, sheltered Zoey Blakeland is free. Now that she's
graduated from high school and can finally escape her
strict abusive father, she flees halfway across the country
to attend ESU, where her best friend Cora is a student.
Now is her time to start fresh.

But meeting Quinn Hamilton changes her dreams. He's
not what she expects, and he unconsciously teaches her
what love is really about. She can't help but fall for him
on that sunny Tuesday afternoon when he asks her to
help him pick out an engagement ring for Cora.

Betraying her best friend is the last thing she'd ever do,
but when it becomes increasingly obvious Quinn is with
the wrong girl, she finds it harder and harder to deny her
feelings.

ACKNOWLEDGEMENTS

There are so many wonderful people to thank! Every day, Mr. Kurt and Miss Lydia put up with a lot of dirty dishes, messy rooms, sporadic meals, and a very distracted Linda so that I can follow my dreams. Without their patience, none of my stories would be possible.

And to the rest of my family, I love each and every one of you. Your support means so much. Thanks Shi Ann and Alaina for always being eager to read whatever piece of rough draft I have at the moment, and Katie for her love of proofreading!

A whole bunch of thank yous go to Mrs. Lindsay Brooks, who is eternally willing to let me bounce the craziest ideas off her and then telling me to go for it.

Thank you to my critique partner, the lovely author Ada Frost, who gave me wise advice on both story and book covers.

Next, I have a batch of the sweetest beta readers possible. My fellow *Teen Wolf* fanatic, Mrs. Stiles...aka Chelcie Holguin: your honest opinion was awesome. Thanks a bunch to Patty Brehm as well. I loved your suggestions. And both Ana Kristina Rabacca and Mary Rose Bermundo: your enthusiasm completely made my day so many times. You are each like a fresh batch of warm sunshine.

A ton of thanks to editor Rosa Sophia and proofreader Shelley at *2 Book Lovers Reviews*, who were both willing to take on a new client on short notice. Thank you.

And the best for last: Thanks to Jesus Christ who forgives every ugly sin I commit against Him and still loves me anyway!

ABOUT THE AUTHOR

Linda grew up on a dairy farm in the Midwest as the youngest of eight children. Now she lives in Kansas with her husband, daughter, and their nine cuckoo clocks. Her life's been blessed with lots of people to learn from and love. Writing's always been a major part her world, and she's so happy to finally share some of her stories with other romance lovers. Please visit her at her website

WWW.LINDAKAGE.COM

Printed in Great Britain
by Amazon.co.uk, Ltd.,
Marston Gate.